Written and illustrated by

Miranda Leek

authorHOUSE®

AuthorHouse™
1663 Liberty Drive
Bloomington, IN 47403
www.authorhouse.com
Phone: 1-800-839-8640

First published by AuthorHouse 7/8/2010

ISBN: 978-1-4520-0620-8 (e)
ISBN: 978-1-4520-0621-5 (sc)

Library of Congress Control Number: 2010904128

Printed in the United States of America
Bloomington, Indiana
This book is printed on acid-free paper.

For my Mom, Dad, and my little sister Stitch, for always keeping the ride entertaining.

And for the roller coasters giving me the inspiration.

TWISTED

1: to turn so as to face in another direction.

2: To alter the normal aspect of; contort.

Part One
Rise of The Red

Behind Iron Bars

Pacing, back and forth from, corner to corner over and over again. As a caged bird wishing to be released. His mind was furious as his wheels made their click clack sound across the iron floor. His fire like eyes burned in rage. Thoughts flooded through him.

"Why! Why me!" The words screamed inside his head.

His restraints started to vibrate in anger as he sliced one of his dagger-like claws into the concrete wall. He pulled back his lips and snarled in frustration as he inscribed hateful words. He shook his head from side to side abruptly trying to overcome the continuing thoughts, ones that sickened him; bringing him closer to the breaking point.

"If I had never met that old man, if I never tried to work for that park! If I never would have -."

He banged his head against the bars and roared in pure rage. He tried not to think, but his will to not do so failed.

"Trapped In this prison! Because of my curse! Where I am from! BECAUSE OF WHAT I AM!!!!"

Chapter 1
New Job

"This is just great!" I said as I slapped a handful of bills onto the table. All those unwanted slips of paper kept piling up, bills from the electric, water, and who knew what else. Everything seemed to be spiraling into a bottomless pit as the miserable minutes ticked by, forcing me to lose myself in my sea of misery that looked like it would never dry out.

All had shifted right after I got fired from my engineering job at the city's local cake factory. I remembered the moment well, my boss calling me to his office for some reason unknown only to tell me those four words: Rodney Philips you're fired! It turned out that I never did wrong; the factory had gone bankrupt making everyone lose their jobs. Now every ex employee was looking hopelessly for work, I included.

I sat at my kitchen table drinking a cup of coffee and munching on a donut. As I took a sip I scanned the newspaper in front of me looking for a new job like I had done for the past five weeks. Every listing was either lousy pay or simply not what I had in mind. I knew I wanted something that I could relate to very well. A job that I would be comfortable doing for a very long time.

As I took another sip of coffee, letting the hot elixir slither down my throat, my eyes caught sight of an ad that I had never seen before. It was an ad that was rarely seen by the public eye. I looked at it carefully scanning each and every printed word.

MYSTIC PARK
WANTED!
ROLLER COASTER ENGINEER
CALL 789-6450
ASK FOR WOODY

Roller coasters, I knew so much about them. I had never actually seen one in person, but I knew more than most who were "coaster junkies". I acquired all the information that I knew from books, television, and the internet. The strange thing was that I seemed to always have an odd attraction to them, and I couldn't explain why. Deep in my mind however, I knew this could be my big break.

I got up out of my seat and grabbed my phone from the counter. I then started to press the keys requested by the ad. I double checked to make sure they were right before pressing send, there was no turning back now. The phone rang and rang, I almost hung up when finally someone answered.

"Hello this is Woody, how may I help you?" A man with a deep scruffy voice spoke. It sounded as if he was out of breath, almost like he had been running.

"Yes, my name is Rodney and I..."

"Would like to try out for the position of coaster engineer, am I right?" he replied interrupting me. It was almost as if he could read my mind.

"Yes sir," I simply said into the receiver, afraid that he was to cut in again.

"Ever worked on roller coasters before sir?" he said, his words quick and sharp. The man was either in a hurry or he was used to random citizens doing the exact thing I was doing. I decided to lie like a trained actor trying out for a specific part in a big-time movie.

5

"Yes." I said holding my breath.

"Then be at Mystic Park around four this afternoon. I will then test you on how capable you are at doing your job. See you then Rodney." He said and then hung up.

At first I didn't know what to think, but then I realized that I had a chance. I would go through with it I wondered as I looked back at the clock. I had a few hours to prepare. I couldn't be late; I was already in a deep hole with little chance of escaping. I couldn't fall any deeper.

When the time came, I grabbed my keys from the hook on the kitchen wall and entered the garage. I pressed the red button on the panel in the dusty corner to open up the door. As soon as the task was done, I climbed into my Mustang and started the engine. I immediately switched the radio on and turned it to my favorite station, blasting the song that was currently playing. I then put on my pair of sunglasses, completing my annual routine as I shifted into gear and drove off.

I sat calmly in my seat listening to music as I steered the sports car along the wooded roads of Huntersberg, a quiet town in which nothing bad ever happened. Huntersberg got its name from the lush woods that surrounded it; the forest was a gold mine for those who desired big game. However, Huntersberg finally got onto the map when Mystic Park was built, making the undetectable city not only for hunters but also thrill seekers as well. I tried to make my way to the summer escape before, but I was robbed of that because of the countless hours I spent at the factory, time that was wasted in the end. Now I was to finally go to Huntersburg's playground; because I had an invitation and a reason to be there.

The song that played faded into an untraceable silence as it ended. I reached down to swap stations for I hated listening to commercials that were useless. I continued to fiddle with the dial, turning it this way and that trying to catch a good tune that was worth it. I came across a rock song that I had not heard since I could remember. I settled on it and then turned my attention back to the road. Suddenly a large buck darted blindly out of the thicket of trees. It was frightened beyond reason; I slammed on the brakes as it traveled inches from the Mustang's hood. The sports car then screeched to a halt, the screaming tires echoing through the woods. The deer then sliced past and vanished into the forest again.

I blinked my eyes briefly trying to comprehend what had happened. Deer were never known to come out of hiding at broad daylight. During the many times I hunted with acquaintances, I had never seen a creature that spooked. I looked to where it had emerged to see a slight rustle of bushes before sighing in relief. Hopefully nothing else bizarre would happen, but then again one could never predict the future.

A few minutes later I pulled up to the park. The grounds were littered with rides and stands, brightening the area with an array of colors. I looked down for a split second as I took the key from the ignition and then put my attention back to rides that sat waiting for their riders. It was then that my eyes caught sight of the granddaddy of them all, the king of the rides, the infamous roller coaster. The scream machine's rails towered over all that stood. As I was looking at the steel coaster in awe, a cold shiver went down my spine and my hair stood up on the back of my neck. A strange stinging sensation ran through my body. Startled, I climbed out of the car.

"Probably nothing, perhaps an adrenaline rush," I said to myself after a brief moment of thinking why that had happened. I quickly put it behind me as I walked through the great iron gates, walking into an opportunity of a lifetime.

My eyes scanned the grounds; it was very prominent that Mystic Park was on its off season; there was no one around except for a few park employees. As I walked my muscles tightened up, feeling a little stronger than they were. Out of the corner of my eye I saw two park employees who couldn't take theirs off me. They looked like they were in their middle thirties. The girl had long silky red hair with a beautiful skinny figure. The boy had brown hair and looked somewhat like a daring teenager. Even as I walked away they couldn't help but to exchange whispers.

Then an old man with long white hair pulled into a low ponytail and a small unkempt beard and mustache advanced toward my position. The sun's rays seemed to make his unnatural white hair glow as he adjusted the collar of his cream shirt covered in an almost renaissance looking vest. He began to smile slightly as he casually stuck one hand into his pocket of his brown trousers. He then held out his smooth hand as a gesture for me to shake it, and I accepted his greeting.

"I'm Woody and you must be Rodney am I right?" he said in his low voice.

"Yep, the one and only." I replied still examining him. To me it was certain that Woody didn't look like your ordinary old middle-aged man. In fact, his body possessed the build of a thirty year old. Every aspect about him was - perfect. Suddenly he leaned closer, putting me on high alert as I knew he was probably about to speak of something very important.

"You are a one and only indeed." He said in a low but serious tone, with both of our eyes bearing into each other's. Finally, I simply nodded as he motioned for me to come into the main office, but only one thing, a simple fact, struck my mind that stood above everything else. His eyes, I thought, they looked almost - unhuman.

Chapter 2
Among The Rails

Woody led me down the hall to an office. Inside, were three other men sitting on chairs. The coaster engineer motioned for me to join them. *There's something weird about him, something beyond explanation*, I thought. Then Woody left the room and began to talk to someone down the hallway. Hesitating, I turned to the man sitting next to me.

"Did you notice anything weird about him?" I hastily asked.

"No not really." He replied.

"Did you look at his eyes?"

"What about them?"

"They look like a – cat's!"

He stared at me like I was crazy then he scooted towards the other edge of his chair, away from me. Was I the only one that could see what his eyes looked like? Get it together! Now is not the time to get scatterbrained!

Woody suddenly walked into the room. He looked briefly at me; His creature eyes flashed me a sense of uncertainty. Could he have possibly heard what I had said? Then he turned and pulled up a chair in front of us, his ice blue eyes looking at everyone in anticipation.

"Gentlemen," he started, "today I am going to do a simple but effective test on you. It will be very difficult to the inexperienced coaster engineer. It's the only thing I'm going to judge you on, so if you can't do it you're done. If you show a struggle you're done. I'll test you one at a time. For most of you, roller coaster walking will be a living hell, but for one of you - it will not." He finished looking at me, letting a sly grin come to my view.

He then guided one of the men out of the room. The few remaining sat quietly talking to each other. Suddenly a small rippling pain shot across my back. Then it went through my arms and legs. I bit my lip and let out a soft hiss of pain.

"You all right?" a man asked, bringing myself to the attention of the others.

"I'm fine," I muttered as I saw all the men's eyes on me. One of them even turned to the hopeful next to him only to whisper a suspicion about "being crippled".

"After this is done, I'm seeing a doctor." I said under my breath. Hours went by. One by one the men left, none of them got the job. *That doesn't mean it's automatically mine, he could still interview someone else*, I pondered. Then Woody came through the door.

"Your turn." He said waving me out.

I nodded and warily followed him from the building and back into the park. My body started to act strange again, my heart started to beat faster. As we got closer to the coaster, it began to hammer in my chest. It went from its rhythmic thump to a completely absurd machine gun like metronome. My health was really starting to worry me.

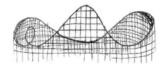

We began our decent up the stairs of the steel coaster's station. My muscles seemed as if they were bulging out of my legs as if they were to burst through my skin at any moment. Something was definitely wrong. However, despite my suffering, I have to go on; I had to have this job! Then we finally reached the heart of the station, the area that actually housed the roller coaster itself, a beast's lair. Without warning, a larger jolt of pain ran down my back, feeling like an aftershock from a baseball bat hitting me in the spine. I quickly stood up and clutched my back, my nails digging into my shirt as I grinded my teeth in agony, my other hand grasping the queue rail in a stronghold.

"What's wrong?" Woody asked, turning around swiftly.

"I don't know, this all started, this will sound really weird and ludicrous, as soon as I saw your steel coaster." I said as I forced out the words.

Woody looked at me showing no expression on his face. He raised a thick eyebrow and looked around briefly for any signs that someone could be listening.

"Walk with me Rodney; I'll explain to you what's going on." He said heading out onto the track. As quickly as it came, the pain receded. I had no choice but to follow him. As we begun our decent up the lift hill, laying a foot only on the stairs that lined the track, my skin tingled and my muscles pumped. Climbing the rails was turning out to be easy. I was even running among them soon I caught up with Woody. I actually felt... powerful.

"Let me ask you a few questions Rodney, Do you feel different walking among the rails?" Woody began as he stared straight ahead with his hands in his pockets, not looking at me once.

"Yeah, I feel power." I admitted.

"Invincible?"

"Yes, if you put it that way."

"Let me ask you this, do you feel the urge to protect? The urge to fight?" He continued.

He was right. I did feel the urges to do things. Some heroic, some crazy, and some daring. What was going on with me? Was I being overrun by a force unknown?

"I do." I answered at last.

"Rodney, you are the only person that I would consider for this job out of anybody."

"Why? I haven't even completed my test yet," I replied befuddled as we broke out in a run down the stairs of the lift hill. How was I able to do this!

"Rodney you will soon learn that you and I have much more in common than you think." He said as we entered a tunnel in the most secluded part of the circuit.

"Woody, would you please tell me what's going on?" I said as we stopped.

Chapter 3
Haunting Change, Haunting secret

Woody leaned against the tunnel wall and sighed deeply.

"You better listen up because I'm not going to repeat myself."

"Understood." I said as I waited to hear what he had to say.

"Rodney we both are from a different world, and we are not human."

"What the hell are you talking about?" I replied, realizing that the old engineer had gotten on a whole new level of weird.

"Listen! There is a place that co-exists within an amusement park, It is known as Amusement Park Between. Where the rides have control, were the impossible becomes possible, and the explainable becomes unexplainable." Woody replied disgusted, his ice like eyes suddenly getting darker.

"Is this for real Woody?"

"First of all it's not Woody - its Thunderbark." He said as he stood there stone still while he barely breathed. He then dipped his head low, letting his long hair drape over his shoulders. The coaster engineer simply stared down, his eyes growing darker still.

"Okay, if that is your real name then don't I have some freaky name if I'm from were you are?" I said letting out a soft laugh.

"Don't mock our names they are warrior names." Woody said crudely. "Your real name Rodney is Railrunner."

"This is very dumb and confusing." I replied sarcastically in defiance.

"I guess when you are in your human form for so long, you forget nearly everything." Woody said under his breath.

The awkward conversation was starting to grow amusing. It was actually really funny. I decided to play along.

"If we both are from a different world, then why are we here?" I said trying to hide a cunning smile.

"It's a long story Railrunner, but I'll try to make it as short as possible. There is a prophesy in our word were the red will defeat the black. An evil tyrant named Ironwheel is currently ruling our world. He kills for his own amusement; he has armies that take control of our kind. Once you came along our world was given new hope. Soon however, Ironwheel learned of your existence and sent his armies to kill you to prevent the prophesy from becoming true. My allies and I decided you would be safe in the real world."

"Who are your allies?" I said trying to hide a snicker.

"They are Merrylegs and Static. You may have noticed them when you came in."

"You mean the redhead and the boy?"

"Yes that is them in their human form. Merrylegs is a carousel horse and Static is a bumper car."

"So am I some sort of ride?" I replied as I crossed my arms.

"Yes. Railrunner, we need to activate your ride form."

"How?" I said as I tried not to burst out laughing.

"We must introduce you to your environment."

"What am I supposed to do?"

"Come closer and I'll tell you." He smiled covertly.

I advanced forward towards Woody. I stumbled on the walkway edge, and fell onto the track. Pain ran through my body. It soared down my spine and my anatomy completely. My body was as hot as fire then as cold as ice. My veins rippled beneath my skin. My muscles bulged as my fingers singed. The pain suddenly stopped. I lay on the rails out of breath; I looked up to see him grinning.

"Your form has been activated."

"What..."

"You'll soon find out. You can meet me if you have any other questions." He interrupted.

"But...."

"You will answer most of them yourself. By the way you got the job. See you tomorrow morning, Railrunner."

Chapter 4
Railrunner Unleashed

A few hours since I left the park, I was forcing myself not to believe what Woody had said. It was stupid and illogical, but what in the world happened to me as I fell onto the rails? Was his story true or was the raging pain a freak accident? Whatever had occurred made me now realize that my co-worker was completely demented.

I was now sitting in the local bar called Snooks with my two friends who used to work at the factory. Buddy and Sly, as they were called, played hearts and betted on money while I drank a beer trying to forget the bizarre day.

"Rodney, when did you get your tattoos and your eyebrow pierced?" Sly said as he layed a card onto the oak table.

I looked at the dragon wrapped around my left arm and the tribal symbol on the other, then felt my piercing.

"It was about two weeks ago."

"Hmm, say how many beers have you had since we got here?" He laughed.

"This one is - my seventh." I finished all wide-eyed.

"That's crazy! You don't look or feel tipsy." Buddy said astonished.

"I'm not really feeling anything. You know they say once you drink that much you pass out." I said looking at the bottle of beer, still bewildered that I had consumed that many and not felt a thing.

"Man, you," said Sly, waving his finger at me, "Are possessed!"

Maybe I am. No, I'm not going to believe that crap again!

"So Rod, where did you get your job?" asked Sly.

"At Mystic Park. I'm the new roller coaster engineer."

"Rodney! Of all jobs, a roller coaster engineer? I thought you were better than that!" He objected.

"Yeah Rodney, you could have had a job working on cars. I hate those damn roller coasters. They piss you off in more ways than one," Buddy laughed.

I felt my head get hot. Suddenly I had the taste for blood. I closed my eyes briefly, trying to clear my mind. I found myself licking my lips and producing more saliva than normal. I glared at Sly and Buddy; I drew my hands into fists, as I was stricken with frustration.

Then on that note both Buddy and Sly's beer bottles shattered in their hands, glass piercing through their skin. They both screamed as spectators gathered around them. What did I do! Did I even do this! What's wrong with me!

Suddenly I didn't feel too good. I felt dizzy and lightheaded. I stood; only to stumble against the wall.

"Are you ok?" a shaken waitress asked.

"I'm not sure." I uttered as I felt beads of sweat coat my forehead.

"Did you drink too much?"

"No," I lied. Then I walked out the door of the bar. Was I finally feeling the effects of the beer? Or was it something else? I went to the back of the bar where my car was parked and started to fiddle with my keys. My hands shook terribly, making me drop them to the pavement. Before I could pick them up, a cat ran from under my car and snatched the keys with his mouth. He then vanished into the darkness. I looked up thinking what next and saw the moon.

Pain sliced trough my body. I felt hot as fire then cold as ice. I broke out in a tremendous sweat. My fingers singed. Pain raced down my back. My skin turned red as blood, my head throbbed. I was getting bigger; thread-by-thread my clothes came apart. My jaw popped out of socket, then pushed forward with my nose, forming a long snout. What's happening to me! My mind screamed. My back ripped through my shirt. Grind! Snap! Pop! The sound of cracking bones, my bones. My skin hardened. My fingers fused together, and then round tips formed at the ends, making - wheels.

"It can't be!" I said finally realizing. Woody was Thunderbark and his tall tale was true.

My shoulder blades shook as seats shot upwards. Then they formed along my back and up towards my head. My organs started to resituate as my tailbone extended. Everything internal and external compressed and stretched. I was changing into my ride form, as Thunderbark had said; I was changing into a roller coaster, a roller coaster called Railrunner, the real me. I felt my mind clearing, being over powered by some unknown force. I was losing control. Pain went through me in spasms. Then it all stopped.

Railrunner fell to the ground in exhaustion. Inhaling and exhaling heavily. The moon hung high overhead, and Railrunner was now running with it. He finally looked up; his fire tone amber eyes caught sight of it. Railrunner stood upright on his middle cars. Then he let loose a bellowing howl unlike any other, loud and powerful. The cat came out of the shadows and stood some ways from Railrunner.

The cat hissed at him its fur standing on end.

Railrunner glared at it. He crouched low to the ground and arched his back up high. Railrunner pilled back his lips, revealing dagger like teeth, and snarled menacingly. Saliva dripping from his jaws, he could smell the cats fear and its blood.

The cat then let out a loud yowl and induced its claws. Railrunner then roared, and went strait for the cat. Before the poor creature ever had a chance to get away, it fell victim to the demon coaster's jaws. Blood seeped into Railrunner's mouth, it tasted good, he realized, like nectar to a god. Out of control, Railrunner then turned and continued his savage raid.

He walked among the concrete; his wheels click clacking. He sniffed; he could smell more fear, more blood. The coaster crept over the bar and gazed down below to see humans. Scrawny and weak, they were no match for an almost twenty thousand pound *living* roller coaster. On the ground paramedics tended to the men with glass shards through their hands. Their red blood, that matched Railrunner's metal hide, dripped onto the ground. Railrunner smiled wickedly, his bloody teeth glistening in the moonlight.

Then the crazed creature leaped down from the building and on top of the parked ambulance. He threw his head back and roared loudly in pleasure. The frightened humans ran into the streets and some into the bar. He the climbed down from the ambulance and smashed through the bars windows. Railrunner then ransacked the pub's interior to bits. The owner of the bar, Geoffrey Calloway, threw a beer bottle at Railrunner's head; it smashed into a million pieces without the glass scratching Railrunner's metal. He paused then turned and barred his fangs at the man. Even though the bar owner was very prominent in Rodney's memory, he found that he could not even recollect his face. *Fool*, thought the roller coaster. He reared back and out of his wheels grew three fifteen -inch stainless steel blades that were perfectly sharp. Railrunner racked his claws across the quartz counter, cutting through it deeply and sharpening them at the same time. Fuming with rage, he went after the man.

The frightened soul ran into the wine cellar with the steel door. I'm safe, Calloway thought, but he was dead wrong. Railrunner's claws slashed through the steel door. They cut through the metal like butter. He then began to pull the door off its hinges.

Suddenly a smoke bomb fell to the floor, making the place vaporous, but Railrunner's eyes could see through it. He discovered the flashing lights of squad cars. His eyes narrowed and he growled low in his throat.

"Come on out with your hands up!" an officer yelled.

Railrunner walked upright towards the entrance. He then pushed the doors off their hinges and stood in the line of fire.

"It's a - roller coaster?" One of the police said baffled, the gun shaking in his hand.

Railrunner crossly walked up to the police. They began to fire, their bullets simply bouncing off of him. He then grabbed the front bumper of the cruiser, and tossed it like a toy. It smashed into another car. Railrunner flung an officer out of his way and roared in sheer amusement. Within a blink of an eye he obliterated the small police force.

Railrunner looked at the mess he had made and snorted in disgust as he thought how pathetic the humans were. Then he looked to the moon and wailed, and ran off into the darkness.

Chapter 5
As The Night Rolls On

Railrunner ran in the shadows. Blood was caked on his wheels, but he took no notice. He ran fast, faster than a car at top speed. He ran with the moon, spirited and free. He took in the air around him. Smells of animals and vehicles reached his nostrils. He could hear anything and everything. Then a somehow familiar scent made him stop, sniff the air, and then change direction. He barreled through the woods, leaping over obstacles as if they were nothing. After he ran as a blur against the forest foliage, Railrunner finally found the scent's source, a dairy farm.

Back at the bar, cops investigated the area. Detective Black walked up to one of the injured officers. He lit up one of his favorite brands of cigarettes and got eye level to the man.

"So, did you see what did all of this?" he said blowing out a puff of smoke.

"I have no Idea. All I can remember was a squad car coming at me." The plump man replied as he kept a hand to his throbbing head.

Black rose up and turned to one of his colleges. "Does anyone else involved have a brief description of what our suspect looks like?"

A tall officer waved at Detective Black "Yes the owner was also involved." He said pointing to a short bald man sitting on the steps that lead to the bar's entrance. Then Black approached the bar keeper with his eyes very dark with frustration. The bar's demolition made no sense. It had been obliterated in record time, without explosives. Nothing seemed to add up.

"What did you see Mr. Calloway?" the detective demanded in a firm yet pensive tone as he got eye level to the owner. The exhausted man sat silently for a brief minute before he answered with his voice shaky.

"You're not going to believe this, but it was a roller coaster."

Black begun to choke on his cigarette.

"Sir, have you been drinking?"

"Heavens no! It was a roller coaster! A *mutant* roller coaster! It was unlike anything I've ever seen! It was red and about seventeen feet tall. It had two cat-like eyes and a nose like a snakes. Its teeth were like a wolves and it could roar like a tiger!" He protested.

"That is quite enough Mr. Calloway." Black said rolling his eyes.

"Detective, I think it may be on the security camera. Here's the tape," Mr. Calloway said as he handed it to Black.

He took a camcorder one of his assistants handed to him and popped in the tape. Then he pressed play and begun to watch. Detective Black's eyebrows raised as his jaw dropped slightly open- dumbfounded.

"He is right…"

Railrunner crouched low in the brambles, and crept along the boarder of the small farm. His demon eyes scanned the cows. He quietly snuck over the fence. The cow's sent flooded his nostrils, but the bovines could not smell Railrunner's, it went undetected. Then he saw what he wanted, a bull. Railrunner crept closer; suddenly the beast looked up and saw him. Then the coaster lunged full force at his target. His teeth snagged its flank and he flung the animal. The bull got to his feet struggling, and looked at the coaster. Railrunner snarled and barred his fangs, challenging it. *What's the matter? You not like red?* He thought tauntingly. The bull charged with his horns lowered. Railrunner extracted his claws and slashed the poor creature's throat; it fell to its side, dead.

He stood upon the bull and sank his teeth into its flesh. Its blood seeping into his mouth and satisfying his ravenous hunger. Within minutes the bull was almost bones. Then from the farmhouse, a man stepped out with his gun.

"Who's out there!" he yelled, his voice echoing in the fog.

Railrunner growled deep in his throat. The man aimed his gun blindly, not knowing what he was shooting at. *He is not worth it; I have already eaten my fill,* thought Railrunner. The man fired, but Railrunner was already gone.

Chapter 6
The Next Morning

I awoke the next morning sprawled out on top of my covers. I hoisted myself up, feeling dizzy. I took my index fingers and placed them just under my eyebrows to massage the area for my head throbbed horrendously. Was I on a hangover? What happened last night? Then it occurred to me.

"It could not have - I must have dreamed it." I said getting up. I didn't feel like my normal self, I was sore and felt like I had gained weight. I looked at myself, my skin had a redder tone and my hair was a tad bit longer. My muscles were huge! They looked like they belonged to an experienced bodybuilder. Did last night really occur?

I got ready and fixed myself a cup of coffee then sat in front of the TV. I switched it onto the morning news. I got up again to get the traditional morning donuts.

"Breaking News! An unexplainable phenomenon has been proven to be real. A video surveillance camera captured the real suspect that destroyed the local bar Snooks, the culprit is a living roller coaster!"

I spun around to face the TV, spilling the donuts onto the floor. I then ran to the screen. The news began to show the video from the bar. My heart started to beat faster.

"It was real! And that was me!" I said, my words struggling to leave my mouth.

" This unusual coaster took many victims on the night of his raid, including five police officers. One of the survivors was bar owner, Geoffrey Callaway. I was pinned in the wine fridge, and it was slashing trough the metal door! Calloway said. It destroyed the whole bar! He continued as he waved his hands in the air. Another event that authorities believe the coaster committed; was the slaughter of a local farmer's bull.

It was sucked dry, it was nothing but bones, but I remember seeing a pair of bright red eyes"

"I'm screwed!" I said as my heart rate skyrocketed.

"Any information on the coaster pleases call 567- 9000. There is a reward."

I turned off the TV. Last night was real. I was a monster that killed for blood! Wait, Thunderbark, he did this to me! But yet he said I was already like this. I 'll get answers from him. I think he is expecting me, he knew ahead of time!

My pondering was interrupted by a knock on the door. I answered it. A girl with silky blonde hair stood smiling in the doorway. It was my girlfriend Clare, and at the worst possible time to.

"Hey Rodney, did you see the news this morning?" she asked as she twirled a long soft strand around her finger.

"Y...y...yes." I said, choking on my own words.

"That has to be a hoax or something, that's impossible." She said pointing to the video on screen.

"Yeah it's got to be," I said playing along.

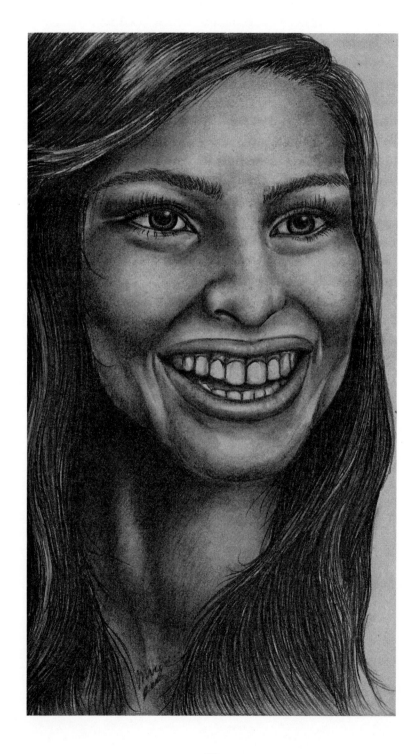

" It's probably the doings of Detective Black, he stretches the truth a lot. Plus he used to be a graphic designer."

"Yeah, he probably did the whole thing by computer." I replied gulping. I could start to feel myself sweat fretfully.

"Exactly, so where are you working now? I heard you got a new job."

" Yeah it's at Mystic Park." I said almost biting my tongue. I didn't even feel like saying roller coaster right now.

"Nice, well I have go, you remember our date at the carnival right?" Clare said smiling warmly.

"Yeah I'll be there."

She kissed me goodbye and left. As soon as she did I grabbed my wallet and headed for the park, I was going to see Thunderbark, immediately.

Behind Iron Bars

He got up again, and started pacing. Cold hard reality was hitting him. Because of his curse, he lost so many things; his home, his belongings, his identity, and his love. He was forever a fear and blood seeking monster. Doomed to live his life as a damned soul and with a destiny that would probably never be fulfilled .

Chapter 7
Cold hard Facts

I made my way to the gate of the park. I stopped to ask a nearby janitor that was doing some extra cleaning a question.

"Do you know where Woody is?"

"He's working on the steel coaster." He replied in a wheezy voice.

"Thanks."

I then started towards the coaster. My muscles began to tighten again and my skin tingled. I headed to the basement of the coaster's station for I knew Thunderbark had a second office there, I had seen it while we were climbing the stairs to the station. It was unlocked so, I quietly opened the door.

"Hello Railrunner." Thunderbark said closing a book. "I knew you were coming."

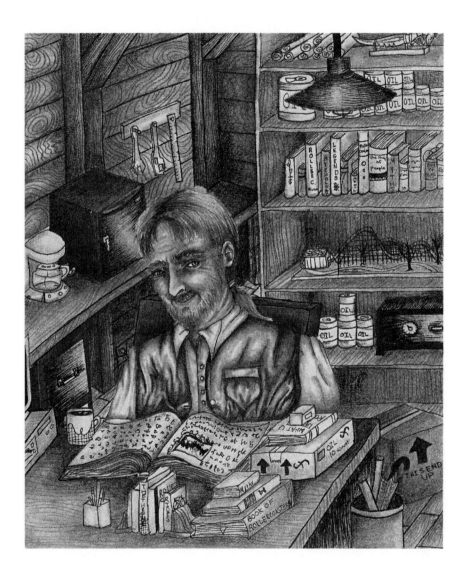

"We need to talk." I said sternly.

"Of course, sit."

I took a seat in front of Thunderbark's desk. He sat down and took a sip of coffee. The "engineer" then looked at me, obviously waiting for me to start.

"I want to know what the hell you did to me." I said pointing at him. Unexpectedly, Thunderbark only let a small smile come to his face.

"Absolutely nothing." He replied.

"Don't lie to me." I retorted.

Thunderbark only looked at me smirking. "So I take it you know what happened last night?" he spoke as he closed a large book on his desk.

"I became a savage beast."

"A roller coaster can be quite a nuisance on its first moon, but I'll get to that in a second. As you know you are indeed a roller coaster. Now I think you should know a few pointers. First of all it is quite an honor to be of roller coaster blood. Both you and I have it."

"So you're a coaster too?" I said finally realizing why he was so strange to begin with.

"A wooden one. As you are steel. Now I need to tell you what you should keep in mind at all times. In the real world, a roller coaster is like a werewolf each night. Your soul has no control at all and you have the taste for blood, until however, when on the night of your first full moon, on the strike of twelve, you will have control but you will still be a coaster. Then after the full moon, you will then have control from every night on."

"The full moon is tomorrow night."

"It is. Now there are other ways to becoming the roller coaster in pure daylight. One is by touching any coaster track. Two is by riding a roller coaster. And three is when you need power the most. And the forth I will tell you when you're ready."

"What about in Amusement Park Between?"

"You're a roller coaster twenty four seven. When you're here in the real world, the coaster is by night and any of the three reasons I told you."

"All right."

"Now a roller coaster has powers beyond humans understanding. We can bend lightening and fire; posses super strength and agility. We can predict when things will happen, exept death, and sense trouble. We can never get sick - ."

"So that's why I never got drunk on all those beers." I said chuckling a little.

"Yes. As I was saying, we are venomous, we can hear a sound from miles, we have the sight of a dragon, and other things."

"Is there any precautions?"

"Of course!" Thunderbark gasped as he threw one of his hands to his forehead. "Railrunner, stay away from civilization at night. Wear gloves and long sleeves when you work on the coasters. And forget about love."

"Why love?"

"Railrunner, you are a roller coaster. Your lover is a human. Once she sees the real you, she's done. Don't even try to conceal the truth from her, she will find out sooner or later. Thunderbark said letting out an provoked sigh. " This is almost a blessing and a curse."

"Well that's not stopping me from going out with her. In fact, we have a date this afternoon."

"Fine then, don't listen to me, but where is your date at?" Thunderbark said with his eyes changing like a mood ring again.

"It's at the carnival."

"Which kind, Railrunner?" he demanded with his icy eyes going dark.

"The ones with the booths and rides."

"Oh boy. Railrunner a roller coaster gains power from amusement parks and carnivals. You also gain power from rides and you can have the ability to control them like their speed and how long they last. If you step on the rails or in a coaster car, you go roller coaster instantly. I would think about that," Railrunner. It's not a good idea to be going there, at all." He said as he crossed his arms.

"I'll be fine." I said getting up and heading for the door.

"You are making a mistake!" I heard Thunderbark say as I shut the door behind me.

Chapter 8
Carnevil

I went home to get ready; I wasn't going to listen to Thunderbark this time. A few minutes later Clare drove up the driveway. As she climbed out and edged toward the front door, I started to get second thoughts, what if Thunderbark was right? Maybe this was a stupid Idea, but I couldn't bail now.

"Are you ready?" Clare asked.

"Yeah."

"Did you want to take my car or yours?" she smiled as she started out the door.

" Yours. Mine was towed last night." I said coming up with an answer that seemed logical. Even though in the back of my mind that was probably what happened.

" Why ?"

"I'll tell you later," I gulped.

Clare and I then got into her convertable and started our departure. A sixth scent kicked in. *I'm stupid for doing this! I shouldn't have even answered the damn door! I can't get out of this now, I'll just get some info on the carnival first*, I thought.

"So, how many people do you think will be there?" I asked.

"Oh, lots! Its opening night."

"What all is there?"

"Well there are games, booths, rides - ."

"Do you know what kinds of rides there are?"

"You know, carousels, ferris wheels, tilt o whirls, roller coasters -."

"Did you say roller coasters?" I said as my heart skipped a beat.

"Yes, do you like them?"

"Well yes and no."

"What do you not like about them?"

Oh boy, how should I put this? I pondered as I rubbed my chin.

"Well I have my reasons."

"Weird, because you are a roller coaster engineer." She laughed as she turned on the radio.

If only you knew, if only you could understand, I thought. I wish if I told you, Clare, that you could accept it and still love me. If only I wasn't a monster.

I tried to relax a little bit; I just have to avoid riding or touching any coasters. Plus be back and away from Clare before the moon rose. If I wasn't careful I could kill her by mistake!

"So how did your car get towed?" Clare asked suddenly.

I chuckled a little, "I parked it in the wrong place." I wasn't really lying on that one.

"Don't worry Rodney, I've been there and done that." She laughed as she drove around the bend. "Another thing, where were you last night? I called lots of times to ask if you were okay since the monster was out."

My blood ran cold. "Well Clare, I was at the hospital with my friends they had to go to the emergency room last night." I said lying through my teeth.

"Oh, hope they are all right."

"They should be."

"Well, we will be there in a sec. It is right around this curb."

"Wonderful." I replied. I was in deep water now.

A few seconds later I saw the carnival, and its rides. Including the roller coaster. A small streak of pain went down my spine even before I stepped out onto the cracked concrete. I've made a big mistake, I thought as a drop of sweat ran down my neck.

"Oh crap," I said without thinking.

"What is it?"

"Ummm, there are a lot of people here." I said coming up with another answer.

"What's wrong with that? Besides lines."

"Well, I'm not so good with crowds."

"Just come on Rodney. She said guiding me out of the car.

"Maybe we should go to the movies or something."

Clare suddenly turned to me. "What is the truth, Rodney? Why don't you want to be here?" She said, her eyes looking deep within me.

"Clare - the truth is complicated." I sighed. "Hard to understand as well."

She didn't reply she just continued on guiding me into the carnival.

"Come on Rodney, lets at least try to put our problems aside us." She said walking through the admission gates.

If only I could, Clare.

A little while later Clare dragged me onto a ferris wheel. As soon as I sat down, my feet and hands started to tingle. I'm feeling the power, I realized. I need to keep in control at all cost and maintain stability.

"This is fun," Clare said as we slowly went up.

"Um, Clare, I have to go home before night falls." I said suddenly as I stared ahead at the horizon, not even flinching once.

"Why?" She questioned.

"I have to go to work."

"Really? Odd, I'm sure we can work something out."

When the ride was over, we went on a few more. The coaster was getting more and more power by the second. My body was feeling more unstable by the minute. Clare had not mentioned the roller coaster yet, thank god.

"I'm saving the best for last Rodney, the roller coaster."

So much for forgetting all about it. I need to make her be distracted. Do something other than a ride. But what! The performances? No, something that could keep her attention. A game! That's it! I needed to keep her busy. How to get away? Now there was a question that I still had no answer to.

"Why don't we do some games?"

"Oh alright"

We got in line for one of those games were you throw a ball at a pile of clay pins. Clare was up first.

"I suck at this, so don't you laugh Rodney!"

"I won't." I smiled at her. She then threw the ball at the pins, missing them by several inches.

"Crap, well it's your turn." She said handing me the ball.

I took it from her and looked at the bottles. I could suddenly see their pressure points. Where I needed to hit them in order for them to fall over. I took aim, and then released the ball like a cannon blast. It hit the bottles, making them fly through the air, the ball went straight through the tent. I began to feel embarrassment on top of everything else.

"Dang, said the perplexed host, well here is your prize," he said handing me a giant stuffed panda. I nodded in thanks then handed the bear to Clare.

"That was amazing! She said grasping my arm. She stopped and ran her frail fingers among my skin, puzzled. "Rodney - have you been working out? Your muscles are huge!"

"Um - sort of."

"Hey you want to go on the roller coaster now?"

"No. How about uh, the house of mirrors?" I said, blurting out the first attraction I saw.

"Fine." She said a little disenchanted.

Maybe I could lose her in there, I thought. We started to walk towards the maze. It wasn't busy; Clare and I were the only ones going in. The operator let us through.

"See you at the exit!" she said heading into the maze. I started, but as I looked into the mirrors, I saw the face of horror, Railrunner's. My reflection was the real me. I looked around; I had a roller coaster reflection in every single one! I began to run, Railrunner running with me, as my reflection. I must get out of here! No one can see me for what I really am! I ran faster, my lungs expanded and compressed as I let out huge puffs of air. I stumbled out of the exit and landed on the dirt ground, right at Clare's feet.

She grabbed my hand and pulled me up, and started to yank me across the lot.

"Rodney, we are riding the roller coaster now, no exceptions." She said forcing me to follow her.

"Clare no! I pleaded. My spine began to ache as we stood right in front of it.

"What is it Rodney?" She said glaring at me.

"You really want the truth! I'm a monster!"

She rolled her eyes mischievously and climbed up the platform, still pulling me along.

"Clare you don't understand! You could get killed!" I pleaded.

"Rodney, you are most likely to drown in your bathtub than falling off a roller coaster any day." She laughed.

But Clare! You don't -." I didn't finish, she pulled me into the car with her.

Rodney broke out in a tremendous sweat as the car climbed the hill. His body started to shake. Clare looked at him frightened.

"Rodney! What's wrong with you!" she screamed.

"Clare, I told you… I'm a monster!" Rodney said wincing. The car traveled faster, Rodney shook violently, and his form had been activated. His skin began to singe and peel, exposing a mixture of metal and flesh underneath. Clare screamed horrendously. Rodney was changing and getting stronger. He lifted up his restraint, and as the car rounded the curb, Rodney tumbled out. He hit the concrete without breaking any bones or scaring his body. He then started to scream.

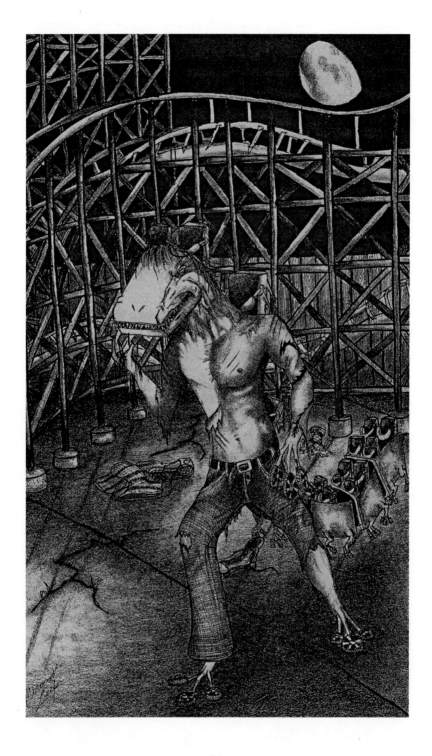

Rodney began to change. No! he screamed. I will not be overpowered! He fought the beast that he really was. His change began to slow, but it could never be stopped. Clare stood several feet away from him watching in horror. Rodney's sholderblades vibrated as seats sprouted along his back. The skin was ripping off his chest and, he was slowly losing his sanity. His hands and feet fused together to make wheels. His tailbone extended as his teeth grew into fangs. Still, his own will was in control, but not for long.

Clare walked up to him.

"Rodney!" She yelled.

He turned and looked at her. He was only half roller coaster at the moment. His skin dangled from him and his hair falling out.

"Rodney, are you a - ?"

"Clare!" he said in a rugged voice. "This only happens at night! And when I touch a coaster. Clare you must go!"

"I need to protect you."

"NO! Clare I have no control until the full moon, until then I can kill you!" he finished as a rippling pain raced through his body. He wailed like a dog and started to rip off his excess skin. He was losing it.

"Clare... RUN!"

He grew through his clothes and towered over Clare. His jaw popped out of socket and then pushed forward, forming a snout. His eyes burned as they became unhuman. He roared to sky signaling that Railrunner had returned.

Clare stood motionless looking at her lover. She didn't want to believe what she was seeing.

"Rodney?" she said to him dumbfounded. He started to recover from the rapid change, and then his eyes met hers. Railrunner snarled and extracted his steel dagger-like claws.

"Rodney! It's me!"

"Its Railrunner now." The coaster spoke. He edged up toward Clare. Then he threw back his head and howled. Then before Clare could react, he lunged for her. She was frozen in fear and couldn't move...

Chapter 9

The Rampage of a Roller Coaster

Suddenly detective Black jumped in front of Clare. He held a rifle aimed at Railrunner, and then he let loose the gun's power. Clare ran for her life while Black was firing. Railrunner landed in front of him and raised his claws, and nailed the detective, sending him crashing through a tent. Railrunner let loose a roar as he leapt onto the top of the fifty foot lift hill.

That's when they all saw him, blood on his wheels and grinning wickedly at the carnival guest. His tail lashed back and forth like an angry cat, and his eyes narrowed. Then all hell broke loose as Railrunner leaped from his perch and the people ran wild.

Just outside the carnival stood Thunderbark and his allies. They were behind a bus watching Railrunner's rampage.

"Got a plan Thunderbark?" asked Merrylegs.

"We need to take action; we don't want this news reaching outside the city!" Static spoke.

"Static you are right. Even though Railrunner disobeyed me and came here with his girlfriend anyway, we must help."

"What are we gonna do then!" Static interrupted.

"Fine. Here is the plan. Merrylegs you go and save the girl, she is at the most risk because Railrunner will seek to destroy the closest to him. Static, cops will arrive shortly, stall them anyway you can. As for me I will try and stop Railrunner."

Merrylegs agreed and Static nodded. Then Merrylegs started to change. Her hair and legs got longer. A brass pole grew out from her. Then her jaw and nose became a snout and her ears pointed. She became a yellow carousel horse. She reared back on her hind legs and flicked her lion like tail and bolted into the park. Then Static started his transformation. His skin hardened and turned green and blue. His tailbone became a long cable with a wire on its end. A steering wheel grew from his back. He doubled over and became a bumper car; he too headed for the park.

"Railrunner," spoke Thunderbark to himself. "You are an ignorant fool who has a lot to learn and a long way to go." He said while watching his comrades arrive unnoticed in the carnival. "Despite you poor decision I am giving you another chance."

He took off his old cowboy hat, his silver hair shone into the moon and his dragon like eyes sparkled. Then he began to turn into his true self. Seats sprouted along his back and his teeth became fangs. His hands became wheels and his jaw popped out, becoming a snout. His skin hardened and the final details occurred. He became a snow-white roller coaster with ice blue eyes. A silver lightning bolt ran across them. He let loose a ghostly howl and then ran for the carnival.

Static rolled behind a wall and took observation, a line of police cars had just pulled up. He simply grinned at them. He thought he should destroy news crews if they arrived along with the police. He stood and transformed back into his human form and walked out of his hiding place with his hands casually in his pockets.

"Kid! What are you doing! This area is under complete lockdown!" A cop scolded.

"I'm just passing trough dude." Then he glanced at their cruisers. "Aren't those Chargers?"

"Kid, we are warning you!"

"Funny, I never get along with cars to well…"

A policeman placed his gun on Static's back. And with that, Static released a painful shock into the man's body, knocking him unconscious. He fell backward, reveling Static's cable tail.

" What the hell?" an officer said as he stared motionless at the unexpected appendage.

Static then turned into the rest of his bumper car form. Then he floored it towards the police cars. Within minutes he destroyed them.

"Damn I'm good!" he laughed.

Railrunner ran through the carnival, destroying nearly everything in his path. From toppling over small rides to completely obliterating food stands. People continued to run in panic. Railrunner could smell their fear and blood. He roared in pure pleasure. Off in the distance he saw flashing lights and heard sirens. It was police and swat teams. How Railrunner hated them, how he despised them! *Come on, challenge me! See if you're brave enough to come after me!* Railrunner thought laughing to himself.

He left the midway and traveled deep into the fair. He entered the area where the creative arts and agricultural buildings stood. Driven by his ravenous hunger, Railrunner leaned full tilt towards the livestock. Scent of pigs and cattle flooded his nostrils. He began to stalk his prey, silently walking inside the large barn. He went undetected, he had no scent nor was he seen. His eyes scanned the plump cows, Railrunner began licking his chops. Then he found his victim, a fat black and white dairy cow.

He slowly crept behind her, she could not smell him, but he could smell her, her blood. She suddenly felt his shallow breathing on the back of her neck; she turned and came face to face with her worst nightmare. Railrunner nailed her, the cow put up no struggle. He dragged her out of the barn, her body leaving a bloody trail. He stopped in the middle of a main walkway, and lay down the cow. *Let them see me feast, let their fear overcome them,* He thought angrily. The demon roller coaster sunk his dagger like teeth into the cow's carcass. Flesh and blood poured down his throat as he devoured his prize. He continued to detatch flesh from bone, satisfying his hunger.

He then heard footsteps behind him, he grinned to himself. *You're in for it.* He then looked up and at his stalker. It was a swat team member. Blood dripped from his jaws as he stared at him, his eyes full of hatred. The man aimed his gun at Railrunner, who reared backward and extracted his claws. Then he charged as a juggernaut at the succorless man. Before the swat team member could fire, Railrunner's claws pierced through his chest. He fell with a soft thud on the concrete. Railrunner snorted in disgust then he turned and saw, Clare.

Railrunner crouched low and started to growl. Clare stood frozen, crying. She trembled as Railrunner crept toward her.

"Rodney it's me!" She said as tears were rolling down her face. She was still in shock ever since Rodney had transformed. She was so transfixed during that time that she did not remember what he had told her.

"Rodney, why?" she asked. "How did this happen?"

Railrunner growled even louder. There was something familiar with her, but he could not process the mere thought.

"How Rodney, how!" She said whimpering.

Railrunner barred his fangs and prepared to strike, but before he could make a move a bright yellow carousel horse darted in front of him. He looked at it, watching it force the girl to get on its back. *It's stealing my prey*, he thought angrily. The horse ran off with the girl. He roared and went after them.

I carried Clare through the gallows of the carnival. Railrunner was hot on my trail. I ran through the sprinklers, for I knew they would disguise my scent. I galloped under the stadium of the dirt track, Clare still grasping my brass pole in fear. Poor thing, she had no idea. I ran into an underground storage room and forced Clare off my back. I then became human and locked the door. And shut the prison window across the room, peeking out the blinds.

"Would someone please tell me what the hell is going on!"

She said looking at me in pure terror. I walked toward her, she only scooted back away.

"I am not going to hurt you, Clare. I'm here to protect you."

"What's going on? How do you know my name? You person… horse, or whatever you are."

"First of all quit yelling! Second of all I'm a carousel horse. And third like you I have a name, Its Merrylegs."

"Well Merrylegs, what is going on with my boyfriend Rodney? Why is he a roller coaster!"

I sat beside Clare. " I can only speak a few answers. Rodney like me is not human, he is a ride from Amusement Park Between, an amusement park that can exist within any amusement park and is only accessible by those who are of its blood. In our world every ride is alive."

" Ok, but what is up with Rodney?"

"Well Rodney's real name is Railrunner. As you could see, he is a roller coaster, the highest authority in our world, and the most powerful creature. If he dares to touch or ride he transforms no matter what. In our world he is a roller coaster twenty four seven, in your world he is coaster by night."

" I just can't believe this is really happening."

" Best believe, this legend is real."

She looked up at me, wiping away tears.

"Hop on, we are getting out of this carnival." I said as I changed and whisked her away into the darkness.

Railrunner sniffed the air and snorted in disgust. He had lost the carousel horse. He stood alone among the empty buildings. Suddenly a new scent worked its way into his nostrils. Detective Black quietly snuck up behind him, a large machete in his hand. He raised it towards Railrunner's back and prepared to stab him but, to his dismay the coaster turned around and clasped the machete in his wheels. He roared into his face, and hit him with a heavy blow, knocking the detective out cold.

"Railrunner." Said a deep voice behind him. He turned to see a white roller coaster. Railrunner let out a nasty snarl, threatening him.

"I warned you, Railrunner." It continued. You deliberately disobeyed me, now you're paying the price on several accounts."

Railrunner turned around completely and barred his teeth and arched his back. He suddenly stood up and generated lightning on his wheels; he directed it at the other coaster. Then it was released in a bolt that headed strait for Thunderbark. The white coaster somehow stopped it, redirected it, and hit Railrunner. He screamed in pain and fell to the concrete. He then blacked out.

Miranda Leek

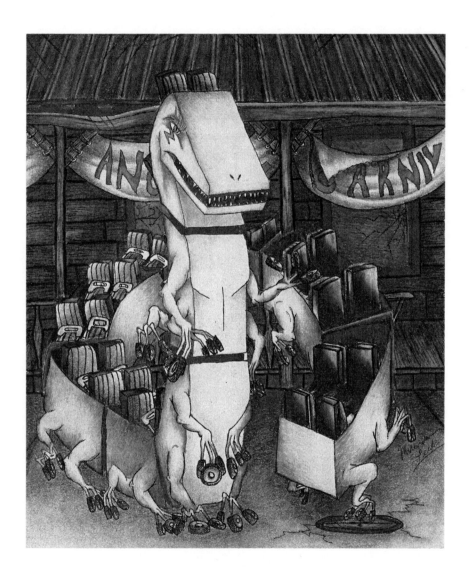

Thunderbark thought to himself as he looked at the red coaster. *I redirected his lightning. His lightning was powerful enough to knock him out. It takes a long time to learn even how to generate lightning; it takes years for an experienced roller coaster to generate that much power. Railrunner achieved that on his second night! And he wasn't even in control! He is probably going to be more powerful than I ever had imagined him.*

Chapter 10
Why Must It Be This Way?

I woke up blinking my eyes briefly, my head throbbed and my muscles ached. It felt as if a bronco kicked me. I opened my eyes a tad bit more to see Thunderbark standing before me. I moaned loudly.

"Railrunner, say something, let us know you are with us."

I looked at him, my eyes narrowed.

"You're an ass." I growled.

Thunderbark rolled his eyes. "He's fine," he sighed.

I sat up to see that I was in a hotel suite. Merrylegs leaned against the wall combing her thick red hair while Static sat in front of a TV playing video games, a racing one. All he did was crash into the other opponents. Merrylegs laughed.

"Have you ever tried not crashing into things?"

"Hey! It's in my nature." He objected, looking back to the screen.

I sat up in bed and turned to Thunderbark. I took a long deep breath then reluctantly decided to speak to him. But he spoke first.

"I have never seen a young roller coaster as powerful as you. You were able to bend some of the most incredible lightning before you were even able to learn it. It takes years for a coaster to even get a small spark."

"Well is there any particular reason why?"

"You are the red. Like I said before, you are a one and only. You are destined for greatness, Railrunner."

"Whoop dee." I grumbled.

"You need to work on your manners, and definitely your language." Thunderbark groaned. I simply ignored him.

"Whatever, so why are we here in this room?"

"There was a possible witness that could have seen you during your transformation yesterday, and he is in the position where he could arrest you." He sighed.

"Detective Black."

"Right, if he saw you he could expose you, and get you imprisoned, ruining our chances of defeating Ironwheel." He said with his eyes changing dark blue in frustration.

I got to my feet to get ready and prepared to walk out the door.

"Where are you going?" Thunderbark said sternly.

"I'm going to talk to Clare, and help her understand what's wrong with me, why I am a freak." I said shutting the door behind me. I wanted to make things right with Clare; I just hope she accepts me for what and how twisted I was.

I walked out of the hotel, to my right was the police impound lot, and there was my car. The black Mustang, it was as shinny as the day I bought it. I'll go get it out; besides, Clare's house is a long way away from the hotel. I walked over to the police station and passed trough the double doors. I saw lots of officers roaming about. I felt so unease, I now considered these men as my enemies. There were posters of wanted people on a large wall, but in the middle of them was the biggest poster of all, the one of me as a roller coaster. I tried to ignore it, and then I walked up to the desk.

"May I help you?" a middle aged lady asked with a smile on her rosy red face.

"Yes, I need to get my car out of the impound lot." I said trying to sound normal, and appear that way.

"Ok, what car is it?"

"The black Mustang GT" I said as I stuck my hand into my pocket.

"What year?"

"2008." I replied as I pulled out my tattered wallet.

"It will be two hundred dollars, sir."

I handed her a wad of money. She stuck it in a safe and smiled back at me, but I could sense that she was leery.

"Well looks like your all set, by the way. We found your car parked in the back of Snooks, on the first night that the roller coaster attacked. You know anything of this?"

"Well, I wasn't really there, a friend drove me home, I was pretty drunk," I lied.

"Okay, but good on your part." She chuckled.

I nodded and followed an officer back into the building and out into the lot. We walked up to my car and he handed me my keys.

"Really nice ride. You're lucky the roller coaster didn't destroy it," he laughed. It was a complete paradox that the enemy was talking to his biggest foe without even knowing it. This only made me more solicitous.

"Thanks. Hey where is Detective Black?" I asked out of curiosity.

"Oh, well he got mauled by you know who last night; he's still in the hospital. They said his injuries were not life threatening though."

"I wish him the best," I said climbing into my car, wanting to snicker at my last comment. I started the engine and drove out of the lot. They were on high alert that's for sure. As so was I.

Clare wandered around her house in a daze. She still was suffering from what happened the night before. She could not convince herself it was a dream, because the scratches lay on her arm. The brutal memory of Rodney transforming still lingered in her head, she shuttered at the very thought of it. Then the doorbell rang making her jump. She looked through the peephole to see Rodney standing on the doorstep.

Clare fell back against the wall in surprise. Her heart began to hammer in her chest, she could almost hear its loud thud as it pounded over and over again.

"Clare? It's me, Rodney; I want to talk to you." Rodney called from the other side of the door. Clare begun to panic, then she quickly walked into the kitchen and began to dig around in the silverware drawer, her hands shaking.

"Come on Clare, I know you're home. Could you please answer?" Rodney called. She shoved several forks out of the way and pulled out a kitchen knife. She hid it up in her sleeve and began to walk to the front door. She did the whole process as if she was in a trance.

Clare slowly opened the door.

'Come in," she said quietly.

Rodney walked through the doorway, shut the door, and stopped to take off his shoes. Suddenly Clare pulled out the knife and brought it down towards his chest. Rodney had no time to react, the knife went into him and Clare stumbled backward gasping in fear. Rodney sat on the floor breathing harshly. He tugged at the knife sticking out of his chest; he pulled it free and lay it aside. Blood seeped through his shirt; he unbuttoned it and reveled the nasty wound.

Then the gash started to shrink, till it was no longer visible, Rodney had healed himself. Clare stood unmoving. She gasped as she realized her mistake.

"I'm so sorry!" She sniveled as Rodney got back up and popped his neck. Rodney looked at her, he unexpectedly smiled a little.

"Clare, I've looked worse, believe me," he started to laugh.

"Like last night?"

"Yes, like last night."

"Clare I came to explain what's going on with me. Care to listen for a minute?"

"I don't mind," she said sitting on the couch. I walked over and sat in the chair in front of her. I wiped my face then sighed aloud. Then I began my story.

"Clare, I wasn't born here, I was born somewhere else, a place called Amusement Park Between. There all the rides are alive -."

"Merrylegs told me that part already. I want to know how you became a coaster, and what a coaster's characteristics are." She interrupted.

"Fine, I will start with how I became a roller coaster. It all began when I went to Mystic Park to get a job, I met Woody. He and I went coaster walking. Then we stopped and Woody said his real name was Thunderbark, and mine was Railrunner. Then he told me where I came from and the legend of Amusement Park Between. And I was the key to some kind of prophecy. Then, it happened."

"What."

"He tricked me, he made me touch the rails, and he activated my curse."

"That's how you became Railrunner?"

"Yes, I become a coaster at night or when I interact with them. I don't have control until the first full moon when the clock strikes twelve and when the moon is at the highest point in the sky, which is tonight. However, in Amusement Park between I'm a coaster always."

"Have you been to Amusement Park between?"

"No, not yet."

"So can you do anything in your coaster form?"

"Yes, I can heal myself; I have extreme strength, agility, and senses. I can bend lightning and fire, which I did lightning and nearly killed myself last night. I can't ever get sick; I can predict when things will happen. And others."

"What is it like being Railrunner?" She asked quietly as she nervously pulled at her sleeves.

"Clare, it certainly has its ups and downs. Right now I have no control and I have a taste for blood. I feel damned, I feel like my soul is being stolen. I feel so heartless. And yet, I feel so invincible, like nothing can stop me, even though that is true. I feel the urge to get revenge to fight. At the stage where I'm at, its like Dr, Jeckel and Mr. Hyde."

"That's when you're not in control, right?"

"Yes, I haven't felt what it is like when I'm in control."

Then all was quiet for a minute, and then Clare looked at me tearing up.

"Rodney, I mean Railrunner, I think your other side might come between us."

"What?" I said startled.

"Railrunner you are very good to me, but unfortunately you are also very bad. You almost killed me last night."

"Clare, I didn't…It's not my fault!"

"Railrunner, this will never work. You have people that can't accept you for what you are. You have people that want you dead!"

"Clare!"

"Railrunner, our love is - forbidden. We can't carry on any longer. A roller coaster cannot be in love with a human!"

"Clare please!" I said coming to my knees.

"Railrunner, we are done, no more." She said with tears rolling down her cheeks. She pulled a pink rose out of a vase and handed it to me, and then she disappeared into the house. I stormed outside and climbed into my car. I sat in the seat holding the rose.

"Why does it have to be this way?" I said in sheer frustration. Why me!"

Chapter 11
Monster in Disguise

I sat in the car, furious. I glared down at the rose in my hand. Frustrated I flung the rose to the passenger seat next to me. I started the engine and quickly backed out of her driveway, almost running into Clare's mailbox.

"My god why!" I said trying to hold back my anger. "I am a monster! I almost killed her! She tried to kill me! I am of roller coaster blood! We can never be together! Never ever again!"

I drove faster, running a few stop signs. My dark thoughts filled my head. My heart was broken, ours was broken. This is all coming too quickly. My life suddenly shifted, taking a completely unheard of route. Nothing made sense anymore!

I pulled into my driveway and ran into my house. I went up to my bedroom. I kicked my bed and knocked my lamp off the end table. I went into the bathroom and hunched over the sink. I turned on the faucet and splashed water onto my face. I looked into the mirror above me. My true reflection appeared.

"Not Rodney, Railrunner! Railrunner did this!" I yelled, breaking the mirror with my fist. I fell backward against the tub.

"But yet my name isn't really Rodney and I'm not really human. My name is Railrunner, a roller coaster. And I've been a coaster all along."

I couldn't think straight. One thing meant this, another meant that. I went back into my bedroom and lay onto my covers. Thunderbark was right; I needed to forget about love. Then my eyes shut and I fell into a deep slumber.

I woke up again at one, and decided to go for a walk. Maybe I could get my mind off Clare that way. I got ready, walked out the door and stretched. Then I ran in the opposite direction of Clare's house.

I ran for about an hour. I then realized I was getting near the carnival. In a way I wondered what it looked like. I barely could remember last night. All I could recollect was Clare's look on her face. The look she gave me as soon as I became my beastly self. That horrible image! I must get it out of my head!

But I couldn't, because the next thing I saw was the carnival. A shiver went down my spine, so did a small ripple of pain. Many officers, firemen, and locals stood around or walked into the ruins. Firemen removed scattered and destroyed rides. Police examined the premises. Onlookers questioned each other and some spoke of last night's invasion. Out of all the people, I spotted Buddy and Sly. Their hands had scratches on them as well as bandages. They talked to one another as the stood a little ways from the rest of the crowd.

I decided to walk over and join in; make them think I have nothing to hide.

"Rodney!" Sly announced. "Where the hell have you been?"

"I've, been on a business trip," I said making up a quick lie.

"What happened that night you left the bar? Right as we got glass in our hands, you disappeared!"

"Okay, I started to feel drunk and I felt the beer coming back up so yeah." I said wanting to laugh at my response.

"Of course Rodney. Good thing you were in the bathroom praying to the porcelain god when that demon coaster showed up." Buddy said looking at the aftermath of the carnival.

"You know anything?" Sly asked.

"No." I said hesitating a little. Then news crews started to arrive and began to set up their gear.

"For all we know that coaster could be right under our noses." Sly announced. "Watching our every move."

My heartbeat quickened. The news crews began to make their broad cast. They started to interview a tubby police officer that kept pulling at his belt.

"Sir, what do you and the police force plan to do since there has been a second attack?"

"Well, I'll make it simple. We are going to stop at nothing to find this demon, like the community, we want it dead and gone. We will search every square inch of the town. We will get the FBI involved! We will learn it's every trick. It will be brought to justice!" The policeman proclaimed.

I gulped. I looked over at Buddy and Sly.

"Serves it right," Buddy started. "Look what it has done!"

"Yep, going around and destroying everything, killing people…"

"I think we get the point," I interrupted. I looked at my watch. It read five-thirty, at least two more hours till the moon rose. "Well I best be going, I have things to do."

"Take care Rodney." Sly called.

I ignored him. Now because of my actions the FBI was coming! And the police were hot on my trail! I had to be more careful as Railrunner for now on, but was that possible for an eight and a half ton living roller coaster? I kept on running, not daring to look back behind me. The sky was turning to shades of pink and orange. The sun was going to set soon. The day had raced by so quickly that I barely had enough time to comprehend it.

I was now almost home, I ran through the lonely streets of the outdoor shopping mall. Few cars sat in the parking lot and all of the stores had closed. Suddenly I heard a struggling scream coming out from one of the alleys between the shops. Curious, I ventured closer. I peeked my head around the corner to see five men trying to rob a young lady. As I looked closer I realized it wasn't an ordinary girl, it was Clare.

Clare was in trouble, she needed help. Besides of what happened earlier I walked out of my hiding place and towards the pose of men.

"Hey! Leave her alone!"

One of the men turned and looked at me, he let a smirk appear onto his face.

"This your boyfriend sweetcheeks? This your prince charming coming to rescue you?" he taunted.

"Rodney what -." Clare started to speak, but suddenly one of the men put a knife to her throat.

"Gentlemen, I am the wrong person you want to deal with." I said without thinking. Before I knew it, one of the men struck me from the side. I fell to my knees against the brick wall. He started to kick me square in the ribs over and over again. Blood came into my mouth. There was a pause. I struggled to get to my feet. I stood up to only get punched in the jaw, blood spurted in various places.

"Wrong person to be dealing with? I don't think so!" One of the men laughed. I wiped my blood off my face. I looked at the sky, just a few more moments, then these men will get what they had coming for them. I could already feel my wounds healing; I turned and popped my neck. These men had their weapon in numbers, but I had a big one, a really mean and nasty one. An unstoppable force from hell.

"I am warning you gentlemen, your gonna get your ass kicked in a minute." I said smirking.

"Oh, so you haven't had enough?" The man laughed. Then the biggest ruffian came rushing at me. I moved him out of the way and slammed him onto the wall; I was getting more powerful, more unstable. I grinned at him; I could feel my front teeth were suddenly fangs. The man looked horrified, before he could say anything; I hit him upside the head knocking him out cold. The gang looked stunned.

"Come on Railrunner!" Clare shouted without thinking.

"What woman? Who the heck is Railrunner?"

"That is me." I said looking at the sun. It was setting. I had to hold these idiots off for just a few more seconds!

"That is you? Why in the hell are you called that?"

I laughed a little. "You're going to see just as the moon rises, you will witness my true power and the monster that I really am. My disguise will be uncovered, and you will see the error of your ways."

"What the hell are you talking about?" He said staring at the sky.

I glanced backwards, the moon had risen, the full moon and all its power. I laughed aloud.

"This!" I said. Power flooded me from all sides. My pulse rose as my heart raced. My blood boiled as my mouth began to salivate. I grew too big for my skin, so I began to tear it off in strips. My tailbone extended as my teeth became fangs. My organs rearranged as my nose pushed forward to make a snout. My shoulder blades shook as seats sprouted from them, and then they grew along my back. I was losing control, my will. Then it all stopped, I finished roaring, to the night sky, to the moon.

✝ ✝ ✝

Railrunner glared at the criminal, their eyes making contact.

"My god! You're the monster! The roller coaster!"

The coaster took a few steps forward.

"Umm - Railrunner! Please spare me!" the leader cowered.

"You feed on the blood of the innocent, I feed on the blood of mere humans, even if they are damned or not." Railrunner spoke with a crazed look in his eye. He then lunged forward and snapped the man's neck, killing him instantly. Railrunner turned and roared at the dead man's followers. They stood in fear as he revealed his claws. They ran but Railrunner was quicker, his claws sunk through human flesh, and he spilled human blood. Clare watched in fear as Railrunner one by one slaughtered the men, as he was on his genocide. Then the man he knocked out earlier ran, he headed for the square of the outdoor mall. Railrunner caught sight of him, and began his pursuit. Clare came out of shock and followed Railrunner close behind.

The man ran into the square and glanced behind him. The roller coaster was nowhere to be seen. He pulled his gun out of his pants that he forgot about and held it up. He was ready. But even as he stood there, Railrunner hid within the buildings. He watched the man eagerly.

The gunman could only hear the gushing water out of the fountain behind him. His heart hammered in his chest as he continued to wander the dead silent square. Railrunner quietly crept forward between the stores. He could sense the man's blood and fear. The robber trembled and so did the gun in his hand.

"Where are you demon?" He whispered to himself.

Suddenly there was a rustle behind the man. He turned and fired the gun, but instead of a mutant coaster, there was only mist. Railrunner grinned at him, thinking what a fool the man was.

Then the crazed human also pulled out his knife. Then he fired a shot into each alley, the bullets only echoed in the night. Then he pitched the knife into the darkest alley behind him. He fired more rounds, and then his gun ran out of ammunition. He dug around in his pockets for more, but found none. He slowly backed up toward the fountain.

"Maybe I lost it." He said.

Then Railrunner landed on top of the fountain, the vibration of his impact was so great that it knocked the man off his feet. Railrunner grinned at him, and then he pulled the man's knife out of his chest, the man watched in awe as the wound instantly healed.

"You know, it's not very wise to be playing with knives." Railrunner said tossing the utensil aside. Then his claws slowly appeared. *"Unfortunately for you, I do anyway."* Railrunner smirked as his claws extended to their full length.

The man got to his feet and started to sprint. Railrunner leaped from his post and jabbed his dagger-like claws into the robber's back. The robber began to choke on his own blood, and then he fell to the ground dead, his body lying in a crumpled heap.

Railrunner snorted in disgust as he licked the blood off his wheels and claws. Railrunner's forked tongue going between every groove. He purred with pleasure, as he licked his lips with satisfaction. Then his keen hearing heard the siren of an approaching squad car. His eyes narrowed as he looked off in the direction of the warning. *I'll give him what he wants, a glance at me, but he won't like it.* Railrunner thought to himself as he crept forward.

The cop had received a call about an armed robbery that happened several minutes ago. He scanned the buildings; they seemed uncomfortably quiet and eerie. It was just him and his partner.

"What a minute what's that?" The one in the passenger seat asked. They stopped the car to see the body of a man. Looking to their left they saw the corpse of another.

"My god. What the hell happened here?" The other said. Then a strange howl sounded.

"What was that? The driver questioned.

"It was him." The officer said as he looked around nervously.

"Is it playing with us?"

"No, it's setting us up." He replied.

On that note Railrunner landed on the hood of the car, he roared in the officer's faces.

"Floor it! Floor it now!" the passenger screamed.

The squad car fled in reverse. Railrunner followed it, charging at full speed.

"Oh my god! It's gonna kill us!"

"It won't if you keep going." The cop said firing his gun through the windshield, the bullets only bounced off of Railrunner's hide. "You know Harrison, I wanted to see this thing, but not like this! Swerve around and go forward!"

The car swerved sharply and turned frontward. Harrison drove the car towards the city, the cop continued to fire bullets trough the back windshield. Railrunner rammed the car from behind, as the men took a curve onto a busy road, nearly making them lose control. The chase headed toward traffic. Harrison blared his horn, and turned the sirens up full blast.

"Get outta the damn way!" he yelled. Railrunner had his eyes on the car; he was not trough with them yet. He sliced trough obstacles. People screamed and ran. He pushed large trucks out of the way. The cop car veered in front of a semi, narrowly missing it. Railrunner leaped over its trailer and landed partially on the roof of the squad car. He sunk his claws through the top of the automobile , going between the two officers inside. They looked at each other in trepidation. Harrison swerved sharply again, and headed down a dark alley. Railrunner was flung off the car, but still he pursued them.

The squad car sped blindly. Railrunner leaped off buildings and their walls. He was furious! Like a volcano that was to erupt at any moment!

"Come on you son of a bitch!" the officer yelled at him.

The car smashed through a chain-linked fence. Railrunner was just a few seconds behind.

"Where now Rob! I can't lose him!" The driver whimpered.

"Go down Jefferson. It enters into the Mystic Park's campgrounds; we should be able to get rid of it there."

The car sped down the road. It headed into a heavily wooded area. Railrunner ran up beside them and bumped the cruiser. The car went off balance, but still didn't flip. They finally entered the campgrounds.

Railrunner felt a strange gain of power. He was near the park. His heart pumped. He would end this pursuit now.

Gathering strength he leaped over the car. The men looked at him horrified. Railrunner turned, he raised his tail and smashed it down on the cars hood, stopping it completely. The men climbed out and prepared to make a run for it. Railrunner raised his claws high in the air. The officers awaited their fate, but suddenly Railrunner retracted them and clutched his chest. With it throbbing, he turned to see that the moon was at its highest. Time for him to be in control.

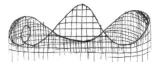

Railrunner threw his head back and screamed a deafening wail. The policemen grabbed their ears, seizing the chance they fled. Pain sliced through Railrunner. A red mist descended over his eyes as he fell backward onto a tree. His seats shook as his wheels singed. He could feel his own will slowly coming back. His chest bulged as he doubled over onto the ground. He reared back his head and wailed once more. Pain went through him in spasms. He gained more control by every passing second, suddenly it all stopped.

I stood up feeling woozy. I looked down at my wheels; they had dried blood on them. I clutched my forehead.

"Shit, what the hell happened?" I said. That was when I suddenly realized those were my words. I looked at myself all over again. "Am I in control now?" I questioned. I looked ahead to see Mystic Park and all its rides across the lake. The moon hung high overhead. I blinked my eyes briefly, trying to get them into focus.

"I am in control."

I then heard a twig snap behind me. I spun around to see Clare. She hesitated, but then she realized I meant no harm.

"Railrunner?" She asked coming to me.

"Yes," I replied in a surprisingly velvet voice.

"Are you - well you know?"

"I guess I am." I said glancing at the moon again. I walked over and sat at a base of a tree. I breathed hard in exhaustion from the change. Clare walked closer.

"What did I do to deserve such a thing? Why is it me that has to carry this burden upon my chest?" I said aloud. Clare held out her hand towards me. Her fingertips touched my metal.

"It feels so different; it's warm and not cold." She said as she continued to run her fingers down my chest. She stopped on my "breast". Her hand pressed firmly against it.

"You have a heartbeat." She said looking into my eyes. "A heart. Not clockwork."

I got up without a reply and walked to the edge of the lake. Clare warily toddled up beside me.

"You know Clare, you are right let's just be friends."

"Are you mad at me?"

"I'm not sure Clare; I'm still confused why I am what I really am. I haven't been able to focus lately." I said.

Clare did not reply, she got on a different subject.

"Ever rode on them?" she said pointing to the track.

"No."

"Strange, a roller coaster not running on rails."

"Clare, I'm not what you call a normal roller coaster." I said admitting a small grin.

"I can see that Railrunner, can I ask you a favor?"

"What"?

"My car is back at the mall, and I need a vehicle to take me home - so, can I have a ride?"

I turned and looked at her, was she really serious?

"Clare I'm not a car let alone a charter service."

"Railrunner, you're a vehicle."

"I am a monster"

"Come on Railrunner." She said almost begging.

I thought about it some more, I decided to give in.

"Fine. Hop on."

She nodded as I lowered myself down where I was on all of my wheels. Clare climbed into my first car (my head). She sat on my leather seat and took a long deep breath.

"Watch your head." I said bringing my restraint down again. She obeyed as it went over her small body.

"Okay."

"Keep your hands and feet inside the *vehicle* at all times." I said a little annoyed. Clare was trying to get on my good side after she had blown me off. I was still upset with her a little ever since this morning. I bolted into the woods; it went on for miles and passed by Clare's house. My wheels dug into the mossy forest floor as I ran.

In the distance I heard sirens, but the police were nowhere near us. We were nothing but a blur against the dense vegetation. I thought to myself as I ran. As a roller coaster, I was living under no rules and regulations. I was experiencing true freedom for the first time; I was running with the moon. The wind whistled as I moved. Out of the corner of my eye I saw Clare. She gripped tightly on my restraint and there was a happy expression on her face, grinning from ear to ear and letting the wind blow through her blond hair. Just like her expression she made speeding along the track. However, this coaster she was riding now did not always run on rails. This coaster was more than just metal and leather; it was also flesh and blood. This coaster was for more than to just scare and thrill, it was formed for combat and sorcery. Clare was riding on a twisted coaster, the roller coaster of Amusement Park Between.

A few minutes later, I arrived at Clare's neighborhood. I crept undetected among the houses. Only the insects stirred because of my heavy steps. Then I entered Clare's yard. I stopped, and she hopped off and unlocked her backdoor.

"Thank you Railrunner." She said shutting the door. Then I sensed something within Clare, she still loved me.

I simply nodded. "Clare" I began.

"Yes Railrunner," she said through the screen.

"Do you promise to not tell anyone about the real me?"

She smiled. "I do, good night Railrunner." Clare finished waving.

I watched her disappear inside her house, looking back once to smile before disappearing. I then turned to leave, Clare's cat, Mittens, hissed at me. I crouched low and gave a dragon-like hiss in return. Mittens yowled in fear, awakening the dogs. Their barks upset their sleeping masters, I left before I was seen. I wondered about Clare, deep down we both still loved each other. But the real me was tearing us apart. Where am I going to go to ponder my thoughts? And spend the remainder of the night? Then referring to Clare's words, I had an idea.

A few minutes later I stood at the gates of Mystic Park. I climbed over them easily and into the park itself. A reassuring comfort entered my body. I walked through the unfilled buildings and kiosk. It felt strange to see this place deserted. As I navigated through the park I felt myself getting stronger, before I knew it, I was standing at the foot of the steel coaster.

I walked up the stairs into the boarding area; the unliving trains had been put up for the night. I looked up the lift hill, I climbed up the stairway that I walked on when I was coaster walking. I wanted to get on the rails at the top to see what would happen. Then I reached the peak.

I placed a set of wheels on the track; a jolt of power ran through my body. Curious, I got completely onto the rails. Power flooded my body, rattling it to the core. The power I was experiencing was different, it was more - concentrated. Then instinct took over.

Wind whipped my face as I sped down the hill. Power now was at its greatest point. I felt like I could never be restrained. I raced along at blinding speeds; I rocketed up the next hill and jumped the rails, only to land on the base of the hill. I rounded a helix, leaving the rails again, doing a move like I was on a skateboard. Only this was a different matter and I was my own wheels.

I looped upside down and went through a corkscrew, roaring in pleasure as I did so. I felt better than I did in my entire life. After the ride was over, I ran the circuit some more; I lost count on how many laps I had done. I entered the station for the last time. I got off the track and prepared to head home, it was nearly morning.

"So how do you like it?" a voice asked behind me. I figured out it was Thunderbark.

"How did you know I was here?" I said turning to see the white coaster in the moonlight.

"A roller coaster knows when one is rolling. As I asked before, how did you like it?"

"It was - unbelievable."

"Yes a coaster is most powerful if it is one with the rails."

"Interesting."

Then Thunderbark placed his wheels on the track, they magically adjusted to fit the rails like a normal coaster's would. However they didn't fit quite right. "Of coarse since I'm a woodie they are not going to fit." He said. Then Thunderbark walked up to me, he looked around to see if there was anybody about.

"Railrunner, we have a task to do. You know where the history museum is right?"

"Of course."

"Meet me there first thing tomorrow."

"All right," I said leaving. Then a thought crossed my mind. Why did he say we had a task to do?

Chapter 12
Investigations of separate species

The next morning I got up early to yet again see myself on the news. After getting tired of hearing it, I got into my car and headed for the museum. After my arrival, I parked and locked my door and then turned to see Thunderbark behind me. He held two photography cameras and press badges.

"Thunderbark, what are we doing exactly?" I said raising an eyebrow.

"We are acting as members of the press, they are the only ones allowed in today. Railrunner, the museum is hosting a new exhibit, Unknown Artifacts."

"So -."

"Here are your instructions," he said handing the gear to me. "Don't speak unless you are asked to, and follow my lead. Got that?"

"Umm, sure." I said trailing him to the entrance of the museum. A man at the entrance asked us to hold up our tags, we passed through undetected. Thunderbark guided me to the elevator, he pressed floor 6. The doors opened and we stepped onto the new level. There was scarcely anybody around. Only one or two press members. We began to walk among the exhibit's artifacts; however we didn't stop to snap any pictures. Thunderbark was looking for something, something important. Then we went into a very secluded dark room containing jewelry. Pieces were displayed in separate cases with their own lighting system. Then we arrived at the back of the room. Thunderbark stopped and gazed at the thing in front of us in awe.

"The Augu Ra." He said.

Inside the case was a golden necklace. Ancient writing was on every bead, even the moon shaped amulet that hung on the chain. Then Thunderbark spoke up again.

"Rodney, the Augu Ra is the necklace of the red roller coaster. It will give you the power to transform in this word whenever you want. It has powers that are very vital to you and to be discovered."

"So you're saying this big chunk of gold is mine?"

"For one thing it's not gold, Rodney. It's made out of the rarest metal of our entire world. Firinium." He said taking his ring off. It matched the necklace, same eerie markings.

"All Amusement Park Between residents need a bit of Firinium on, before they enter our world. Every ride has a ring."

"Woody, how come I have a necklace?" I asked perplexed.

"Because you Rodney are a red roller coaster. They only come along after another dies. Reds are automatically destined for greatness. The Augu Ra has belonged to every red coaster there ever was, all the way back to the beginning."

"Again, interesting."

"Now help me snap some picks of the area." Thunderbark said bending down and taking odd picks of the room's corners and ceiling. Every image containing a surveillance camera, making me wonder.

"Why are we doing this?"

"Rodney, the reason why is we have to steal the Augu Ra is in order for us all to get back into Amusement Park Between."

"WHAT!"

Detective Black passed back and forth across the meeting room of the police station. Five of the sheriffs sat at the meeting table drinking coffee. Everyone anxiously awaited the arrival of the FBI. Then Detective Black sat down at the end of the table, he scanned through photos, he suddenly put them down as the men he inquired about came through the double doors.

"Morning gentlemen, take a seat." Black started. The FBI's men sat at the remaining spots, their captain sat at the other end, a lean man with silver hair and a solemn stare. He then cleared his throat to speak.

"All right Detective, give me some details on this abomination."

Detective Black walked over to the dry erase board and took a remote from the shelf that housed the markers. He then switched the projector on. The frightening image of Railrunner appeared. All of the men from the FBI gawked and pointed.

"Dear god is that the thing you are talking about detective!" He said befuddled.

"Yes, that is the red roller coaster. It's terrorized us every night since Tuesday." Detective Black announced as he changed from one image of Railrunner to the next.

"Let me ask you Detective, is this a hoax you made up?" the captain said changing his outlook.

"You say this is a hoax?" Black replied as he played the video of Railrunner ransacking Snooks.

"Well then, what do you make of it Black? Robot or beast?" The captain said, staring deeply at Detective Black.

"Captain," Black started sternly, "No technology in the world could be this advanced."

"So this is a beast then?"

"Yes. There are various things to support this statement. It only attacks at night, so it seems to be nocturnal. It eats meat, particularly cattle. It has organs and senses. And a predatory drive. Plus I've seen this thing a little to close, I've fired at it, and it made me bleed my own blood." He stated as he pulled up his shirt to reveal the slashes made by Railrunner. Several men gasped in horror.

"Hmmm - very interesting detective. Is there any other pieces of information that is valuable?

"Yes sir, after further investigations, we think an individual is involved with this."

"Really?" The captain questioned.

"Yes." Black said putting an image of Rodney on the screen. "This is Rodney Phillips. Witnesses say he was present at Snooks at the night of the attack. Some say he left a few seconds before the coaster arrived. He was also present at the carnival right before the attack and some affirm that they saw him at the mall on the night Mr. Roller Coaster decided to go shopping for flesh. Point is he is our main concern for one big reason."

"What is that Detective?"

"His job is at Mystic Park, as a roller coaster engineer." Black smiled deviously.

The FBI captain rubbed his chin in thought. "All right here is what we do. Our forces will search the city for the coaster by day; we want to catch that bastard off guard. Have Rodney interviewed, I want every one of his secrets squeezed out of him."

"Captain we have no records showing where Rodney lives and we can't get him at work because the park is on its off season."

"Damn it Black! The captain said standing and shouting. "Do you have any other suggestions!"

"Well sir, I know where his girlfriend resides." Black replied. He suddenly smiled wickedly to himself.

"Good! Gentlemen!" the captain announced. "We will capture this monster, and show no clemency!"

Thunderbark and I walked out to my car. I got in the drivers side as he got into the passengers. We shut the doors, and then started talking.

"Thunderbark! This is insane!"

"I know, but it is a risk that we will have to take, Railrunner." Thunderbark replied sympathetically.

"So you're just saying bust in and take it! That will lead the police here faster than I don't know what!" I objected.

"I have a plan. You and my troop will carry it out. Static will disable the alarm, when he is done, Merrylegs will guard the first floor, allowing nobody entry. She will destroy the video cameras on the first floor and the second, Static will do the rest. That is when you and I will fetch the Augu Ra."

"You are fanatical, but - this may be possible. Say did you drive here?"

He laughed. "No, I don't ride around in silly vehicles like this, I have my own wheels."

I smiled at him.

"I wouldn't have bought a car if I had known I had wheels earlier." I replied.

Clare sat on her couch wrapped in her blanket drinking hot coco. She watched the news broadcast, Railrunner was always the top story, always breaking news. Nowadays it was always about her love. Clare was uneasy and on edge, the cup vibrated a little in her hand. She had not eaten well in the last few days and felt drained because of it. All because she had accidentally found out Rodney's secret, or should she say Railrunner's.

Suddenly there was a loud knock on her door, making Clare jump in surprise, almost spilling her hot chocolate. She got up and walked to her front door, and peered through the peephole. She gasped, men in suits stood there, the letters FBI were stitched across their overcoats. They are trying to find Railrunner! The words echoed inside her head. She had no choice but to answer the door.

"How may I help you gentlemen?" Clare said as she tried to smile warmly.

"FBI," the captain said holding up his badge. "Miss Clare we are entering your premises to do an investigation and to ask you a few questions."

She hesitated, but then let the men through. Clare sat back down on her couch. The FBI captain sat across from her.

"Miss Clare I am Captain Vick. I am going to ask you a few questions regarding your boyfriend, Rodney Philips. We are recording your responses."

"Ok," Clare said trying to not look nervous.

"We believe Rodney is involved with the red roller coaster, there is evidence to support this. Rodney was visible at all of the locations where the coaster attacked. In addition, he knows their engineering by working at the park here. Clare, do you know if Rodney has had any connections with this thing?"

" He does not have connections." Clare replied trying to remain calm.

"Well, do you ever hear Rodney talking about the coaster?"

"No sir, he only talks about the normal ones at the park." She said lying.

"Clare, we know something is going on with Rodney. You can't deny it any longer."

Clare's heart hammered in her chest.

"Rodney is not involved with any of this! If he was he would tell me." She replied roughly.

"Clare don't over react. Lots of men have deep dark secrets. Those are the ones that they do not dare speak of."

"Rodney tells me everything, even his secrets." Clare said sternly.

"What are they then?" Vick asked leaning forward.

Clare stared at him. She was running out of comebacks. She opened her mouth to say something, but she found herself looking out the window, the sun was beginning to go down, there was not but an hour left in the day. They were running out of time. And she would do anything to stall them.

"Miss Clare, I asked you a question." Vick continued.

"Sorry, Rodney told me once that he was an orphan." She replied, and this time she wasn't lying.

Detective Black sat in his dark office smoking a cigarette and scanning through the coaster case. He constantly looked at pictures of Railrunner, examining him all ways possible. He looked at pictures of Rodney. He opened his mouth and let out a large puff of smoke.

"What are you hiding, that you don't want me to know?" Black questioned himself. He looked at the picture of Rodney again. Then put Railrunner's beside Rodney's on the screen. He looked at them closely, that's when he caught something. He zoomed in on them both. His eyes widened at what he saw.

The tattoos on Rodney's arm matched the markings on Railrunner's. And they both had the same gold eyebrow piercing. Detective Black realized his prediction was wrong.

"Well, Rodney, looks like you've been hiding a dirty little secret after all."

"An orphan?" questioned Vick. "When did he tell you this?"

"Long time ago." Clare began as she started to put Railrunner's missing pieces of his puzzle together.

"Really? Did he say where he was from?"

"Well, let's see," Clare said trying to think of a place other than Amusement Park Between. "He is from Tennessee." She lied.

"Clare, did Rodney mention at any time in your relationship the subject of roller coasters?"

Clare could feel herself sweat a little. There had been many times Railrunner had mentioned coasters.

"No not really," she said.

Vick rubbed his chin. He was getting tired and frustrated. Then he leaned closer to her.

"Clare, how many times have you actually seen the monster? Was Rodney with you?"

Before Clare could answer, Captain Vick's phone rang. She sighed in relief.

"This is Vick." He responded.

"It's Black." Vicks volume was up on high on his phone and Clare could hear his every word.

"Found anything, Detective?"

"Yes, I certainly have. I wouldn't waste anymore time, I looked through old files and found his residence. Meet me at the location, and Captain, bring reinforcements, you'll need every one of them."

Oh my god, Black knows! Clare thought. Vick quickly hung up and scrambled his men out the door. A few seconds later Clare picked up the phone and dialed Railrunner's number. The sun was starting to set.

Chapter 13
Arrest

I walked into the door, and took off my jacket and flung it onto the couch. Suddenly my cell phone rang. It was Clare.

"Clare?"

"Railrunner!" She screamed. They're coming! Black found out somehow! The FBI and the police are heading right for you!"

"When did you find this out!" I said yelling into the receiver.

"The FBI interviewed me! I didn't tell them a thing about you! But somehow Black found out! Go Railrunner! Get out of there!" Then there was a loud bang on the door.

"They're already here!" I replied hanging up. Before I knew it a gun was pressed up against my head and I was held in the firm grip of a squad member.

Railrunner stood stone still as another officer came through the door and shut it behind him.

"Got any more ideas, Rodney?" the officer said.

Railrunner looked at the sky. The moon had showed its face once again. His eyes turned into that of which they were.

"Gentlemen, you just got on my bad side!" he said as his teeth became fangs. Before the man could fire, Railrunner sunk his teeth into the officer's neck, making them both fall to the floor. Railrunner began to change rapidly, his metal hide ripped through his skin as seats pierced through his back. The officer he bit was killed instantly, and the other one died from his own bullet that bounced off Railrunner's metal. Rage built up inside him, as the urge to protect and fight entered his body. His transformation was much quicker than before, than it had ever been. Bigger he grew the stronger he got. His hands and feet trembled as they became wheels. His nose grew into a long snout as his senses increased. Then he settled, he was his true self again.

"Boy I'm tired of you people being arrogant! If you can't accept me, I can't accept you!" I shouted in rage. I gathered my strength and jumped through the roof. Landing in front of the brigade, greeting them with a mighty roar.

The bullets started to fly, each one of them bouncing off of me. Then they ceased fire. I began to laugh.

"My turn." I said, but before I could attack, unexpectedly, I felt a spark ignite from the back of my throat. I opened my mouth, a beam of light shot out like a missile. Shockwaves flew outward from it, destroying nearly everything. Then the beam hit a squad truck, making it explode. The whole ground shook, foundations cracked. The tremors continued, forcing everyone to take cover. Then I realized what I just did, a concussion beam. The blast from it obliterated nearly everything. I suddenly felt weaker, that was probably why Thunderbark said to use the weapon as a last resort.

Remaining men came out of hiding. They began to fire once more. I charged and flipped over their cruisers, flattening some of the unfortunate. My strength seemed to drain from me. I was getting weaker by the second. There had to be someway to recharge myself! Wait a minute, the rails! If I reached them, I could get back to maximum power.

I stopped, and ran in the direction of the park. My legs felt like lead as I moved. I could hear bullets brush past me. Helicopters hung overhead, tracking my every move. I ran in zigzags for thirty minutes, destroying everything at my wake. Finally from a distance I could see Mystic Park. Suddenly I heard a blast like that of a cannon. Seconds later, a great force hit me from above. I opened my eyes to see a blanket of netting in my face. Then the gravity of the situation set in. I was captured!

Railrunner thrashed in the net. He tried ripping it with his claws, but the it was made out of some foreign material. He roared in frustration. Then his keen hearing picked up footsteps, Detective Black stepped out of the shadows grinning triumphantly.

"Finally the great beast has been captured!" Black boomed. Railrunner snarled and bared his fangs.

"Are you some kind of lycanthrope? A new species of were-folk, Rodney?"

The roller coaster started to stand up, looking hideous. He growled deep in his throat, completely ignoring how weak he was. "My name is not Rodney! It is Railrunner!" he roared.

"Railrunner, you are the biggest masterpiece of death I have seen in my life. The most horrible creature I have ever beheld."

"You are the sorriest excuse for a cop I've ever witnessed." Railrunner growled. Then Black let lose a smirk, he pulled out a remote and pressed a red button on it. The net let out an electrical shock equivalent to 100,000 volts. He howled in pain and agony. Electric spasms ran through his entire body, completely draining Railrunner's energy. Black smiled to himself, he thought Railrunner was finally paying for his evil deeds. Then the red coaster blacked out and fell to the forest floor.

The malicious detective laughed and got on his phone.

"The red is down, send a truck." He said then hung up. Minutes later a large semi pulled up to where Black and Railrunner was. With a lot of effort, the brilliant red roller coaster was hoisted into the trailer. Black climbed into his SUV and drove towards the highway. Almost thirty black vehicles followed him. Their secret lights flashing as they escorted the large truck down the road.

Detective Black sat with Captain Vick in the lead car.

"Detective, we are going to take this thing to the most secure prison in the area. We need to get an expert roller coaster engineer to come and examine it. Run a few tests, and hope everything works out like we want it to." Vick began.

"Good. When we arrive I'll call for the engineer. Hopefully we can figure out where this thing came from in the first place."

I awoke feeling woozy and lightheaded. I looked around; I was in a very dark area, some sort of cell. Where am I? Suddenly voices could be heard. I blinked and tried to get into focus. Then I realized, I was in a jail cell, behind iron bars!

Chapter 14
Caged Bird

My heart started to beat faster; I looked around franticly for a way out, there was none. I got up and tried to walk forward, unfortunately chains were attached tightly around my "wrists", I snorted in revulsion. The iron shackles still allowed me to walk to the edge of the bars, there was just two guards sitting at a round table playing cards. I gripped the bars and pulled, I was still too weak from the blast to even bend them.

I backed into the corner of my cell. My thoughts filled me with dread. How was I to escape? Would I ever see Thunderbark, Merrylegs, or Static ever again? What about Clare? What will happen to her? What will these men do to me? Rip me open and experiment? Disassemble? Kill? Just because I accidentally killed their kind? Because their blood was spilled? The thoughts still continued to race. Some sickened, and some saddened me.

I contemplated more. What was going to become of Amusement Park Between, I wondered. Would Ironwheel dominate completely? I shook my head trying to clear my mind; that technique wasn't working out to well. I remembered horrible images, all the brutal things I did. Those poor souls. Those poor people. All because of me. All because of this curse, that I can never transverse for as long as I live.

My pondering was interrupted by Detective Black slamming the doors open. The two guards greeted him, but they were hastily escorted out. He walked up to the cell, standing probably two meters away for his own good. He looked at me with a firm gaze.

"Evening, Railrunner."

I replied with a growl.

"Railrunner, why are you here?" he asked as he crossed his arms in defiance.

"It's not on my own will, detective." I said coldly.

"Then whose is it?"

"You're an ornery one; you'll be hard to digest." I said coming to the edge of the bars. I wanted to play with his mind, make him suffer.

"You are a bit of an ass yourself." He said making a quick comeback. I was glad he was getting his mind off his last question. I couldn't reveal any of the others.

"I take that as a compliment," I replied.

"You're welcome. Where did you come from, Railrunner?"

"Detective, you are being pushy. I am from a place no mortal such as you will ever find."

Black sighed, he was getting frustrated, and I was loving every minute of it. "Well then, were you born or built?"

"That Detective I cannot answer, I don't know that." I answered, but began to speculate, that was a fact I did want to know.

"Why did you kill all those people, Railrunner?"

"A roller coaster is considered out of control on your rails. In our world, when our ride form is activated we are uncontainable till the full moon is at its highest. As you can now see I am stable, and I mean no harm." I sighed, but Black only gave me a grimace.

"But you still had blood on your wheels, Railrunner. You are still going to pay for ruining my life as well as all the others." He finished storming to the exit. "By the way, I'm having an expert evaluate you." He smiled depravity.

I held my middle wheel up. He walked out and shut the door behind him. I wanted him dead now more than ever. Then I wondered who the evaluator was? The door opened again and the two guards came back in, this time with a box of snacks. I got back up against the cell wall and layed down. I sighed watching a mouse scurry by, wishing to run and be free like it.

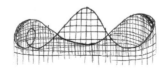

79

It was now ten o' clock. An hour had passed. Suddenly, I heard voices outside the room. The door creaked open, and the two guards stood and walked out. Great, I thought, Detective Black was coming back for a visit. But to my revelation, it wasn't Black, it was the evaluator he called, it was Thunderbark!

My hopes rose, but I tried not to look euphoric. He edged close to the bars, and pretended to observe me. He looked up at me and winked. Thunderbark turned and yelled. "He's a big one! I'll need some time to get a good look at him!" He made sure they were gone then turned to me.

"Railrunner! How on earth!" He whispered promptly.

I let out a whoosh of air. "Long story Thunderbark."

"Tell me later," he laughed, but then he became serious. "Railrunner you can bend metal! Problem is you will only be able to move small amounts, no bigger than a grain of sand. I cannot get you out of here; I can't bend metal, only wood. But you can! You can figure something out."

"Why don't you just transform and pull these bars apart!"

"You are in this horrid place by your own fault!" He said changing his tone. "You used a concussion beam when you weren't ready. If I get captured we are screwed. I would help you out of here, but we will need Merrylegs and Static in order to pull it off successfully. I can fetch them, but in the meantime you need to recharge your energy. You can take some from my ring." He said handing it to me.

"Will I be strong enough to pry the bars apart?" I asked.

"No. But you will probably have enough to bend metal." He smiled.

"So let me get this straight, this is all you can help me with?"

"No, but I can turn off the security cameras and alarms for you. Railrunner, I am sorry, but you need to learn this technique, and this is the time! And we're going to need all the time for tonight! We have to steal the Augu Ra and say our farewells."

"What do you mean farewells?" I interrupted.

"Railrunner, I'm sorry but we must go to Amusement Park Between tonight. There is too much at stake in our world and this one."

I sighed. "Perhaps you are right. I'll work hard to try and bend metal while you round up Merrylegs and Static." I said touching the ring. A small surge of power ran through me. After my body was satisfied, I handed it back to him. He started to head out, but then he turned around and spoke again.

"Remember, you can bend any type of metal, wherever it may be." He smiled.

As Thunderbark exited, I realized he was giving me a hint. I just had to figure it out.

Chapter 15
Prison Break

I sat in the corner of the cell up against the wall. I thought about what Thunderbark had said. What could he possibly be telling me? I looked out at the guards. They were now eating cereal, littering the floor.

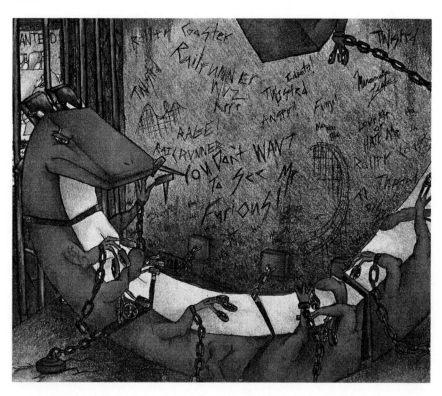

Thunderbark wasn't helping me on purpose. The white coaster wanted to teach me a lesson. Plus he wasn't giving me a helping hand because he wanted me to learn something new. I started to flex my left set of wheels, making them pop. I then peered at the two guards again. A mouse scattered from underneath the table with a piece of cereal. It scampered into my cell and sat in the opposite corner and started to eat. I looked at it, examined it. Then something donned on me.

I glanced back at the guards once again. I zeroed in on the cereal box, and began to read what it contained. A single ingredient caught my attention, Iron. Thunderbark's last words rang in my head. I turned to the mouse; it was eating an item that contained iron. Minuscule amounts of iron. My eyebrow raised, I had an idea, I just wondered if it would work.

I extended my right set of wheels out slowly. I pointed them at the mouse's tiny body. I kept my "fingers" close together, nothing was happening yet. I then pulled my wheels apart, the mouse squeaked in sudden shock. Its fragile bones snapped as it suddenly got on its hindquarters. It cried in pain. I watched in pure amazement, I was manipulating the metal within the mouse's body!

I moved my arm a little, the mouse's forearms stood straight up. I raised it higher; the little animal hovered in the air. Then I made a fist. The mouse's body jerked, then he let out a final squeak as its blood splattered on my wheels. I pulled them back in astonishment, the mouse dropped to the cell floor dead. I looked at my wheels in bewilderment, I had figured out what Thunderbark had told me. I could make others do my every will, by simply bending the amount of iron in their blood.

The door slammed open as Detective Black came into the room once more. I felt a grim smile spread across my face. I watched Detective Black take a handful of cereal and plopped pieces into his mouth. Boy, was he doing the completely erroneous thing.

"Railrunner I am charging you for murder, destruction of private property, trespassing, and other accounts. You are sentenced to be put to further examination and later death. What do you think of that?" He said looking up to me.

I glanced down to see the keys on his belt. I looked into his eyes, and exchanged a grin. "Detective, they say I am a damned soul, but it is yours that is dark and bleak. And there is something else, Detective."

"What might that be?"

I held out my wheels, and extended them apart. Black's body froze and his arms hung in the air like a puppet. He looked at me in horror.

"You need to watch your iron intake." I said making Black grab his keys and toss them into the cell.

"What are you doing to me!" he cried.

"Killing you." I replied making a fist. Black's blood sprayed through his shirt. He fell to the floor like a rag doll. I quickly grabbed the keys and unlocked the cell door. I climbed out and faced rounds of the guard's bullets. I roared and flung them aside. I smashed my way through the exit, catching several officers off guard. I used my body and slammed them onto the wall. More came at me from all sides like an archaic army; I swung my tail, knocking the men down like bowling pins. I ran wild through the halls, using my sense of smell as my guide.

I continued to make my way down corridors. I stopped to sniff the air again, however a cop jumped onto my back. He made his way up to my head. I growled and popped open my restraint, the blunt force knocking the man out. I snorted and continued to run. Finally the exit was in sight, but it was blocked by a barricade of men. I swerved and darted into the garage where all the cruisers where kept. I stopped dead in my tracks. The captain of the FBI stood there like a stone wall with a huge gun. It was a large weapon that fired some sort of missile, either way I did not like where this was heading.

"You may be classified as super natural, but I think a bit differently." He began as he aimed. I bolted right as he fired. I hid behind a squad truck.

"How ironic! It is the roller coaster that is playing chicken!" he said firing another missile. It struck not but ten cars from where I was. I moved again like a soldier on my belly. I slowly made my way toward the opening of the garage. Along the way I passed a light switch, I'd be better off in the dark than him. I switched it, my eyes automatically adjusted to the change of light. The captain looked around nervously.

"Can't you see in the dark, Captain?" I said loudly so he could hear. He turned and fired, once again missing.

"Guess not. To bad for you." I said placing my wheels under a car. I waited till his back was turned and then I made my move, throwing the car at him. I didn't look back to see if the police car met its target. I just ran outside, into freedom.

My wheels sounded like galloping horses as I traveled on the concrete. I glanced back; the police would soon come after me. I did not have long; Thunderbark was to meet me at the museum. From there we would steal the Augu Ra. After that was done, I would say farewell to Clare. My stomach cringed at the thought of all this. I would have to play my cards straight, and go from there.

I took a shortcut through the woods. It felt like the night I spent with Clare, but after this night, those days were over. Never again would that be a reality, only a dream. I ran to the edge of a cliff. It was the one where you could see every bit of Huntersville. I scanned below, within no time, I spotted the history museum. In the brambles behind it, were Thunderbark and the gang. I threw back my head and howled like a wolf to signal that I had arrived. I could feel that Thunderbark was happy as could be. And so was I.

Chapter 16
Robbery

"So, you figured it out?" Thunderbark asked.

"Yes, after a while I did."

"All right, time to carry out the plan. Static if you will –."

"Certainly." He replied rolling toward the back door. He stopped just a few inches away and held his cable straight in the air.

"Might want to cover your ears." Merrylegs smiled.

I obeyed her and anxiously watched Static. An electrical spark ran through his tail. The cable vibrated, making a strident beep. It was very high in pitch, so high that the dogs barked for miles. The sensor at the door began to smoke and hiss, and then it shut down completely, unlocking the door.

"Human technology can be shit sometimes," Static laughed. "The whole circuit should be disabled now, but it will only last, in my calculations, ten minutes. Best if you hurry."

"Thanks Static, now travel to the security room and stick by the controls in case the circuit is switched back on." Thunderbark ordered.

"Can do." He said going inside.

Merrylegs went into the museum next and Thunderbark and I followed. The white coaster looked at all the corridors, and then he signaled for me to adhere behind him. We walked through a long dark hallway to a door on the right. I opened it to reveal a long flight of stairs that led upwards. I started my decent up the shaft, pushing through the stairways at ease; Thunderbark followed a few feet behind.

We finally reached the sixth floor, I burst through the door. Thunderbark climbed out and stood with me. My eyes scanned the area, and then a daunting thought crossed my mind.

"You think the heat sensors are still on?" I asked.

"Let's see -," he said. Thunderbark then bent down and blew out an icy mist. It made the air cold and bits of frost pop up here and there. One by one little red lasers showed up.

"You were right." He said staring in amazement at the web of sensors.

"Damn." I replied. I looked around for some answer to this predicament. I noticed that there were none on the ceiling. I smiled, and then I extracted my claws and stuck them into the wall. I climbed upward, gripping the ceiling and navigating upside down. Thunderbark followed my action.

"Good thinking on your part!" he congratulated.

"Thanks! It's kind of like going through a loop." I replied.

Finally I could see the display case holding the Augu Ra.

"Almost there."

"Good because our time is running out." He said coming next to me.

"How much is left?" I asked, as I carefully pressed onward.

"Three minutes."

"Next time keep that comment to yourself." I groaned. Thunderbark then shook his head.

"Fine, there are no sensors surrounding the Augu Ra, we can drop." He said as he detached from the ceiling, twisting around so he landed on his wheels like a cat would land on its paws. I followed his action, astonishingly, my wheels made a quiet impact on the thick carpet.

I took one of my claws and drew a large circle on the glass case surrounding the Augu Ra just as a spy would. Thunderbark caught the glass as it fell to the floor. He sat it aside, and then grinned at the necklace and me.

"Go ahead, Railrunner, It's yours." He said looking at me with his blue eyes. I sighed and reached my wheels in. Their nylon tips touched the Firinium necklace. A ripple went down my back.

"Can you feel its power?" Thunderbark encouraged.

"Yes, I can." I said taking it from its holders. I pulled it from the case and held it in the air, moonlight from the windows flickered from it, making it shine like sequins. I held it over my head, and then let it fall gently around my neck.

A cold mist raced through me, as my muscles tensed up. Power was restored to my body. I felt stronger than I ever was, except from when I rolled on the track. I let out a deep sigh in satisfaction and pleasure.

"Ready?" The white coaster asked.

"Ready, Thunderbark."

We quietly made our way down to the lobby to where Static and Merrylegs waited.

"We must hurry! Time is getting short! The sun will be up soon!" Merrylegs said galloping to the exit.

"Yeah, we must hurry if we are going to see Clare. Also the police and FBI plan to invade us." said Thunderbark bravely.

We ran as a pack in the direction where Clare lived, the Augu Ra had given me new strengths, but it would not give me support when I had to say goodbye to the one I loved.

Chapter 17
Love Hurts

We prowled quietly among the backs of houses. Clare's neighborhood was silent. Not even the crickets chirped. I led the way through bushes and trees. Wet grass brushed against my metal as we walked. Merrylegs was right; the sun would be rising soon. If it came up before we reached the portal, we would have to wait another day, by then the authorities would capture us and we would be on national news. Dooming Amusement Park Between on so many accounts.

Finally we reached Clare's house, I quietly sneaked over her fence, to find Clare drinking coffee on her back porch.

"Railrunner!" she said dropping her coffee and running to me. She wrapped her arms around me as far as they could. "Thank goodness you are okay! What happened to you?"

"I was captured by Black and the FBI, but later escaped. That is why I haven't got very long to -," I said trailing off. I could not say it.

"To do what?" she asked concerned.

I gulped. "To say goodbye."

Clare looked at me startled. It was obvious that she was tearing up.

"Oh, Railrunner, Why do you have to leave?"

Thunderbark appeared up next to me for support. Clare looked at him in awe. She then watched Merrylegs and Static climb out of the brambles.

"Miss Clare, I am Thunderbark." The white coaster addressed her like a gentleman. "It is so very hard to tell you this. The FBI and the press is on our tails, if we are captured we will be exposed to the public. The worst will probably happen to us. Amusement Park Between will be lost to an evil dictator that wants nothing but the blood spilled from our race."

"I see." She replied quietly. "Will you ever return?"

"I will momentarily after I defeat Ironwheel." I began.

"You mean you can't stay?"

"It is not possible. Most people cannot accept me for what I am unlike you. That's why I love you Clare, because you have stuck beside me for all these years. Through thick and thin, and through our ups and downs." I coaxed, trying to get her spirits up.

"I feel the same way about you. I like you just the way you are, even if you have metal instead of skin." She giggled nervously.

A small smile spread across my face. I wanted to kiss her and cradle her in my arms, but I couldn't.

"Railrunner, I will never stop loving you, I will never love anybody else, and my heart is yours, forever." Clare smiled as a tear went down her cheek.

"And mine is yours." I replied.

She jumped up and hugged me, tears rolling down her face onto my shoulder. Tears produced from my eyes too. They fell onto her soft blond hair.

"You're a strong woman Clare, I greatly admire that."

"I still think you're a strong man, even though you're not human" she said looking up at me wiping her eyes. She then leaned in cautiously and kissed my cheek. I smiled at her and gently licked the side of hers.

"I know that's not considered a real kiss," I said frowning a little.

"Its alright Railrunner, any from you is fare game. You had better get going before they find you." She said as she lowered her head and let more tears stream down her cheeks. I sighed and gently placed a wheel just under her chin; making her look back into my eyes.

"Clare, I'll be back soon. Don't you worry," I said smoothly.

"Soon seems like a long time." She sighed.

"It does not have to be. Your frog prince will be back before you know it."

Clare giggled at my comment. I gave her a final hug as Thunderbark, Merrylegs, and Static said farewell to Clare and headed out the gate. I slowly followed them, I turned to look back to see Clare wave. Suddenly loud sirens pierced through the crisp night air, sounding like thousands of screams.

"Railrunner! Run!" she pleaded. I nodded and ran to join my troop. It was true what they say, love does hurt.

Chapter 18
Final Rush

My heart raced as I ran. Blood pumped at an abdominal rate. Sirens came from all directions and flashing lights lit up the horizon. The FBI was closing in on us. We made a straight beeline for Mystic Park. We started through the forest near the campground. The leaves rustled as we blazed past. The barking of dogs sounded, they were K-9 units. We were slowly being ratted out.

Thunderbark charged into the campground, suddenly a dog ambushed him. He yanked it off and threw the barking crusader into a tree, knocking it out.

"They must already be here!" Merrylegs shouted over the calamity.

"How much time is left, Thunderbark?" I said turning to him.

"We have about an hour left."

"That's more than enough time." I grinned.

"For what?" he questioned, slightly astonished as his eyebrows rose.

"We need to lose these goons once and for all. They probably have video cameras with them, if they film us as we leave. We will be exposed. By getting rid of them we are safe."

Thunderbark rubbed his chin. "You're right, Railrunner." He agreed as he looked toward the entrance.

"They will probably be entering at the main gate, that's the direction where the dog came from." Static said.

"Talley ho then." Merrylegs announced as she reared back neighing. The police were probably at the midway of the park. During my times here as a human, I remembered seeing a ferris wheel near the midway that overlooked the park. I could catch the police by surprise there. With my plan in mind, I veered off from our pack.

I stood at the foot of the giant ferris wheel seconds later. I looked up its steel structure; it seemed to teeter in the wind. It was like climbing up a big spider web, I thought as I went up it. The metal beams creaked and stressed under my weight. This thing wasn't built like a roller coaster track. It felt like it would snap and fall over at any moment.

When I reached the top I tried to balance myself out. Sure enough I was right, hoards of police stood at the midway. Their dogs sniffed the place out carefully. To my right I could see Merrylegs in the "kiddie" section looking for any straggling policemen. I soon spotted Static in the parking lot, disabling cars. I looked around for Thunderbark; I finally spotted him, in all places, the water park. He was looking for something, the portal perhaps.

Then the ferris wheel let out a loud creak of despair. It echoed in the dead silence. A spotlight was shown on it; the beam of light slowly ascended the metal frame. My tail wagged, this time I was ready for them. The light reached me, it reflected off my shiny metal. All of the policemen turned their gaze upward.

"Looking for me?" I said smirking. The men aimed their guns. I leaped off the ferris wheel, doing a somersault in mid air, and then landing on my wheels. Bullets rang out, bouncing off me and hitting some of the misfortunate. I turned to face the police, but a huge armored truck sped at me. The many men shouting and waving their firearms like mad. Quickly reacting, I grabbed the truck's front bumper and hoisted it in the air. The shouts of triumph turned into screams. I threw the truck at the brigade. It hit several squad cars and policemen. I faced the remaining humans and activated my claws.

They fired at me once more. I slashed a nearby light post and used it as a bat. I swung, breaking bones and smashing cars. I then tossed the temporary weapon aside, and began to fight head on. Men ran from the left and right. Static and Merrylegs had arrived to join the party. Merrylegs lowered her horn and Static's cable shot off hot sparks. I watched as the carousel horse's unicorn like horn pierced through the flesh of humans. Static stung people as if they were a scorpion's prey. No matter how grueling, this sight still engrossed me.

I continued to lash out and use my rage and frustration as my weapon. A fleet of officers stood in rows with shields, and their guns aimed at me. I felt the power from the Augu Ra. I started to absorb it, the necklace began to produce a blinding glow. Then the power that generated from it was released in a major blast that came from the amulet, it hit the row of men, completely disintegrating them. Then I watched in horror, as the FBI captain appeared on top of a destroyed squad truck, he held, of all things, a bazooka.

"How did I miss him?" I said to myself.

"Time to bring this coaster into downtime!" he laughed. He aimed the weapon at my head. He placed his hand on the trigger. Before he could fire, a lightning bolt made contact with him. The air started to smell like burning flesh. I turned around to see Thunderbark standing upon the clock tower. He dropped down, landing next to me.

"I found the portal, it is in the water park. We must go there now! Time is almost up!"

I roared to get Merrylegs and Static's attention. They stopped and ran to join us.

"Where heading to the portal!" yelled Thunderbark. "Follow me!"

We ran in a blinding flash. We leaped over rides and booths. I looked over my shoulder to see that the remaining men were trying to track. We entered the water park, shutting its entrance behind us.

"It's this way!" Thunderbark said signaling for us to follow. We trailed after him, at some point it looked as if he was flying he was running so fast. He led us to a quiet area at the back of the water park. It was a relaxation area for adults when they wanted to take a break from the boisterous kids. Thunderbark walked to a Jacuzzi. The water within it was glowing bright blue, and you couldn't see the bottom of the tub like all the others.

Then Thunderbark looked to the horizon, the sun was starting to appear from the back of the distant hills. He then slithered into the tub, disappearing completely.

"Where did -."

"No questions just follow." Merrylegs said jumping into the water. She was followed by Static. I swallowed and took one last look at my world, and then dived into the blue abyss.

Water swarmed around me like a bunch of angry bees. I opened my eyes I couldn't see anything. I could hear nothing. I started to panic and thrash around in the water. My body felt like it was being compressed. It started to sting my seats and metal. I opened my mouth, but no sound came out. I tried to swim upward. I could now see a blinding yellow light. With a sudden kick, I surfaced. My eyes were blurry from the water. I climbed out, gasping for air. Then my senses got back into focus.

I looked to see Merrylegs and Static beside me. I stared forward at Thunderbark, who smiled warmly at me. I looked beyond him, and gasped. We weren't in my world anymore. The vegetation was like a rainforest. Valleys with rides stretched far. The whole place looked like a dream.

"Everyone, welcome to Amusement Park Between!"

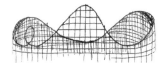

Part Two

The Land of Wonder and War

Dangerous Waters

He gazed at the enemy; their fighting attempts only fueled his anger. He lashed out with his own weapons, striking the enemy mercilessly. Making them pay for the pain they had caused to this world.

He wanted to destroy them, destroy their leader, obliterate his armies and their leaders. He swore he would make them sorry, make them gush their own blood…

Chapter 19
Carousel Witch

My eyes were still transfixed on the scenery around me. Amusement Park Between looked like a place from the most imaginative mind. It was so beautiful and mysterious at the same time. This place looked like a painting from a talented artist. It was completely different than I had imagined it.

"Don't be fooled Railrunner, this place is more dangerous than it seems," said Thunderbark, getting the lay of the land.

"You know, I pictured Amusement Park Between to be all industrial, I didn't know it was like this!" I exclaimed.

"Like Thunderbark says, it may look this way, but there are no safe havens." Merrylegs said softly.

"Ever since Ironwheel came about." Static grumbled.

"What's his motif anyway?" I asked. For a while nobody answered. They all just gave me blank stares. Finally Thunderbark spoke up.

"Railrunner, I'll tell you when we can find a place to settle down, but first we must see a friend of mine before we do anything. After we visit Moonhoof, we will go to the place that I had in mind." Thunderbark said starting down the cliff.

"Who is Moonhoof?" I asked Merrylegs.

"She is the carousel horse that lives in Morbinzin Swamp. Moonhoof is a witch, fortuneteller, medicine woman, and psychic, whatever you wish to call her. Anyway she knows pretty much anything."

"Interesting, how old is she?"

"She is nearly a hundred." Merrylegs replied.

"Shit, how long are life spans around here?" I said amazed.

"Well, carousel horses can live to be about five hundred. I'm almost sixty five."

"What about a roller coaster's?"

Merrylegs chuckled a little. "A roller coaster can live forever if it plays its cards right."

"Really? How old is Thunderbark?"

"He is an older coaster." Merrylegs began "Thunderbark is nearly ninety."

"Dang! So, how old am I? Do human years count?" I smiled.

"No, Railrunner you are not even a week old yet." Merrylegs said laughing.

"I'm a big baby then?"

"Yup."

We ventured deeper into the forest. The further we went the more beautiful it became. Flowers of all colors appeared and so did the strangest. Giant boulders with the same language written on the Augu Ra were here and there. Trees seemed to touch the sky, sheltering us with a lush canopy of leaves.

"Thunderbark," I said walking up to him. "Why is Amusement Park Between - like forest?"

"You ask a great deal of questions, Railrunner, but Amusement Park Between is like this because we love clean air and a non polluted land. However, we have technology that is far more advanced than any humans with the perks of being good to the environment. Put it this way, why do you think some of us live so long?" He said finishing and looking at Merrylegs and me. Thunderbark must have heard our conversation.

After some time, the landscape started to change. It began to look more dismal and swamp-like than a fairy wonderland. Murky water sat everywhere and trees jutted out from the swamp's surface. Thunderbark stopped at the water's edge and bent down to sniff it's surface. Seconds later, he let out a low rumble and looked to us.

"Its safe, we swim from here." He said sliding into the water. He floated on top and let Merrylegs and Static hop on his back. Then he paddled out, moving through the water at ease with his head held high and his body swaying like a snakes.

I stared down into the water; it brushed against my wheels like the ocean would do to a pair of human feet. The water went barely past them as I waded in. I glanced at Thunderbark; he had stopped to wait on me. "Well, if a roller coaster could run on land and rails, then it can swim," I said quietly to myself. I leaped, and plunged into the dark water.

I felt the swamp cover me like a blanket. A thin lens went over my eyes as I opened them. I paused and looked around, the water was clearer than it looked before. I began to swim forward, paddling and moving like I did on the rails. I glided through the water like a seal. Small silver fish went past me as I swam. I could see just as well underwater as I could on land, every detail was present. After about ten minutes I surfaced next to Thunderbark.

"So, what do you think about swimming?" he asked.

"It's different." I said trying to match his speed.

"A neat thing about that is, a roller coaster can hold its breath underwater for about thirty minutes." The white coaster smiled proudly.

"Cool, so how much further?"

"We should be getting closer."

As I traveled, I looked around the swamp. It was becoming apparent that something lived here. Narrow wooden docks cris crossed over the water and wrapped around trees. Lanterns hung from branches and an empty boat floated alone. Then the water started to get shallow as we came closer to the heart of the marsh. A large island covered in large rocks appeared. The opening to a cave was visible, a torn purple cloth hung over its entrance.

"We're here." Thunderbark said as he climbed out of the water and onto the island. We entered the cave quietly. It was a long passageway that led into a large candle lit room. Merrylegs and Static hopped off and stood at my side. I started, but was quickly stopped by Thunderbark. Apparently this was a private matter.

"Wait here until I call for you," he said disappearing into the room.

Thunderbark peeked around the corner of the cave. The room was littered with bookshelves with loads of books. Potions sat on tables and ingredients in wooden cabinets. Glowing candles cast shadows in the poorly lit room. A rectangular table sat on the other end. Candles with wax running down them sat on it along with stray books. Behind the table was a grey carousel horse. She had pale green hair that was longer in the front and got shorter as it went down her spine. Her tail was like that of a normal horse along with her head. Golden piercings and rings were bestowed on her.

Thunderbark entered the room quietly. The horse suddenly turned and looked at him. She had light eyes that were almost solid white, but their irises and pupils were still visible.

"Thunderbark! It has been ages!" she exclaimed.

"Hello again Moonhoof. It's been quite sometime." He replied smiling.

"Indeed it has. What has been keeping you?"

"I was doing an investigation in the real world." Thunderbark sighed in fatigue.

"The real world! None dares tread there! What is it that you came here for, Thunderbark?" She said as her ears pricked forward as the carousel horse rapidly became alert.

Thunderbark took a seat across from Moonhoof's table. He leaned in and began to whisper under his breath.

"Moonhoof, I need to know where the Temple of The Red is."

"Thunderbark, I cannot tell you that! You know it was made a law that it was only for the red roller coaster. We swore never to tell its location!"

Thunderbark sighed. "Moonhoof, would you tell me if I show you why I must know?"

"Depends on what you want to put before me." She sighed. Thunderbark nodded as he got up and walked to the hall and waved his wheels. Seconds later Railrunner stepped fretfully into the room. Moonhoof then saw him, she looked bewildered. Her mouth opened slightly in shock.

"The red roller coaster - it has returned to us." She said transfixed while walking towards him. Railrunner quietly stood where he was as he watched Moonhoof circle him. "Hmm, lets see - great posture, muscular arms, powerful chest, wheels are in good condition." She suddenly stopped in front of Railrunner and looked him up and down. "Decent size, but he might want to work on his wits due to some of the irresponsible decisions he has made in the past."

Railrunner looked at her and responded with a low but slightly threatening growl. Moonhoof took a few steps backward from him. Thunderbark elbowed Railrunner in the ribs.

"Bad attitude," she said continuing.

"And language." Thunderbark chuckled to himself.

Moonhoof laughed. "However that can be a good thing, anger comes in handy sometimes. Altogether, a fine young coaster. He will be a good pupil for you to train, Thunderbark."

"I am honored." He replied glancing at him out of the corner of his eye. Railrunner responded with a feeble smile.

"Now you both get comfortable, I am preparing to tell you one of Amusement Park Between's biggest secrets."

I followed Thunderbark's actions, I didn't want to do something wrong and look dumb. Moonhoof trotted back behind the table and pulled out a large old book. She sat it upon the table and began to thumb through the yellowed and tattered pages. Her pale and inexplicable eyes scanned every word and illustration. I couldn't make anything out of it, since the whole thing was written in the strange language the residents here used.

"Ahh." Moonhoof said sighing. "Here we have it, the location of the Temple of the Red. It is a two days journey from here it sounds like."

"I thought it would be closer." Thunderbark interrupted.

"Indeed. But you and your friends are welcome to spend your night here."

"Thanks." He sighed in slight discontent.

"Well, as I was saying, it is a two day trip and it is at the most remote part of Amusement Park Between. It is under the large island Magmarr that lies in the middle of the Acterbahnn River."

"So the temple is under the island? Underwater?"

"Yes." Moonhoof continued. "The entrance is nearly sixty feet down and is below a great yinkan tree that sits at the water's edge. You will then swim up a long tunnel and that's when you should enter the temple."

"Thank you so much Moonhoof, so where do you want us?" The white coaster smiled genially.

"You can sleep in the abandoned swamp houses. I think you will find them surprisingly comfy."

"Thanks for everything Moonhoof, we will see you in the morning."

Thunderbark then walked out of the room, as I began to leave, Moonhoof stopped me.

"I never caught your name, whom do I have the pleasure of addressing?"

"It's Railrunner." I said smiling a little.

"Railrunner - a true warrior's name and a true warrior of that which you are."

Chapter 20
Moonlit Conversation

The wind whistled outside the old swamp house. The crickets and frogs sang their songs in a chorus that echoed through the night. Soft dappled moonlight beamed down from the high window onto me. Tonight was sleepless, my mind was full and my stomach was empty. My continuing thoughts and growling belly kept me awake. Thunderbark however, was fast asleep in the opposite corner, his nose buried behind his tail.

I let out a long sigh and stood up carefully so I didn't awake anyone. I slowly walked out onto the dock and bent down to peer at the surface of the water. Fish sounded good; besides, it was meat. I glanced back at the house, and then silently slithered into the water.

The warm indulging liquid surrounded me as my eyes adjusted to "water vision". The swamp was dark, but I could see everything. I glided trough the water, scanning for signs of life. I dove to the bottom, brushing the sandy floor. I then caught the sight of shimmering scales. I looked at the fish as it came out of the shadows. It was big, it looked like a cross of a catfish and shark, making the grey fish look very primitive. I watched it swim forward carelessly, and then when it turned its head away, I bolted forward like lightning.

The fish darted at the last second, but I was still not far behind. My predatory instinct took over, I found myself swimming faster. The fish was losing ground and precious time. It then turned and swam toward the dock; I rushed upon it, my mouth open wide. My dagger-like teeth snagged its flesh; I surfaced, with the fish grasped in my jaws. I looked up to see Moonhoof standing on the dock before me, her pale eyes bearing into mine.

"I was just looking for you, Railrunner. I wanted to speak with you. Sorry that I interrupted your hunt." She smiled.

"Don't worry about it," I said lying the dead fish out onto the dock as I climbed out of the water. I began to tear it to shreds; my hunger got the better of me. When there were only bones left I turned to see Moonhoof looking a little sickened.

"Sorry, I haven't eaten anything all day." I admitted wiping the blood away.

"You are fine! Come, I must discuss a few things with you."

"All right," I said following her.

The wooden dock let out loud creaks as we walked. I wondered what Moonhoof wanted to speak to me about. It had to be important if she had been searching for me.

"Railrunner, you are the only thing that has returned hope to our land. I want to talk to you about some things that only a red is capable of."

"Really?" I questioned.

"Yes, a red roller coaster has the ability to perform continuous concussion beams, but in this world only."

"Is that true? It won't completely drain the energy from me?" I asked surprised.

"Yes. Here you have unlimited energy, especially because you bare the Augu Ra." She said as we entered her cave.

"Is there anything else I should know?"

"A mouth can only speak so many words at once, nor are its words remembered to their fullest; a book however, tells a much different story."

"So-." I began only to watch Moonhoof pull out a dust covered box from atop one of the shelves. She then used the key that hung around her neck and opened the locked chest. The carousel horse pulled out a really old book and handed it to me.

"This will teach everything that you wish to know. It is called the Veradagashi, in other words the book of the red roller coaster. It was written by the very first red, if you have a question or need extra advice that Thunderbark cannot teach you. Refer to this book."

"Cool," I said while thumbing through it. Problem was, it was all written in that bizarre language! But then I saw a translator in the back, relieving me from my worries.

"Now there is something else, Railrunner. Did Thunderbark ever tell you where the residents of Amusement Park Between come from?"

"He hasn't yet." I realized.

"All right, well the rides here come from being tossed aside in the real world. When they have worn out their life there, they are put aside by humans. They lie in rest, doomed they seem, until they are given a new life in Amusement Park Between."

"So, I was once a regular old roller coaster that nobody wanted?"

"No, not you. Defiantly not a red. No ride knows where the red comes from. They say the only rides that know are roller coasters, and you might want to ask Thunderbark that."

" I'll make sure of it."

"Good, now there are some rides you should know about. The worst of all the rides. They are the ones, who were either destroyed or were involved in a deadly calamity. They are known as The Fallens."

Fallens, that suited them well. Like angels cast down from heaven for their errors, becoming damned souls cursed to walk the earth living a life of evil. Fallen rides were living in their own personal hell, forced to take out their anger on the ones who did them wrong. Just like fallen angels.

"Glad to know that." I replied after my brief thinking.

"Another thing before I bid you good night, you and your friends will be traveling through various cities and villages on your journey. Railrunner, if the Fallen see your flaming red metal all hell will break lose. So, here is a trench coat and vest that should cover you and keep everyone out of harms way. You don't have to wear it all the time, just when you go through a town."

"Good," I said gathering my stuff together.

"One more thing before you leave!"

"Yes?"

"Take this," she said handing me a vile full of a dark blue liquid. "Use this only as a last resort when you are battling Ironwheel!"

I thanked her and took the vile and wrapped it in the trench coat . I said good night and headed back towards the swamp house. Then I got to thinking, was Ironwheel one of the Fallen? If he was, could he have been somehow tortured by humans in the real world? Badly enough that he wanted revenge on them?

Chapter 21
The Assassin

The following morning, the sun shinned brightly in the sky, and there was not a cloud in sight. This morning I had woken up and thought about going to Clare's house to visit, but I forgot I was in fairy tale land where nothing made sense anymore. I was starting to miss Clare and everything about her. I wondered what she was doing or if she was all right. I felt sickened that she wasn't within my reach.

Today I wore my coat and vest; Thunderbark said we would be traveling into the village of Trenzon. There we would get supplies and the like. He said it was at the bottom of the mountain, and it was a small town with less than forty rides. I walked beside Thunderbark while Merrylegs and Static brought up the rear. I kept my hood down; I would pull it up and over my head before we entered Trenzon. That way I was hidden and nobody could see any red metal, not even my "hands".

Then Thunderbark crouched behind a large rock at the edge of the mountain. He peered at the nearby city below him. He smiled and looked to me.

"That is Trenzon, Railrunner. I'll be watching you closely as you roam around. Don't do anything stupid! Keep to yourself and don't speak unless you are addressed to. Here is some money," he said handing me a small bag of coins. "Spend it wisely."

"Where did you get money?" I said as I peered into the bag.

"First of all our currency is called g's. Second, I got them from Moonhoof."

"Oh, well anything else you would like to share with me?"

"Keep your head down but be alert! Finally watch our backs. Now, let's get moving, we have lots of ground to cover." He finished springing forward.

I nodded and pulled my hood over my head.

Within the next thirty minutes, we had succeeded in reaching the base of the giant mountain. Trenzon was right in front of us now. Its appearance looked like carnival booths that had a modern and old world feel. The buildings were ten times the size here than in the real world. Steel was also heavily used, from structures of buildings to art sculptures. The strange letters were written among them, from small to large characters.

We walked toward Trenzon's entrance, two large stone sculptures that were in the shape of a tooth jutted out of the ground. Together they looked like an unfinished arch.

"Those are called Bast; they are positioned at the entrance of every city, village, or town. The larger the city is in rank, the taller the Bast are," said Thunderbark. "So you may run along, I'll get you when I'm done."

"I'm not a baby."

"Really? You said you were one yesterday." He smirked. I rolled my eyes and walked forward. Merrylegs and Static had already wandered off in the randomly placed bazaars. I looked around; there were all sorts of rides here, from carousel horses to roller coasters. They all seemed to stare at me, stopping whatever they were doing just to get a glance. What to do first? Then I spotted a sign above a shop, three of the strange letters were on it, from reading the book I was given, I knew they said "bar". That was where I was heading; I had to get my mind off a few things for a while.

As I entered the bar, everyone looked at me suspiciously, and then they went back to whatever they were doing previously. I sat next to a white carousel horse at the counter, a blue roller coaster stood behind it bartending.

"What will it be?" He said not even turning to glance at me like he was used to this sort of thing all the time.

"What you got?" I replied not looking up.

"You traveler?" The coaster asked in a profound voice.

"You could say that."

"Hmm, We have beer, wine, but for you, I suggest a Red C."

"Lay it on me."

Within seconds, the coaster bartender whipped up the drink. Then he took it and sat it on a hovering disk, next he gently gave it a push and it floated towards me. I picked it up off the disk; it magically floated back to him. Thunderbark was right; this world did have more advanced technology.

I lifted the cup to my lips, I felt the cold liquid slither down my throat, it tasted tangy and sweet, a surprisingly remarkable combination. It felt relaxing and satisfying.

"You like?" asked the bartender.

"It's good."

"You know, it was named after the red roller coaster." He smiled.

"Really?" I replied sounding surprised.

"Yup, now that's six g's."

I dug in the bag Thunderbark had given me, and pulled out six silver coins. The coaster took them and thanked me, and then he turned his attention to another customer.

I continued to sip the beverage down. I checked my surroundings, but suddenly the blue coaster walked back over with an adequate smile.

"So," he started. "Where you from?"

"Out of town," I replied not really lying.

" Hmm, we do get a lot of travelers here, Trenzon is kind of like a pit stop. Any reason why you're wearing that cloak? The temperature is quite warm."

I almost choked on my drink. " Well - it is because I have a scar that runs down my entire body, it's real embarrassing." I said making the shit up as I went along. I felt more unease by the second.

"Sorry I asked, I would have done the same thing."

I nodded, but then a horrible image popped into my head. Merrylegs was being attacked, being held against her will. I shook my head trying to clear it, but nothing worked.

"Something wrong?" he asked.

"I -."

Then I heard Merrylegs's terrified nay. I looked at the exit startled. Wait a minute, didn't Thunderbark say I could predict the future! So Merrylegs was in trouble! I got up quickly and stormed out the bar's doors. Static came to me in a panic.

"Merrylegs has been kidnapped, Railrunner!"

"Who was it!" I demanded.

"I don't know! It was a grey go- kart!"

I growled in anger, I tasted the air for Merrylegs's sent; I found hers along with the nasty odor of her kidnappers. I got on all my wheels and ran at full speed.

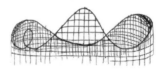

I navigated in and out of buildings, as fast as I could. I was going to make sure Merrylegs's life wasn't going to be stolen. I rounded a corner and came to a grinding halt. The grey go-cart was holding her pinned against the wall; he was going in for the kill.

I let out a nasty snarl; the assassin stopped his deadly attempt and looked in my direction.

"You're not very smart; kidnapping her was a bad move, very bad indeed." I hissed, arching my back and creeping toward him.

"Excuse me, you dare speak to one of the Fallen?" he said, I could sense he was constrained.

"Why do you taunt me so? Dare you argue with a roller coaster?" I continued as I stood and extracted my claws.

"Dare I do." He said as he sprung at me. His teeth sunk into one of my seats through the coat, he had made a terrible mistake, I thought to myself. I flung him off and chased him through the alley. He darted into the open, spectators fleeing in fear as he turned to face me. He lunged at my head; he landed and started to beat me with his big tires. I raised my arm and pried him off and threw him at a steel pillar.

He started to turn around for another attack, but I ran up on him and stuck him with my claws. They went strait through the pitiful ride him and the pillar. I pulled them out and watched the go-cart drop dead. I licked the blood off, and sighed in relief.

"Oh my -." I heard someone say behind me. I turned to see Trenzon's residents pointing and staring at me.

"He killed a Fallen!"

"Is that -."

"It is!"

I felt my face, my hood was down! They could see me!

I stepped backward in shock; Thunderbark came running up beside me.

"Railrunner! How could you be so careless?" He scolded.

"Thunderbark, I was being attacked!"

The crowd exchanged comments again.

"No wonder he was wearing a cloak." I head the blue coaster say to himself.

"Please stop!" shouted a voice. A green bumper car rolled out in front of everyone. Despite the calamity, he smiled broadly.

"Greetings, I am Mayor Storm. I apologize red roller coaster for this inconvenience. What is your name might I ask?"

I looked at Thunderbark, unexpectedly he told me go ahead.

"It is Railrunner." I finally replied.

The Bumper car then turned to the crowd. I raised my eyebrow as I wondered what he was to do next.

"Let it be known that today is the day the tyrant, the red roller coaster, Railrunner, has returned hope to Amusement Park Between! Let him bury the Fallen, Freakshow, and the evil king Ironwheel!" The residents of Trenzon applauded in an uproar. Then Thunderbark walked up to the mayor and whispered into his ear. "My loyal subjects!

Railrunner's teacher wishes me to address you this message. His identity must be kept secret! If word got out that he has returned; all hope is lost! No one under any circumstances lets the word out of our city!" The audience nodded in approval. Then the mayor turned to me.

"All hail Railrunner!" he said kneeling. Everyone behind him followed his action, kneeling down in rows like dominoes. I found this incredibly embarrassing.

"Well done." Thunderbark said in approval.

"Thanks. I wish we could stay, but you, Merrylegs, Static, and I know we must continue and find the temple. Like he said, we've given hope to Amusement Park Between." I sighed, the white coaster then patted my shoulder.

"Well put my friend." Thunderbark said as he smiled in favor.

Chapter 22
Origin

The day faded into night as the blue sky turned black. We had made a lot of progress today; Thunderbark said we should arrive by morning. Clare's absence left me with a feeling that there was something missing. And I couldn't bare it. Along with that I still did not know the most important things about me, this world, and others; information that I seeked terribly.

We all sat around in an awkward silence at our campfire. Nobody said a single word. It was Static who finally spoke.

"Merrylegs and I could get more wood, we are kind of running low on it." He said getting up. Merrylegs followed him into the forest, now it was just me and Thunderbark. I looked into the fire, watching its flames lick the air, spitting out sparks. I then glanced at Thunderbark, now would be the time to ask him.

"Thunderbark?" I said quietly.

"Yes, Railrunner?"

"I want to ask you something - something that Moonhoof brought up."

"What might that be?" He beamed warmly.

"Moonhoof told me where the residents here come from, but she said I came from a different source. She said you might know."

Thunderbark looked at me, his light eyes simply stared into mine. His mouth remained in a firm grim line as Thunderbark sat there like a statue. He then sighed and gave in. Obviously disclosing a subject that he did not feel comfortable speaking about.

"Most everyone thinks that the red was a science experiment. A super coaster in other words. Alas that is wrong. Others say the red is a god made from the blood of dead coasters. That is wrong, too.

Moonhoof is right, only a roller coaster knows where the red comes from."

"Where?" I asked so quietly that not even the creatures of the night could hear.

Back in the real world, Clare sat in a dark room lit with a single light. She nervously twiddled her thumbs on the table. Clare was at a police interview, and she prepared for Captain Vick; collecting up her loose words and thinking of what to say.

The city had been on high alert for the past two days. Squad teams and even the army patrolled the streets like predators looking for prey. She knew that the FBI wanted more. They were going to ask her of Railrunner's whereabouts, any information they could squeeze out of her

Then the door creaked open and the Captain invited himself in.

"Evening Miss Clare." He said grinning and sitting down. She only looked and didn't reply. He placed a box of donuts on the table. Clare's face turned red in vexation.

"Are you going to pull the good cop bad cop card?" she said disgusted.

The Captain narrowed his eyes. Then he went on with what he was doing.

"Mam, you seem to know the most information about the roller coaster. In fact, last time you didn't mention some of it. For example - it was your boyfriend!" he finished in an uproar.

Clare gulped in response.

"Clare, can you explain his motive. Explain why he killed all those people." He said looking into her eyes.

She hesitated. Clare's heart rate went up.

"Answer me!" he yelled at her.

"It wasn't his fault!" She screamed back in his face.

Captain Vick slammed his fist on the table.

"What do you mean it wasn't his fault!" he said frustrated.

"He had no control!" she winced. Then she repeated her words.

"Why?" he demanded.

"He told me he did not have control until the first full moon. When he is in control, he wouldn't hurt anyone!"

The Captain was silent. He then started again with a question that only made Clare's heart beat faster.

"What else did he tell you?"

"Railrunner didn't tell me anything else!"

"So - the coaster has a name." Vick said rubbing his prickly chin.

Clare gasped and put her hand over her mouth.

"I'm not as stupid as I look mam; I thought you would know more."

Clare simply looked at him in horror.

"Where is he Clare?"

"I don't know."

"You know!"

"I don't!" she cried.

"Tell me!"

"What is the point! No one can reach it!"

"What is it!"

"Another universe!"

"Space?"

"No! It is a world that is only accessible by those who are of its blood!" she screamed.

The captain got in her face and sighed.

"What is this place called Miss Clare?"

She swallowed and wiped away her tears.

" Railrunner calls it Hell."

"What is it Thunderbark?" I demanded.

He let out a long tired sigh. His icy eyes went from the mesmerizing flames back to me again.

"Railrunner, the red is the only ride that is born, not from magic, but of a womb." He finished. I however continued to stare bluntly at him.

"That has got to be the stupidest shit you have said to me since we got here! I mean, how in the hell is that possible!" I laughed.

Thunderbark snorted in disgust and looked at me then continued.

"Here anything can defy logic and explanation." He grumbled under his breath.

"How does it happen then?" I asked almost wanting to snicker, even though Thunderbark was probably telling the truth. What the white coaster said was so bizarre that it was hard to believe.

"I goes like this, after a red dies; a few years later a female coaster is selected. She is chosen because she is the purest and has the nicest heart towards others. Amusement Park Between summons her to the Temple of The Red. The whole time she is in a trance and doesn't have a clue what goes on or happens. Some spirit thing occurs, but I not entirely sure on that one. Next morning she returns home with amnesia. Then its twelve months of patience, after that the red is born and all hell breaks lose." Thunderbark finished.

"What happens next?"

"The red is sought after to be killed by the Fallen or an evil sort. That is the reason why I and my troupe had to take you to the real world, so you wouldn't die."

"Bizarre, interesting, yet weird as all get out." I replied. Then another thought crossed my mind. "Thunderbark, who was my mother?"

He sighed again and poked a stick into the fire. He seemed to be thinking, trying to recall who she was.

"Railrunner, I believe your mother's name was Angeltrack." Suddenly Thunderbark's eyebrows raised in shock he straitened up and gulped. "My god, now I remember -."

"What?"

"I remember when I found you; I remember your mother's death."

I looked into the fire and thought deeply to myself. This was something I wanted to know, but yet did not. However, my thoughts pushed me.

"What happened, Thunderbark?" I said with my tone just above a whisper.

"Well - here it goes. I was hunting alone in the forbidden forest, hence the name; I was minding my own business when a roller coaster ran past me. As I peered down from the tree, I noticed she had a bundle in her mouth. I decided to watch her every move, because I sensed trouble. She suddenly hid her bundle in the crevice of a large boulder; after that she took off. The next second I found out why she was running."

"Why?" I asked wanting to know more.

"Freakshow. She was after Angeltrack, chasing her with claws extended and fangs barred. I got down from my perch to assist, but the second I touched the ground; I witnessed the most bloodcurdling screech I had ever heard. From that very moment I knew I was too late, Angeltrack had been murdered in cold blood. I remember Freakshow's maniacal laughter as she left."

"What happened next?" I asked concerned.

"I remembered the bundle she hid in the rock. I went to investigate, and found you. That was when I knew Ironwheel was after the red, and I knew I had to help. So I gathered Merrylegs and Static for assistance. We decided you would be safe in the real world."

"Ok, but how did I end up alone?"

"Well, we decided you should be with humans, to be raised as a changeling. It was for the better, because we wanted you to know their background and deal with them, learn their lifestyles, and culture. That way you would seem normal to society and nothing would look equivocal. We secretly watched you over the years, but when you were adopted we lost track. Finally we found your whereabouts just in time, when Amusement Park Between was being tortured by Ironwheel."

"That's why you put the ad in the paper."

"Correct, because we knew you couldn't resist."

I chuckled at that one, but I still had another question for Thunderbark.

"Who is Freakshow?"

"Who is she?" he said looking at me sternly.

"Yes."

"Freakshow is one of the Fallens; in fact she is the general of Ironwheel's main army. She is sly and stubborn, and has one of the worst reputations in all our land. She was put together out of scrap parts of other roller coasters, some of steel coasters and some parts of wood, just for kicks. Humans tortured her mercilessly; finally they destroyed her. And when she entered Amusement Park Between, she hated them and all of their kind."

"Hmm, what does she look like?"

"None of her cars match, none of her wheels do, and she has one blue eye and one green."

"All right. I have one final question, what is Ironwheel's motive?" I asked, my question only making Thunderbark swallow apprehensively.

"Ironwheel has the deepest hatred for humans, even more than Freakshow's. He wants to gather his armies and get his revenge on the humans. He wants to rule Amusement Park Between and make every ride and man his slaves!"

I nodded and stood up, Thunderbark watching me eagerly.

"I want revenge and justice. I want to kill Freakshow, because she murdered my mother and probably countless others. Most of all, I want Ironwheel dead! I want to burry him in his grave! I want to make him pay!"

Chapter 23
Temple of The Red

The following morning was peaceful and just. The strange birds sang their songs and the vegetation's dew sparkled in the soft rays of the sun. All of us were currently walking along a heavily wooded path that looked as if it had not been used in quite some time. Thunderbark led and Merrylegs followed close behind him. Static and I brought up the rear.

"What were you and Thunderbark talking about last night?" He said suddenly. "I could hear you both speaking, but I couldn't make out any words."

"Shouldn't you be minding your own business instead of listening in on others?" I said in reply somewhat angry that he was poking his nose into things he shouldn't.

"Sorry," he replied sounding ashamed.

"Well, he was only talking about information on Amusement Park Between." I lied.

"Like where things come from? For example, how the regular multicolored animals or stuffed toys won at fairs that nobody wants?"

"Yeah, stuff like that, Static."

"Sorry again to bother you." Static said abashed.

"Your fine." I replied. Then I smelled something, it was bland yet sweet.

"You smell that, Railrunner?" Thunderbark called from ahead.

"Yes." I yelled back to him.

"Its water, we must be getting nearer to the Acterbahnn River. That means we are close."

Thunderbark's words made my heart beat faster. I was about to see something that apparently has been unseen for years. A place that possessed my heritage and history. A place that was mine. A haven that I was to inherit like the others before me.

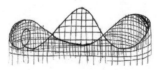

The vegetation became less dense as we walked. My anticipation rose higher as we proceeded forward. Then we exited the forest into a beautiful clearing; a glittering river cut through the land like a knife. Thunderbark walked to the edge of the Achterbahnn , and then he looked at the large island in the middle of it.

"Come on," he said as he began to walk along the bank; His eyes still on the island that stretched for miles.

"Didn't Moonhoof say the entrance was under the great yinkan at the river's edge?" I asked following him.

"Aye, she did. When you see it, notify me."

I nodded in reply as I scanned the island with him. I glanced at the murky water, nothing was visible. Suddenly I saw a collection of great limbs stretching above the river.

"There it is!" Thunderbark announced exultantly.

"The entrance?"

"Yes! Now, everyone stay here, I will dive down and see how far we have to swim."

"Good idea." Merrylegs agreed.

I watched Thunderbark breath in and out deeply, concentrating each one. Then he jumped bravely into the water, disappearing underneath the crystal surface. Minute by minute ticked by, still there was no sign of his white head bobbing above the water. I prepared to go in after him, but finally he surfaced.

"Yes! Found it! It's a long way down and out I'll tell you that! Put it this way, try as hard as you can to hold your breath for over ten minutes." He said as he climbed onto the bank, breathing hard.

"Ten minutes!" Static exclaimed. "I can't hold my breath that long!"

"Me neither," Merrylegs hastily pointed out.

"Good thing I thought ahead when we visited Trenzon. Merrylegs and Static, I picked up you both some air candy." Thunderbark laughed as he pulled out a regular bag of cotton candy.

"What is that supposed to do?" I asked.

"It can allow anyone to conceal their breath for fifteen minutes."

"That's just ordinary cotton candy isn't it?"

"Nope, it is our version, Railrunner." He finished watching Static and Merrylegs consume the desirable treat.

When they were done, the two climbed onto Thunderbark's back. He told me to follow him closely, he then took a deep breath and jumped into the river, and I dove after them. I opened my eyes in the water after I was under its roaring surface. Thunderbark was gaining ground; I sped after him so I wasn't to be left behind. The Acterbahnn's current was strong; I fought through it, swimming surprisingly swiftly.

Thunderbark motioned for the bottom of the river; here the current was not as strong. Still however, Merrylegs and Static had their tails wrapped around his lap bar clinging for dear life. As we continued to navigate through the giant rocks at the river's floor; bizarre multi-colored fish swam out of our wake, even brightly colored dolphins and seals moved aside. But there was no time to gander.

Thunderbark entered a dark tunnel with me following closely, fearing that the tunnel could suddenly fork and I would lose him. The tunnel went on and on, seeming like an eternity. My lugs started to ache terribly, feeling like they were being compressed together by a ludicrous force. *How much further away was the surface!* I thought tensely. Then the tunnel got lighter and lighter, a wave of relief fell over me. *Finally!* With a quick burst of speed, Thunderbark surfaced, seconds later I appeared beside him gasping for air.

"I take it you didn't get a good breather before you hit the water." He chuckled, giving me a sly grin.

"Well, I tried to hurry." I replied.

"Railrunner," he sighed. "You must learn to make good decisions! Instead of the many stupid ones - like the carnival."

"Point taken, Thunderbark." I said in a melancholy tone.

"Good, now we just have to walk to the end of this cave and we should enter the temple."

"Yes," Merrylegs sighed to herself.

"Had enough?" Static asked her.

"For the moment." She replied, trying to rid the water from her mane.

We walked along the dusty floor. It was clear that nobody had been here, the temple had, after all, had been undisturbed for several decades. Water dripped from the old rocks and small cave creatures rustled in the shadows. We then reached the end of the tunnel, there stood a great golden door that had tarnished from time. It looked like a giant coaster wheel, but around the edges was a language that I had not seen since we arrived in Amusement Park Between.

"Any idea what it says, Thunderbark?" I asked the white coaster.

"Not a clue, I've never seen that language before."

"Damn." I replied.

"Railrunner!" he scolded.

"Sorry, geez -."

I put my attention back on the door, suddenly the letters seemed more familiar, and then I remembered the key in the back of the Veradagashi. It must be a language that only a red would know. I studied the words more, one by one their meanings popped out at me. Maybe it was a command that could open the door.

"*Herbracador vershila merkommen macmarr ransullen.*" I hissed. The door let out a loud moan, and then from the left side of the wheel, a miniature gold coaster train rolled out; making a circulatory path around the door. As it passed a spoke in the wheel, the spoke pulled toward the center. Finally the small coaster disappeared where it had started and all the spokes were pulled into the center. Then the door slowly swung open.

"Nice work." Thunderbark complemented.

"Thank you." I replied watching in amazement. Finally, the Temple of the Red…

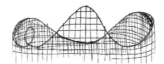

My eyes began to adjust to the changing light, getting them into focus. I felt my jaw slightly drop at the sight before me. The telltale pair of Bast welcomed all who entered, only that they stood several feet taller then the ones in Trenzon and were solid gold. The temple was illuminated with giant lustrous crystals that grew from both the ceiling and the floor. The temple "dwellings" looked like they were out of Eldarado; the same tarnished gold as the door. They were large and grander than even the castles back in the real world. It was like a giant palace of gold, something that King Midas would be fanatical for. The landscape was like a rainforest as like Amusement Park Between, but more beautiful. Light pools of blue glistened like diamonds from the light, waterfalls fell continually. Grand statues of roller coasters stood untouched by time.

"Wow, it's beautiful," Merrylegs commented.

"It's like a world within another," Static said in awe.

"This is Amusement Park Between's most sacred spot, of coarse it is amazing." Thunderbark corrected them. He then walked up beside me smiling. "What do you think?" he asked me.

"Holy shit, it's cool."

"Railrunner, what did I tell you about cursing?"

"Give me a break; I've been living in the real world for thirty-six years." I laughed.

Merrylegs and Static ventured forward into the temples lush landscape. Thunderbark and I decided to tour the inside of the temple. We walked up about thirty stairs or so into the temple's actual entrance. It was dark and I couldn't see but three feet in front of my nose. Thunderbark felt the side of the wall, and then out of a dark crevice he pulled out a torch. He then held out his "hand" and pulled his wheels apart. A small flame aroused from his fist and traveled to the top of the lantern, lighting both it and the hallway. He looked at me and smiled.

"How did –."

"I'll teach you later." Thunderbark spoke as he led the way.

We continued to walk through the temples halls, artifacts were everywhere and large rooms like an England palace presented themselves to us. The whole time Thunderbark behaved different, he would glance at me every so often with a grim look. Could he be jealous for some reason? But I suddenly sensed it wasn't jealousy, but worry, why?

Then we came to a large door at the end of a corridor. It was even more astounding than the temple's entry standing nearly as tall as the Bast outside. The door had an image of the red on it along with the letters that I only knew.

"Master suite?" I laughed.

"Could be," Thunderbark said looking at the giant door. "I guess you should open it." He continued as he peered at me from the corner of his eye.

"Guess I should." I replied examining the letters. After about a minute I had the whole thing translated.

"*Megoria farnger sheip trorgan horserp naria.*" I hissed. The door opened, slightly faster than the one before. It revealed the most amazing room in the whole temple. It was a "master suite", stunning in fact. The bed was at the far end of the wall along with heavy iron and gold furniture; it had everything that a real world bedroom would have plus some.

"I think this is my room." I said in a slight daze as I walked further into it. I paused at the bed and glanced around. Thunderbark walked up to my side. He stared at me vigorously.

"Where did you learn the language to open the doors?" he asked with his eyes bearing into mine.

"Well, a book." I replied nervously, slightly worried what Thunderbark was getting at.

"What is it called, Railrunner?" he demanded.

"Veradagashi, Moonhoof gave it to me." I uttered.

"The book of the red, no wonder-."

I raised an eyebrow. "There something wrong, Thunderbark?" I asked confused.

"Railrunner, there is a rumor about that book." He said austerely, the white coaster's eyes bearing into mine.

"What?"

"Can you pull it out and turn to the back of it?" Thunderbark said as he pointed to my messenger bag.

"I guess." I said prying it out of my cramped bag. I opened it and turned it to the back, but there were several pages missing, making Thunderbark's eyes widen.

"Just as I thought. I'm going to tell you something that you will have to know for your sake and everyone else's."

"What is it?" I said as I sat on the colossal bed.

"The previous red, a coaster named Moonblood who was probably the most well known red at the time, was looking through the book one night. He came across the pages that have now been ripped out."

"Thunderbark, what was on those pages?" I asked.

"On the ten pages were various maps on where each portal to the real world was located. He knew if Ironwheel were to get a hold of them, it would be disaster for everyone in this world as well as the real one. So he ripped them out and hid them someplace and the pages haven't been found since."

"Smart, Thunderbark what exactly happened to Moonblood?" I said looking at him. The coaster then sighed in defeat.

"His destiny was to kill Ironwheel as it is yours. In combat Moonblood was savagely murdered by the evil bastard that Ironwheel is."

This made me gulp in uncertainty. Thunderbark then smiled and sat next to me.

"Don't worry Railrunner; you are the most powerful red roller coaster that I have ever beheld! More powerful than Moonblood for sure. Plus you have something that he did not." He grinned to himself.

"What might that be?" I asked.

He laughed as he exited the room. "A trainer."

Chapter 24
Training Train

I woke up the next morning under the satin sheets of the iron bed, mainly because Merrylegs's smooth nose brushed against my shoulder. I gave in and raised my head to look into her face.

"Why did you wake me?" I grumbled as I yawned.

"Do you remember your session with Thunderbark this morning?"

I sighed and sat up. I asked her if I could sleep in more. Merrylegs then shook her head in denial.

"No, Thunderbark wants you in the courtyard. You better be glad that I woke you up and not Static." She finished turning to him. Static smirked and chuckled, his tail shot off small sparks.

"Trust me Merrylegs, If Static woke me up, he would find himself in deep trouble and off the map." I said eyeing him tauntingly. He winced in response. I climbed out from under the covers and followed them both out of the room. My eyelids were heavy from little sleep. Lately there had been too much on my mind. Where was Freakshow, Ironwheel, but most of all Clare. I worried about her safety and what was happening to her. I wondered what she thought about me now, I found myself missing her more and more.

Minutes later, we exited the temple rooms and into the courtyard. My eyes adjusted to the change in light quickly. I soon spotted Thunderbark leaning casually against one of the roller coaster statues.

"Morning metal head." He said cheerfully.

"Morning," I moaned.

"Don't worry today we are just going to go over some basics."

"Fine," I replied sitting in the soft lush grass. I stared at him waiting for him to start his "lesson".

"I think I am going to initiate on lightning, you should know it already. Now if you will, stand up in front of me."

I did what he ordered, I prepared myself, my muscles tightening.

"Ok, Railrunner see if you can redirect this." He said waving his arms, lightning generated on the tips of his wheels. Then he shot the lightning toward me.

I felt a surge of power run through my body, I held out my arms. My brutal instinct overpowered me, I redirected the lightning in a bigger amount toward Thunderbark. At the last possible second he ducked, the lightning narrowly missing him by inches, only to obliterate the rock behind him.

"You are stronger than before," he said getting up sighing in relief. "Now I will have you generate lightning on your own, see if you can hit those gold idols I placed on that wall over there." He said smiling like a kid who had just been given candy.

I stared at them and concentrated, I then took a deep breath and began to produce lightning. It seemed to dance wildly among my wheels, then I aimed and extended my arm towards the miniature statues. It sliced through the air and hit all the idols at once, damaging nothing else in its path.

"Very impressive." Thunderbark commented. "Now let's continue."

For the next two hours I worked on lessons with lightning, mastering each skill as I went through. Thunderbark said I was unnatural at this, that I was gifted.

"Now, I think I will teach you fire."

"All right, how do I do that?"

"Bending fire is a lot harder than lightning, mostly because fire is powered from the heart and barely the mind. Do you see where I'm coming from, Railrunner?"

"I - think so." I responded as I still tried to comprehend what he had said.

"Well, I'll just go through it step by step. First take a deep breath and concentrate your breathing like you do lightning. Then think of something that puts a spark in your heart. That should be easy for you, Railrunner." He smiled.

He meant Clare, I realized.

"Then while you exhale, act as if you are punching something. Watch closely." Thunderbark finished repeating the process of what he just spoke of. As he threw his wheels forward, a large fireball shot forth like a missile. It hit one rock, smoldering it.

"Cool, now can I try?" I said as I watched the flames lick the air.

"You certainly may." He replied moving to the side.

I breathed in air, I thought of Clare and her comforting words, her soft skin and gentle touch of her hands. Then I breathed out and punched in fury, a massive inferno torched everything in its path. I sighed in a long satisfied whoosh.

"Well done!" Thunderbark congratulated me. "Now we must play with fire more."

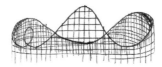

The next technique was fairly simple and easy to master. Thunderbark taught me how to manipulate fire so that it could move around like a flaming strand in the air like a deadly streamer. He told me that the particular skill was best as a whip. Next, he taught me what he demonstrated last night with the lantern, how to bend small amounts of fire. The technique was used for my own pleasures rather than in battle, but it could still come in handy at times of combat.

"You are very good at this, Railrunner. You are easy to teach." Thunderbark said with his icy eyes sparkling in anticipation.

"Thank you."

The white roller coaster then nodded in response. "Now I'm going to teach you something that might be slightly harder to do. It's called Fire Fury."

"What a cheesy name." I smeared.

"Very funny," he said with his voice very low. "The Fire Fury is a release of all your anger, all your frustration. All of that is released in an explosion, a searing inferno. I will not teach it here, because it will destroy the temple."

"So now what?"

He suddenly shifted, changed his mood. "Well, I think I had better teach the Fire Fury to you when it is safer to exit the temple."

I sighed slightly aggravated. "If you think it is best, Thunderbark."

"It is. I'm going to teach one more thing to you before we end our session."

"Fine." I said disappointed that we were not done. It was past noon and I had never gotten a nibble.

"This exercise is like what we did with lightning, only that I want you to hit the rocks separately and not all at once. Think of it like this, when you are preparing to attack an enemy an alliance could be near them. Kill the evil and not the good."

"I see your point," I replied, not really knowing how to respond.

I repeated my process I did before, thinking of Clare. How I missed her, Clare's absence was making me more miserable by the hours that ticked by. I held out my arm and aimed, hitting the rock alone. I smiled in confidence. I hit three more perfectly, and then I went for the final two. I messed up by hitting the rock I had my sights on and smoldering the one next to it.

"Do over." Thunderbark demanded.

I growled rudely, my stomach was getting the better of me. I found five more rocks, this time I did it with no mistakes.

"Good work, Railrunner. Now we can call it quits for the day, but that doesn't mean I won't give you homework."

"What! I'm not in elementary school Thunderbark." I said bluntly, making Thunderbark raise an eyebrow in defiance.

"Yes, you heard me. I simply want you to work on your bending. Also it is wise to be practicing with metal, as you know I cannot teach you that."

" I will," I gave in. Then we went off to do whatever we pleased in the temple. Today's lessons were exciting, but most of all they were depressing. Bending fire required me to think of Clare. It sickened me deeply. I ventured to a peaceful spot; the great pool with the giant waterfall. I lay at the waters edge munching on a recent catch. Merrylegs unexpectedly walked up beside me.

"Hi Railrunner."

"Hello," I muttered, still looking into the blue water. There was an awkward silence between us for several brief moments. Then Merrylegs spoke up again.

"You miss her don't you?"

I looked at Merrylegs; her eyes were full of worry.

"How can you tell?"

"Well, it is kind of noticeable." She said slightly embarrassed.

"I do miss her a lot." Then I thought of a strange reference, but it could possibly help Merrylegs understand more. "Do you know the story of *Romeo and Juliet*?"

"Yes. I read it during our time in the real world."

"Well, at the very beginning, in the prologue William Shakeshere calls the story "the tale of the star- crossed lovers". I and Clare's love is very similar, forbidden by forces that neither of us can deny."

She simply nodded. "You'll see her again." She encouraged.

"I hope so, and if it is possible."

Chapter 25
Hidden Secrets

About two weeks passed since my first training session with Thunderbark. We had lessons everyday since then on bending. I improved greatly as I learned more, knowing almost everything and every trick. But during that time my longing for Clare grew greater, I found myself even dreaming of her almost every night. It now seemed there was an empty hole in my heart.

This morning and, some of the night before, I was working on something that I had wanted to do to the place ever since we stepped into it. It would be for the greater good I had decided; it was my own project and I was almost finished with it. At the minute I hung upside down from a raft on the ceiling fiddling with wires. Then I heard Thunderbark approaching, yawning a sleepy yawn.

"What are you doing, Railrunner? It is four o' clock in the morning." Thunderbark moaned.

"I'm updating. In other words, modernizing the temple." I said finishing up and hopping down.

"What did you do?" he asked looking at me, his eyes placid.

"I'll show you," I said walking over and flicking a giant switch. One by one rows of lights switched on, brightening the entire temple.

"You added electricity!" he said excitedly, perking up as the light lit up the dark halls.

"Of course," I said but then I noticed a hidden door that I had not seen earlier.

"I'm going back to sleep, I'll give you a two hour delay for rest, since it looks as if you have stayed up all night." Thunderbark finished as he headed into his bedroom.

"Thanks Thunderbark," I spoke as I pretended to head to my room. I waited till he was out of sight before I proceeded to the hidden door. It was at the very end of a dark corridor and it barely looked like a door at all, in fact it looked like a wall only with writing on it. I whispered the words:

"*Killomarg reza yern diz xiloikr.*"

The door didn't open as well as the others; I had to pry it open. It was a dark and narrow hallway; I generated a small flame on my wheels. Then I went inside, following the cobweb-ridden walls. The halls opened up into a large gloomy room.

I continued to control my flame, it feeling like a little heartbeat. As I examined the room, I noticed that it wasn't gold like the rest of the temple. It was marble and stone, it looked a lot older than the rest of the temple. I glanced around some more; there were nine coaster statues, four on one side and five on the other. They were made of solid marble; I walked up to one to examine it. I now saw that each one was different, probably sculpted to be each red that there was. Turned out I was right, a nameplate was placed at the bottom of each statue. The one I was looking at now was Moonblood.

"So this is you." I said, my voice bouncing off the walls like an echo in a cavern. I looked at it up and down again. I realized he was pointing at something, they were all pointing. I followed their wheels; they went in the same direction. The stone roller coasters were pointing at another door.

"Wonder what else this place has to hide." I chuckled to myself. I motioned for the door; it was by far the shabbiest; it being made out of rusted steel. I didn't have to speak my language to open it, but as I did I made a shocking discovery.

It was a large room, probably thirty gymnasiums put together. It housed the wildest looking roller coaster track I had ever seen.

"Shhiii…" I said staring at it, my words disappearing in my throat. I was so transfixed on the rails that my flame fizzled out in a quiet puff.

The track was smooth silver, its rails looking like a spaghetti bowl. It rose high off the ground of the enormous room, four hundred feet was the highest point. Below the track was the temple floor, littered with the most impressive statues of the entire temple. Pools of glowing water stationed themselves in patterns. My eyes darted back to the track again, like a vampire to blood, I couldn't resist. I instinctively lunged for the rails.

Power ripped through my body like a sudden surge of lightning. My mind raged in fury, images flashed in my head as my wheels screamed along the rails. I found myself roaring and laughing horrendously in amusement. Up and down, around and around I went. Reaching preposterous speeds, which were far past illegal in the real world. My spirits rose as I moved, myself was growing more powerful by the minute.

I continued to get my fix, fix of power and adrenaline. I went trough inversions that would otherwise be impossible in the real world. When I came across dangerous curves, I leaped and rebounded off of statues and back onto the tracks. I laughed in pleasure. It felt so good to run the rails again.

Then moving along a tight bend, I noticed another secret door on the ground below. I sighed; the rails would have to wait a little bit. I dropped down onto the stone floor, I glanced for witnesses but there were none in sight. I made my way to the door, it gently creaked open to yet again a dark room. I lit a small flame and quietly ventured inside.

"Hmm - a weapons vault. Why is there a need for this?" I said questioning myself. On the shelves that lined the wall were what looked like rusty guns. Funny that these were here because it seemed that roller coasters were already well equipped. I cautiously picked one up, and examined the old gun that was falling apart. I tossed it aside not giving a care. From my engineering experience, I could tell that these guns were completely useless, none of them would ever work again.

"What was the point of even -." I began with my voice trailing off again. At the far end of the room on a stand was a sword. And it didn't look anything like the ones used in the Middle Ages either. Its blade curved in several spots making it have various different points. I touched my hand on the golden handle, and raised it up off its pedestal. It gleamed brightly in the soft glow of the firelight. It was amazingly beautiful, but yet so deadly.

"I wonder why this was hidden in this dark and vague place. Hidden away from the rest of the temple." I spoke softly. Then I decided to take it back to my room to keep it there. I could research on it easier in the cozy environment. I took an old sash from the dust-covered floor and wrapped it around the weapon. I tied it with some stray string that I also found in the vault. Finally I tucked it away under one of my seats. It was too late to run on the rails anymore, plus Thunderbark would be looking for me soon.

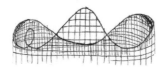

Back in my room, I shoved the sword under my bed to join the book. Then I climbed back into it and slipped under my covers. I felt my eyelids grow heavy, then they fell over my eyes as I went to sleep.

A high- pitched wail seared the air. Clare ran as fast as her legs could carry her. She struggled for her vital breath, gasping uncontrollably. I ran after her. My wheels thundering across the blood stained earth. She stopped in the darkness staring straight ahead. I screamed her name as she vanished. From behind me, dagger like teeth closed in…

I awoke sweating terribly. I breathed in and out rapidly. Thunderbark was at my bedside looking at me in worry.

"What happened?" he said putting a set of wheels onto my shoulder. It took me a minute to calm down before I finally decided to speak about my dream.

"I had a nightmare about Clare." I said still huffing and puffing.

"Tell me, Railrunner." He said sternly.

"Well, there was lots of blood, her scream was horrifying. I ran after her, but I could not catch her. Something happened - she vanished and *something* came after me."

He let out a long deep sigh. The white coaster looked at my face again, his eyes full of sorrow. "I think your dream means something." He said finally.

"What?"

"I don't know, I can't clarify that. However, it could still very well just be a nightmare."

"Hope your right." I replied climbing out of bed.

"Well come along, Railrunner. I have something that we must work on."

"Coming," I said following him out of the room. I was missing Clare more than ever now. It was- unbearable.

Chapter 26
Duel and Decision

The images of my dream still haunted me as I walked out into the courtyard to meet Thunderbark. I had a bad feeling in the pit of my stomach about today's session. From a distance I saw the white coaster standing on the small island in front of the great waterfall. Weird, we had never practiced there before.

Merrylegs and Static joined me, seeming somewhat excited. Static had a wide grin on his face and Merrylegs trotted happily.

"Why are you two so -."

"Excited?" Merrylegs finished.

"Yeah."

"We're going see something we haven't witnessed in a while, It's something that will prepare you for your fight with Ironwheel."

"What is it?" I asked.

"You are going to duel Thunderbark!" Static blurted out.

"What!"

"Yes, he told us this morning before you awoke."

"Wonderful," I said coldly. I didn't like the whole idea of it. I had never actually dueled another roller coaster before. I didn't know how I would comprehend the mere fact.

Thunderbark welcomed me as I stepped foot on the island. I grinned nervously in response.

"I think they already told you what we were doing didn't they." He began collectedly.

"Yeah - they kind of did," I said joking a little.

"To let you know, I'm going to go easy on you. There are a few rules I have to explain first before we get started. First, no bending of any kind. Second, no claws. Third, no teeth. What we are doing is like karate, you get my point, Railrunner?"

"Yes."

"Good, now let's begin." Thunderbark said as he loosened his muscles

My body tensed as we moved back and forth like sumo wrestlers. I felt myself letting out a threatening snarl. Thunderbark looked at me astonished. His only response was a loud hiss like that of a breaking train. I lunged quickly for him, my wheels ready for his throat, nevertheless at the last second with a hard shove, I was thrown to the ground. I turned and glanced back at Thunderbark.

"That was pitiful, dazzle me." He said in a playful tone. I then got up and darted to the left and attacked him from the side. It worked at first, but then I was thrown to the ground once more.

"Railrunner, you have to trick your opponent. Make them have no idea what your next move is."

"All right -." I said suddenly bending over and swinging my tail, hitting him across the face. Thunderbark lay on the ground. He struggled to get up, when he finally got in a sitting position and spat out blood.

"Nice one, you caught me off guard." He said spitting out more blood. "Like in the real world we use the element of surprise, but here we use it for a different matter." Then he swung his tail without warning, this time I saw it coming and I dodged his attack.

"Caught you trying to pull a fast one." I laughed slightly.

"Very good, that is the most important thing in battle, stay alert." He chuckled.

"Of course." I said making another move when he was in the process of getting up, but he hit me right back, knocking me off the little island and into the water.

Then it happened very quickly.

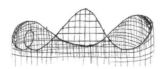

Rage suddenly built up inside me, my blood got hot.

Anger flowed like a river and my heart beat faster. Blood pulsed and my mind raced. Hatred came into me in a rushing fury. I was losing myself, instinct was taking over. My bloodlust returned...

I sprang up and over the island, landing on Thunderbark's back. The force was so great, we both landed in the water on the other side of the island. And I sunk my teeth onto his arm. He wailed in agony, and then my mind snapped, bringing me back into reality.

I staggered backward holding my head, as Thunderbark looked at me in horror.

"What just happened?" I said dazed.

"You bit me, Railrunner." Thunderbark uttered in pain.

"I did?" I said confused.

"You did, do you not remember?"

"No - I don't know what just happened."

"Railrunner I think you are starting to suffer from Jyronatropy."

"What's that?" I said with my memory returning.

"Every so often, usually about three weeks after you gain control, a coaster will sometimes experience some sudden spells where they lose control again. This could go on for about one week."

"So when I'm angry or upset, it triggers me to lose it?"

"Yes. But sometimes it happens from withdrawal of something."

"Well ok, hey we had better get that wrapped up! You're bleeding really badly."

"Yeah, I'd better." He sighed in exhaustion.

Then it donned on me, why wasn't his wound healing as it should?

"Can't you heal yourself, Thunderbark?" I asked confounded.

"I can't. I forgot to tell you, a roller coaster can be harmed or killed by another coaster."

"I'll *definitely* keep that in mind!"

We took Thunderbark to his room, and tended to his nasty wound. He lost a large amount of blood, but Merrylegs said he would make a full recovery in time. He now lay asleep, aided by some pain medicine.

"He will be in bed a few days," Merrylegs said to me. "It's not like it was your fault, Railrunner. You couldn't prevent your nature even if you tried."

"I still feel like it's my fault." I sighed.

"It's not," Static cut in.

"Whatever you say, I think I will get some rest now." I replied sheepishly with Merrylegs giving me a weak smile.

"All right, we were about to do the same thing. Good night, Railrunner."

"Night," I called as I walked out of the room. I thought more about what Thunderbark had told me. A factor why I snapped was, withdraw, and I knew what from, Clare. I pondered more. Thunderbark was bedridden for a few days. I had a clear schedule. It was then that I made my mind up, tomorrow I would go and visit Clare.

Chapter 27
Daring Move

Before the break of dawn I pulled out a piece of old parchment and struggled to write a letter to Thunderbark. With a quill I wrote:

Dear Thunderbark,

I'mgoinghuntinghavenoideawhenIwillreturnmaybetomorrowmorningDon'tworryhave my cloak. See you soon.

Railrunner

It was difficult to write the letter with wheels instead of hands, but at least it was still legible. I snuck quietly out of my room and walked down the long dark hall. I was the only thing that was active in the temple, nothing else stirred. I silently entered Thunderbark's room; he slept soundly in his bed. I silently sat the letter on the end table with all the medication. Hopefully Merrylegs would find it. Then I left the room.

Minutes later I stood outside the temple. I slipped on my trench coat and took a sip of river water. I glanced back where we had lived for several weeks, and then I bolted forward, disappearing into the forest.

It took our group about three days to get from the portal to the temple, and that was when we walked. If I ran, I could get to the portal by - maybe eight o'clock. Hopefully earlier. Amusement Park Between was quiet, but at least its silence was not eerie. Within the next hour and a half, I reached Trenzon. Mist hung in the empty streets, and all of its carnival lights were out. I looked at the little town hall, remembering the day that I slain the Fallen go-cart and when they found out I arrived here. However, I did not have time to gander and ponder memories. I had to get to the real world.

Running and running, my heartbeat kept rising. I knew it was only a matter of time before Thunderbark would find out that I had vanished. It would be even worse If he had found out I had gone to the real world. Hopefully the police forces had disappeared. Maybe I could be right; after all I had not made an appearance there in three weeks.

I was getting nearer to the portal, I could feel it. It would only be a matter of time then. One good thing on my timing was that I would arrive in the real world by early morning, and I would be human. The downside was that I had to leave before nightfall, or else everyone would witness what I truly am.

An hour later I had finally reached the portal. The strange blue florescent glow shone bright even as the dark began to fade. I took one last glance at my home, and then I concentrated my breath, and plunged into the water.

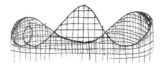

This time I knew what to expect as the water swarmed around me. My body went numb, as I continued to hold my breath. I could feel myself compress and shrink. I was becoming human, I thought. Everything shifted and changed as the seconds went by. My lungs started to hurt, I started to panic. With a jolting kick, I surfaced into the real world.

I climbed out of the water, my body was sore. I looked down to see that I had human hands and feet. I felt my face, it too was human. I had on the last outfit I was wearing before I transformed and my cloak became a black hoodie. The strangest thing though, was that I was completely dry. I took one quick look around then started my journey in the real world.

The rays of the sun softly beamed down onto my back. I walked along the empty streets with my hood up. Then I heard the roll of wheels, was it the cops? I turned around to see Sly driving a new Chevy truck. To my dismay, he rolled down the window.

"Hey sir, do you need a lift?"

I turned around and smiled at him. His eyes widened as he realized who I was.

"Rodney! Where in the hell have you been!" he said excitedly opening up the passenger door. I climbed in; I had to be the least bit suspicious.

"I've been to Germany, on a business trip." I said lying.

"Really? Your job has been paying off."

"It is, but I can see that yours is, too." I replied as I glanced at his truck.

"Yeah, I decided to invest in what I had in opening up a shop. I sell sports gear."

"Interesting."

"Yep, bought me something I really needed. This baby is fully loaded!" Sly said as he patted the dash.

"I can see that." I replied laughing. But then I saw that we were approaching a police sting. My senses told me that they were searching for the red.

"Drive faster, Sly." I demanded.

"Why? What is the problem?"

"Just drive."

"Tell me why -."

"Just do it!" I ordered him. I almost was yelling.

He stepped on the gas petal and drove away quickly. We rounded a corner, and the cops were no longer in view. I sighed in great relief.

"What the heck was that all about!" he said looking at me strangely.

"I can't really tell you. I'm sorry for yelling."

"That's fine, say where am I taking you?"

"To Clare's house."

"Clare's? She has been so troubled lately. The FBI, police, and even the army have interviewed her. I don't know why."

"Huntersville is still obsessed with m- madness over the roller coaster?" I asked, almost screwing up big-time.

"Yeah, they are on high alert, they are ready for it. Hope that bastard gets what it deserves." Sly said as while he never took his eyes from the road.

I looked to the floor, my theory was wrong. Everyone was out to get me.

"Rodney?"

"Sorry Sly I zoned out."

"That is also fine, by the way, what were you doing walking this early?"

"I always walk in the mornings." I replied. I really wished he would hurry up and get me to Clare's.

"All right. I forgot to tell you that your house was destroyed and your car was repossessed." He said wincing.

"Screw it." I said.

"You're not angry? I thought you would be furious!"

"You don't want to see me furious." I said under my breath.

"Pardon?"

"Nothing."

"Well we are here. Nice to see you Rodney."

"Right back at you."

He nodded and drove away, as I sighed again in relief. He was starting to ask me too many questions. I turned to the front of her house. I began to walk up her perfectly paved sidewalk, when Mittens jumped out and hissed at me. I rolled my eyes and barred a set of gleaming white fangs at the cat. Its hair stood on end as it ran away yowling. I smiled a little in amusement.

I cautiously strolled up to her front door. I reached and rang her doorbell, then stepped back and waited quietly. My keen ears heard footsteps, her footsteps that sounded like a melody to my ears. Then I heard her turn the knob. The door creaked open. Then her beautiful self appeared in the doorway. She looked at me in shock; tears began to run down her face.

"Railrunner?" she said gasping with her hand over her mouth.

"It's me Clare." I said smiling from ear to ear. She pranced forward and hugged me tightly.

"Come on in, it is safer, I don't want those horrid people to take you from me." She said guiding me in. Her house had not changed a bit. I could smell breakfast from her tidy kitchen.

"Thanks, I said lost in a little bit of thought. I still couldn't believe I was here.

"We can sit down and discuss your travels and what has been going on here at breakfast. You still like pancakes?"

"A little bit," I said slightly frolicsome. She smiled and showed me to her kitchen. I sat at the table and Clare went to the stove to check on the pancakes and to fix extra.

"Clare, I would help you, but I'm afraid I'm a bad cook. Maybe I can get us drinks?"

"That's fine; the drinks are in the garage in the fridge out there."

I nodded and made my way to its interior. I found the fridge easily. I opened it and grabbed Clare a coke, for some reason she liked that instead of coffee. I was going to grab me a coke but my eyes caught the sight of a can on a shelf. It was a can of motor oil. I found myself liking my lips. I hesitantly grabbed it off the self. I held it in my hand; temptation caused me to open it. The thick black liquid looked strangely -*appetizing*. My lips touched the can's rim; I tilted it backward, the oil slithering down my thought. I licked my lips in satisfaction, it tasted good. I rejected my coke and took the oil instead.

I carried our drinks to the table and sat them down, and then I helped Clare with gathering the food. We sat at the seats, across from each other. I took a sip of oil and Clare stared at me eccentrically.

"Your drinking motor oil!" she laughed.

"Yeah, it's actually good." I replied.

"Well then what happened after you left ? I take it you and your friends made it to the portal."

"We did. However, we got involved in a big brawl with the police and the FBI. Thankfully, we made it to the portal in the nick of time, just before the sun rose."

"Really? So how is Amusement Park Between?"

"Oh, Clare I wish you could see it! It's like a fantasy world! It is the most beautiful place I have ever laid eyes on. It not industrial like you would think its all forest! The technology is phenomenal, much more advanced than anything a scientist could invent. It is a place were anything is possible."

"What about the evil ruler you mentioned?" she asked perplexed.

"Oh, I forgot about that," I said starting to get depressed. "I might as well start from the beginning."

"That's all right, Railrunner. I'm all ears."

And so I explained Amusement Park Between in great detail. How the rides come to be and what they became if they are destroyed in the real world. I told her the legend of the red roller coaster, how I was created differently. That I was born and not built. I told her the prophecy again, I told her my destiny. Finally I told of Ironwheel and his armies. I told her of Freakshow and Ironwheel's servants. Most importantly, his motive.

"Hmm, sounds like your world has its ups and downs like ours."

"Yeah," I laughed. "I think that is enough about me for a while, what about you?"

"Well our world has been chaos since you left," she began. "First the FBI got troops down here, they've been ratting this place out like wolves. I've been interviewed numerous times. Captain Vick has tried to find out where you have disappeared. He knows you are from another world."

"Does he know which one?"

"I didn't tell him about Amusement Park Between when he tried interviewing me about that. I told him you were from hell."

"To some it seems as if I am." I replied.

"Well, I'm really glad to see you; I've missed you so much. I think I am suffering from withdrawal." She sighed

"I think I am too."

"Really?"

"Yes, but withdrawal is different for me. I get out of control at some points. Like Thunderbark said every once in a while I get spells like that. I turn into a killer again for a brief moment."

She seemed too fearful of what I just said. I took another sip of oil, and gave her a crooked smile to let her know she had nothing to worry about. She seemed slightly relieved.

"You want any butter for your pancakes?" she suddenly asked.

"That would be fine." I replied. I didn't really like pancakes anymore. Clare's dog, Huck, sat by my side begging for food with sad eyes. When Clare had her back turned, I scooted the pancakes onto the floor for Huck. He picked them up and ran out of the room with his tail wagging.

"Never mind, Clare. I ate them anyway." I lied.

"Really? That quick?"

"Yeah."

She smiled and sat back down taking a drink, and then took a bite of pancakes.

"I have something that I never got the chance to ask you, Railrunner."

"What might that be?"

"I asked you what it was like to be a coaster when you were out of control. Now what is it like when you are in?"

"Well, I'll put it like this. I don't feel like somebody's poured a liter of acid into my brain that's for sure!" I smiled.

She laughed, and then I continued.

"It's kind of like- well- concentrated. It's like a vampire. They can choose who they suck blood from, but yet they have all the power they could want at their disposal."

"Oh I see what you mean." Then there was a loud knock on the door. I already knew who it was.

"Oh no! There're coming for you! You must go, Railrunner!"

"But -."

"Just go please." She whispered. She looked at me tearing up.

"I want one more thing before I leave -." I said starting to lean in toward her lips. They met mine, and we kissed. The police got impatient outside, they started to bang on the door and yell. Our courtship was vaguely interrupted.

"I will come back I promise." I hugged her.

"I know you will." She sighed. Then I said my final goodbye and escaped out of the back door.

I ran, no man noticed me at first till one saw my face. From there the chase was on. Without thinking, I ran into the road. I stared into the eyes of Captain Vick. He smiled evilly.

"There you are, Railrunner." He said simply. "Any reason you are in disguise?"

I flipped him off and bolted into an alley made between two apartment complexes. It came to a dead end, and the humans were not far behind. I looked around desperate, I spotted a fire escape. My agility was still in use even in this body. Like a cat, I leaped straight onto the second level of the fire escape. I climbed it with ease, making it to the top in less than a few seconds. I began to run across the rooftop, a helicopter now joined in the pursuit. My heart started to race, I reached the edge of the six-story building. My muscles bulged within my legs. I acted on instinct, and jumped across the gap between the buildings.

I continued to move, leaping over gaps at ease. The force was hot on my trail. I had to lose them! I climbed down the sheer face of the building I was currently running on. I darted to my left. A big warehouse stood about two hundred yards away from me. Maybe I could lose them there.

Luckily the place was open. I locked the door and sat a big wooden crate in front of it. I turned around to see that there was no way out. I hid behind a tower of crates. As I gasped for air, the men could be heard outside. They were lining up, ready to blow me to pieces. Could this really be the end?

Suddenly, my palms began to sweat. I looked down at them, they started to tremble and shake. The Augu Ra glowed brightly. My skin began to flake off, exposing my flaming red metal underneath. My eyes burned as they turned into that of the beast I really was.

"Showtime." I growled.

Captain Vick stood outside the warehouse, nervously. As he waited to make the signal, he expected for the worst to happen. He knew he was dealing with the most powerful supernatural creature that he could ever believe. He signaled his men to aim their guns at the warehouse.

A very loud bang sliced through the air, Vick's heart hammered in his chest. Suddenly, the wall of the warehouse was wiped out like it had been hit by a bomb. Out of the smoke emerged, Railrunner. His fire like eyes glared intensely at Vick. His lips peeled back into a nasty snarl. It was clear that the roller coaster was defiantly not too pleased of the men's presence.

"Well, surprised to see me *Vick*?" Railrunner spoke; his voice was rugged but yet turned velvety at its end. The Captain didn't reply, he could only cower in fear. "Coaster got your tongue?" Railrunner mocked. "I'm sure you are, and yet I'm surprised to see you *alive*."

"And I'm surprised to not see you dead." He retorted.

" I can't die." The red roller coaster smiled.

"We shall see." He said signaling to fire. Gunshots echoed through the air, being heard for miles. The bullets simply bounced off of Railrunner. The demon coaster waved his arms.

"You'll now learn that I play with fire!" Railrunner yelled. A searing inferno completely wiped out the first row of helpless men. All Vick could now see was the hungry flames in front of him. But out of nowhere, Railrunner sailed over the tank that Vick stood upon. He landed untouched on the other side.

The roller coaster headed for the portal, but out of the consuming fireball he had created, emerged six tanks full of angry humans. Railrunner turned to face them, he was ready. All at once the tanks fired missiles. Railrunner simply knocked them off course. He then bended them back to his pursuers. It eliminated one tank. Railrunner smiled, then he let loose a concussion beam. I rid him of his problems and the city could feel its massive shockwave. Railrunner continued his escape route.

Minutes later he arrived at the portal, and did not hesitate diving in.

Dangerous Waters

His mind was furious. The enemies sent flooded his nostrils. The foul odor only made him angrier. Revenge was a priority now, no doubt about it. He roared in fury, and it could be heard over the crack of the waves and the shrieks of the helpless.

Chapter 28
Tempers Flare and Fizzle

Merrylegs stretched as she awoke out of her sleeping position. It was time to check on Thunderbark, and how well he was healing up. As she walked out of her room, she had a hunch that something was missing. Merrylegs thought for a long while, but decided to ignore it.

She entered Thunderbark's room silent as a mouse. He was still asleep. He looked uncomfortable as he sleep lightly. Other than that the coaster looked a lot better. Merrylegs nudged his side with one of her hooves. Thunderbark awoke immediately, blinking his eyes briefly. He yawned, showing his sharp white teeth.

"How are you feeling?" Merrylegs asked.

"Better, my arm still hurts. Railrunner's venom seems to be disappearing though."

"That's a good thing. However, I'm still going to give you some pain medicine for your arm just so we're on the safe side."

"Sounds good." He replied.

As Merrylegs reached for the medications, she noticed a neatly folded up piece of parchment. She carefully opened it and began to examine it.

"What's that?" Thunderbark questioned, suddenly alert.

"It's a letter, from Railrunner."

"What does it say?" He said sounding alarmed.

"He left to go hunting." She said quietly as she nervously waited for the white coaster to respond.

Thunderbark's eyes narrowed into slits. A low growl sounded from deep within his chest. He barred his fangs and began a threatening snarl, making the carousel horse jump.

"*I know good and well that Railrunner is not hunting.*" He hissed with his teeth tightly clenched together.

"How can you tell?" Merrylegs asked nervously as Static entered the room.

"Odd, where is Railrunner?" he asked.

"THAT IGNORANT FOOL!" Thunderbark suddenly shouted. His temper was flaring.

"What is wrong!" Static asked Merrylegs.

"Railrunner went hunting, he left the temple." Merrylegs replied.

"He did NOT go hunting." Thunderbark said climbing out of his bed. He stormed for the door to his room.

"What?" Merrylegs and Static asked at the same time.

"*He went to visit Clare!*" The white coaster answered angrily.

"Thunderbark! You probably don't want to be livid at Railrunner. He probably took you to seriously about suffering from withdraw." Merrylegs protested.

"Yeah, he's really young, reckless, stupid, and takes things to literally!" Static said, receiving a glare from Merrylegs.

Thunderbark's rage seemed to lighten a bit. Suddenly he turned angry again.

"The thing is, he knows better! If he screws up once, we are doomed! Hell, I've told him a thousand times not to leave!"

Merrylegs couldn't argue with that one, Thunderbark had told him repeatedly not to leave the temple. Merrylegs knew Thunderbark had to be careful on what he would say to Railrunner. Right now the young coaster was like an explosive , bound to explode when the fuse reached the bomb.

Thunderbark entered the temple's courtyard, and Railrunner just came through the entrance. He stood staggering a bit, his cloak was burnt at the ends. He looked exhausted as could be.

"Why in the hell did you go and see her?" Thunderbark demanded.

"From what I can remember, you said it would heal me." He snapped back.

Railrunner could barely hold himself up, from all the running across Amusement Park Between and the real world.

"What! Railrunner, that move was completely careless! You could have died!" The coaster growled.

"*Why would you care?*" he replied in a low voice.

That made Thunderbark EXTREMELY angry.

"*I do care for your information! I was the one who trained you! I was the one who watched over you for years! I was the one who saved your life!*"

Railrunner did not respond. He simply looked at Thunderbark. His eyes were full of shame. Then he couldn't stand any longer, falling to the ground at Thunderbark's wheels.

I awoke lying in my bed. I must have collapsed from exhaustion. Then I remembered my argument with Thunderbark. Why did I do that? Why in the hell did I say what I did? I felt horrible, not sick, but completely stupid! How could I be so heartless after what all he had done for me?

I sat up and clutched my head in agony. I growled at myself.

"Why am I such a hothead?" I questioned. I looked up to see Thunderbark standing in the doorway. He looked as if he had calmed down from the incident earlier. He came and stood beside me. He smiled a small smile.

"Sorry for yelling at you, I was in the wrong." He said. It sounded like he meant it.

"It's fine." I replied sighing.

"I guess the thing that scared me the most was the simple fact –."

"What."

"The fact on what can actually kill a coaster."

"What can kill us?" I said already knowing the answer.

"The only thing that can kill a roller coaster is another roller coaster."

"So that is why you didn't heal up from my attack?" I played along.

"Exactly."

"I understand now, Thunderbark."

"I'm sorry." The white coaster apologized again.

"Well Thunderbark, I've actually kept something from you too."

"What?" he asked concerned.

I climbed out of bed and pulled out the sword that I wrapped up in cloth.

"What is that?" he said eyeing it carefully.

I unwrapped it, Thunderbark's eyes widened.

"Where did you get that!" he said whispering in excitement.

"I found it. It was in a secret alter. I discovered a hidden door that led to a room full of statues of the previous reds. Then I went through a door at the end of the hall and found a track! A big steel roller coaster track."

"Really! Did you find anything else?"

"Yes, I found old weaponry. The only useful weapon was this sword." I finished with Thunderbark looking at it in awe. He then grinned widely.

"That's not just any old ordinary sword, Railrunner. That was the sword used by Moonblood. The sword that is said to hold a very powerful secret."

"Cool." I replied, it being the only response I could think of.

"Well, I guess I need to discuss something with you. I have already announced this to Merrylegs and Static. Tomorrow we are leaving the temple now that you have completed your training. We are going to Ferris Harbor in order to sail up the Acterbahnn to the nearest city, Zegria. We are going to my home. Mainly because I need something important from there."

"Okay. I am with you. I'll pack tonight."

"Fine, we leave on the crack of dawn. And Railrunner -."

"Yes?"

"Be prepared and watch our backs. We don't know what could happen."

Chapter 29
Ferris Harbor

The next morning was foggy and muggy. The sky was grey and bleak. Merrylegs, Static, and I were standing in an alley between two shops. Ferris harbor was nothing particularly special. It just had small businesses and various merchants. The dock, strangely enough had no ships. In fact, there were none in sight.

Thunderbark stood speaking with one of the rides that rented ships. I listened intently on their conversation.

"I need a ship, a big sturdy one if you please. I also need a crew."

"That is going to cost you a bit." The old green go cart replied.

"How much?" Thunderbark demanded.

"Well, I'm gonna say about seven thousand g's."

"That is quite a bit." Thunderbark sighed in disappointment.

"I can't help you there." Was his only response.

Thunderbark looked to the ground; he let out another sigh of defeat. I walked forward, my hood over my face. Thunderbark turned to glare at me. I pulled out a brown cloth bag and dropped it in front of the grouchy ride.

"I think this will cover it." I said in a low voice. I gave the go cart a crooked smile.

He carefully opened the sack. His yellow eyes grew bigger as he pulled out a solid gold block. It gleamed brightly even in the cloudy atmosphere. He smiled at Thunderbark and me.

"There is more where that came from, if you supply us with what he demanded." I said smiling.

"Whatever you wish, I will have a ship and a crew for you within the next thirty minutes."

"Thank you." Thunderbark replied. Then as he left, Thunderbark turned to me.

"When did you get that!" he said in an excited whisper.

"Before we left. I decided to use my brain."

"I wish you could use your brain more." He said smirking.

I growled at him.

"I'm just messing with you, Railrunner." The white coaster spoke as he slapped me on the back.

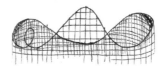

Our group stood at the river's edge waiting for our boat. I played with my sword, tossing it this way and that in one set of wheels, not even looking. Merrylegs and Static ate as Thunderbark kept scanning the surface of the water.

"Why are you doing that?" I asked him.

"You will see in a second," he replied not looking at me.

I followed his act and scanned the water, too. Suddenly in front of where we were standing, thousands of air bubbles foamed at the surface. Then a BIG creature gradually rose like a god out of the water. I recognized it as a swinging ship. It had the head of a dragon or sea serpent that formed from the ship's bow. It had four legs with webbed feet that jutted out from the ship's underside. The creature shook its big head like a dog would to rid itself from water. It opened its mouth and let out a bellow like that of a bison.

"See?" Thunderbark said finally looking at me.

"Sure do," I replied watching our crew ready the ship.

We walked by to help out and discuss matters with our captain. He was a roller coaster, wooden like Thunderbark, and his name was Bandit. His appearance looked like that of a large raccoon, adding humor to his name. The ship we were sailing on was called Nessie, another ironic combination.

After about an hour and a half we finally moved out. We stood in Bandit's office, Static was poking into things he shouldn't, Thunderbark was looking over maps with Bandit, and both Merrylegs and I peered out the window. I could feel that our captain was suspicious of me since I still wore my trench coat and my hood up.

"Well, Thunderbark would you like to introduce your friends? I would love to know their names while we are together." Bandit smiled.

"All right." Thunderbark started. The tone of his voice told me he was nervous. "There is Static over by the cabinet. Merrylegs is the yellow carousel horse. And - that is Railrunner standing with her."

"Nice to meet you all. Can I see your face, Railrunner? I like to know everybody by his or her name and appearance. It sort of feels weird when I don't."

"You can remember me as the one with the coat." I replied stuttering a little. Thunderbark was staggering a little bit.

"Come on!" he said ignoring me.

"I'd better not."

"Please?"

Why was he so eager to see me?

"Might as well, Railrunner." Thunderbark said surprisingly. He might want to know why we are in a hurry."

I sighed; I looked at Bandit who was anxiously waiting. I slowly removed my hood. Bandit's mouth dropped open a few inches.

"My apologies, Railrunner. This is the first time I've ever seen a red in person, I have dishonored you."

"No Bandit you are fine."

"Thank goodness! I thought you would be angry with me."

"I'm not."

"Good. Now everyone, I will try to do my best so that you get to where you want to go quickly and safely. However, safety could be an issue if we do not look out."

Chapter 30
Water Hazard

It had been three days since we sat sail. Each second we were getting further away from the portal. This meant I was getting farther from Clare. During the days passed, the weather surprisingly improved. The clouds parted and there was nothing but clear skies.

I gazed out from the edge of the deck at the crystal water. I eagerly watched the multicolored fish swim by. My boredom level increased while being on the ship. In fact, from the look of it, my friends and the crew were very bored. The rides either played cards or some other game native to this world.

Thunderbark walked up next to me. He was just like every member on this ship. The coaster started to toss shiny pebbles into the water. He turned to watch Merrylegs and Static, and then he returned to focus on me.

"Tired?" He asked.

"Mostly exhausted, how much farther is it?"

"Well, Bandit says it will be a few hours." He sighed.

I grumbled in response. I was sick of being on Nessie.

"At least we are together to pass the time." Thunderbark added. He was trying to cheer me up. It was quite obvious. I then decided to get on a new subject.

"If you say so. This is sort of random, but I have wondered this for quite some time. Where did you, Merrylegs, and Static come from?"

Thunderbark was silent for several minutes. He then sighed like he always did right before explaining something bad or important to know.

"I will start with Static." He began. "Static worked at a traveling carnival that hit all the major cities every year. He was the oldest of all the bumper cars. The humans acquired him when the carnival first started out. It was 1968 when he couldn't work anymore, so the humans cast him aside in storage. Then our world took him in."

"What about Merrylegs?"

"Merrylegs came to us in the year 1946. She was thrown aside after years of abuse. Humans did not treat her well, but she still loved the children. They were the only ones she liked for a long time, until I made her see goodness in adults. She was put into storage forever for several accounts. Her yellow paint was chipping, her mane was falling out, and cuts scarred her wooden body. Also for her indifference."

"All right, what about you?"

Thunderbark let out one of his classic sighs again.

"It is quite a tale, but I will shorten it as best as I can, Railrunner. It goes something like this- it was the year 1920. I was the fastest and most furious coaster around at the time. My "keeper" loved me; I was like a car to him. A prized jewel. He would wax and polish me weekly. His name was Henry White. He would brag about me as I ran across the rails. I was the "thing" back then. As the years passed, times changed. Henry grew sick, and was bed ridden. I waited in storage for I had grown unserviceable. Amusement Park Between worked its magic, and I transformed into the beast that I am today. After the first day in Amusement Park Between, I found out I could go back into the real world as a human. On the day that I did, I visited Henry.

"What happened?" I interrupted.

"I was in the hospital with him. He lay dying. The nurse told everyone to get out as he drew his last breaths. I entered when everyone left. Henry was still alive and conscious enough to hear me. I told him who I was, and he was happy to see me. But seconds later he died."

"That's it?" I asked.

"Yes, Railrunner. All of us rides have a story to tell on how we came to be. Yours overall is the most special. I have to admit." He smiled.

I didn't know how to respond to that statement. I simply nodded and said thank you.

Nessie unexpectedly bellowed loudly, the swinging ship began to rock. Bandit scrambled up to calm her. My heart started to race as Thunderbark became suddenly vigilant. Every ride aboard grew wakeful.

"Something is wrong Thunderbark!"

"I know! I sense it too!" He replied. Merrylegs and Static joined us. The crew scattered in fear. I watched in horror as three dragon-like heads rose gradually out of the water. Finally all of the swinging ships emerged. The middle was the biggest one of them all; its monstrous head looked hideous. Then I recognized it from my raid at the carnival. Before I became a roller coaster, I rode on it with Clare. When I transformed, I destroyed it. That was when I found out our pursuers were the Fallen.

Behind me, Bandit roused up the crew, preparing to battle. Thunderbark told Static and Merrylegs to go in the cargo hold for safety. However they resisted his request. I looked back to the advancing enemy. A terrible mocking laugh sliced trough the air like a knife. There, on the bow of the center ship, was a mangled and mismatched roller coaster. I knew at once who she was.

"Freakshow!" I snarled.

Thunderbark snorted in disgust. "That bitch! Railrunner put your hood up! Freakshow cannot know what you are!" Thunderbark yelled over the calamity. I immediately obeyed him. Good thing Freakshow had not noticed me yet. This was going to be a fight to the death, I thought silently to myself.

Our ship moved forward in a frantic retreat. Freakshow laughed menacingly, and then she waved her arm to send a massive fireball toward us. It landed on the deck of our ship, Nessie wailed in agony. Thunderbark ran up onto the stern, and sent out a bolt of lightning in response. Like a trained acrobat, Freakshow flipped out of the way. Then she rained more fire towards Thunderbark. I leaped in front of him and put my wheels together, splitting the stream of the deadly blast. Freakshow glared at me, I smiled in response.

"Fire!" she yelled to her crew. From all the ships, cannonballs were induced. Nessie swerved wildly in the water to avoid them. When one of them hit the water, it sent a rippling wave across the river. One flew just over the deck of our ship, barely missing Static. Then we decided to fight back. Bandit brought out a big bazooka from the cargo hold. He aimed it at the swinging ship on the right, and fired. The missile met its target. Rides on board, were shot in the air from the aftershock of the blast. One down, two more to go.

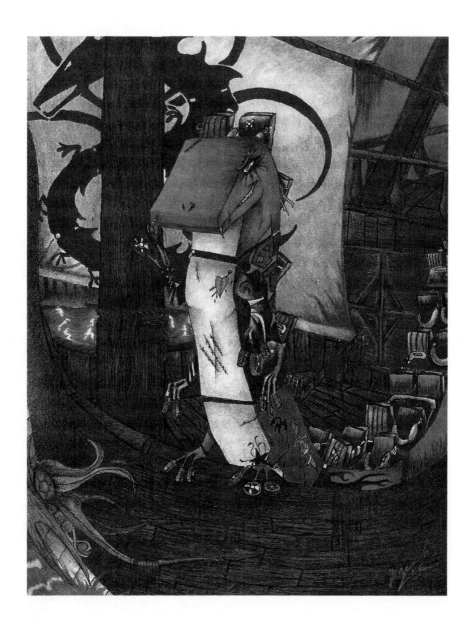

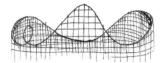

I turned around to see that the ship on the left was right next to us. We were side by side, a hell raising moment for everyone on Nessie. I extracted my claws, and so did Thunderbark.

"I want their blood to stain the wood on their ship!" Thunderbark snarled. Some of our crew leaped onto their ship and began to quarrel with the enemy. Unfortunately some of the Fallen boarded our ship. We began to fight once more. I dug my claws deep into the evil's flesh. I slaughtered different rides, no matter how big they were. I backed up and put my wheels on my sword, but Thunderbark stopped me.

"No! If you bring that thing out, everyone will know!" He said over the agonizing screams. I nodded, and then I turned away from him and began to bend like mad. Electrocuting, scorching, and playing with metal in deadly ways. Static used his shocking cable furiously as Merrylegs brought down heavy hooves onto the backs of the Fallen. Even the ship itself was doing its share, tangling with the other. The sent of blood was heavy in the air, overpowering the sent of the sweet water.

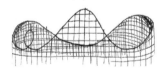

I turned to see Merrylegs fleeing from one of those little planes you would see on a kiddie ride. She galloped at full speed into the interior of the ship. Outraged, I followed her, plowing down any unwanted ride in the way. I rocketed down the stairs, and into the cargo hold. Merrylegs stood against the wall, the plane walked toward her like a prehistoric creature. Blood and saliva dripped like a faucet from it mouth. The thing must have bitten Merrylegs, because she had a nasty wound on her leg. With tears of pain in her eyes she screamed in defeat.

I lunged for the plane, my claws out like a tiger. The next split second, I had the ride pined on the ground like a pitiful bird that had been caught by a cat. I enclosed my teeth around its neck, snapping it, killing the stupid creature instantly.

"Are you all right?" I said rushing to her aid.

"My leg," she moaned. "Railrunner -."

"I can get the blood off and wrap it up for you."

"Do it! Lick the shit off and wrap it please!" she said with tears running down her face. My forked tongue ran over her wound, I hated to taste her blood, blood of the good. I liked the blood of the enemy. I wanted to taste it so bad, especially Freakshow's. Even more, Ironwheel's. I ripped off the cloth from a flour sack and carefully wrapped her leg.

"Thank you so much Railrunner." She said. "You saved me."

"It was no trouble," I replied to her. Gruesome thoughts suddenly flashed through my mind. They fueled my anger and rage. My mouth started to water as I thought about tasting my enemy. My mind screamed to become the savage beast that I truly was, and to take my enemy out. I swore on that, swore I would make the Fallen and the rest of those mongrels pay. It would be the ultimate price, death.

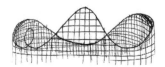

Another Fallen entered the cargo hold, this time a go-cart. I simply raised my arm and sent out a bolt of lightning. The ride dropped dead before it could reach Merrylegs and me. Static then entered the room completely out of breath and shocked to see Merrylegs in her condition.

"Watch her, Static. Don't let any one of those assholes get near her! Understand?"

"Roger that." He replied bravely.

I then rushed back out onto the deck. Thunderbark was wrestling with a big roller coaster. I held out my arm and did what Thunderbark had done to Captain Vick. The attempt worked perfectly.

"Thanks for that."

"Now I don't owe you anymore," I smiled. Then my grin faded when I saw the center ship not but about a hundred yards from us. The ship's mask suddenly tangled up with ours. I watched in horror as Freakshow smirked and started to descend up the mangled pole.

I snarled, and backtracked the way I had come, hopping over the many unfortunate. Then I leaped into the sails and bounced back onto the mast, clawing my way up. When I reached the top, Freakshow was already waiting for me. Now that I had a better view of her, I could see that every car was indeed different. Her head being purple, her next car black, green, then blue and so forth. None of her wheels matched, some of them were steel and some wood. Every restraint was different; some were patched up and sewn poorly. Her eyes did not even match, one being green and one being blue. Freakshow was a sorry excuse for a roller coaster.

"Nice day to sail." She said in a cruel tone. "What, might I ask; are you hiding roller coaster? Under your cloak?" she laughed.

I barred my teeth and snarled.

"Oh come on! We are all freaks! All monsters!"

"Look who is talking on that one." I retorted.

Freakshow gave me the "I've got bodies in my freezer" glare.

"Come on," she said waving for me to come closer. "Let's talk." She said playfully.

"Ladies first!" I laughed. Freakshow then charged and delivered the first blow, however I returned the favor by knocking her off the wooden pole. To my dismay she grasped the wood and flipped herself up onto where she was like a trapeze artist.

We kept going at it. I threw left hooks and rights as she did so. I bended against her. Lightning and fire searing her back and metal. I could taste the blood in my mouth from hits to my jaw. I extracted my claws again, cutting through her arm and chest. A big gash on both of them, blood pouring out of both the wounds. It pleased me to see the blood of the enemy, and to cause them pain and suffering.

We both swung at each other again, hoping to give the final blow. I felt excruciating pain as I was hit in the chest at the same time I hit Freakshow. The attack sent us both backwards across the wooden "balance beam" about fifty feet from each other. I tried to hull myself up, but the pain was horrible. When I finally succeeded, I turned around to see my worst nightmare: Freakshow staring at me with my hood off.

For a brief second all we could do was stare at one another. It seemed that the world around us had froze in time in which every thing stopped.

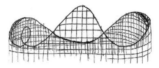

Freakshow opened her mouth to speak, but no sound came out.

"Yeah, you missed me before."

"Well, I'll make sure to not miss you this time, red!" she snarled. In the blink of an eye, she let out a concussion beam. Instinct overpowered my body, and I let out a beam in response. Then in a sudden rush, they collided. The explosion rocked Amusement Park Between, in a relentless earthquake. Destructive waves ripped through the water. I felt myself flying through the air. Then the hard slap as I hit. I surfaced, but I could barely keep my head up. I could only see the shattered remains of the ships, and the smell of blood filled the water. I felt myself going under. But then a familiar voice reassured me.

"Railrunner!"

Then everything went black.

Chapter 31
Ultimatum

I woke up with Thunderbark, Merrylegs, and Static standing around me.

"It is nice to see you conscious, Railrunner," said Thunderbark.

"And alive." Merrylegs added.

"Same to you, how long have I been out?" I asked insubstantially.

"About an hour or so."

I sat up clutching my head, it was throbbing still.

"Were there any survivors?" I asked

"Most of them did, but they are long gone now." Thunderbark replied.

"What about Freakshow?"

"Unfortunately she is still at large." Thunderbark said annoyed.

"Figures." I growled.

"Nice to hear that you did not cuss." Thunderbark laughed.

"If I recall, Thunderbark, I heard you swear on the ship!"

Thunderbark sighed, realizing he had been caught in a lie. We kind of all laughed at him. He only chuckled as he helped me up.

"Now, that we are all fine, we shall start heading to my place. There we can fix Merrylegs's leg and tend to our battle scars. Plus get the most vital thing to our journey."

"What?" I asked him as we began to walk upriver.

"The map to Amusement Park Between."

Inside the dimly lit hallway of the castle trotted a purple and black carousel horse. His legs shook nervously as he prepared to speak of something that was forbidden by standards. The two guard rides let the nervous messenger inside the throne room.

The horse walked as quietly as he could across the stone floor, cautiously stepping over the occasional bone. He could only stare at the throne, and the big black roller coaster sitting upon it like a gargoyle.

The coaster's pupil less red eyes stared at the horse. He broke out his claws and began to rake them across the arm of the stone chair. He barred his teeth in anger.

"Why have you disturbed my rest, horse?" he demanded.

The horse bowed to him. The coaster snarled.

"Weren't you supposed to do that earlier?"

"Sorry King Ironwheel, but I have an urgent message from Freakshow."

Ironwheel picked up a skull from the floor, a carousel horse skull to be precise. He held it in his wheels, Ironwheel's claws going in and out of the eye sockets.

"Humor me." He said in a rugged voice.

The horse gulped. "Well, there was an incident on the Acterbahnn. Three of our ships were destroyed, Freakshow and Bones being the only survivors."

"Hurry and get to your point." Ironwheel interrupted. His claws scratching the skull.

"It was all destroyed by one ride," the horse gulped again and prepared for the kings claws to tear him apart. "Sire, the time we have dreaded has arrived."

"What?" Ironwheel said angrily through his teeth.

"The red has returned!" the horse cried.

Ironwheel roared in pure fury, his cry echoing through the castle and Amusement Park Between.

Part Three
Bloodlust

The Line of Fire

The sky seemed to be lit in a blaze. Innocent and guilty blood was spilt on the soil. Thousands of screams seemed to have become one. Blood glistened on his teeth and wheels, his mind in a fury.

He swore the city would not fall into the hands of his enemy. And to get back the soul that had been stolen.

Chapter 32
Defunct Den

Darkness surrounded me. Clare walked forward out of the abyss. I was glad to see her, until my eyes caught the sight of her blood running from slashes. I screamed her name. But my voice went unheard. She seemed to sink back into the never-ending blackness. I tried to run, but my legs felt like lead, as if I was in slow motion. She disappeared, but then a black figure emerged. I saw that it was a roller coaster, his metal black and decorated in thousands of silver skulls. Both of us let out growls, and charged at each other with the taste for flesh.

I awoke with a sudden start. I was sweating all over and gasping for air. I sat up off the leaf-covered ground and shook my head, trying to rid myself of the horrible nightmare. I looked to see my allies standing around me with worried expressions on their faces. Apparently, I had been making quite a fuss.

"Are you all right?" Thunderbark asked with a hint of agony in his blue eyes.

"You don't look to good," Merrylegs added in.

"I think I just had a bad dream," I replied with my wheels still on my head.

"I've never seen anybody dream quite like that," Static said turning to Thunderbark for answers. At first Thunderbark did not say a word, he only stood there rubbing his chin. For some reason I had the feeling he knew, but he did not want to say it in front of Merrylegs and Static.

"I'm not sure what to tell you, Railrunner. I guess we will have to keep it under investigation," he said at last. However, when he turned to head out, he still kept his eyes on me. He was going to talk later, I could fell it.

We started to travel silently among the trees again. The morning atmosphere was pleasant. The birds fluttered up in the canopy as the beads of dew began to disappear. The temperature was perfect, nice and warm but not to hot. Today we were to pay a visit to Thunderbark's house. The day before, he said something about retrieving a map. I still had no idea what to expect of his territory because Thunderbark had not lived there for several decades.

Merrylegs and Static walked side-by-side talking to each other. I could only guess on what subject they were speaking of, me. Because, every once in a while they would glance back out of the corners of their eyes at Thunderbark and I. Then the white coaster suddenly slowed his pace and let Static and Merrylegs venture on ahead.

"I want to talk to you, Railrunner."

"I knew you would, I could tell." I replied.

"You thought right. I think I know why you are having such intense nightmares."

"Why?" I asked curious.

"Well, if I remember right, one of the reds had frequent nightmares. I believe her name was Redrail, the fifth red." Thunderbark spoke as he rubbed his wheels along the bark of passing trees.

"Are you saying there might be a pattern here? Every five reds, the fifth one having dreams that leave them in pain?"

"Exactly. Tell me if you have any more dreams, Railrunner. I have a few theories, but I cannot be clear on them yet."

"I'll let you know if it occurs again," I said. Now it seemed like I had more to worry about.

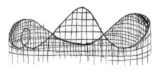

About an hour later, the forest got suddenly denser. Little light came through the treetops and there was no activity from Amusement Park Between's wildlife. Then I spotted a barely noticeable rotten roller coaster track. It was covered in layers of moss and trees sprouted through the gaps between its rails. Vines tangled the scaffolding. It was in such bad shape that it looked as if was about to sink into the earth.

"We are here." Thunderbark said as he started to lead the way. Merrylegs and Static continued to mess around the brush. The white coaster walked over to the track and put a set of wheels onto the rails. There was no apparent change in him.

"Humph, no reception," he sighed as he pulled his wheels away.

"Excuse me?" I asked him politely.

"Since this is – damaged, the track cannot support me with power."

"Wonderful."

"Why wonderful?" He asked astonished.

"Some helpful information to keep in mind." I continued; Thunderbark began to smile at that comment.

"I think I'll just settle for some good old barrel aged oil." Thunderbark said as his grin became bigger.

"So, oil is a delicacy?" I said snapping my wheels like a human would with their fingers.

Thunderbark then raised his eyebrows astounded. "Yes, had it before, Railrunner?"

"Yeah, I found a sudden liking to it."

"Good, because I have some in my cellar. Oil is like wine, the longer it sets the better it is. Plus it serves as an energy drink," he said.

"Really?"

"Yup. Now the entrance is somewhere around here," he continued as he searched high and low. Merrylegs and Static came over to join me, both of their faces coated in worry.

"I smelt the enemies scent." Static started.

"Fresh or stale?" I demanded.

"Static says it is stale. Thunderbark might want to find the entrance quickly, we don't know if the place has been ransacked or not." Merrylegs said with a hint of concern in her voice.

"It's all right," Thunderbark called. "There is no way that those *parasites* can get into my den," he boomed from across the clearing. It was obvious that he thought that was funny because he was chuckling to himself. I turned to see that Thunderbark was standing next to a tunnel that could barely be seen because of the underbrush. It blended in perfectly with the rotten track.

"You found it?" I asked.

"Yes, now I better explain, or rather show you what I meant earlier," he laughed as he fished around inside the tunnel. "You could say I have a really good security system," he said as he pulled out one of the biggest spiders I had ever seen.

"What -." Merrylegs started, but she choked on her words.

"Merrylegs, everyone, there is nothing to treat," he began while the gigantic spider crawled around in his wheels. "These spiders are harmless to rides like us, you see when they catch a Fallen's scent, they'll come running. If they bite a Fallen, he or she dies within an hour."

"Cool," Static said edging in for a closer look.

"How far can they smell a Fallen?" Merrylegs asked, becoming less fearful.

"From about fifty yards, but it is enough to scare them out of their wits!" Thunderbark laughed as he returned the spider.

"Thunderbark?" I asked.

"Yes, Railrunner?"

"If you said that only a roller coaster could kill a roller coaster, what effect do these spiders have on them?"

"Good question, it can only paralyze one for three days."

"Oh, that really comes in handy then."

"You bet it does Railrunner. Now if you all follow me, it is somewhat of a tight squeeze." Thunderbark said as he walked on all his wheels into the cave.

The passage in the tunnel was narrow, the spiders were proving to be hard to avoid. They would only move out of the way at the last second before you stepped on them. Then Thunderbark suddenly made a mesmerizing sound like that of a low cell phone beep. Miraculously, they moved out of the way, clearing a path so we could pass through at ease.

"Problem solved," he said. "It is not much further now."

"Good," I retorted. I was tired of my seats rubbing the top of the tunnel. I could tell that Merrylegs was not too crazy about the situation either, because her pole would scrape the roof and dust would fall into her silky red hair. Then we finally reached the end opened a brass door to reveal a small (in some standards) cozy den.

"Now, I know my place isn't as fancy as Railrunner's temple, but it still suits most." Thunderbark said as he started to tap the floor with his wheels, he must have been looking for something again.

"Still Thunderbark, its antique style gives it a relaxing atmosphere," Merrylegs said as she shut the door behind her.

"Well, they do say when you are built in the 1920s, you stay in the 1920s." Then Thunderbark found what he was looking for. He then told us to stand back as he pushed in a lone rock that stuck out of the den's wall. Shockingly the floor pulled away to reveal the passageway to a VERY high tec vault. "But I don't always have to be old fashioned!" Thunderbark laughed, his voice echoing off the den's walls. He then led us down a large and wide spiral staircase to the area outside the vault. The trapdoor slid shut overhead as we all arrived. The walls were solid chrome and blue lights flashed among the interior. It looked like something from the movies. He walked up to the big heavy-duty door. To the right was one of those eye scanners that you see in all the spy films. Thunderbark leaned in and put his right eye up to it. A green ray of light sailed over his pupil and a split second later the door opened.

The room was cold and mist leaked out of the pipes. Against the walls were four gigantic barrels.

"This is your oil cooler?" I asked him.

"Well, partially. It also hides a secret; he said opening a little compartment on one of the barrel's sides. Then another trapdoor released in the wall behind the fourth barrel. Then we ventured inside.

It was a very empty room with only a steel chest in its center on a podium. Thunderbark ran his wheels over the chest's smooth surface. He then fiddled with the combination lock, it was a touch system and all of its numbers were like the language that I saw all over Amusement Park Between. Then the chest popped open to revel a steel rod that looked like a mailing tube.

"This is it." Thunderbark said holding it up for all of us to see. "The only map of Amusement Park Between."

About an hour later, all of us sat around Thunderbark's table drinking oil (except Merrylegs) looking at the map; our eyes scanning every line, valley, city, every single detail. The map looked as if it had been hundreds of years old with its yellow tint. For many years it seemed to be guarded heavily by a god like creature, or rather machine.

"Amazing isn't it?" Thunderbark asked me.

"Sure is. I did not know that this place was THAT big!"

He laughed one of his belly laughs; it seemed that Thunderbark would only laugh like that after he fulfilled one of his needs. To me, it was somewhat hilarious. It also seemed that he was laughing at me. Sometimes it look as if like I was an excessive toddler that kept asking questions and demanded answers. At other times to Thunderbark it was like I was a savior, a powerful warrior the answer to all Amusement Park Between's problems. Most of all, a companion or ally.

"I think it is getting late," Merrylegs said yawning.

"It is, let's get some sleep. We have a long day of traveling tomorrow." Thunderbark said getting up.

Minutes later we got settled down into the four bedrooms. I lay awake in the bed pondering. I was suddenly weary; I had the feeling something bad was going to happen soon.

Chapter 33
Capture

The next morning I awoke to see Static and Merrylegs feasting on breakfast. The whole night I had a bad feeling in the pit of my stomach. I looked at what they were eating, something vegetarians would die for. Now that I truly was a scream machine I had grown to dislike greens completely, my diet was strictly meat.

I sat there and did not eat a thing. My mind was in a haze again, I was once more distracted by my own thoughts and worries. I thought about Clare, about the strange dreams, and the fact that everyone thought differently about me because of what I was —a *roller coaster*. I shook my head to get my mind clear, it only worked a little.

I started to believe that the main thing that I wanted was Clare to be with me. If there was some way she could live with me here -

"Railrunner, have you seen Thunderbark?" Merrylegs asked, cutting into my personal thinking.

"As a matter of fact I haven't." I said after a long pause. I then ran into his bedroom to look if he had left a note like I did. Sure enough there was one.

Dear Railrunner, Merrylegs, and Static,
We have no good meat, so I am going down to the river to fetch us some fish. I'll be back soon, and Railrunner, don't do anything stupid.
Thunderbark

I could only gawk about how beautiful his writing was; I guess it was because he had been writing with his wheels for years. Then suddenly my head began to burn, like I had an extreme temperature. Then an image of Thunderbark came into my mind, my heart started to race after I witnessed the whole vision. I ran back into the room where Static and Merrylegs ate. They looked at me as I burst through the door.

"Thunderbark is in Trouble!"

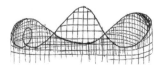

I ran with my muscles pumping. I was furious! The way I felt when I left to the real world and gotten myself into deep trouble. Was Thunderbark possibly trying to get back at me? No, there was no way, couldn't be, not after that horrible image! I leaped over the rotten track pieces like a rocket. I followed Thunderbark's familiar scent, without warning another joined his. I felt my nostrils flare as I smelt the foul and sour odor of a Fallen. I snarled as I thought about sinking my teeth into them.

The scents got stronger and stronger, and then I burst into a clearing where Thunderbark was wrapped up in some kind of strange net, with Freakshow grinning wickedly beside him. I glanced at Thunderbark, tears came through the corners of his eyes and blood seeped out from various scratches. I stood up and gave Freakshow an ugly sneer.

"Looks like I have captured the great white." She mocked. "What do you think about my prize, red?"

"First off, I have a name, it is Railrunner. Get that through your *dismembered* skull. Second, Thunderbark is *not* a trophy!" I growled.

Freakshow stood motionless at my crude comment. A black carousel horse that had the pattern of his skeleton all over his body emerged from behind the mismatched roller coaster. He smirked, so that I could see that he had fangs like a vampire. I rolled my eyes in response.

"Hello Bones, would you like to meet Thunderbark and - *Ra-lrunner?*" she hissed.

While she wasn't paying attention I hit her with an unexpected lightning bolt. She screamed in agony as she fell to the dirt. She arched her back and snarled, then threw a fireball at me. It missed by only a few inches. I turned to see that she pulled Thunderbark to the edge of the river to be loaded on a swinging ship. Two other roller coasters yanked him over the ship's side.

"Lets use him as bait for the red herring!" she laughed. "I'll deal with him later. Now move!" She finished as the ship swam off.

I went as fast as I could possibly go. I couldn't let them have him! I heard Thunderbark's desperate cries for help. I sped along the river's edge like a bullet. The world was a blur as I ran, the fastest I had ever run. Determination kept me moving at full tilt.

Then I saw Thunderbark leaning on the rail of the ship with several rides trying to keep him restrained.

"I'll be fine!" I heard him yell.

I'm not letting them get away! I thought.

"They will keep me alive! They...GRRARH...are using me as bait! I... will be... all right!" He said as the Fallen dragged him from my view. This time I wasn't going to listen to him. Gathering all my strength, I lunged up into the air and aimed for the ship with my claws outward. Freakshow snickered, and aimed a concussion beam at an overhanging tree limb.

The blast's aftershock sent the limb back towards me. It hit with such a force that my path stopped and I tumbled down into the water. My ribs burned from the impact as I surfaced and hung over the floating log.

I glanced at the ship, which was miles ahead. Frustrated, I banged my wheels onto the wet bark. Thunderbark was gone, but he dropped me hints like he did in the real world on how to save myself. This time however, the tables were turned. He was dropping hints on how to save him.

Chapter 34
Definition

My life: sucks
Too bad it lasts forever.

Chapter 35
Aggravation

I limped back to Thunderbark's house. Merrylegs and Static watched me worried. Everything was silent; my wheels trembled as rage built up inside me. I felt myself growling from deep within my chest as I walked quickly.

"Railrunner -."

"DAMN IT!" I yelled slashing the rotten track into, my claws digging deep in the wood.

"Railrunner!" Yelled Merrylegs. "What is wrong?"

"THAT DAMN BITCH TOOK THUNDERBARK!" I shouted furious.

Merrylegs looked at me blankly, so did Static, they had no words to speak.

"YEAH, YOU BOTH HEARD ME! THOSE ASSHOLES TOOK HIM! HOW IN THE HELL DID SHE CATCH HIM! NONE OF THIS SHIT MAKES SENSE!" I said cutting a tree in half with one swipe.

"Railrunner, calm down!" Merrylegs tried to coax me. I snarled and chucked a boulder like a cannonball.

"I agree, calm down and for crying out loud Railrunner, quit cursing!"

"SHUT THE HELL UP!" I then turned and ran.

I followed closely behind Railrunner. Trees had fallen onto the path and some were muddled. Railrunner was so strong, probably deadly when he was throwing one heck of a roller coaster tantrum. I had seen him mad, but never like this!

I could not get over the fact that Thunderbark had been captured! Of all the bad luck! I knew Thunderbark too well; I knew how he would handle this. Railrunner on the other hand was an unstable molecule. I could hardly keep up with him; my legs were starting to grow numb! Then he unexpectedly slowed and veered to his right. I followed him, half fearing for my life.

Railrunner ran to the edge of the cliff that overlooked the Acterbahnn. He then roared the BIGGEST earth shattering roar I had ever heard, Thunderbark couldn't even top it. His roar echoed all through Amusement Park Between, powerful sounding, threatening. His mouth was completely open, showing all of his razor teeth, the thought of them going into me, made me sick to my stomach. Railrunner's roar then died down into a whine. He hung his head low and breathed hard. Hesitantly, I bravely ventured forward.

"Railrunner?" I said in the most calming voice I could muster.

"*Go away Merrylegs.*" He hissed, not even turning to look at me. He then sat down and stared at the horizon with one of his deadly glares. I galloped over to Railrunner and positioned myself before him. I gulped.

"*You have a lot of nerve to stand in front of me.*" Railrunner growled.

"You're being a jerk!" I said to him without thinking. I saw him start to tremble again. Trembling in anger, so ready to kill me. I waited for the roller coaster's teeth to rip out my throat. I still wasn't finished speaking my mind, so I continued.

"Why are you being such a hothead! Railrunner, you have an anger management problem!"

He snorted in disgust, and gave me a threatening grimace.

"I didn't ask for any of this, Clare!" he retorted. My eyes widened. Then he realized what he had said and hung his head in defeat. Then there was nothing but an awkward silence between us.

I fought back my feelings. Everything seemed even more messed up than it was before. All of my memories bothered me to no extent. Merrylegs continued to look at me, her eyes showed pity. I sighed.

"I'm sorry Merrylegs, I couldn't control myself. I can get out of whack sometimes. I am just really stressed right now."

"I know you are. You've been the same way since you found out what you were. Maybe - I should–take a look." Merrylegs said after a short pause.

"What do you mean?" I asked her a little confused.

"Railrunner, they say that unicorn carousel horses have the power to see what's in ones mind. I am no different. If you don't care, I think I should have a gander."

"Go ahead."

"Lay down." She said.

I obeyed her command, I still had no idea how she could "read ones mind". I watched quietly as she trotted forward and bent her head down. Then the tip of her pearl colored horn touched my forehead. Merrylegs inhaled and then shut her eyes, and mine seemed to have a black shade go over them as my body trembled. My wheels burned and my head started to throb. My skull felt like it was on fire. I gritted my teeth. My senses seemed to vanish, but I could still hear Merrylegs, she seemed to have labored breathing, every once in a while she would whimper. Then we both couldn't take it anymore, and we broke from the connection.

I got back to normal in no time, however Merrylegs shook with fear. She breathed hard and her eyes watered.

"I- have never seen ANYTHING like that. Your head is filled with horrible memories! I saw everything."

"Everything?"

"Everything, from anytime."

"Interesting," was all I could mutter.

"Now since I have seen what lies within your head, I understand what Thunderbark told me."

"What?"

"He said that you were, different." She smiled tenderly.

"Different as in how?"

"Different as in special."

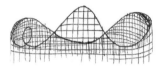

I walked with Merrylegs back to our "base". Static looked up from the meal he was currently engorging himself on. He swallowed a mouthful of food, and then opened his mouth to speak.

"R -."

"Let's just keep comments to ourselves, and forget that event even happened." Merrylegs interrupted.

"What about Thunderbark!" Static said ignoring her completely. I growled a warning. I wasn't in the mood to fool with Static's nonsense.

"Static, we haven't completely forgotten that fact," Merrylegs went on. "We're going to have a meeting to decide how we are going to proceed."

"Well, if we are having a meeting, Railrunner better take a chill pill first." Static said under his breath. I snarled and edged for him. Merrylegs ran to stand between us.

"Don't you push it, Static!" she scolded.

Static sighed. "I will go to the meeting, if Railrunner promises not to be a gutter mouth."

"Don't press your luck, Static! I snarled through clenched teeth. I moved closer to him still, he began to roll backwards in retreat.

"Static, you seriously don't need to carry it on. Railrunner is very stressed as it is." Merrylegs said in her reassuring voice. There was an awkward pause as the two continued to stare at one another.

"You read his mind didn't you?" he said quietly.

"Yes, I did." Merrylegs replied. It was the only answer she could think of.

I continued to glare at Static. Why was he acting so stupid? Merrylegs thought the same thing as me, I could tell. Then she turned and headed to the entrance of the den, and I followed close behind her.

We sat around the wooden table. Odd that there was an empty space. I was used to seeing the wise old white coaster sitting there. Merrylegs sat across from me and Static at the end. I sat alone, afraid that I would get pissed off and snap again.

"Now," Merrylegs began. "Do we have any clue where the Fallen could've taken him?"

"I do." I said.

"Shoot."

"Thunderbark knew, he gave me hints to where those bastards were taking him."

Static rolled his dark eyes. I gave him a warning glare, and them flipped him off. Funny, because that expression did not exist in this world. I could flip every one I hated off on a continental basis, and no one would know. However, my allies sitting before me and Thunderbark were the only ones who knew that gesture. To them it meant back away.

Suddenly, Merrylegs reared back and smashed her hooves on the table. Our attention came off each other and onto her.

"Boys! Stop this nonsense! You are both being immature children!" She yelled. "Static! You are the one who started this! Shut the heck up!"

Then it was quiet, Merrylegs still stood in her defensive position. I looked at the wall and Static stared down at the grains of wood on the table. I turned to look at him, he snapped his head up to see me. I let out a long sigh.

"Sorry. Sorry to you both. I should have never acted that way. I couldn't get a hold of my temper, but give me a break I'm a roller coaster. I can be downright sour and crude sometimes." I finished hoping that Static would apologize, too.

At first I thought he was going to send me a dumb remark, but he surprised me.

"I'm sorry Railrunner. I am just flabbergasted by the whole fact that Thunderbark is gone. You may continue."

"Apology accepted. Now as I was saying, Thunderbark gave me hints where he was to be taken."

"Maybe Freakshow took him to Zjoir Prison. That's the Fallen's most heavily guarded, and the most feared. All kinds of war heroes have been kept prisoner there." Merrylegs suggested.

"Maybe." Static agreed.

"Couldn't be." I interrupted.

"Why do you say that, Railrunner?" Merrylegs asked confused.

"Thunderbark mentioned they were going to use him as bait. Heck, even Freakshow mentioned it. She said, that he was for the "red herring". Oh my- I think I know where he has been taken!"

"Where!"

"Freakshow had her men transport him to Ironwheel's lair. She knew I would go after him. Ironwheel will use Thunderbark as bait to get to me."

"Railrunner- I think you are right." Merrylegs said pulling out the map. "Ironwheel's castle is at least a hundred and fifty miles away. Up in the Dread Mountains, the most barren place in all Amusement Park Between."

"Everyone says that is where hope goes to die." Static moaned.

"I don't give a rip how dangerous it is. Thunderbark needs us, and so does this world. We are going to Ironwheel's lair no matter what."

"It will be a long way." Merrylegs sighed.

"Do we have money to get some supplies?" I began, worried what the answer was.

"We don't." Merrylegs said disenchanted.

"Well, where is the nearest city?"

"Zegria. It is fifteen miles away. It has various opportunities to make several g's." Merrylegs replied as she began to perk up.

"To Zegria?" I asked.

"To Zegria," she replied.

Chapter 36
Arena

The following morning was cloudy; looking like it was going to rain. The wind had picked up and I could tell it was going to storm later. However, it didn't really bother me. I was used to it, being outside in horrible weather while training with Thunderbark. It was a lot different without him walking at my side, or anybody else's.

I wore my coat with my hood up. Merrylegs walked partially under it, she still was being close to me ever since yesterday. Personally I didn't need protecting; I didn't have to be babysat. But yet, Merrylegs could just be hanging around me because she missed Thunderbark. She was suffering from it, so she stuck with me. I actually liked her company; I could tell she was trying to be a better friend.

Within the next forty-five minutes we arrived on the outskirts of the city. Zegria was about the size of the shopping mall back in Huntersville, and our mall was gigantic! Zegria was about ten times bigger than Trenzon. In fact, there was enough room for superior rides such as ferris wheels. The place's style was different, too. More like the modern and ancient world mixed together. Modern of the USA, and the ancient worlds of China and Japan. Odd, but yet in this whole world nothing was normal.

"Well, how should we start?" I asked Merrylegs.

"I guess ask some of the locals who own shops if they need help, heck they probably do." She replied watching the rides roam about.

"I could ask somebody if they need any electrical things fixed." Static laughed.

"All right. Should we meet somewhere by the end of the day?"

"Probably, Railrunner. How about the square? In front of the fountain?"

"Sounds good to me." Static remarked. "Although we might pass by each other during the day!"

"Could, I mean it's possible." Merrylegs laughed a little.

"I guess we should get to it then." I said turning in another direction.

"Right, see you both later." Merrylegs finished as she galloped off. Static zoomed to his left and was quickly out of sight. I stared at everyone walking around. I took a deep sigh and set off into the crowd

Finding work turned out to be harder than I thought. Because of my "grim reaper monkey suit" every ride was deeply suspicious. All eyes seemed to be on me, I felt like shooing everyone off, but I could not screw up and blow cover. I glanced at merchant shops; owners gave me an unwelcome stare. I sighed and kept moving.

An hour passed and still no luck. Merrylegs and Static must have been doing better than me. Way better. It started to sprinkle and then it poured down. I swore under my breath and looked around for shelter. I quickly spotted a local bar, without hesitation I entered.

This bar was much classier than the one in Trenzon, with big screen plasmas and grander interior. I sat at the bar and waited, a silver coaster asked me what I wanted. I told him the same thing I had gotten in Trenzon, a Red C.

"Excuse me sir," I muttered.

"Yes?" he asked.

"Where can you earn a heaping amount of g's really fast?" I said with a crooked grin.

"You are broke!" the coaster growled, speaking really low and snatching the drink from me. I only laughed quietly.

"Trust me; I'll be worth your time." I said sliding up my sleeve slightly to show my red metal. He glared in shock at me.

"You're a –."

"Shhh - you say –it, and I'll cut your restraints off." I said with an earnest tone.

The coaster grinned in return; he seemed to be taking my side. He then leaned closer to me.

"What's your name?"

"What's yours?"

"Highrider."

"I am Railrunner. Now, how about that question I asked you?"

"A really easy way for *you* to make money is at the Arena. It's past the clock tower, and about a block from the restaurant. Like I said, easy earnings."

"Ok, this conversation never happened and I was never here." I smiled furtively.

He nodded and slid me the drink.

"On the house." He winked. "Oh and go around the back, that is where you sign up. Good luck."

"Thanks." I said as I was exiting. I took the last gulp of the Red C and then threw the glass to the ground. I then headed for the Arena, still wondering what to expect.

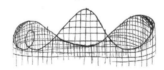

I walked up to a big dome like building; it was bigger than any sports arena I had ever seen. I stood a ways from the entrance watching eager rides go inside. Highrider said to enter from the back, where I would sign up. He said this was easy for me, I sure hoped he was right. I changed my direction and headed for the building's rear. There was a line of about twenty rides waiting. They were all thrill rides, the worst of the worst. I felt my teeth quiver and my mouth water; instinct was wanting to take over.

As the line moved, a tin-lizzy, an antique car ride that was used to provide pleasure for small children, took names. I watched intently as I became next in line. The ride in front of me finished and entered the dome. I walked up to the table. The diminutive ride stared at me strangely.

"What are you doing here kid?"

"Please don't start that shit; friend said this was a good place to catch a few g's." I said somewhat annoyed.

"I think you should go upon your way." He grumbled.

"Sign me up before I shove your head up -."

"Fine, your name please?" he said giving in.

"Railrunner, and you might want to keep that filed so you don't forget it!" I said through clenched teeth. My instincts were playing the main role suddenly, probably because I was not in the mood for any balderdash. I had to get g's quickly, so we could make our way to Thunderbark, and I hated to make him wait.

"All right," he said coldly. "You may enter."

It would be my pleasure, I thought as I went through the double doors. The next thing I saw, shocked me, it was a battle arena. A big stone surface was the "fighting zone". All around the arena rides sat and cheered. On the big stone platform two rides were fighting, a blue, jewel-incrusted roller coaster, and a green coaster dueled. The blue one then threw the other into the wall, and he fell below the platform. A carousel horse walked out to the blue coaster.

"Once again the undefeated champion of the Rumble of the Rides is Rozrail!" he finished as the valiant exited the arena. "Now, a new series of rides will duke it out for the top and the one left standing will face Rozrail for the title!"

"Wonderful." I said to myself.

For the first match I was to be paired with a ride called, Spiderleg. Winner would face the victor of the previous match, and so on. Until Rozrail, of course. Then after a loser was hauled out of the ring, the announcer walked out.

"Ladies and gentlerides, the next match is between the returning contender, Spiderleg, and the unknown mysterious, Railrunner!"

A gigantic spider ride waltz out into the stone platform, its movement similar to a real arachnid's. As I knew a "spider" ride is a ride that has a mechanical center with eight hydraulic arms jutting from it. On the end of each arm is a pod where humans sit. When in motion, the pods move up, down, and around, in a circular pattern.

The one before me walked on its pods, and was solid black, kind of like a black widow. It even had the red hourglass shape on its underside.

The stupid thing had four eyes and a gaping hole with two large fangs. I wanted to laugh at it; I found the ride somewhat humorous.

I edged my way out onto the stone platform. I could feel everyone's eyes bearing down onto me. From under my hood I could see the audience pointing and gawking. Spiderleg only stared at me in pure uncertainty. I felt my wheels tremble in temptation. Then a gong was rung, signaling for the rumble to begin.

Spiderleg began to circle me, taunting me. I stood my ground, alert and ready for anything.

"Why do you wear that rag? Do you think you are threatening?" he taunted.

I only chuckled.

"Do you think you are funny? Do you think you are a god of some sort?"

"Depends on what your definition of "god" is." I replied.

He now stood in front of me, holding back a hiss. I felt my muscles tense up.

"You're just a hot shot," he continued. "Who thinks he is all that, heck that is what all roller coasters think of themselves." He went on.

"If that is what you think." I said really low. My wheels trembled more, the bloodlust was returning.

Then Spiderleg raised one of his arms and brought it down toward me. The pod, going for my face. I caught it before it hit me, the spider ride looked surprised. I then slung him with all my strength; he flew succorless toward the wall. He hit with a loud crack, the wall cracking with him. The ride then fell into the pit below the platform. I turned to see that the audience was silent, the carousel horse walked up to me in shock, apparently that was the fastest time that anyone had ever defeated another.

"I present the victor, Railrunner!" the horse announced. The audience went wild; their excited cheering put a large smile on my face. I looked at every one of them, but my smile faded when I saw Merrylegs and Static, each with an angry scowl on their faces.

Chapter 37
Confrontation

I leaned against the wall, waiting. I knew that any second Merrylegs and Static would walk up really angry, probably going to ask me what the hell I was thinking. Well, I DID have something that could change their mind.

Sure enough I was correct; they both strutted up to me, pissed as all get out.

"Railrunner! What where you thinking!" Merrylegs said up in my face.

"You could blow this whole mission!" Static scolded.

"Hey! I couldn't find work! I was told that this place was an easy way to make money. So, instinct drove me here."

"You know, most of the time your *instinct* isn't always right!" Merrylegs whispered angrily.

"Well, I suppose you two made a heaping amount of g's."

They both stared at me silently.

"We did not make anything." They admitted.

"Lucky for us I made quite a bit," I said holding up a bag of gold coins.

"Railrunner, how much is that?" Static asked.

"About eighty g's."

"Oh my!" Merrylegs said excitedly. "Maybe we were wrong; I think you should carry on. If you keep this up, we will have enough for the round trip." She finished.

"You both with me then?"

"Absolutely, especially for the fact that we are doing this for Thunderbark." She said smiling now.

Suddenly out of the corner of my eye I spied Rozrail walking towards me. I felt a growl caught deep within my throat, I knew he was going to say something to me. I felt my hood to make sure it was over my face.

"Well, well, well, if it isn't the fastest vanquisher, Railrunner." He started in a swaggering tone.

"What do you want, Rozrail?" I demanded trying not to lose my cool.

"I want to let you know that I own the ring and all the prize money, not *you*." He said putting a wheel to my chest.

"Did anyone ever tell you to keep your belongings to yourself?" I riposted.

"We are not born and raised, Railrunner. Only a red is, and nobody has seen a red in thirty six years."

I could only snicker, I found this funny.

"You have a lot of nerve to laugh at me." Rozrail growled.

"You have a lot of guts to poke fun at me." I replied.

Rozrail leaned closer to me, his eyes narrowed. For some reason he sniffed me.

"You smell like a bar." He said disgusted.

"You smell like shit." I snarled.

He raised a set of wheels and prepared to punch me. I elicited my claws. Merrylegs and Static gasped as officials ran in to break us up.

"Save it for the ring." One of them said.

I shook myself loose from their grip and walked toward my allies.

"I will!" I yelled back to them.

Chapter 38
Check and Mate

Countless battles I fought, countless battles I won. Money filled the bag. Merrylegs and Static cheered me on up in the stands. I imagined Thunderbark with them, supporting me. I wanted him out of his confinement, fighting like a dog to reach him, and Clare.

"More water sir?" an assistant asked me.

"Sure, thanks." I said as I took the water from the little ride. I leaned against the entrance to the ring and took long satisfied gulps. The final match was between Rozrail and I. What that bastard said earlier made me more angry, more up to beat him. I wanted his blood on my wheels, just like I wanted Ironwheel's. A roller coaster's predatory instinct was as mad as a werewolf's; I was no different. Tonight I had been putting it to good use. I would also use it in the near future.

Minutes wasted away as I stood there watching. I felt confident, more than ready to fight, to draw blood. Rozrail behaved like a Fallen, for that I would treat him like one. Greed had driven him this far, to hate mercilessly, and that would cost him dearly.

"Two minutes," a ride told me, I nodding in reply.

Two minutes till his doom, hopefully not two minutes till mine. I could now see him from where I was. He yelled at his assistants, treating them as if they were dirt under men's shoes. How I hated him! Him and all his dull glory.

"I hate that coaster." One of my assistants said looking at Rozrail.

"He makes drunken fools look smart." I replied.

The ride laughed and went on his way. I turned my attention back to my opponent.

I kept my lips in a firm line as I watched him push and shove. Should I kill him? No, I wasn't going that far. Only to hurt him, I thought. Only to teach him a lesson.

Finally the clock ran out. Rozrail walked out onto the "battlefield". No ride cheered like they did with me, it was all silence. Rozrail snorted in disgust. Then I made my way outside into the open, glaring at Rozrail with my fire-red eyes. They seemed to burn with hatred as I fought back a snarl. We stopped fifty feet from each other. Rozrail smirked and raised one eyebrow. What a jerk, I pretended like I did not care by cocking my head.

"All right, you both know the rules; the one that gets knocked across the barrier line loses. Winner gets ten thousand g's. Remember, anything goes but no concussion beams. Wait for my signal." The carousel horse finished. He then walked back to the tower and situated himself. I looked to the stands to see Merrylegs and Static giving reassuring gestures.

Then the giant gong rang, echoing all through the dome. I now did not take my eyes off my stubborn opponent. This was just like training with Thunderbark, I told myself. However, for some reason he did not attack, I figured he would speak his mind before he did so.

"Any last words, Railrunner?" Rozrail asked.

I flexed my muscles and prepared to bolt. I began to laugh, laughing at the face of fear.

"Catch me if you can!" I said loudly so many could hear.

Rozrail snarled and sent a stream of flame straight at me, I leaped up into the air and did a back flip; landing on my wheels. Rozrail only stared at me, shocked. I grinned and then ran to my right. He stood his ground and sent more shots of fire. All of them missing me. When I had the chance, I generated lightning on my wheels and directed it at Rozrail. He ducked, the lightning almost searing his back, it hit the wall and cracked the stone all the way through. He roared angrily, again, I only chuckled.

He jumped back up and let loose more fire. I turned and rained more lightning down like Zeus. Rozrail then made an attempt to redirect the lightning. I remembered from training, that my lightning was much more amped up from a regular coaster's. Rozrail's body stuggled tremendously from the sheer force of my attack. His wheels shook trying to move the lightning away from his body.

This was a perfect chance. While Rozrail was stressed, I could attack him. Not with a lightning bolt, that would surely kill him. Fire would be a better option; problem was it was amplified, too. A small dose of it was equal to a normal coaster's. Again my brain processed a faint image of Clare. A small flame grew from my wheels. I then sent an engulfing fireball straight at Rozrail, who was too consumed to even notice.

He screamed in agony as the blast scorched him. My lightning that he was currently fiddling with traveled in all directions. I ducked, the dangerous strikes tearing up my cloak so it was littered with holes. Then there was a pause, and the whole arena was silent once more.

Rozrail hauled himself up off his belly; he glared at me with blood dripping from gashes and burns. He breathed shallowly, it was clear that he was getting weaker. I stood eagerly watching him from a distance.

"Do you honestly think you have me beat?" he said coming to a stand.

"That depends on what some call defeated." I replied.

He growled and sent a big blast towards me. I held my arms out in front of me and placed them together, like I was going to dive. The blast split in two and went around me. I then took both streams of fire and guided them back to him. He barrel rolled out of the way and assaulted with fire once more. I punched towards his assail; the blast vanished into a cloud of smoke.

Suddenly I felt the Augu Ra heat up from under my vest. It glowed faintly from under the fabric.

"No! Not now!" I whispered to myself. If Rozrail saw it, he would know I was the red! Everyone in the whole arena would know! The Fallen already did, I didn't want to make matters worse. Yet, it might do the rides good to see me. Let them know I had returned; let them have something to hope for.

Rozrail sent another shower of flames, I dodged and redirected. This only made Rozrail angrier, more uncontrollable. My heart raced faster as we continued to duel. The arena began to smell of smoke, and even a hint of scorched leather. The Augu Ra glowed hot from under my vest. I looked down, a faint hint of light peeped through. Usually when that happened, something was bound to occur. Rozrail got furious as his blasts missed me or were bended back in a counter attack. He ran and tried a different tactic.

We were now inches apart; Rozrail did "fire punches" at me, I could feel each one's heat as his wheels brushed past my face. Any chance I got, I scratched him with my claws.

"*Why can't I get you!*" He screamed as he swung his tail. I jumped backward to avoid the move plus to keep my distance. Then Rozrail opened his mouth, I could see a small spark from the back of his throat. The Augu Ra glowed brighter, its heat burned my chest. I looked back to see that Rozrail had fired a concussion beam. I did not even have time to react, but suddenly the Augu Ra let loose a blast of yellow light, like it had back in the real world. The light hit the beam's core, it completely disintegrated the deadly attack to a small ash that fell to the ground like a firework that had fizzled.

I groaned, a little woozy from what had just occurred. I focused my eyes back on Rozrail, who stood motionless, glaring at my neck. I gulped and again looked down. The Augu Ra was visible for all to see.

"What -." Rozrail started but then trailed off.

I sighed, looking around to see that the audience was pointing at me. They already knew, there was no point in keeping it a secret now.

"Well, let the thirty six years come to an end." I said. Rozrail looked at me bewildered. I rolled back my sleeves, making the whole arena silent. I raised them to my hood. I slowly lifted it back, letting the burned cloth fall loosely around my shoulders. Everyone, including Rozrail, gasped. Merrylegs and Static's faces were blank.

"You're the red roller coaster," Rozrail said with his green eyes widening and one of his wheels pointed in my direction. I then took off my cloak that was pitted with holes; throwing it aside. A rustle of murmurs ran through the audience.

"Indeed I am." I said shrugging.

"I would have never done...knew...attacked...my apologies Railrunner." Rozrail said kneeling. That act always looked strange to me. It also made me very uneasy, in, which I really was at the moment. I nervously looked back to the audience, every ride had bowed. This was embarrassing as hell, I thought to myself.

The carousel horse trotted up to us, he smiled at me with excitement in his eyes.

"Since Rozrail broke the rules by the use of a concussion beam, Railrunner the red roller coaster is the victor!" he announced as he handed me a bag full of crisp bills. The whole arena applauded ecstatically. After about a minute everyone was silent once more, they seemed to be waiting for a speech. The horse handed me a fancy microphone, I wasn't expecting to speak! I had no idea where to start or what to say!

"Sorry I have kept everyone waiting. Gosh, I don't know quite were to begin with the basics!" I laughed.

I paused to glance at Merrylegs and Static. They were actually grinning? But why? Then I continued.

"I don't know if anyone knows this or not, I was raised as a changeling in the real world. I finally realized about a month ago that I was never human. I then was found by one of Amusement Park Between's great warriors, Thunderbark."

There was an outbreak of whispering from the rides. Then I continued.

"Thunderbark trained me day in and day out. However, just recently, Thunderbark was captured by the Fallen and taken to Ironwheel's castle. I swore from the moment he was stolen I would rescue him no matter what. I also swore when I first stepped into this world that I would rescue each and every ride from Ironwheel's wrath!" I finished with a dramatic end.

The audience cheered endlessly, their screams bounced off the stonewalls.

"Another thing, I would like to thank you all for your support, especially Merrylegs and Static, who secretly watched me over the years. Again, I thank each and every ride in here, and all over Amusement Park Between!" I added. Rides went wild in the stands, all of them giving me standing ovations. I looked down to see that Merrylegs and Static had joined me by my side.

"Nice job, Railrunner." Merrylegs said smiling up at me.

"You're not mad?"

"No, we knew Amusement Park Between would find out sooner or later."

"Yeah, they already know in Trenzon, plus the Augu Ra revealed the true you." Static put in.

"The reason why I decided to reveal myself fully was because I feel that Freakshow has already told Ironwheel of my presence."

"I hate to say this, but I think you are right."

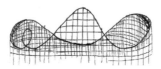

Chapter 39
Nightmares and Never Dreamscapes

For the last remaining hours of the day, it seemed like I had spoken to hundreds of rides. It felt as if I was a presidential canadate, being bombarded by lots and answering numerous questions. I didn't really mind, but I felt that I gave them witty and smart facts. I thought I had proven myself to many, proven I was capable of fulfilling my destiny, doing what I was made for.

We walked among the empty streets of Zegria. The storm had ended and now there was nothing but the occasional raindrop that fell on your forehead. There seemed to be no activity going on, except for the great amount of rides that partied in local bars.

"What next?" I asked Merrylegs with a yawn.

"I think we should go to one of the hotels here and get a room. I am tired, plus I cannot see in the dark."

"I agree with the tired part." Static yawned. "It really has been a long day."

"All right, what can we afford?"

"Shoot anything!" Merrylegs chuckled.

"Well, which is the nicest place? I don't know any hotels here." I laughed.

"Might I suggest The Silver Spoke?" said a voice behind us. I turned to surprisingly see Rozrail. He was covered in bandages and had gashes all over him. He was a sorry sight.

"Look, I'm really sorry about -."

"No need to apologize, Railrunner. My ass deserved to get kicked. I am the one who should be apologizing. For the whole thing, being a complete jerk and all. You made me learn my lesson. I am NEVER fighting in the ring again, I am getting a real job." He said.

I started to doubt him, I began to read the truth like I did with Clare, turned out he wasn't kidding.

"You are forgiven, Rozrail."

"Thank you."

"Now, what hotel did you say again?" I asked.

"The Silver Spoke. Really classy place. Beautiful rooms with a view, really splendid restaurant bar and drinking bar. Everything you could want is there."

"How much is it?"

"With all your money you earned, you can afford pretty much any room. I suggest the penthouse suite."

"Is that expensive?"

"Not for you, it is about six hundred g's. That is only a teeny bit of what you have."

"Okay then, Silver Spoke it is."

"It is just straight ahead, Railrunner. It sort of sticks out like a sore thumb. Big stone building with the fountain in front."

"Thanks Rozrail."

"Don't mention it. Oh, and I am really happy to see the red has returned. I'm rooting for you all the way."

"Thank you, hope you have a nice evening Rozrail."

"You too. Good night to all of you."

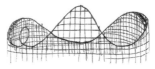

The Silver Spoke was at the end of the street just as Rozrail had said. It was large indeed, about the size of a skyscraper in New York. The hotel was very different from the rest of the buildings in Zegria. It was stone, but had a hint of woodland style. The Silver Spoke looked to be about thirty stories, that was probably not much in the real world, but here everything was super sized.

A large perimeter fence surrounded the beautiful hotel. At the very front was the gate, a "bellboy" that stood there letting rides inside the walls. I gulped as we made our way to it. The bellboy suddenly snapped his head up. He looked at me like everyone else did, shocked. He blinked his eyes several times trying to take it all in. Then he opened the gate and bowed.

I smiled to him as we passed through. Then I turned to Merrylegs.

"I HATE it when everyone does that!" I hastily whispered.

"Why? You actually don't like rides bowing for you?" she said to me.

"No, I don't like it because I don't feel special. I'm just like every coaster here, except for a different color."

"Railrunner I don't think you understand fully." Merrylegs spoke up.

"What do you mean?" I asked.

"You were created differently than any ride here. You are of the most pure form, the quintessence of the rides. Railrunner you are a combination of real blood and the spirit of Amusement Park Between itself."

"Weird," I sighed. Merrylegs rolled her eyes, and then something dawned on me. "Merrylegs! How did you know how I was created!" I whispered.

"Thunderbark."

"Why did he tell you!"

"He did not mean to. Thunderbark got a little out of his head when you bit him."

"Oh, does Static know?"

"I don't think so. He wasn't around when he said it." She replied

"All right." I sighed.

" Whelp, guess we should head in."

I nodded in reply. To tell the truth I was glad that only Merrylegs knew about me, Static wasn't all that good at keeping things to himself.

The Silver Spoke's lobby was just as grand as the outside, the log cabin theme continuing into the interior. All of us walked up to the reception desk where a bright hot pink carousel horse stood scanning over files. Merrylegs cleared her throat making her look up.

"Oh I'm sorry -." she trailed off as she looked at me. "Oh my goodness! Don't even bother paying! What room would you like great red?"

"I guess the penthouse suite, friend of mine said it was nice." I said rubbing my neck.

"Penthouse it is!" she announced, handing us a little round sphere with a blue button in the middle.

"Thank you." Merrylegs said taking it from her. I then began to walk in the opposite direction they did.

"Railrunner where are you going?" Merrylegs demanded.

"The fun zone."

"And where is that?" She demanded, raising her eyebrows.

"There were three words that jumped out at me. Bar and restaurant bar. Besides I haven't eaten all day. I can bring you both something up later." I smiled charitably.

"Fine, I'll have a salad." She said walking into the elevator that was as big as a house. I then turned around and headed for what I considered a jollity.

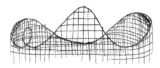

About four hours later, I began to walk back to the room. I held Merrylegs's salad in one set of wheels and Static something in the opposite. I halfway hid a bottle behind my back. During the period of time that I spent down there, I drank and ate to a full extent. I could never get sick, so I didn't really care.

I made it up to the thirtieth floor with ease. The penthouse suite wasn't hard to find. It had big brass doors and it was labeled like every room here. I did not have the key so I gently knocked in case they were both asleep.

Merrylegs finally opened the door after several seconds. She looked like she had been sleeping because her hair was a "rat's nest" and her eyelids were heavy.

"Where in the world have you been!" she whispered angrily.

"I was eating." I replied in a tone just above a pin drop.

"You were drinking, too." She said as she spied the bottle I hid.

"Fine you caught me, but I brought you a salad. I had no idea what Static likes, so I got him a variety of things."

"Thank you," she said as I entered and placed the dish on a nearby table. Static lay on the rug in the center of the sitting area. His cable lying flat on the floor, twitching occasionally. Merrylegs had been lying in the other bed clearly because of the ruffled sheets.

I flopped down onto the large empty bed that overlooked the balcony. I rolled over onto my side, burping deeply in my throat as I did.

"Sorry." I said to Merrylegs. "Excuse me for that one."

"Its fine, I don't blame you." She said after swallowing a bite of salad. "I do admire the fact that you actually used your manners. Its like you never do."

"Very funny, Merrylegs." I said rolling over onto my back.

"Har har. Well, good night Railrunner."

"Night."

I stared at the ceiling for a brief moment. I went over plans and events secretly in my head. I thought about things that I had on my mind for weeks and days. Such as Thunderbark and Clare. Then my eyes got heavy, eventually closing all together.

I stood there in the never-ending blackness. Blood poured from the sky as rain. Blood ran like a stream, bubbling at my wheels. I looked around in a panic. Where was I? Why was I in this horrid place! I tried to run, but yet again my legs felt like lead. Clare's screams rang out in the darkness. I shouted her name. For the first time she responded by yelling mine. Her voice only made me run faster.

The further I ran, the more blood there was. I stopped when I saw Ironwheel's obvious figure. I felt myself gasp when I saw Clare lying limp in his arms. She suddenly looked over to me, and held out her hand pleading for help. A ripping snarl sounded through my barred fangs. Then I lunged, roaring in pure rage.

I woke up to see that Merrylegs and Static stood over me. I was shaking horribly. Sweat coated my metal and leather. I sat up with labor like breathing.

"Railrunner! Are you all right!"

"I guess - so. I'm not totally sure. I had one of those damn nightmares." I wheezed.

"You gave me such a scare! You looked like a human having a seizure!" Static said alarmed.

"It was the same topic wasn't it?" Merrylegs asked concerned.

"Yes." I said finally catching my breath. " Only this time this one was intense. I think they might be getting worse."

"They could be. I wish Thunderbark was here, he would know more about it than I would."

"That's the problem, he was still puzzled on them the last time we spoke about it." I said sitting up.

"I don't quite know what to think; of course I'm not a roller coaster either."

I gritted my teeth as I carefully stood. I was dizzy, really dizzy. I felt the room spinning, images were mirrored. Gravity felt disrupted. I grabbed a glass of water that stood upon a table. I took long gulps, and hunched over against the couch. When the dizziness passed, I walked out onto the balcony for some fresh air.

"You okay now?" Merrylegs asked me.

"Yes, I guess. That was the worst dream I think I've had so far. It felt so -real."

"Hmmm -maybe there is something within your book that says some information on these horrid dreams."

"You know about the book too!"

"Yep, Thunderbark again."

"You might be right Merrylegs. I'll catch up on my reading. When should we head out?"

"As soon as the sun rises. That way you're not bombarded. Or bowed at." She giggled.

"Again, very funny Merrylegs."

Chapter 40
Pirates

At twilight we left the Silver Spoke just as decided the night before. Railrunner seemed to be much better than he was last night. I had to agree with him, the frequent nightmares were getting worse. I just wish there was something I could do for him to ease his suffering.

We currently were deep in the forest once again. All of us had settled down to enjoy breakfast, a meal that Railrunner had taken from the bar before we left. I silently ate my fresh salad and secretly glancing at my two counterparts. Static was a messy eater as always, not bothering to use any manners of any kind. Railrunner however, was not eating. Was it possible that his nightmare still bothered him?

"Aren't you eating?" I asked him.

He laughed one of those belly laughs like Thunderbark used to do; Railrunner then patted his stomach and smiled.

"Hell, I ate so much last night, I forgot to leave room for breakfast!" he said grinning with all of his snow-white teeth showing.

I laughed a little in response. Could I have been wrong? Did he not care about his dream anymore? I bent back down to take a nibble, but out of the corner of my eye I saw Railrunner reaching into the bag and pulling out the book slightly. He then sighed quietly to himself and slid the book back. Now I knew he was hiding all of his tension. He was indeed still worried.

I was still hooked on that stupid dream that I had the night before. I looked down to try and forget the whole thing. I stared at my stomach;

I pictured it being ballooned out due to how much food I consumed yesterday. Oddly it was normal, flat. Maybe roller coasters didn't get fat neither. That was a plus. Sadly that attempt to rid my mind of the previous night did not work.

I looked at Merrylegs and Static. I was so eager to know what secrets were hidden in the book. Then I had an idea how to unlock them. I stood up slowly; Merrylegs stopped eating and paused to look at me.

"Where are you going?" she said smiling.

"Oh, I'm just heading to the river to get some fresh water. It's not very far from here, so I won't be long." I said lying.

"Okay then. Hurry back."

When she looked away, I picked up the bag that contained the book. Then I quietly made my way into the dense vegetation. Thorns and leaves brushed my metal hide. Vines snagged my restraints over and over again. I pulled out the sword and began cutting like an explorer. After slicing my way through the jungle like area, I found a nice peaceful spot upon a rock that overlooked a lily-covered pond. I put the sword back into place, and then lied down on the huge stone. I sighed as I opened the book and began to thumb through its yellow pages.

My eyes skimmed each section. Finally I came upon the part on Redrail. I began to read every paragraph. Most of the section told about Redrail's life. How she was the first female red out of the cycle. Then at the end of the section, there was a paragraph on the dreams that both her and I had. Those dreaded nightmares that caused me pain and mental suffering. I began to read:

Redrail is the only known red to have strange nightmares that were of the same thing each night. Ones that caused mysterious pain that could not be explained. There is not much I know about them. The following information is for any future red that may experience this strange gift.

I tried to read Redrail's journal to find out more, but unfortunately she set it ablaze long ago. However, I was able to recover a single page from it. It shocked me on how bad the nightmares would become. She would get dizzy, having throbbing migraines, and run a scorching temperature. In some of the most extreme cases, she would pass out or even go into a coma!

Also for any red that has this, Redrail did write down an antidote to bring her back to normal if her condition went too far. She would drink...

I was sure as hell I didn't see that last word coming.

Blood.

That was the last thing that I would have thought of. Of all things! I didn't have a problem with drinking it. Just a problem of where to get it from. I couldn't drink the blood of the innocent! That was nonsensical! I only seeked the blood of the enemy!

At the beginning of my new life, tasting blood seemed like a delicacy. Now it was nowhere near civil! I was made to protect Amusement Park Between. I couldn't rob blood from any ride that supported me! Sure I could drink the blood of the Fallen, but what if I had one of the extreme nightmares that could make me black out? Or put me in a coma? What if there wasn't any Fallen blood at my disposal? I could get blood from one of the animals here, but that would require hunting. I had to figure something out; I did not want to be labeled as "bloodsucker", "vampire", "beast", or the worst one, "monster".

Wait a minute; did it have to be fresh blood? Or could it be blood that was saved? I had an idea, next time I took a Fallen down, I would gather its blood, afraid it would come in handy. That was now on the list of things to do. Like rescue everyone from a ruler's dictatorship.

Suddenly a petrifying neigh sounded in alarm. I easily recognized it as Merrylegs. I gathered my belongings in a flash, and then made a beeline for our camp. I ran silently, moving like a ninja. Then suddenly Merrylegs met me face to face.

"We are being robbed!"

"What! By who!"

"They are called pirates! They support neither Ironwheel nor the Amusement Park Between alliances. They steal and do bad for their own benefit!"

"How many are there, and what are we dealing with?"

"There are six. Two carousel horses, a go cart, two kiddie planes, and a roller coaster!"

"Figures."

"What should we do?" she said in a fury.

"Get them. They have something I want." I growled.

"What do you mean by that?"

"Let's say I caught up on my reading." I said as Static joined us. We snuck up to our site, peeking through the leaves of bushes. The thugs were ransacking the area, taking everything, including our money.

We charged forward at once, rearing on our hindquarters. Static hissed and sent sparks off his cable. Merrylegs reared back with her nostrils flaring and her legs flaying. I retracted my claws and barred my teeth, then roared a powerful threatening roar.

The intruders looked up. Their leader, the green and yellow roller coaster, saw me and signaled his fleet to retreat. In his hand he held the bag of g's, rage build up within as I charged for him, and then the chase started.

Merrylegs went for the go-cart as Static went after the carousel horses. The wooden coaster was not that fast, his build made him slower than a speedy steel. I soon caught up to him, when I got the chance I tackled him like a lion. The two of us rolled over in the fallen leaves. Then we broke apart and stood opposite from each other.

"Har! A red! Where have you been for the last three and a half decades?" He laughed.

His question caught me by surprise.

"In another world, but now I am protecting this one, from the likes of you." I retorted.

"Oh, that is harsh." He smirked.

"I want my money and I want something else to."

"You can't have what's finder's keepers, and what is that other thing?"

I laughed, kind of like I did when I did not have control.

"Your blood!" I said lunging for him. My teeth sunk deep, his blood pouring into my mouth. Trashing and bashing, mauling each other like fighting wolves. The forest seemed to spin under me.

I slung the hellion then I grabbed him in an iron grip around his head. I squeezed like an anaconda; a horrible cracking sound came from his skull. At the last second he threw the bag up into the air. I dropped him to the ground and reached for the packaged g's. Unexpectedly, a plane caught it and flew up into the canopy.

"Stupid!" I yelled as I went after it. The plane flew among the branches, and that was where I was headed. I launched myself up a tree's trunk and ran across its limbs as nimble as I could be. The plane flew further ahead. The tree's branches were coming to an end, summoning strength; I leaped onto the neighboring tree and continued the hunt.

Jumping and jumping onto trees and more trees. The plane was beginning to lose speed. I had to end this now; I couldn't get to far from my friends. Then the plane paused and hovered in front of a large kinkajou tree. This was my chance.

I paused and remained quiet. The plane looked around, thinking I was gone; it landed huffing and puffing on one of the moss covered branches. I silently pulled out my sword. I aimed, and then trust it forward like a tomahawk. The ride looked up in surprise, but it was too late. The sword pierced through its chest, pinning the creature to the tree.

I pounced onto the limb and picked up the bag of g's. I then grabbed the sword's handle and began to pry it out. When I succeeded, I began to lick the blood off. That reminded me to collect the antidote.

I pulled out the bag that held the book, and then searched for some kind of container. There was the vile that Moonhoof gave me, but that was far too important. Finally I found the bottle that I kept from the Silver Spoke. I twisted the cork off and poured the remaining liquid out. I then held the bottle below the dead plane, letting its blood drip into the bottle, when it was full; I started to make my way back to camp.

I now saw that the fight had ended, Merrylegs and Static were picking up the pieces.

"Oh thank goodness, Railrunner!" Merrylegs said relieved. "I see that you got our money back."

"Indeed, it wasn't really that hard to get." I replied chuckling.

"It seems that was all the bandits were after. After checking, we found that they did not steal anything else."

"It is better than them having the book." I said.

"Right. There is no telling what evil they could have done with it." Static cut in.

"So what is the death count?" Merrylegs said as she picked up stray materials.

"I killed the coaster and one of the planes." I said.

"I took out the go cart."

"The horses are dead." Static added.

"Hmm, weren't there two planes?" I asked suddenly.

"You're right, Railrunner." Merrylegs spoke. "That's not good at all! It could get the word out!"

I suddenly heard a rustle up in the treetops. I shot a lightning bolt upward, a few seconds later the plane fell down at our "feet".

"It's dead." I sighed.

"Nice one." Static complimented me.

"Thank you." I said nodding my head in response.

"Welcome."

"Where to next?" I asked Merrylegs.

"I guess we should stop at the next town, Xzerma. We can stock up on food there."

"But Xzerma is watched by the Fallen!" Static complained.

"I know, that is why Railrunner must wear his cloak."

"It is mangled and looks like hell!" I protested.

"You might want to get a new cloak then, because all of the remaining cities have been claimed by the Fallen."

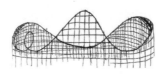

In The Line of Fire

This city now looked like the fiery pits of hell. Fire had burned bodies and buildings. He stood up without fear. His wheels were soaked from the blood of many, the blood of damned souls. He let out a bellowing howl and signaled his army to charge.

Chapter 41
Judgment

I followed the lines that were on the map. Xzerma was not but a few miles away. I continued to look at the map as Merrylegs and Static picked up the last remains of our camp. Then I put on my trench coat that was tattered and torn. It was acceptable, the holes weren't that big so any ride could see my metal.

This time Merrylegs covered up, too. She wore a cloak that looked like it was from India. It was red and yellow with patterns all over the fabric.

"Why isn't Static covering up?" I asked her.

"Static doesn't stand out, he looks more ordinary than we do."

"I see." I replied.

"A few minutes later we walked among a dirt path through the forest. Merrylegs and I keep our hoods over our faces. Rides passed by, but they took no notice. That was a good thing. The scents of more rides made its way to my nostrils. We must have been getting close. I then spied a clock tower that appeared from above the trees.

"We're here," announced Merrylegs.

The dirt path became a brick one as we entered Xzerma. It looked to be an older city due to its many fields that were still farmed, but for the Fallen. It looked a lot different from Trenzon or Zegria. It was more like an old English town, in fact its appearance looked like Transylvania. Rides here were skinny and malnourished. They looked skuzzy and rough, but most of all miserable.

I sniffed, the Fallen's foul odor was everywhere. It was hard to distinguish the smell of the good from the bad. Here we were to be extremely cautious.

"What now? Are we together?" I whispered to the yellow carousel horse.

"Yes, first of all you need a new coat. I remember a clothing shop around the corner." Merrylegs said over her shoulder.

"Let's go."

We trotted across the brick walkway. Rides with sad eyes glared at us.

"Welcome to hell," an old bumper car muttered.

Merrylegs guided me into an old stone building. Inside were racks of different fabric. A huge fireplace was on the wall to the left, from behind the large table, rolled an old tin-lizzy. His appearance was no different than any ride here. He was dull grey, and had a small beard growing from the front of his bumper. His eyebrows were also overgrown. All in all he was an eyesore.

"May I help you?" he croaked.

"Yes sir," I replied kindly. "I need a new cloak."

"You do not treat me like vermin? You don't carry the sent of the Fallen either." He responded as he looked at me seriously.

"I don't fellow ally." I said as I made my voice sound soothing and reassuring.

"Come with me young coaster. I shall show you my wares. By the way, I am Ashsoot."

"Nice to meet you, I am Railrunner. These two are Merrylegs and Static."

"Good to see some nice rides like you three, now follow me." He said. Ashsoot guided us to the back room. He then began to look through different fabric.

"Where is my best seller!" he said.

"Maybe I could help -." I started walking forward. Suddenly my tattered cloak snagged a nail on the floorboard. A big tear emerged up it, all the way to my shoulder. Ashsoot turned to see my flaming red metal.

"You... you...are the...red!" He said in surprise. "Hurry come quickly! I must take you all to a more secure place!" Ashsoot hastily explained.

The car then opened up a secret door that led to a set of stairs. As we got to the bottom, Ashsoot sealed us into a cramped room.

"Good, we are safe down here."

"Nice." Static said as he sighed in relief.

"I need to give you something I have been waiting to give." The small car whispered.

"What?"

"This," he said pulling out a chest from a secret nook. He unlocked it by combination, then opened it up to pull out a leathery cloak. It was well kept, the black leather looked to have been shined daily. "It is yours now, great red roller coaster." I took it from him and slipped it on. It was comfy, a perfect fit. It looked like a goth rockers with studs and spikes, very intimidating. It was also nice that it had pockets.

"I like it, it looks threatening." I told him.

"Glad to hear that. Mainly because this was Moonblood's."

"Really?" I said shocked.

"It was, now it goes to you."

"Thanks."

"You're welcome. I did do one patch job on the cut that Ironwheel made with his claw. That was the blow that killed the red."

I looked down at the slash. I imagined Moonblood crying in agony and his blood gushing out of the wound. Then out of nowhere a horn sounded.

"What does that mean?" Asked Merrylegs with her ears pricking forward as she became alert.

"Oh no! It is the Fallen soldiers! They are here to take prisoners, or even kill!"

"What!" Static yelled.

"Go! You have to leave at once!" Ashsoot said running out of the room. He then went outside and joined the others. I pulled my hood up and followed Static and Merrylegs out of the cramped quarters. We hid in an old barn, watching through a crack.

Roller coasters and go carts appeared in a fleet. They wore armor like a knights, except for the helmet looked like a skull. Then Freakshow appeared in the middle of them. She wore only a smirk as she stared at the line of frightened rides.

"Captain," she said. "What do you make of these rides?" She said to the orange coaster next to her.

"I think they are a bunch of bloody cockroaches, general."

"Good answer." She replied as she walked down the line of rides. Ashsoot quivered, he was terrified. Freakshow then started to speak again.

"I suppose you worthless souls have heard that the red has returned, but don't get your hopes up!" she laughed wickedly.

I quietly snuck out of the barn and stood at the end of the line. Surprisingly Merrylegs and Static joined me. When Freakshow and her troops had their backs turned, I leaned to the miniature train next to me.

"When I attack, you all go for her goons, tell everyone." I whispered as I rolled up my sleeve slightly. His eyes got big, and then he started to spread the word.

Freakshow began to walk in our direction.

"I suppose you -." She paused as she stopped in front of Ashsoot. Freakshow bent down to sniff him. The aggressive coaster must have smelt me! Her face went into a disgusted grimace. "Ashsoot, you carry the stench of the red!" she said slamming him to the ground. He slowly got back up, fighting tears. The pain in his face angered me.

"Where is he!" She yelled as she smacked his face.

"Hey leave him alone!" I snarled. Freakshow stopped and hurriedly strutted up to me, her eyes ablaze with anger.

"Why do you speak roller coaster?"

I did not answer, she then smacked my face.

"And you wonder why we don't like your kind. Especially not *me*." I said pulling off the cloak and lunging for her. Freakshow and I fell to the earth, slashing each other in a fury. I heard screams of triumph come from the attacking rides.

Freakshow and I got up and started to fight mercilessly, my claws making deep cuts into her metal. Suddenly she broke free and bolted into the fields. I went after her, Merrylegs and Static followed, unfortunately so did two of the go-cart soldiers. My allies soon noticed them, and began to track them down through the tall crops.

Freakshow was losing ground. Her mismatched body was not built for speed. I quickly caught up to her and sunk my teeth into her back leg. She yelped like a dog, then turned and bit my back. I let go and clamped my teeth down onto her throat. Freakshow cried in pain, and then she swung her tail and knocked me away, breaking both of us apart.

"Let's see how noble you are, Railrunner!" she said pulling out her sword. I did the same and charged like a gladiator. We collided again, fighting like knights. My blade blocked hers from slashing my hide. Then her sword got caught in one of mine's many points. I twisted it around, flinging hers out of her wheels. She then sent a bolt of lightning after me. In a split second it bounced off my sword. With luck, it hit Freakshow, but it was not enough to take her down.

She ran again, still I hunted her like prey. I leaped in front of the coaster and scratched the side of her face with my claws. Blood ran down her cheek and it continued down her entire body. She then hit me with a heavy blow from her wheels to my jaw. She then closed her teeth onto my neck. I swung my tail onto her head. As she let go, I rushed at her again, continuing our brutal one verses one match.

Now the fight had gone on for three minutes, but it seemed longer. We had bitten each other numerous times. Slashed each other for hundreds. Pain was very prominent in my body.

I swung my cars and knocked Freakshow onto a boulder. I enclosed both sets of wheels around her neck, holding her arms down with the others. She squirmed, but went nowhere. Then she stopped and stared at me with her strange eyes.

"Do you feel any effects, Railrunner?" Freakshow moaned. "From my venom? If so, why do you still fight?"

"Because my thirst for your blood is still raging," I said biting onto her neck like a vampire. Suddenly she raised her arm and drove one of her claws into one of my seats. Pain ripped across my back, tears came to my eyes. I then slammed my claws into her shoulder. She screamed her lungs out and reluctantly let go.

"Damn you!" she said spitting blood. I suddenly felt weaker, I could barely stand up. She was right; I was feeling the effects of the venom. It looked like she was worse, staggering toward me like a drunk and looking pale. She was sweating and was also dark under the eyes. I looked back, to my horror we were nearing a cliff. Then I turned my attention back to Freakshow.

Suddenly the dizziness grew worse, my vision blurred. Then without warning, I felt the ground fly out from under me. I now lay helpless at the edge of the cliff. Then Freakshow worsened even more, she couldn't even stand. Her eyes rolled back into her head. She then began to fall forward, onto me. Gathering the strength I had, when she impacted, I flung her off me and over the cliff. Freakshow was now falling helplessly to the earth below, to her death.

I stared up into the cloud filled sky blankly. I inhaled and exhaled harshly, completely out of breath. I tried to get up, but my body would not respond. My cuts and burses stung terribly. I tried to cry out for help, but I did not utter a word.

I felt everything within me slow, like I was going into hibernation. My eyesight seemed to dull, was I dying? I couldn't have been. Thunderbark said that only humans suffered severely to our venom. Hope he was right. Then my sight dulled even more. Soon it turned into "tunnel vision". Now I could only see faint shadows like the ones over me. I heard voices, but to whom did they belong to? I couldn't make out the words; they sounded gibberish, like extreme mumbling. Then everything went crashing into eternal blackness.

Chapter 42
The Pack

The red coaster lay in a deep sleep. Bandages wrapped around him in various places. Tubes ran into his arms, hooking him up to fluid sacks that were attached to a machine. He had been lying there for quite a while in the large bed draped with white sheets. The room where he rested was quiet, the firelight flickering against the walls of rock.

A lime green roller coaster stood over Railrunner. She had been tending to him since he first arrived. She continually checked the monitors.

"Looks like the venom count is decreasing." She said inaudibly. Then she turned and wrote in her records of his condition. Then she turned again, watching for signs of movement. The coaster could still not believe, even after all the time she spent watching him she could not grasp the mere thought that he was actually *there*. The legendary coaster had convinced her that the rumors that the red had returned were true. She did not believe any of this was happening, even though it was.

"Chainlink." Spoke a deep voice.

Chainlink turned to see a navy coaster standing in the archway.

"Yes Razorblade?"

"Some of our members believe they found who was accompanying him. I'm going to let them enter, to see if they can recognize him."

"Not to object, but does that seem a little risky?"

"Yes, but the two claim to know him, plus some of the members say they saw these rides with the red." Razorblade said stepping aside. Merrylegs and Static walked quietly into the room.

"Railrunner!" cried Merrylegs as she ran up to him. Static followed her. Merrylegs brushed Railrunner with her nose, but he did not wake.

"What did you do!" she pleaded with Chainlink.

"I'll explain," she sighed. "We found Railrunner unconscious after we saw him battle Freakshow. There was no one around to help him, but two members of our pack. They brought him here so we could revive him. So far, we are making slow progress."

"Is he in a coma?" Merrylegs questioned.

"No, he is just under a lot of anesthetic. I took it off him to see what will happen."

"Okay, but what is really wrong with Railrunner?"

"During the battle, he was bitten many times. He has a high venom count." Chainlink continued as she grasped a pole.

"Will he be all right?"

"Yes, but in time."

I stood there looking at Railrunner in disbelief. He looked as if he were -dead. Except for the occasional breath he would emit every few minutes. Of all the time we spent looking for him, he was here, in submission. He seemed to be in silent hibernation.

"How long do you think it will be before he recovers?" I asked Chainlink.

She raised one of her wheels about to answer, when Razorblade walked in.

"So?" he asked her.

"Yes, they are the ones." She replied.

"Good. Now, If you both would follow me, I need to show you a few things you must know." He said motioning us to come along.

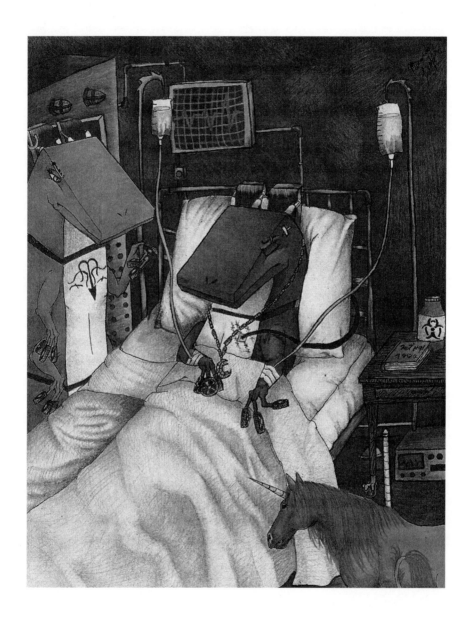

I looked at Chainlink for her answer. She simply lowered her head and shut her eyes. That probably meant she was uncertain.

Razorblade guided us into the long hallway again. As we walked I looked among the wall, the same language that was in the temple was all over. There were some illustrations here and there of roller coasters. All in all, it looked like caveman writings, but why was it here?

"Ancient battles." Spoke Razorblade.

"What?"

"The drawings you see are records. Records of war."

"Oh." I replied.

"It will all make much more sense when I show you this place." He chuckled deeply.

Then the tunnel opened up to a balcony that overlooked a large room. Dozens of roller coasters worked, on weapons: Swords, maces, axes, any instrument of death that was ever on blueprints.

"This is where -."

"You make weapons." I finished.

"Correct. If you haven't figured it out already, we are a pack."

"Like wolves?"

"Only smarter and much more deadly." He laughed to himself. "Now, I am the alpha, as you know I am Razorblade."

"Okay."

Then we started to walk again, out of view of the large room and down a big flight of stairs.

"Our pack works to protect the citizens of Amusement Park Between from the likes of the Fallen. We have waited over thirty years for Railrunner to arrive. He is the key ingredient, if you know what I mean."

"Of course."

Razorblade led us to different rooms. Finally we came to a large door that was at the deepest part of the whole place. There were two guards at the door holding sharp spears. They nodded to Razorblade and let us pass. We entered the largest room of all. It was circular and lit by dozens of torches. Columns surrounded it; in the center was a large stone chest. Carvings of roller coasters appeared on the surrounding walls. The "temple language" was everywhere, even on the ceiling and floor.

Razorblade walked up to the stone chest. As we got closer I noticed the writing was microscopic and the chest was as big a roller coaster itself. Razorblade ran his wheels over the lid.

"What is this?" asked Static.

"This is one of the most sacred places in our world, a tomb." Razorblade spoke with his tone suddenly turning serious.

"A tomb for whom?" I asked befuddled.

"Well, the coasters on the walls are actually generations of reds. The one in the center, behind me there, is Moonblood."

"So -." Static went on looking at everything.

"This," Razorblade said rubbing the chest, Is Moonblood's tomb."

"Whoa and why do you live here if this is a tomb?" I said in shock.

"You are not really supposed to be doing that," Static added.

Razorblade sighed. "We were forced to live in this place after the Fallen drove us out of Alcator; we discovered this place on accident. One of our members fell into a hole that led us here."

"Oh."

"Since then we have been preparing for revenge against Ironwheel." The navy coaster said as he stood taller.

"What kind of revenge?" I asked.

He smiled cunningly "You will see once our leader awakens."

Chapter 43
Arise

The state of pure peace was so relaxing. It seemed that the quiet comfort surrounded me in never ending warmth. Was this heaven? Sure felt like it. I looked to see if I sprouted wings, nope. Was it hell then? Sure did not look like it. Maybe the place was an air lock between the real and unreal. Well, wherever I was, I liked it.

Here, it felt more weightless than airtime. Everything seemed light as a feather. Suddenly I felt the comfort slipping from my grasp. All of the harmony was being pulled away from me. Faint hints of pain returned, they got greater as they seemed to overcome everything. Then all seemed like it had shifted, I realized I had thudded back to reality.

My eyes were closed. I could see nothing but blackness. I gradually forced them open. Everything was blurry; I could only see faint colors. I blinked my eyes once. I could now see outlines. I blinked again, my eyes finally got into focus. I was in some sort of chamber. Across the room was a green coaster and Merrylegs with their backs turned to me. Where in the heck was I?

I looked down to see that I was in a bed with white sheets. It suddenly came to mind that I ached everywhere. I tried to shift, moaning as I moved slowly.

"Railrunner?!" Merrylegs said running to my side. "I'm so glad you are awake!"

I sighed and tried to sit up, however something pulled me back.

"Easy, just relax," said the lime green coaster.

I looked to see that I had IV's in several arms. I gave up and lied back down.

"Merrylegs, where in the crap am I?" I asked while staring at the ceiling, and then I turned to her for an answer.

"It is probably better if Chainlink explains that to you." She said looking at the coaster.

"All right, Chainlink, I want to know what's wrong with me and where I am." I demanded.

" Is he always like this?" she asked Merrylegs. I rolled my eyes and gave a weak smile. Merrylegs laughed and nodded.

"Anyway," Chainlink began. "You are being held in our pack's lair under close surveillance. We have kept Freakshow's venom from overpowering your system. I can say this, we are very happy to have you here."

I let out a deep sigh. I popped my neck as I tried to get comfortable.

"How long have I been here?" I asked looking at Chainlink.

Merrylegs glanced at her, gulping. Chainlink swung her arms in hesitation. Then she shrugged and looked at me.

"A week."

"What?" I said sitting up again. "I've been asleep, for a week!"

"Well - yeah. You will probably be bedridden for several days still. Railrunner, you are not ready for combat yet."

"Wonderful," I said throwing my arms up, unfortunately I forgot about the IV's. "Ouch! Damn it!" I spoke in frustration.

"My apologies, Chainlink. He can be cranky."

"I can see that." She laughed.

"I guess it is just the fact that I have spent a week here doing absolutely nothing, while Thunderbark rots in hell." I grumbled. I lay back down again and started to twiddle my wheels. "Sorry for swearing." I said taking a deep breath.

"That is quite all right, Railrunner. I understand." Chainlink replied.

Then Static rolled into the room.

"Morning," he spoke to Merrylegs. Static must have not known that I was awake. "How is Railrunner?"

"Dandy." I said. Static looked up in surprise.

"Nice to see that you are finally up!" Static laughed. "Razorblade wanted me to check on you."

"Who is Razorblade?" I asked puzzled.

"Pack leader."

"Oh."

"Anyway, he said if you were awake, he wanted to speak with you."

"Tell him I'm up then." I yawned. Static nodded and exited the room.

I stared at the ceiling again, my body felt like it had been tossed around in an ocean surf. It still felt like it was too, with never ending swaying movement. Then a navy blue coaster entered the room. He stood looking at me grinning, and then he started to kneel.

"You don't have to do that, I'm nothing special," I interrupted him.

"Sorry if you do not find that- likeable. It is just that you are the most pure source of energy in all Amusement Park Between. You are a blessing."

"I am only a different color." I said laughing slightly.

"If you say so, my lord. Might I ask how you are this morning?"

"Still sore and hurting a bit. You said you wanted to see me about something?"

"Ah, yes. We want you, Railrunner, to lead our pack in the invasion."

"Excuse me?" I replied, not sure if I heard him right.

"The Fallen are planning to attack Amusement Park Between's biggest city, Alcator."

"But isn't it a Fallen city already?" Merrylegs interrupted.

"Yes, but the Fallen are going to raid it in three days, killing all who live there. Our plan is to first break in the prison and gather troops, then siege Alcator right as the Fallen move in."

I crossed my arms. "Sounds like one hell of a move, Razorblade."

"What is your further opinion, Railrunner?" He replied while raising an eyebrow.

"I think we should go through with it. Shall we discuss tactics?"

"Yes, we need to figure out how we should enter the prison unnoticed. I am going to hold a meeting tomorrow night."

"That seems good, I might be better if you know what I mean." I said as I scratched my chest where the Augu Ra rested. Razorblade's eyes still transfixed on it; completely overwhelmed I was here.

"Yeah, it is settled then, you are going to lead us to victory?"

"Certainly."

Chapter 44
Nightscare

Static and I stood in our room. It vas very late at night and we both couldn't get to sleep. We lay awake talking about what was to happen in the future.

"Do you think Railrunner is - ready–for this?" he asked.

I thought about Static's statement, did he not believe in the red coaster? "Yes, he has trained hard for the very moment. Thunderbark taught him well. I think he can pull it off."

"His attitude towards things worries me though." He sighed.

"A bad attitude can come in handy."

Static giggled. "You are right Merrylegs; I need to stop thinking about that. It is just the choices he made in the past are, well, not so good."

"They got us here didn't they?" I objected.

"You are right again. I need to quit doubting him."

"Now, we should -."

Suddenly Chainlink burst into the room. She was out of breath and shook up, her eyes lit with terror.

"Come quickly! Something is wrong with Railrunner!"

We ran in a blur down the hall, I heard Railrunner's agonizing cries. Not this! Anything but this! We entered the room, I feared the absolute worst.

That's when I saw him, his eyes closed shut and gripping the side of the bed, bending the frame. Beads of sweat were all over him. He tossed and turned, flopping like a fish. It was apparent he was having a nightmare.

"Wake him up!" I yelled. Static touched him with the cable and emitted a painful shock. Railrunner didn't wake up, Static tried again with no success. He then gave the most powerful shock he could muster, Railrunner awoke, but he wasn't in the best condition.

Railrunner's limbs shook and he was soaked in sweat. Blood seeped out of his arms from ripping out his IV's. His eyes were bloodshot and had dark circles under them. He stared strait ahead clinching his teeth. His body swayed, apparently he was very dizzy.

"I... I don't...feel like...myself." He said stuttering horribly. Suddenly he fell backward onto the pillow; Chainlink rushed over and applied ice to his forehead. Railrunner looked around wildly, like somebody was coming for him.

"What did you dream!" I yelled to him so it would register. He looked at me with dark eyes, they seemed like they were almost black rather than the fire coloring like they usually were.

"D... death...Ironwheel...Clare."

It was the same as the rest. Railrunner was like Redrail, the dreams were making him reach the breaking point. Without warning the machine that he was hooked to started to go crazy. The red coaster's heart rate went wild and so did his brainwaves.

"We are losing him!" Chainlink said.

Railrunner started to grow weaker, his body started to go limp. Then he suddenly turned to me.

"Merrylegs."

"Yes Railrunner?"

"Get my bag...I need something...from it."

"Okay!" I said without hesitation. The bag was hung on a hook at the other side of the room along with his coat. I quickly pulled it free and handed it to Chainlink.

"What now?" The green coaster asked.

"Pull out the bottle." He demanded.

Chainlink fished around the bag, she then pulled out the bottle full of a red substance.

"Blood?" she asked him.

"It is the antidote." He spoke softy.

Chainlink pulled out the cork and opened Railrunner's mouth more. My stomach churned as I watched the red liquid go slowly down his throat. Railrunner lay there motionless for a few seconds. Suddenly he started to perk up, he then sat up in bed and looked at us, and then he admitted a weak smile.

"I've looked worse," he said.

"You scared the hell out of me!" I told him. "Are you all right now?"

"I believe so. I had a bad dream." He said as he let out a whoosh of air.

"So was it about -."

"Yes it was. Worst one yet too."

"You said there was death." I questioned.

"Yes, I did." He breathed heavily.

"Who died?"

"I don't want to say it."

"Come on!" I whispered.

He stared at me blankly, then surprisingly he got up and walked to the balcony. He hung his head low. I trotted up to him, he looked at me with sad eyes.

"Who?" I asked again.

"Clare."

Chapter 45
New Worries

The following night was the night we were to take action. It was late in the afternoon and we were to start the meeting soon. All day we had spent readying ourselves for war. I had been nervous about two things: Commanding an army and the dream I had last night. Merrylegs had asked me information about it, but I didn't want to say anything in front of Chainlink or Static. I wanted to speak to her alone, now.

I slipped on my trench coat and walked out of my room. I looked over the balcony to see that half the pack was down in the large weaponry room; Static was talking to Razorblade, which was a good thing. It meant that he was away from Merrylegs. Their room was downstairs, she was probably still in it. I continued to walk down to their level where the room was located. I had only been there once, so it took a couple of tries before I could find it.

I opened her door slightly, sure enough Merrylegs was there. She simply stared down at her suit of armor; I could tell that she did not want to do this.

"Merrylegs you care if I talk to you for a minute?" I said quietly so I didn't startle her.

"No, come on in, Railrunner." She replied turning to look at me.

"Merrylegs, I feel that- I can only talk to you about last night." I said walking to her side.

"Ok," she replied getting comfortable.

"Well," I started. "I dreamt about Clare and Ironwheel."

"I think you mentioned that already."

"Oh, right. My nightmare went like this: I was running through the real world after Ironwheel. As the dream went on, I realized that he was carrying Clare."

"Then what happened?"

"All I can remember is that I and Ironwheel were scaling the clock tower. I recalled Clare screaming for her life, screaming my name. Then I looked up to see Ironwheel laughing manically, then -."

"What?" she asked.

"He dropped her. I could not catch her; she fell into an ocean of blood. She never surfaced, and then I knew she was gone." I said sighing heavily.

"That is all that happened?"

"Yes, Static woke me up after that."

"I don't know what to tell you, Railrunner. I wish Thunderbark were here to help, but I do appreciate you considering me as an honest ride." She smiled warmly.

"You're welcome Merrylegs." I said to her.

"I would like to see your dream Railrunner, may I?"

"Read my mind?"

"Yes, I want to see it this time, I want to get as much information as I can to help you."

"Fine," I said lowering my head to Merrylegs. I waited for the sudden shock of pain when her horn touched my forehead.

It happened like before; when Merrylegs read my mind after Thunderbark disappeared. Every part of my body seemed to freeze. I could hear Merrylegs trying to fight back a scream, then she pulled away and it all stopped.

"I hate reading your mind!" she said gasping.

"Then why did you want to read it?" I laughed.

"Like I said, I wanted to help you. I think your dream means something, like it is trying to tell you -."

It had finally dawned on me. Merrylegs gave me enough info I needed to figure this out. How could I have been so stupid and not seen it!

"Merrylegs, my nightmares are telling me the future!"

"But aren't roller coasters supposed to already be able to do that?"

"Thunderbark told me that yes," I said quickly. "However, he said that was only for practical things like the weather. I think I can predict death, he said no coaster could do that! I think my nightmares are trying to tell me that -." I shut my mouth because we both knew at once. We were silent, the only thing that could be heard were the voices in the background.

"How- could it be possible?" Merrylegs questioned. "How could Ironwheel get into the real world when he doesn't even know where the portal is?"

"I don't know! The thing is I don't understand how he found out about Clare!"

"That, I am not even going to attempt to answer!" Merrylegs replied, stamping one of her hooves to the ground.

I snarled in frustration and began to pace back and forth angrily.

"How far is it from Alcator to Ironwheel's castle?"

"Not far at all, in fact it overlooks the city."

"Good, I'm going to kill him before he can reach the real world and Clare."

"I'm with you. I can help."

"Tell Static and see if he is in." I said motioning for the door.

Merrylegs started to follow. "Right, I'll find him. Is it all right if I tell the parts about you're dream?"

"Yeah, now that I know what they were trying to tell me."

Chapter 46
In The Dead of Night

As I walked to the weaponry room for the meeting, my mind was furious and full of questions, questions that I had no answer to. How could I have been that dim-witted and not seen the truth before? It was so easy to figure out! I just didn't catch it! Why am I such an idiot! The fact that Clare could possibly die, made me wish I never became a coaster in the first place! Yet Clare still was in love with me after she learned the truth. Maybe there was a way that I could change the future. Perhaps get to Ironwheel before he got to Clare. I knew I had to accomplish two things: Save Amusement Park Between and save my love. I couldn't screw up no matter what.

During the last hour, I concurred some of the basics we could use for our battle plan. I would have to speak to Razorblade about further tactics. I stood in the hallway looking out into the room. All of the pack was there, including Merrylegs and Static. Then someone tapped me on the shoulder, I turned to see that it was Razorblade.

"Nervous?" he asked.

"Not really," I lied.

"Well, I heard about last night. You must be like Redrail."

"Unfortunately." I sighed.

"It can come in handy if you think about it." Razorblade said as he tried to cheer me up.

"You know I can predict death?" I asked surprised.

"Yep, I think it could be useful in battle if you know what I mean."

"Oh, maybe it can," I said seeing his point.

"I have made a map that we are going to look at, that way we can determine our maneuvers."

"Sounds good, Razorblade."

"Ready for the meeting then?" He said walking to my side.

"Ready," I replied.

Razorblade and I stepped into the great room. Every coaster looked up; they all gave me the usual emotions. Some stared, gasped, and there was the occasional smile. Then they started to bow, but then Razorblade flicked his tail, making them stop.

"Railrunner says you should not kneel to him. The red states he is like us only a different color."

I could feel myself get hot with embarrassment. All the coasters looked at one another, and then they nodded in approval. In the center of the room was a large circular table. It was solid smooth steel with a chrome top. Razorblade then held out his wheels. To my surprise, figures rose out of the top. They consisted of trees, buildings, rocks, and so forth. The mountain was at the far corner of the table, Razorblade made a "flag" come out from it.

"We are here," he said. "The prison is about twenty miles west." He continued while making a large stone building appear. Then a dotted line ran across the table. "That is our desired path. It is the most secluded and safest one by far."

Then Razorblade cleared the whole table, and made a large-scale model of the prison. You could see every detail as if it was a hand crafted dollhouse.

"This is the prison. It is surrounded by guards on the outside and inside. Whatever we do, it must be done quickly and silently. We don't want Ironwheel to know until it is too late."

I looked at the board, where every guard was stationed. I then had a plan that just might work.

"I have a suggestion," I said.

"Go ahead general." Razorblade said moving aside.

"It goes something like this. We should split up into two fleets. That way we can advance from behind. However, we are going to need a few from each group to take care of the watchtower and guards outside."

"How are we going to do that without being spotted?"

I smiled and laughed deeply in my throat. "We disguise ourselves as Fallens. During our time in Xzerma, I witnessed what the Fallen soldiers' uniforms looked like."

"How quaint, we happened to seize twenty suits of armor the day we found you in Xzerma." Razorblade laughed.

"Perfect, you and I will wear one any of you who are brave enough to enter a Fallen lair." I said turning to the pack. Several of the biggest coasters stepped forward, including Chainlink.

"Thank you all, now is everyone clear on the plan? All fleets invade as soon as we exterminate and give the signal."

"Yes," they replied.

I took the armor that Razorblade handed me. I slipped it on under my trench coat.

"Tonight is the night we will take back Amusement Park Between! Now, let's move out!" I said putting on the skull- like helmet on my head. It was now the time to get what was lost.

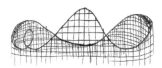

The rides in the "special unit" were suited with Fallen armor and swords. The rest of our fleet wore our own colors, red and black. We were now hunting like wolves, moving silently through the forest. I led them, keeping myself alert. I listened for even the slightest snap of a twig, and I kept my wheels hovering over the handle of my sword.

The moon hung high overhead, it's light reflecting off our metal and armor. The moon's presence gave me slight comfort like it had in the real world. Then the Fallen's foul scent came into our wake. It was greater than even in Xzerma, for our safety I sniffed and listened intently. No ride was around except for us.

"We are getting close," Razorblade spoke softly. "It is just up that hill."

"Good," I said under my breath. "Very good." I continued as I licked my lips, I wanted to taste their blood and get our revenge, and soon I would have it.

We advanced to the top of the hill. Razorblade on my right and my two friends from the beginning on my left. Below us was a prison that looked like Alcatraz. The model back at the pack's lair looked like an identical twin. Their guards were at either entrance. Then I turned and started to speak to our army.

"All right, half of you with Razorblade and half with me. I need ten of our "Fallen" soldiers and the rest with Razorblade. Let's move out." I whispered just before we headed in the direction of the back entrance. The coalescence force then split, putting our plan into action.

Within minutes we stood, hidden among the trees, at the edge of the forest. Three roller coaster guards stood in front of the giant iron door. I looked up to see that the ride at the tower wasn't paying much attention either. I stood and so did all the other rides in disguise.

"Call me warden." I said giving them a crooked smile.

"Funny you should say that because, you look just like him. Coat and all, Railrunner." Chainlink replied.

"Maybe we can use that to our advantage."

"Well said." She nodded.

"Come on." I started as I advanced into the enemy's lair.

My counterparts walked beside me as we motioned into the open. The guards looked up, they then stood straight and prepared to take orders. Chainlink was right; I did look like the warden.

"Awaiting orders sir." The grey and yellow coaster in the center announced.

I smiled wickedly.

"There has been a slight change in plan, boys. King Ironwheel wants to lay off a few of his servants." I started as I altered my voice a little.

"W…what?" he stammered.

"That's right, I am firing you." I said snapping my wheels like I would fingers. My allies suddenly drew their swords and slammed them into the guards. The grey soldier stared at me in shock then back to the sword that stuck out of his belly.

"Unfortunately we have to do it in the most gruesome way possible." I smiled as he fell to the dirt ground dead. Then I turned to my team. "Three of you take their places; move these bastards out of the way so that they are unseen!" I whispered.

Three of us took the corpses to the woods while the watchmen had his back turned. The pack members stowed them away secretly where they could not be seen or smelt. We then quietly entered the big iron door. We were now treading even deeper in dangerous waters.

There was no guard in sight. Now was the perfect time to execute another plan.

"I need three of you to travel through this place and exterminate any guard you come in contact with. Open any cells when you get the chance. Tell the prisoners to head for the edge of the forest."

"Yes sir." They replied running off.

"Let's go this way," I said turning to Chainlink and the others. They nodded and started to follow. The halls were dark and eerie. It was so silent that you could hear a pin drop. Then we approached three guards than were walking side-by-side, not aware that we were stalking them close behind. I signaled with my wheels to move in. In no time I was just inches away from the guard's back. I waited for my allies to get into position. Quick as lightning, we pulled out our swords and slashed their throats. After their demise, we safely stored them away.

"Nice work," I whispered. "Now let's get these cells open." I said extracting my claws and obliterating the heavy iron hinges. Inside was a carousel horse. She looked petrified and backed up against the wall.

"We are not here to harm you. This is a search and rescue. Proceed to the edge of the woods where our party awaits." I said stepping aside. She seemed to get the point and bolted out.

Cell by cell we opened. Rides made the quiet escape into freedom. Our plan was functioning well so far. At the moment I worked on a lonely cell at the end of the hall. I lifted the door free from the wall to find a surprise.

"Don't hurt me warden sir!" Ashsoot cried.

"I'm not the warden! It's me, Railrunner!" I said lifting my helmet up a few inches. Ashsoot then beamed in relief.

"Oh thank goodness!" He sighed.

"Listen head down the hall and out into the woods. Our army is waiting there; tonight we are taking Amusement Park Between back."

"Roger that!" he whispered excitedly, he then went as fast as he could in the direction where the others were traveling. I then turned to an advancing guard, that was not our own.

"What do you think you are doing!" he demanded. He raised his spear, ready to strike. I quickly stuck my claws into his chest and threw him aside.

"We must work quicker! There are starting to be more of them!" I said prying a door off its hinges. All of my team nodded and began to work quicker than ever.

Soon we had opened a little more than a hundred. We had killed nearly thirty Fallen guards. Both numbers were rising by the minute.

It was getting close to midnight. The moon was at its highest point, making me stronger than ever. Chainlink hung close behind me. The team had opened so many doors to let prisoners out, we even ran into Razorblade's fleet at some points. Then I spotted a passageway that we had not seen before.

"This way. We haven't been up there." I pointed up the shaft-like staircase.

"Ok," she replied as we descended.

The steps went up in a spiral, at their top was an iron door with a small window to look through.

"Wait a second." I told her. She obeyed as I peered beyond the glass. To my dismay I saw the real warden and five of his allies. One of them ran up to him out of breath, fearing the worst, I listened.

"Sir, I think there may have been a security breach."

"What!" The big roller coaster said alarmed and angry.

"Yes, we found some of the cells empty!"

"How in the hell did they get out!"

"We don't know!"

I put my wheels on the doorknob.

"Railrunner!" whispered Chainlink. "What are you doing!"

"You will see." I said opening the door. I stepped out onto the large rooftop of the prison. At first, Chainlink and I went unnoticed. Then the warden finally turned around. I felt a smile of dignity spread across my face.

"What is going on here!" He said looking at me in resentment. "Who are you?"

I didn't answer. I simply stood there leaning casually.

"Answer me!" he demanded loudly. Then he drew his sword and charged, just what I had been waiting for.

I felt the spark in the back of my throat, at it went upwards, it tickled my tongue. I opened my mouth and let out a concussion beam. Its shockwaves cracked the surface of the roof and the foundation of the prison itself. Its blast echoed through the night. The warden was sent flying backwards into the prison yard below.

The other guards looked at their deceased leader and back at me. I took off my helmet, and Chainlink came out from behind, bending fire and lightning. I then tilted my head back and released another concussion beam to the dark night sky, signaling for the pack to attack.

A hundred screams it seemed, went off like an alarm. From my stance, I could see the trees rustling by force. Then suddenly dozens of our army members burst through the bushes with swords drawn and ready to clash. Chainlink and I watched as many of us climbed over the walls and barreled through the iron door. Our troops spilled into the prison yard. Fallen soldiers raced out of the corridors, completely unaware that they were outnumbered. It was clear, that we were winning.

I watched with a slight grin as I saw the Fallen being slaughtered one by one. It was like two rivals packs fighting for territory, which it indeed was. Soon there was not but six soldiers left. I raised my arms and brought them downward, shooting out several bolts of lightning. All six Fallen soldiers were hit like targets. There was now none left, my heart fluttered when I discovered we had won.

Razorblade looked up from below, everyone followed his gaze. He smiled and took a flag, bearing our colors, and raised it high in the air. He then roared as he drove the flag's pole down onto enemy turf, claiming that this was now ours.

I found myself letting out a bellowing laugh, mainly because I knew that there was finally hope. Hope that could put the citizens of Amusement Park Between back on top.

"Well done general!" Razorblade shouted. I looked to see that Merrylegs and Static now stood next to me.

"See Static, I knew he could do it." Merrylegs said to him.

"Yeah." He replied simply.

"Did you two bet on me or something?" I questioned them.

"Not really- never mind Railrunner. You did great, better than I expected." Merrylegs smiled.

"Good, thank you. Now there is just one important order to say before we proceed."

"Go ahead," she said grinning.

I looked back to the army again, I raised my sword high in the air, and like dominoes they all followed me. The ex-prisoners cheered in triumph, and then I gave the command:

"To Alcator!"

Chapter 47
Apocalypse

Time was now limited, everything was transforming into something that was thought to never be possible. My head was spinning from my continuous worries. Such worries made my whole focus on things cloudy or foggy. Soon I would see Ironwheel and his entire wrath that he would rain down on me. Soon I would see Thunderbark again; I was expecting the worst there. Trapped for weeks in a confined cell had to be hell for him. He had been waiting endlessly for me, could it be possible if he had given up hope? Maybe, maybe not.

It now seemed like I was the balance to this world. A force that was to keep things at ease, harmonizing the good and bad things that I seemed to have no control over. Yet I had no control over some of the things that had to do with me. I had the dreams that caused pain; I had *different* abilities than any other roller coaster. There was also a predatory instinct, making me lick my lips when I saw blood, laugh when I saw my enemy's death. Why? Was there something wrong with me? Couldn't be, I was the way I was because I was born and not built.

I continued to linger among my thoughts as we marched toward Alcator. I seemed to be thinking all those thoughts because I believed it could be the end, but I wasn't going to let it end! I shook my head to clear my mind completely, this time it actually worked.

We moved silently in the tall grass in the light of the vanishing moon. Merrylegs padded silently beside me, I could feel the vibration of her heart. It was fast, much faster than normal. Merrylegs must be uneasy, and I could see why. I was too.

"Merrylegs?" I asked her.

"Yes, Railrunner."

"I can tell you don't want to do this." I said looking to the horizon.

"Well, it is that and something else."

"What?"

"The fact that you can predict death makes me wonder if I am to die today." Merrylegs mumbled.

"Merrylegs! Why would you ask me that?"

"It is the principle that you can."

"Listen, if I knew you were going to die I would have told you already."

"Oh, well silly me." She said sheepishly.

"Static is not going to die either before you ask me that question."

"Good. Is anybody?"

"You are pressing your luck." I said raising my pierced eyebrow.

"Sorry Railrunner, I just want to know." Merrylegs whispered quietly.

I sighed. "Some are, yes."

"Okay, I just wanted to know, I won't ask you anything else." She replied inaudibly.

"That is fine, how much longer?"

"We should be there in about an hour."

"Hmm, I don't really have a plan on how we are to evade, hate to say."

"I thought Razorblade had one." Merrylegs spoke.

"Really?"

"Yes."

I turned to see that he was not far behind us, I called his name. He quickly came running up to me.

"What do you wish, general?" he said in his deep voice.

"I want to know if you have any plans."

"Yes, I actually do, general. I arranged to have a few of our planes circle the city and see what the Fallen are up to. Then if we get the "green light", you give the order to attack. If by any chance that we need help, I have reinforcements that are close by. Let's just say that they are a blast." He finished chuckling quietly.

"Good."

About fifty minutes later the city of Alcator had appeared above the horizon. Even still the sun had not shown its face and the city's fog lights were still shinning brightly.

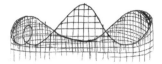

In little time we reached the edge of the river that almost surrounded the peninsula where Alcator sat. In the not so far off distance I saw the huge outline of a dark castle that was precariously perched on the edge of the cliff. I growled deep in my throat, that was Ironwheel's lair.

"Hush, save it Railrunner," Static said in a low tone. "You will get your chance."

"I'll make sure I do." I replied.

Razorblade snuck out of the bush to where I laid. He crouched low to my level.

"I am sending out our planes now," he said. I watched as five planes fluttered from the trees and toward Alcator, their wing beats silent as a moth. I watched them eagerly as they circled like vultures above the city's infrastructure. At some points they became specks in the melancholy sky. Then they became larger as they flew back toward us. The two landed with a soft thump on the grass in front of me.

"The conditions seem good, there are very few Fallen soldiers around, in fact, they seem almost sluggish."

"Thank you, spread the word to the back flank, we are moving out."

"Aye, sir." They said as they took off again. Razorblade slowly crept into the water; I let Merrylegs and Static hop onto my back as we advanced. The water that surrounded Alcator was murky and had a rotten odor; I did not even want to know why it was that way either. Probably threw bodies in here, I thought. Then Razorblade climbed onto the dock at the other side of the river. I soon met him; we peeked over the edge of the wood. Then Razorblade started to move in, my heart hammering in my chest because I knew that this was it.

We waited outside the city gates unseen until everyone was out of the foul smelling river. Then the pack leader charged forward like a bull, he head butted his way through the iron gate. Once inside, he turned to look at me.

"Sound our battle cry!"

I didn't hesitate, I ran forward and roared. All of our army motioned forward, ready to kill. The battle had begun.

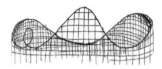

I watched as the others raced forward and started to smash up various things. The remaining Fallens rushed out of their hiding spots, only to meet their fate. My bloodlust rose as I watched our troops beat the Fallen to their roots. Then I couldn't hold back myself, I charged forward.

I started to rip apart things and throw it at my opponents, I burst through gates, harming any damned soul that got in my way. I watched as Razorblade pried apart a door and threw it in the distance. He didn't aim at anything, he just chucked it.

"Why are we just making a mess!" I yelled to him.

"Because we wanted a fight! We are going to attract the king's men!"

I nodded, the main army was the one who we were supposed to hang out to dry after they were stained with their own blood. The Fallen came toward me in a big rank, I let lose a concussion beam, bowling them down like pins. Concussion beams seemed the way to go, after all I had plenty to spare!

I did more blasts; my throat began to tire after about twenty or so. My beam's aftershocks badly damaged the city, again I found myself laughing in pure amusement. I looked up, to my horror a hundred fallen soldiers were coming down from the castle, arms up and ready. This was it.

Then all of Ironwheel's soldiers charged, letting out cries to intimidate. I snarled, then roared, signaling for our men to move forward. Everything then turned brutal. Both forces, good and evil, clashed like tractor-trailers in a head on collision. I ran to join them, as everyone lashed out at each other like angry predators.

I ran up the face of a building, my claws digging deeply into it, I then lunged for a neighboring skyscraper. Then I leaped from each of their sides, like a tree frog hopping from branch to branch. I then climbed to the tiptop of the tallest building. I ran to the edge and glanced for a split second at the chaos below. I snarled, and then dived downward into the sea of soldiers.

I extracted my claws, and started to obliterate. Thirty minutes past, and our numbers were wearing thin. My wheels were soaked in bright red blood and so were my teeth. The sky seemed to be lit like fire and everything was burning to the ground. Then I heard Razorblade's call, I looked around but he was nowhere in sight. Suddenly the ground trembled, the buildings behind us collapsed. Then suddenly out of the smoke appeared five swinging ships. They walked on land like alligators, but their was a major difference, they had big cannons standing on top of them. They were Razorblade's reinforcements.

The cannons fired, the sound was deafening to sensitive ears. Soldiers fell to the ground without a struggle. Blood's sweet scent was heavy in the air and was sprayed all over the grass. Then the Fallen struck once more, this time the coasters used their best weapon as a last resort. Then it all went down hill again as the two sides fired at each other. Screams were all that could be heard. Death was all that was seen.

Anger filled me, I thought of the ones I loved, my friends. Fury replaced fear. I felt myself grow hot, almost burning. My blood boiled. I felt myself grow light, then I hovered a few feet in the air. What was this? Then I remembered Thunderbark's teachings, it was the biggest fire blast that this world was to ever know. I watched flames spread around me. They whipped around like a tornado; I raised my head, and wailed. All my eyes could see was an explosion that went up into the smoky clouds and the battlefield.

I felt the power leave me, and I floated back to the earth. I opened my eyes to see that burnt bones littered the ground. Was everyone dead? I looked some more, then one by one our army popped out of the smoldering ashes. The familiar faces of Merrylegs, Static, Chainlink, and Razorblade looked around in confinement.

"Railrunner! You saved us." Static cheered.

"Not quite, Ironwheel is still on the chess board." I growled as I looked at the castle.

"Oh no. Forgot about that. "Razorblade sighed.

"If Merrylegs and Static would come with me, I think that would be taken care of." I smiled cunningly.

"Of coarse general, thank you, it was a privilege to fight along your side." Razorblade saluted.

"As it was with you." I replied.

"Now Railrunner, I think you should get going."

"Message received."

Chapter 48
Twisted Truth

The lair was fairly easy to sneak into, since all the guards were dead. Now first thing was first, we had to find Thunderbark.

"Where do you suppose he is?" Merrylegs asked.

"Let's see." I said. I raised my head and sniffed a load of air. I tried to distinguish the scents from each other; finally I recognized the white roller coaster's.

"This way!" I said running though the castle's gloomy halls. I turned this way and that, going down floors and floors. Thunderbark's scent got stronger and stronger. Then I paused and looked at the room we were about to enter. Cramped cells were closed with extremely heavy iron doors.

"It is a dungeon. Look around, he has to be here!" I said rushing forward looking through each cell's bars. Piles of bones were in every one. Hopefully Thunderbark's were not part of those piles. It wasn't until the last door that I spotted a solid white coaster lying in a crumpled heap in the corner of the cramped room. I knew at once it was Thunderbark.

I stuck my claws completely through the door, and lifted it off the hinges. Then without hesitation, I barged in and kneeled at his side.

Thunderbark slowly raised his head. He looked dreadful; his eyebrows were longer and unkempt. He had a slight beard growing from under his chin. He was skinny and looked beaten, in fact he was covered in bruises and scars.

"You actually made it, Railrunner." He croaked.

"Thunderbark! I am so glad to see you!"

"I take it you defeated his armies?"

"Yes, I figured out the fire fury that you told me. Plus I had some help from a pack of roller coasters."

"Well done, I knew you could do it. Railrunner," he said suddenly. "I have to tell you something." The white coaster said as he shut his eyes in agony.

"What is it?"

"I have thought long and hard while I was here. I need to tell you the truth, and all of it." Thunderbark said looking up to me in pity.

"What do you mean Thunderbark?" I asked confused.

"The truth about how your mother died and not a lie. And - how I knew you so well."

Oh boy, here we go. With the bizarre material once again.

"Tell me. Tell me the story."

"All right. I actually - knew Angeltrack for a while. She was good friends with all of us, in fact she used to be part of our group."

"She did?" I asked as I raised my eyebrow in bewilderment.

"Yes, as I was saying, one night she disappeared. Then she returned acting eccentric. We knew something was not right at all. Time slowly ticked by, and the old legend of the red roller coaster was starting to come into play. As -."

"I know." I cut in. "I know what happens."

"Good that means I don't have to speak as much. Well, that was when we found out she was having you."

"Oh damn here it goes," I blurted out loud. Thunderbark rolled his eyes, but reluctantly started again.

"Months went by, and we stuck by her side. You allowed her to enter the temple for safe keeping."

"Because no one must know."

"Exactly. Then at the very end it all went to hell. When she well - delivered. Every coaster in our world knew."

"Even Ironwheel."

"Unfortunately. When he heard you had been born, he sent Freakshow and her troops. We found out that they were going to kill us and headed for the real world. And then the worst happened."

"What?"

"Freakshow caught up to us. Just as we got closer to the portal, Angeltrack stopped and headed in the opposite direction. She then told us that she was going to stall them, in other words, die to save you. But right before she did she told me that I was now considered as - your godfather."

"What the hell! Why didn't you tell me earlier?" I said utterly baffled.

"I knew you couldn't accept it." Thunderbark sighed.

"I'm shocked, I would have never known. This is like finding out you have some deadly illness!"

"I know it is a bit hard to comprehend, but it is the truth and all of it. I really should have told you that when I found you, guess I didn't want to overload your brain. I made a mistake, I know. Can you forgive me, Railrunner?" he said slowly standing.

"Yes, I can." I said putting my wheels on his lanky shoulder.

"Good, now I know where Ironwheel's throne room is. I can take you to it, Railrunner. It is time that the red put him into his place."

Chapter 49
Corruption/ Eruption

We raced through the castle as fast as we possibly could. Ironwheel's lair was like a maze, confusing to figure out. My heart was high up in my chest, figuratively speaking. I was so nervous about-facing the evil king. Out of everything, I was more fearful of my friends. Even worse I was terrified for Clare.

"So, where were you? I hate to admit, but it took you longer than I expected, Railrunner." Thunderbark began.

"That was because I killed Freakshow, but received big-time damage to myself, I was in a small coma for a week."

"Wait a second; did you say that you killed Freakshow?" He asked alarmed as his eyes grew bigger.

"Yeah, I threw her over a cliff."

"Railrunner- she is still alive. I saw her yesterday when she came to beat me in my cell." The white coaster said softly. I then got angry.

"How could she have survived our match! More or less a fall of a damn cliff!" I said stopping in the middle of the dark hall. Thunderbark looked at me sincere as Merrylegs and Static both seemed shocked.

"Railrunner, you forgot the most important rule! A roller coaster can only be killed by another coaster! Not even a fall from a five hundred foot tall cliff!"

"I know! You told me, I think - three times. Guess I should have paid attention." I said shrugging.

"Well, lets get to Ironwheel's throne room, it is not much further." He said running up a set of stairs. I quickly caught up to the coaster and ran by his side. Out of the corner of my eye, I watched him. Thunderbark looked like an oriental dragon with his small beard and eyebrows, all he needed was a mustache to pull it off. The fact that he was my godfather, was so - implausible. I had mixed feelings, it was strange, and yet it was exciting all the same. It was kind of well, neat really. I never had a real family and he seemed like he was family, I don't know , guess he was.

Then at the top of the stairs was a small room with a circular door. The knob in the middle resembled a skull.

"I hate this place." Static said.

"Trust me Static, everyone here does," Merrylegs whispered to him.

I reached for the knob, its surface was hot but it didn't stop me. I turned it slightly, the door slowly swiveled open. The room exited into a great hall full of armor, it lit by small smoldering torches. We entered and as soon as I took a whiff, I smelt the worst smell ever. The smell of decaying corpses and above all that was the foul odor of the Fallen. My heart rate rose rapidly, Ironwheel was just behind the door at the end.

"That is it, Railrunner." Thunderbark spoke quietly.

"Here we go." I growled to myself as I walked forward. Thoughts of the dreams I had flashed in my mind. I blinked several times trying to get rid of them. No! I won't let any of that happen! A splurge of anger and rage went through me like a thousand volts. I grabbed the handles of the big copper doors and yanked them open, splitting their hinges as I did so. I snarled as I got my first ever look at Ironwheel.

The king sat upon his throne glaring at me with piercing pupiless red eyes. He was a BIG black roller coaster with silver "tattoos" all over his body. Ironwheel had piercings in his eyebrows and lips, even his nose. Big rings were on his "fingers" that held stones of dark colors. Some of his teeth stuck out of his mouth, including his front canines that made him look like a vampire. He was a complete monster, not from his looks but from all the evil that he had done.

"Finally the red roller coaster had appeared on my doorstep." Ironwheel said in a voice that sent shivers down spines. He crept down from his gargoyle stance to the center of the room. He then sat down and lashed his tail back and forth like an angry cat, or should I say panther.

"Where have you been, roller coaster? You've kept all these - freaks waiting for decades." He said taunting me.

I narrowed my eyes in anger. "My name is Railrunner, you asshole." I snarled.

"Hmm," he laughed. "Spirited, you seem confident, *Railrunner*." Ironwheel hissed.

"You are pathetic, pestering me, how childish."

He snarled. "You are going to fail, just like Moonblood."

"I'm not like him, like they all say, I am unique." I said extracting my claws.

"Put those things away, boy. You are wasting your time."

"I am not." I said thinking what a stupid comeback that was.

Ironwheel then stood up from his previous position. He extorted his jagged claws, my muscles bulged and I prepared to strike.

"Any last words before I gut you?" He growled.

"I have a question, what do you want with Clare? Why do you want to kill my love out of all the people in the real world?"

The evil king stared at me bluntly. "Clare? Who is she? This human you speak of is your girlfriend? I will look for her after I'm done with you and am off to the world where humans walk." Ironwheel laughed.

Wait a minute, did he not even know about Clare! Was I seeing her death because I - told him of her existence! So her death was my fault? Or was Ironwheel lying? Hope it was the second one.

"To bad you are never going to leave this room!" I roared as I went for him.

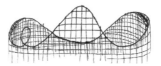

We both clashed like titans. I stuck my razor sharp claws into his metal hide. I felt excruciating pain as he slashed me with his. I opened my mouth and enclosed my teeth around his neck. Ironwheel screamed in agony, but then he used his huge arms to lift me high into the air. He threw me across the room with great force. I landed with a bang on the stone floor. I turned quickly to see that Ironwheel had a mass of lightning bolts dancing around him. Then he sent them to me, I scrambled out of the way of the bolts then hit the floor with a thundering crack.

Before I could stand, he picked me up again and threw me into a column. I split it and landed in a pile of bones. I got up and barred my fangs.

"See! You are weak! Just like all the others!"

"I told you! I wasn't like them!" I said generating a dangerous amount of lightning on my wheels. Like the great Greek god, I sent them raining upon him. They were so amped up that they lit the room in a blinding white light. The bolts hit Ironwheel, knocking him into a wall.

I got on my belly and arched my back like a cat, my restraints vibrating in rage. I watched Ironwheel pry himself from the wall; I smiled, I was glad to see the jerk in pain. I stood up quickly again and hit him with a blast of fire. Ironwheel disappeared within the inferno, but then he leaped from the flames and onto me. I struck him with hot claws, he yelped in pain, his blood dripping from his wounds. He reared back to hit me with a heavy blow, but I pulled out my sword and pointed it at his chest.

Ironwheel snorted and swung his wheels at the sword, knocking it completely out of my arms. The sword flew across the room, but when it hit the floor the handle broke free. Ironwheel and I turned our attention to it as we watched a scroll tumble out of the inside of the sword's blade.

"Moonblood!" Ironwheel said as he leaped off me and ran to retrieve the scroll. I watched him unroll it, a wicked grin spread across his face. " What do you know, the missing pages from the book. All of them stitched together just waiting for me." He laughed. "See you, never!" He said as he burst through the ceiling and out back into Amusement Park Between.

Thunderbark and the others ran into the room. He looked at the roof, to the sword, and at me.

"What happened?" he began with a fearful expression on his face.

"Ironwheel discovered that the missing pages of the book were in the sword all along." I said picking it up and looking into it. I suddenly spotted another small rolled up piece of paper. I pulled it out and began to read. As I scanned the words and illustration, a big smile spread across my face.

"Thunderbark, there is a way that only a red can make a portal! A portal to where they can go to any park they want!"

"Well get to it!" He said excited.

I ran to the wall of the room and pulled out a skull, and crushed it into dust like the instructions said. Then I sprinkled them around into a circle. I read more, I then frowned.

"Looks like only a red can travel through this." I said turning to them.

"Don't worry, Railrunner. We can meet you there later. I know where another portal to a place that is close to Mystic Park." Thunderbark spoke.

"Well, okay here I go. Wish me luck." I said

"We do, Railrunner. Be careful. Whatever you do, don't do anything stupid." He laughed.

"I won't Thunderbark, thanks for everything, all of you."

"You are welcome, but you might want to get going."

I nodded and breathed in deeply, and then muttered the words that were inscribed on the page. *"Hergan duoir fizx saropre bimmesh."*

The portal opened up as a blue pool.

"To Mystic Park," I said taking a deep breath. Then I leaped into the abyss, leaving behind this twisted world and into the real one.

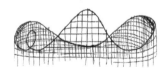

Part Four
Adrenaline Rush

Fatal Attraction

He moved like lightning before the storm, dodging his enemy. Over and over again he attacked; again and again he missed. He thundered across the rails at blinding speeds. It came to his mind that this was a fight that he did not know if he could win or not. It was a fight that would determine everything.

Chapter 50
Reunion

It felt like I had fallen into a dunk tank. You expected it to come and yet you didn't. The water surrounded me faster than ever before, like a ferocious beast was swallowing me. I felt the water rush by me, I now realized I was traveling in a current. I waited still, letting it take me.

As I moved, I comprehended that my body was not changing. It did not compress and shrink like it had before. My body remained stable; it didn't change into its human form. Maybe in the real world it was still night. That could be either a good thing or bad thing.

As I held my breath, my lungs began to hurt. I started to stress, what would happen if I didn't make it? Hopefully that would not transpire. Then I opened my eyes out of force and worry, to my relief I saw that the blue water brightened. I kicked hard, tiring to speed up the process. Then my wheels touched something, a floor. My seats poked up out of the surface of the water. It grew shallower, and then there was not but a foot deep up ahead. Suddenly I stopped on a dime. I rose my head up out of the water, to see that I was back in Mystic Park.

I looked around to discover that I lay in the wave pool. The water rolled in gentle tides against my metal. I slowly stood to get a better look at things. I was still a roller coaster, not human. The moon hung high in the misty sky. I had been right, when Amusement Park Between was experiencing day, the real world had night and vice versa.

I walked from the wave pool and dried instantly, and then I had a thought. When I become human I would be wearing the same clothes I had when I last changed. That was way back when the FBI bombarded my house. If I transformed, I would be wearing the exact same clothes, meaning the humans would be able to track me down easier. Then I had an idea.

I started to break for the ride warehouse; I had remembered that it was near the middle of the midway but behind several buildings and rides. I knew Mystic Park stored the ride vehicles there for the winter and all the décor for the park. I also retrieved faint images of engineer uniforms. I could take mine, and when I turned human, I could change into one of those. Plus I would have my trench coat that would become a hoodie.

The ride warehouse was right where I thought it was. The building was old and rusty. It had a dull grey color and was surrounded by thick weeds. I opened the garage door, almost bending the metal as I lifted it from the bottom. The inside was pitch black, a human could not see past their nose, but I was much different. I could see everything as if it were day. I walked along the concrete floor. There was a section where every type of ride was housed. Parts sat on shelves gathering dust as the long cool months slowly rolled by.

I passed a roller coaster with its upstop wheels removed and sitting on a platform like a car that was being worked on. I looked long and hard at it, wondering what it would be like in the future. It was somewhat funny that Amusement Park Between somehow knew that rides were being stored for the cold months. It was like the spirits could tell when they were wanted and unwanted. I looked at the lead car and tilted my head in amusement.

"You and I are alike in many ways, but yet we are different." I said to it, funny I was talking to one that wasn't even living. I turned around and began to continue my search for the uniforms. From across the room, I spotted them along the wall behind a carousel horse that leaned against the bricks. I looked for my name among the navy suits, but I forgot that I was looking for my fake name. I found it at the end of the rack; I held it up to see that on the front pocket my "name" was stitched in bright neon letters. I found it above the words, roller coaster engineer and Mystic Park. I took it along with my coat and rolled it up into a tight ball, and tucked it away under one of my seats. I then started my search for Clare.

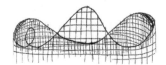

I ran along the deserted streets of the real world. It seemed that the night here was lifeless, except for the chirping of crickets and the fluttering moths. I looked back; Mystic Park started to disappear in the black of the night. I paused and looked at my surroundings. I stared at the clock tower in the not so far distance; it read two am. That meant that it was in the afternoon in Amusement Park Between. It would probably take Ironwheel several days to arrive. Thunderbark predicted that the king would pick the portal of Mystic Park, because it was the simplest to find.

As I continued to look around I heard the sound of an approaching car. I got out of the road and into the bushes. A light blue convertible whizzed past me. I recognized it easily as Clare's. What was she doing out this early? I didn't hesitate; I decided to follow her.

Clare didn't drive very far, only to the corner gas station. I hid behind the car wash and watched as Clare parked by the air pump. She emerged out into the lot. Clare was perfectly dressed and looking normal. She walked into the gas station, a man smoking a cigarette watched her silently as he leaned against his truck that had seen better days. Suspicion swelled up inside of me, why was he looking at her like that?

Then Clare exited the store with two beers in her hand. Her nerves must be bad; Sly had even mentioned that when I rode with him in his truck as he drove me to her house. Then Clare fiddled with her keys and finally opened her car to put the beers in the seat. The wind picked up suddenly and blew her door shut. Clare sighed and searched through her keys again.

Out of the corner of my eye I saw the man walk over to her. My senses told me that something was about to happen. The man looked sort of intoxicated as he tapped on her shoulder. Clare turned around in surprise.

"Hello there miss, you look beautiful this morning."

"Ummm - thanks." Clare spoke nervously.

"How about you and I visit my place and share those beers?" He said as he leaned casually against her car.

"Rather not." Clare said opening it back up.

"Come on!" The man said grabbing her shoulder.

"Quit it! Leave me alone!" she cried, struggling from his grasp. This made me VERY angry. I let out a tremendous growl. The man and Clare looked around in alarm.

"What in the hell was that?"

Clare raised her eyebrows; she somehow knew it was me. "Railrunner." She whispered under her breath.

"What?" He said shaking her shoulders again.

Clare looked him deep in the eyes. She smirked. "You are in for it." She replied under her breath.

With her words, I sprang forward. I landed and grabbed the man by the neck. I snarled in his face as he choked from my tight grip.

"What do you want with me!" the man screamed.

"Stay away from my girl." I said through clenched teeth. I tightened my hold on his neck, his eyes seemed to bulge, and I found that amusing. I roared in his face, upsetting everyone around. I turned and slung the dim man through the gas station's windows. I snorted in his direction and then turned to Clare.

"Railrunner"! She said running up to me. Her arms wrapped around my body in a hug. She then rested her head on my hot metal. I carefully gave her a return hug.

"Um, Railrunner, you're sort of crushing me."

"Sorry, Clare." I said letting go. She stood up strait and popped her back, and then she smiled.

"I really missed you." She smiled.

"I did too." I replied, then I glanced at her car, it was completely totaled. "Oh crap, I'm sorry about your car too." I said scratching my neck. I suddenly became nervous that she would be angry with me.

She unexpectedly laughed. "That's all right; it was getting up there in miles anyway."

"Shall I give you a ride home then?"

"That would be wonderful." Clare said climbing onto my back and situating herself. "This is one nice vehicle." She said leaning on my hood.

"Very funny, Clare. You know most people can't stand me." I said with a classic crooked smile. Then I heard the sound of sirens, which meant it was curtain call. Clare and I left silently toward her house.

I walked quietly with Clare among the empty streets. Minutes ticked by as we talked in conversation.

"So Railrunner, what brings you back?"

My blood ran cold. "It is one of things that I would rather say later. In a more private area if you know what I mean."

"There is no one out here, Railrunner."

I looked to the ground wondering what to say next. "Clare, something bad is about to happen."

"What?" She spoke quietly.

"It involves you." I swallowed.

She grew silent like her cat had a hold of her tongue.

"Tell me." She whispered.

I let out a long sigh as Clare hopped off of me and glared at my eyes. She was expecting an answer.

"Ironwheel is coming here, and he will be looking for you." I gulped. "I am going to guard you, be your bodyguard in other words."

She put her hand on my cheek. I looked at her intently. There was a short pause as we stared into each other's eyes.

"Thank you, I think you can beat him. You are the most vicious roller coaster I ever knew, but most of all the bravest."

"You are the greatest and most beautiful human I ever met." I laughed.

"Thanks, now I have something for you at my house."

Chapter 51
Scripted and Unscripted

Clare and I moved silently through her neighborhood. It was now five in the morning and still no one stirred. The only things that did were dogs, cats, and the occasional scurry of a mouse. The sky was turning lighter as I felt my strength drain from me, I would be human any time now.

I carefully climbed over Clare's fence and into her small back yard. She got out of my seat and dug in her purse, once again seeking her keys. Then her cat walked out from behind an old pot, and hissed at me. I barred my teeth and hissed back loudly, making Clare jump.

"Railrunner! You are going to have to warn me next time"

"I think I scared your cat more." I chuckled.

"Do roller coasters not get along with cats?" she asked finally finding her keys.

"I don't know; I think we get along with dogs better, if they are friendly of coarse."

She laughed as she opened her back door. "You coming?" she asked.

"Wouldn't it be better if I was human first?"

"Oh right, forgot. I guess come in when you are ready, that gives me time to get your surprise." She smiled.

I nodded in reply and looked to the horizon. In the far off distance I could see the faint rays of the sun. Then the whole process started. A rippling pain went across my back as my head throbbed. My wheels singed and my ribs hurt. I felt everything compress and shrink. Metal softened and changed color as locks of jet-black hair went over my face. The transformation quickened and soon it all stopped. I was "Rodney" once again.

I slowly got up and looked at my hands, human hands. It was weird not seeing sets of wheels; fingers just looked so fragile. Being human was weird, really weird as I now saw it. I then walked into her kitchen, still tidy as ever. I looked around for Clare, but I didn't see her.

"Clare?" I called.

"Sorry, Railrunner. I'm back here." She announced from in the bedroom. I walked down her long narrow hallway into her master where she stood holding a box. She handed it to me and waited for me to open it. I popped off the lid to find a set of keys; I realized they went to my Mustang.

"You got back my car?" I asked puzzled.

"Yes, it is in the garage, I figured you would need it during the day."

"Thanks," I said. " Clare do you mind if I do a wardrobe change?"

"I don't, do you have anything to change into?"

"Yeah, I'll be back in a second."

Minutes later I walked into Clare's living room with my uniform on. The trench coat became a large leather jacket that I held in my hand. Clare looked up from messing with her DVD player and laughed.

"Hate to say it, but that looks very conspicuous." She said giggling.

"Well, I guess I could still wear the jeans." I sighed. "You wouldn't happen to have any really big shirts that could fit me?"

"I think I have the shirt that I was going to give you as a Christmas present. I'll go get it, you need it anyway." She said running into the bedroom again. She came back with a black t-shirt with a guitar on it.

"Hope you like it." Clare smiled slightly as she handed it to me.

"I didn't get you anything, though." I shrugged.

"Don't be ridiculous, you presence is enough." Clare said returning to the DVD player. I quickly changed again and found her on the couch. She was wrapped in a blanket and sipping coffee.

"Come watch this movie with me, I think you might like it even though it was made in 1977. I haven't actually watched it myself; I wanted to watch it with you so I waited."

"What is it called?" I asked sitting next to her.

"I bought it at a used movies place, it is called *Roller Coaster*."

"Fancy that." I laughed.

Clare then pressed play and the movie began. Thirty minutes into it, and I knew the storyline. It was about a brainless terrorist who blew up coasters just for money. The special effects were probably state of the art back then, but now it was cheesy.

"This offending you, Railrunner? If it is I'm sorry. I didn't know it was like this, I'll take it out if you want."

"I'd like to kick that guy's ass." I muttered staring at his face on the screen. "That bastard doesn't even know what he is creating."

"What?" she asked.

"Fallens."

"I forgot what those were and how the rides came about, could you tell me again." Clare asked sheepishly.

"Sure. As you know, the rides in Amusement Park Between come from your world. The ones that are good come from being in storage when they are no longer needed. The ones that are evil have been destroyed in the real word, we call them the Fallen."

"Oh I remember now, and you were the only one that was created different. The only one that was born."

That reminded me. "Clare, I need to tell you something that I just recently learned."

"Go ahead, Railrunner."

"Well, I found out the truth about me. It is really weird so just play along."

"Trust me Railrunner I have seen stuff that is beyond weird." She laughed. I knew exactly what she meant.

"Good we are on the same page then; I am the - well, mixture of Amusement Park Between and real blood. This is really hard to explain." I said as I scratched my head in deliberation.

"I'll try to understand the best I can." She smiled tenderly.

"Okay, Thunderbark, the white roller coaster, Merrylegs and the little bumper car, Static, knew my mother very well. When they discovered I was, this is stupid, coming as some would say, my mother had to be hidden for her own safety. When time passed and finally I was born, all went into turmoil. You see, when I had arrived, every coaster knew, including Ironwheel. He sent his armies to kill me and everyone involved. We left to the real world, but soon Freakshow, Ironwheel's best general, was hot on our trail. My mother, Angeltrack, sacrificed herself to buy us some time, to save us in other words."

"That is really sad; I shouldn't have even bribed you to tell me." Clare said leaning on my shoulder and looking to the floor.

"It was something you should have known anyway. But the freakiest part of the whole thing was what Angeltrack said before she left us."

"What?"

I gulped. "She made Thunderbark my - godfather." Clare then smiled.

"What do you know, you had a little family and you did not even know about it!" she laughed almost spilling her coffee.

"Am I the only one who thinks this is dumb!" I said throwing my arms into the air. Clare looked at me a brief second, then continued.

"I have to admit, it is a bit strange, but it is the truth and it is real." She said laying her hand on my shoulder.

I sighed. "I just have to accept it I guess. I only found this out a few hours ago, I'm just flabbergasted about it." I chuckled slightly, putting my arm around her.

We continued to view the rest of the movie. It was long that was for sure! At least this was a good moment with her though.

"Do you this life is a disaster movie?" I asked as the credits rolled. "It sure feels like it with everything that has happened to me."

"No, I think it is more of an adventure movie. Your life has every aspect of one. Action, suspense, romance, a destiny." Clare smiled to herself.

"You are right, Clare. As you are always right." I replied in a smooth tone.

"I am not." She laughed quietly, leaning towards my lips, I went the rest of the way and the next second we locked in a kiss; something that I had not had in a long time. It was so very, lovely.

Then there was a loud knock at the door. We stopped, fearing the worst.

Chapter 52
The Alliance

The knocking continued as Clare and I got to our feet. She raced to the door as I prepared to make a run for it. Clare looked through the peephole and then put her hand on the knob.

"I think it is your friends." She said turning to me.

"Which ones? Is it Buddy and Sly or is it -."

"It is an old man with, a young girl, and a boy."

"You can let them in," I sighed in relief. "That's Thunderbark, Merrylegs, and Static."

Clare opened the door; Thunderbark took off his cowboy hat and asked her if I was here.

"Yeah, he is. You all can come in." Clare invited them.

"Thank you Clare," Thunderbark replied as he stepped into the living room along with Merrylegs and Static.

"I see you made it in one piece, Railrunner." Thunderbark said as he put his hat back on. I could barely remember his human form since I had not seen it in a while.

"Wasn't that hard," I smiled.

"Now that we are all here, I believe we must discuss tactics on how we are going to handle this situation." Thunderbark began.

"Right."

"Can I get any of you something to drink?" Clare asked us.

"Railrunner told me about some oil that you had Clare, is it possible by any chance if I could have a bit of it?" Thunderbark said sitting on Clare's couch.

"No problem," She laughed. "Anyone else?"

"I hate to say it, but wine would be wonderful for me, if you have it that is. If you do not, I'll just have water please." Merrylegs admitted.

"As a matter of fact I do actually; I'll drink some of it as well." Clare said heading into her kitchen.

"I'll help you," I followed her.

After Clare and I rounded up the drinks we sat around her living room. Thunderbark cleared his throat and prepared to speak.

"As we all are aware, Ironwheel is coming to the real world. We know he is going to use Clare to get to Railrunner. We need to figure up a plan on where to take her so she can be safe. Another thing about Ironwheel is that he will use the ones closest to his enemy to get to them."

"Like Buddy and Sly?" I said in alarm.

"Exactly. We need to put these subjects under surveillance. Does anybody know of a place that is far from Mystic Park and well hidden?"

"I do, Sly lives outside of town in a cabin. It is deep within the woods. It's very far from the park so it might be ideal." I said standing up.

"Seems perfect Railrunner, is it big enough?" Thunderbark asked.

"Sure, it is a really nice cabin. I have actually been there a few times in the past." I replied as I took a sip of oil.

"Thing is," spoke Merrylegs. "What are we going to do when night falls?" she said as everyone in the room became silent. The white coaster then sighed in defeat.

"Sly might have to know, it would be for his own good really." Thunderbark unexpectedly said. I then realized what he meant.

"Now that I think about it, he should." I sighed. "So are we just going to show up at Sly's or what?"

"Yes, you might want to - wait a minute is he married?"

"No."

"Good, I don't want anybody else involved. Railrunner, just call ahead of time and don't take no for an answer."

"Yes, Thunderbark." I said. However, out of the corner of my eye I saw Static gawking at the news.

"Guys, you might want to look at this," Static said turning up the television.

"Citizens, we have breaking news again. The red roller coaster struck a gas station in the early hours of two in the morning. There are many injuries and one dead. Everyone is advised to be cautious. Police and troops are now setting a perimeter, yes everyone, the red is back."

"Railrunner!" Thunderbark said angrily. "What did I tell you!"

I hesitated at answering; I didn't want to see his piercing eyes. "I had to, Clare was in trouble. The human assaulted her."

"It is true." Clare said backing me up.

"Well, it does totally ruin our chances of taking your Mustang. Since the police know it belongs to you." Thunderbark said rubbing his head. "Any ideas on where we are to find a car?"

"We could buy a car." Static spoke.

"Last time I checked Static, we are broke!" Merrylegs said rolling her eyes.

Then I had a thought. I reached into the bag and pulled out the sack that had all my g's in it. I slowly opened it to see several sets of one hundred dollar bills, lots of real world money.

"Thunderbark," I began. "How much is ten thousand g's in real world currency?"

"I think, a hundred thousand dollars, why?"

I dumped the bag out onto the floor, the stacks of bills hit the hardwood with a thud. Everyone's mouths, dropped wide open.

"Where in the hell did you get all that!" Thunderbark said excitedly.

"Won it, to the dealership then?" I said as I put on my jacket.

"Yup."

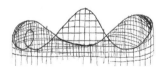

Hours later we drove out of the lot with my new car. I liked it, so did Clare, and Static. However, Thunderbark and Merrylegs thought differently.

"I cannot believe you bought a Hummer," Thunderbark said crossing his arms.

"It is an armored Hummer to be precise." I pointed out. Thunderbark however, still continued to grumble.

"We kind of stick out." Merrylegs said looking out the window.

"You guys need to learn how to have fun," Static laughed. "I like the twenty four inch chrome rims the best."

"Stupid." I heard Thunderbark say under his breath. I sighed.

"Look on the bright side, it is a big plus it is an armored car. So it gives us extra protection in case we are ambushed at all. The thing about it is, lots of people have done the wildest things to their rides here, so nothing to worry about."

"Wait a minute, aren't armored cars the ones used by the secret service?" Merrylegs asked.

"Exactly, that is why I could not pass this up. Trust me think, *James Bond*."

"Oh, I see now! Good idea Railrunner." Thunderbark said suddenly. "I know what you are talking about now, forget I said anything."

"Will do." I smiled.

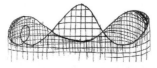

A little while later, the afternoon hours had settled in and the sky turned to various shades. Merrylegs, Static, and Clare were asleep in the back seat. Just Thunderbark and I were awake in the front.

"I need to tell you something, Railrunner." He said as he kept his eyes glued to the road.

"What?"

"Do you remember the night when we were stealing the Augu Ra?"

"Yes. Of course." I replied as I recalled the old mission.

"You remember the chilling ice breath I made?"

"Yeah."

"Every roller coaster has a special talent, even the red. Mine is ice, I can freeze things; control it like fire and lightning."

"Is mine having those nightmares?" I grumbled.

"No, that is not included. You will discover your special talent when you reach your most desperate point."

"Thanks for telling me." I said looking out the window at the overgrown landscape.

"You're welcome." Thunderbark replied quickly.

Deep in my mind, I already knew when that was going to be.

Chapter 53
Unexpected

Thunderbark and I sat in silence as we veered off the highway and onto our exit. The road became narrower and more hazardous. It now seemed that we were driving in the mountains with the large cliffs and surrounding trees. One false move and we could go over.

"It is getting cold; I'm turning on the heater." Thunderbark said as he reached for one of the many buttons.

"Wait! That's not -."

The radio turned on full blast, waking everyone up. I quickly turned it off.

"Whoops." Thunderbark said almost choking on his laughter.

"Well, we are up now." Merrylegs yawned.

"We are almost there anyways; I think I'll call Sly now." I said pulling out Clare's cell phone. I dialed his number and waited.

"Let me talk to him, Railrunner. I have an idea." Thunderbark said holding out his hand for the phone. I reluctantly handed it to him, right as Sly answered. After his greeting, Thunderbark began to handle everything like a pro.

"This is Woody Jackson of the US secret service. For federal investigations we will be staying at your residence. The situation concerns you and the ones known as Rodney and Clare. Several of our agents will serve as your guards until further notice." Thunderbark said in a serious tone. For a minute there was a long silence between the two, and then he unexpectedly smiled and hung up.

"We're in." Thunderbark said handing the phone to Clare. I looked at him astonished, surprised that he actually pulled it off successfully.

"That probably is the best bullshit I have ever seen anyone pull off."

"I'm pretty good at it," he laughed.

"What did he say?" Merrylegs asked.

"He basically just took it all in, plus he still gave me directions in case you didn't remember where it is." Thunderbark finished looking to the sky. "We don't have much longer, we need to hurry."

"We are here anyway." I said pulling into Sly's driveway.

I climbed out of our car and slammed the door shut behind me. The rest of the crew followed me to Sly's front door. All of us stood on his porch and waited on an answer. Finally he did.

"It has been a while Rodney." He said with a grin. "Come on in, it is going to be night soon, and you know what that means." He said with his voice stricken with worry.

"Don't I ever," I mumbled out. Suddenly I heard the faint sound of tires running over dead leaves.

"You hear that?" I asked Thunderbark.

"Hear what?"

"Never mind, let's get inside." I said walking into his warm house. Sly sat in his big chair by the fireplace as everyone else surrounded the edges of the room. I tried to gather up my words before I spoke. Thunderbark took a seat at my side, preparing to back me up on anything. Then I sighed and started.

"Sly, we are here because -."

"Because of what?" he interrupted.

"Well, you are involved with - the red roller coaster case." I said, the words tickling my tongue.

He stared at us blankly, and then he finally spoke after a brief moment.

"Why am I involved! I had nothing to do with it! I didn't create it is that is what you people think!" Sly objected angrily.

"Should we tell him?" I asked Thunderbark.

"You should, I'll correct anything you missed." He replied.

"Sly, you better listen up, I am not repeating any of this, and you must tell no one!" I said in a way that Thunderbark would have.

"Fine, do you know information on that thing?"

"You could say that," I said biting my lip.

"Go ahead, I'm listening."

"There is a place called Amusement Park Between. It is the afterlife that rides experience when they are no longer used or destroyed. The bad ones, the ones that were obliterated, are known as the Fallens. They are pure evil and are under the rule of King Ironwheel. There was only one ride in particular that could kill him, the red coaster."

"Wait a minute!" Sly interrupted. "Are you saying that the red roller coaster is a good guy!"

"Trust me, I know." I said smiling. "As I was saying, the red is the only one that was born, he wasn't like any of the other rides. The red is - special, a key to their prophecy."

"Then why was he here and not in Amusement Park Between!"

Thunderbark nodded for me to give him permission to speak, I agreed and he started.

"Well the red was actually in Amusement Park Between for about a week after he was born, but little did his mother know that when he was brought into the world that every coaster knew, even Ironwheel. So the evil king sent out his armies and his best general, Freakshow, to kill the red. The ones who practically raised him, left to hide the red in the real world for safe keeping. The troops soon caught up to them, but his mother sacrificed herself to save them. Then when they arrived here they secretly watched over him for thirty six years."

"How in the hell could they watch him for thirty six years without being noticed!" Sly cried in shock.

"Their race is a lot more advanced. Plus they can disguise themselves as humans."

"It is official, this is a new level of weird."

"It is true, better believe it Sly." I said.

"How do all of you know this?" He asked.

All of us looked at one another for an explanation. All of a sudden the front door flew open. A cop entered and pointed a gun at my face. Everyone stood in alarm, backing up to the walls, Clare looked horrified. I stared at the officer; my heart skipped a beat when I discovered that he was Buddy.

"Buddy? You're a -." I said holding my hands up into the air.

"I am now, you made a mistake in buying that car, signing your name on the dotted line." He cut in.

"Damn it!" I said frustrated, thinking about how careless I had been.

"Yeah Rodney, since I joined the force wanting to exterminate the red, I learned a few things."

"What the hell is going on!" Sly said franticly.

"I learned what you really are - *Railrunner.*"

I went completely silent and so did all my allies. Clare glared at Buddy angrily. I had now been fully exposed to my best friends.

"Are you telling me that Rodney - is the roller coaster?" Sly said as he finally realized.

"Yeah, and his real name that he is known as is Railrunner."

"Wait," Sly began. "Does that mean that all of you are -."

Thunderbark unexpectedly nodded. Sly and Buddy's eyes widened.

"Crap, it is a rat's nest!" Buddy growled in pure rage. He then pressed the gun closer to me, I glanced down to examine it. I smiled, seeing something that I had missed before. Then I looked out the window to discover that I had only a few seconds left. I could already feel the change coming.

"Buddy." I stammered.

"What?"

"How are you going to kill me if your gun is on safety and that I'm immortal?" I growled.

He looked at his gun in disbelief. I quickly turned and kicked him out the front door, hitting him in the ribs. I peered out to see that the moon had finally risen. I doubled over in pain as everything started. It raced through me quicker than before. I felt my hands turn back into wheels and the rows of seats sprout along my back. I grew less and less human, more like I really was. Then all the pain stopped and I became whole again.

I sprang out the door and stood over Buddy. I lowered my head and bared my fangs. I then let lose a rippling growl in the man's face. Buddy looked at me horrified, he then picked up his gun, but before he could fire I placed a set of wheels onto his wrist so he could not aim it fittingly.

"I would not do that if I were you, the bullet will just do the boomerang effect." I said prying the gun from his hand. Buddy fought for custody of the weapon, but he lost. I flung it aside into the bushes. "I'm not going to kill -."

Out of the corner of my eye I saw Thunderbark as his true self racing toward me. He shoved me off of Buddy and glared deeply into my eyes with his.

"What did I tell you about over doing it!" he scolded.

"He was going to kill himself! Ever notice that bullets simply bounce off of you and hit the shooter?" I argued.

"I'm not blind Railrunner." He growled.

"So, you owe me an apology!"

"Sorry." He said crossing his arms. "What are we going to do with *him*?"

I looked back at Buddy, his eyes went from me to Thunderbark over and over again. Then Merrylegs and Static joined us along with Clare and Sly.

"This is - absurd." Buddy said aloud.

"I know, I thought it was stupid too when Thunderbark here told me the story." I said holding a set of wheels for him to pull himself up.

"Why did you kill all those people, Railrunner?"

"Allow me to explain that one," Thunderbark started. "When a roller coaster enters the real word for the first time, it cannot change into its real self; it remains in its human form. It stays human until it touches the rails or rides an actual coaster. Then its ride form is activated and the roller coaster's own will is not in control, kind of like a lycan. It remains that way until its first full moon where it gains control from then on."

Buddy shook his head trying to get the better of things. Sly then came over and helped Buddy up.

"It is real, Buddy. It took me some time to believe it too. Clare is the same way. If you come inside, they can explain to you what is going on." Sly said with a hand on Buddy's shoulder.

"Before we do anything, we have to know if you are with us and not with the force." I demanded.

Buddy sat there for a minute, he then reached for the radio from his belt, I prepared to make a move, but he shocked me. Buddy took the radio and threw it from the cliff along with his cell phone.

"I'm in, because you stuck with me through all kinds of misfortunes." He said holding out his hand to me.

"Don't shake unless you seriously mean it." I said sternly as I held my wheels before him. Without hesitation, he shook them. Then he took his badge and threw it down into the ravine.

"I quit." He smiled.

"Then I guess you won't need this!" Thunderbark said leaning against the squad car. He lifted it up and tossed it down the cliff along with the rest of his belongings. The car landed with a loud thud against the many trees.

"The brakes stuck anyway." Buddy laughed.

"Come on, we'll explain this whole mess." I said walking into the cabin. Everyone followed me inside, ready to hear the whole story again.

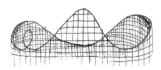

After my story was told and the confinement was cleared, I prepared to tell the reason why we were all here. I remained quiet sipping a beer while Thunderbark finished up. Sly and Buddy occasionally looked from Thunderbark to me. Their eyes looked me up and down completely; I could tell that they were still having trouble grasping the truth.

"Your turn Railrunner, just tell them why we are watching them."

"Wait, your babysitting us?" Sly remarked.

"If you will listen, you'll know why." Thunderbark growled.

I cleared my throat as I sat the bottle on the end table. "I fought with Ironwheel about two days ago; he escaped with a map showing where the portal to your world is. The portal is in Mystic Park."

"It is?"

"Yes, Ironwheel is looking for me, and he wants to kill me. In other words finish off what Freakshow started. Ironwheel will use the ones closest in my life so he can reel me in. He did that with Thunderbark while in Amusement Park Between. Ironwheel will not take any chances, he will do it here."

"So that's why you all are watching us then?"

"Yes, it is for your own safety." Merrylegs said.

"Any comment?" I asked them.

Buddy raised his hand.

"Yes?"

"How in the hell did your mother get -."

"Don't even ask. Not a single one of us can answer that!" I said holding back laughter. "Even though I am a roller coaster, I think that is the stupidest thing I've ever heard!"

This time everyone in the room laughed, even Thunderbark himself.

Chapter 54
Shift

I stood on the back balcony overlooking the woods. The moon hung high in the sky casting a luminescent glow among the trees. Nearly everyone had settled down for the night except for us rides. Merrylegs paced the halls in front of the sleeping humans while Static stared blankly at a late night show. Thunderbark suddenly appeared next to me. He looked up at the moon, his icy eyes sparkling. He then turned to look at me with a grin on his face.

"Nice night, don't you think?" he asked.

"It is." I replied.

"Do you think we can trust Buddy?" he said, his tone changing.

"I read him for the truth, looks like he did give up police work."

"Good, it would really be horrible if the authorities got a hold of the information we just revealed."

I nodded in reply. My stomach suddenly growled loudly, it just now dawned on me that I'd had not eaten in almost two days. I clutched my stomach and sighed aloud, I then realized Thunderbark had heard me.

"Hungry?" he asked.

"Yes."

"You can hunt, I'll watch the fort. Ironwheel should not be in the real world yet. You'll need your strength for the future anyway. You might want to consume as much as you can without overdoing it." He said.

"Thanks Thunderbark, I owe you one." I said leaping off the balcony onto the soft patch of leaves below.

"Don't do anything stupid, Railrunner!" he called down to me.

"I won't!" I said as he went back indoors. I watched the door for a few seconds, and then I bounded off into the lush forest.

The wilderness was the same as always with the scurrying of small creatures among the leaf covered ground and the continuous chirping of crickets. I knew this woods well, Sly and I once hunted here together using some guns he had recently acquired from a friend. Tonight was much different than that night from many years ago. This time I was hunting as a *beast*, machine to be more exact. There were no guns, just me, myself, and I.

I stopped in the middle of a clearing that housed a small pond. I knew this was a popular hotspot for animals such as deer, which sounded really good right now. I sniffed the air, there was hundreds of smells to distinguish from the others. Some were stale, some were fresh, but most of them were long expired. Could I have had an effect on them, too?

I went over my plan; maybe I should go on further and hope for better luck. Then there was the fact that I couldn't go to far from the cabin. I sniffed again; my nose caught the sent of an approaching deer. My mind was made up, I was to stay here. I hid in secrecy up in the trees. Minutes later, a doe walked out of the brambles and towards the pond. A buck would have been more ideal to kill, does were responsible for making more deer. Sadly, I couldn't stand my empty belly any longer.

The deer positioned itself at the lake's edge, it looked around for predators. Then she slowly lowered her head into the water and began to drink. I cautiously started to decline, and then one of my seats caught a branch, snapping it. I held my breath as the deer looked up in alarm. Then after a minute or so she returned to drink. I felt saliva form in my mouth as my stomach complained again. I could not stand the urge any longer.

I leaped from my perch and on top of the deer. My teeth clamped down onto her neck, snapping it and killing her instantly. I licked my lips in satisfaction and began to feast. I peeled flesh from bone at a fast rate. Animals in the real world did not taste as good as the ones in Amusement Park Between, still they were eatable.

I swallowed the last strip of meat, and then I walked to the pond to wash it all down with a drink. The cool water soothed my throat, plus it washed off any unwanted remains of deer. Suddenly out of the corner of my eye, I saw a dark shape looming among the trees. I sniffed; to my surprise it was the foul odor of a Fallen. My mind went into a haze, how could they be here already! My legs tensed up, a growl escaped my throat. The thing stopped and stared for a split second, then ran. I bolted after it, why now! My mind screamed, I was ready to get on with my killing spree with the vermin. The thing slowed and finally stopped on a cluster of large boulders. I paused jut a few feet from it. The object was a black carousel horse with a skeleton painted along his body, and I had recognized him before. He was the carousel horse that hung around with Freakshow, Bones.

"You decide to show up?" I growled.

"I didn't want to miss anything." He spoke, his vampire fangs flashing me a smile.

"Do you mean Ironwheel's funeral?" I mocked.

"No! Your death!"

"I don't put up with assholes. Who is all here?"

"Thanks to you, it is just me, Freakshow, and Ironwheel. We are the last of the Fallens!"

"What a big honor, now where are they!" I said standing up and extracting my claws. Bones then grew nervous, he turned and tried to run again, but I grabbed his pole and held him to my face. "Do you want to talk now?" I said pressing my claws to his neck. He looked at me fearful, then he started whimpering.

"They are simply roaming around for a place to settle! We just arrived and they sent me to find a resting area! It is the truth I swear!" he finished. I read him, surprisingly he looked like he actually was telling the truth.

"Thanks for telling me Bones." I said sticking my claw into his chest. He looked at me in shock, then his eyes rolled back into his head as he died in my arms. I dropped him back onto the rock and set his body ablaze, ridding any evidence. When his body was burned to a crisp, I seized my flame and ran back to the cabin, straight to Thunderbark.

I made it back in less than two minutes running at full speed. I feared the worst, what if they had already arrived? What if they were all- no do not go there. I scaled the back balcony up to the first floor. To my relief they were safe, everyone sat up watching the television except for the humans. I hammered on the sliding glass doors. Thunderbark looked up and quickly ran over to let me in.

"What the heck are you doing?" He demanded in an aggravated whisper.

"You are never going to believe this Thunderbark, but they are here!" I said shutting the door behind me. I pulled the drapes over them; I turned back to Thunderbark who stared at me with a fearful expression on his face.

"What do you mean they are here! That is impossible!"

"Guess they ran as quick as they could to the portal."

"Who all are THEY!"

"Ironwheel, Freakshow, and I killed Bones while I was hunting."

"You saw Bones? Did he tell you this?"

"Yeah! I forced him to before I butchered him!" I said to the white coaster, then realizing we both had woken everyone up due to our yelling.

I felt Clare's eyes burning into me with horror. Thunderbark hung his great head low. He did not speak a word for several seconds. He was tiring to come up with some sort of plan or explanation, I thought.

"Time to leave everyone." He said turning and gathering a few things. "Get any item that is dear to you but is light." He said to my human friends. "Here is what we do, Clare you drive the Hummer carrying Merrylegs and Static. Sly you drive your truck and have Buddy as your passenger. You carry the belongings, except ours along. Railrunner and I will follow till morning. As we turn human when the sun rises, we'll play it by ear." Thunderbark finished as he headed out the door. I caught up to him as everyone loaded the vehicles.

"So after this, we go on from there?"

"Railrunner, I say that because I don't know what will happen." He sighed with worry in his voice.

I watched as he exited. "I thought roller coasters could see the future?"

"They can, but that's only certain things." He said turning away. "This is not one of them."

I could only imagine what those things may be.

Chapter 55
Demands

It was sunrise and Snooks had just opened. It had been in repair for weeks, but now it was reopening its doors. Mr. Calloway stood behind the bar wiping the counter. He had spent all morning getting the place into tip top shape. He did have an odd feeling, however, that something was imminent. His nerves were on edge ever since the night that Railrunner had bashed the local bar. All because he stared death in the face.

Suddenly two strange people walked through the double doors. It was a man and a woman, and they did not look the least bit ordinary. The woman had short black hair that went into a Mohawk that was died purple at the tip. She was tall and skinny, but the most striking thing about her was the woman's skin. It looked like it was from many different people all stitched together. Even her body parts were not identical, her hands did not match nor did her eyes. The man was wrapped up in a cloak that only reveled from his nose to his chin. He too was tall, but extremely muscular looking. Both of them were very suspicious.

The characters took a seat next to each other at the bar. Mr. Calloway watched them smirk at each other as he walked up to them.

"What can I get you?" he asked nervously.

The woman looked up, her smirk getting bigger. She looked at her partner for his answer, but he simply nodded.

"Information." She said in a voice would make babies cry.

"What kind? Who are you two anyway?" Calloway spoke shocked.

"My name is Fern." She said with the smirk still on her face.

"I am Iro." The man said in a voice that sent shivers down a spine.

"Anyway, we are - investigators, on the case of the red roller coaster, named *Railrunner*." She said almost hissing at the end.

The bar owner stood silent, those words struck fear into him. The image of the night he was attacked came into his head again.

"I know some things." He said finally.

"Like what?" Iro demanded.

"Well, I know that he has the same markings on his arms as one of my past customers."

"Really! What is the man's name?" Fern said with her smirk growing into a wicked smile.

"Rodney Philips. Come to think of it he has the same eye piercing as well."

The girl said nothing else, she just turned to her counterpart again, and he nodded for a second time.

"There anyone he hangs around with?"

"Yes, his friends Buddy and Sly. There is also his girlfriend Clare."

"Good. Do you know where they live?" Iro spoke quietly.

The bar owner gave them the location of their residence. Both of them smiled evilly, suddenly Mr. Calloway wondered if he should have told them this or not.

"Do you want to sire, or can I?" Fern said to Iro. Calloway stared at her strangely, why did she call him sire? What was she even talking about?

"I will - I would love to, I like it fresh." he hissed. Suddenly his mouth opened wide and his teeth became fangs. He then lunged for the bar owner, sinking his teeth into his neck. With a jerk, the man's throat was ripped out instantly. Iro stood and licked his lips, wiping every inch of blood off his face.

"Freakshow, do you know how good that felt?"

"Very good, sire?"

"Hell yeah. Now as we now realize Bones went to search for Railrunner late last night. He hasn't returned, I think our target murdered another one of us."

"I believe so, he would have to be back by now. He was in the forest on the west side of town when he disappeared. Railrunner and his allies must be in that region." Freakshow said.

Ironwheel growled. "The bastard must be! I will make him pay! I'll strike his heart, and I will taste his blood! Make him dead!"

Chapter 56
Warned You

I slowly opened my eyes to see the stitching in the Hummer's seats. I lay there for a brief second looking at all the treads, and then I turned to see Thunderbark driving. I moaned as I sat up straight in the seat. I yawned as I looked in the back to see that everyone was still asleep.

"Nice to see you up late." He said staring at the road in front of him.

"Late?" I asked slightly confused.

"Yeah, it is four in the afternoon already. You fell asleep almost as soon as you became human again." He said chuckling deep in his throat.

"I haven't really slept well for the past two days. One night I had a nightmare that almost put me back into a coma, and I was raiding a prison and sneaking to Alcator."

"Hmmm - did you say you had another nightmare?" Thunderbark asked concerned.

I let out a whoosh of air. "Yes, worst one by far."

"Tell me."

"Well, I saw Clare - die. All those dreams led up to her death. The morning after I had my last one, I knew I could predict death. It was a pattern after all, every five and the fifth predicts death."

"That's how you could see what happened to Merrylegs in Trenzon. As for Clare I have some advice for you."

"What?"

"You can't rebuild your past, but you can rebuild the future." He said as he let a slight grin escape onto his face.

Thunderbark's words ran through my head over and over again. I then put together what he was trying to tell me. Unexpectedly, Thunderbark turned into the parking lot for a gun and pawn shop.

"Why are we stopping here?" I asked him looking around.

"Your friends are only human; they need a way to protect themselves if they run into trouble."

"From what I recall, roller coasters cannot be harmed by guns."

"Right, but there is someway they can be." He said as he climbed out. Thunderbark entered the store, I watched him for several seconds before I turned my attention to something else. I saw Thunderbark talking to the clerk at the counter about guns. Sly's truck was parked behind my Hummer; I decided to speak with them until Thunderbark returned.

I opened the door and closed it as I moved to the driver's side of Sly's truck. Buddy sat in the passenger seat eating old candy as Sly fooled around with his GPS.

"Hey guys." I said leaning on the door.

"Oh, hello - Railrunner." Sly smiled.

"First thing first, don't let anybody hear my real name. Just use Rodney when we are in public." I said glancing around nervously to see if anybody caught that.

"Whoops, sorry! You slept a while, does being a you know what, rob of sleep sometimes?" He asked almost whispering.

"It really depends on what I am doing." I laughed.

"What does it feel like?" Buddy asked with an even softer tone.

"Well, it's wild and crazy, but you get used to it after a while." I replied.

"Do you ever regret it?" He continued, his question making me think deeply.

"Sometimes." I said after a brief second. Then out of the corner of my eye I saw a man in his middle twenties look into the window of the Hummer.

"What does he think he is doing?" Sly whispered not taking his eyes off the man.

Then another man walked up to the driver's side of my car. He too, looked through the window. Then his hand slowly reached for the handle. I growled and strutted for him, my hands trembling, I knew I did not have much time left.

"What in the hell do you think you are doing!" I said into the man's face.

"A little game of what you see is what you get," he laughed.

"I'm not the guy that you would want to mess with, especially not at this hour." I said almost reliving the mall incident over. Merrylegs and Static climbed out of the car in alarm, Sly and Buddy rushed to my side. Thunderbark finally looked out to see me in an impending scuffle, he ran out to my aid.

"Do you honestly think you are outnumbered?" the man said as ten others stepped out of the shadows. I looked to the sky to see it fading; they did not even know what they were getting into, more so what they were dealing with.

"I'm warning you, it is not very smart to be tangling with us." I continued. The man only looked at me and laughed. Thunderbark glared at them with one of his stern and serious gazes.

"You should listen to him, you boys better run along home, it is gonna be dark soon." He said in agreement.

"The Altered love the night life." The man sneered, using his gang name.

"The Twisted do too. I live for the night and the presence of the moon." I said almost laughing again.

The man just gave me a strange look. He then turned to his colleague to say something, but he only pulled a fast one by slamming Thunderbark against the Hummer. It all spread like a wildfire as a huge brawl rang out between the two sides. Merrylegs punched a man in the jaw as Static got kicked in the ribs. Buddy and Sly were pinned against the wall while Clare was in a catfight with a woman follower. Thunderbark stood over a man with a knife pressed to his throat. I watched the fight go on, I glanced to the sky; the sun was sinking below the hills. Our time was coming ever so quickly.

I suddenly turned to see the barrel of a gun pointed at my face, an all too familiar sight to me.

"Not so tough are you now pretty boy!"

I smirked at his face, and then like lightning I grabbed the man's hand and twisted it; throwing his gun from his hand. He cried in agony and grasped his broken wrist. I then elbowed him in the nose making him fall backward in to the alleyway. The man quickly got to his feet, his nose was bleeding all over his face and his wrist was turning black and blue. He swung at me with his good arm, missing as I ducked as the last second. I turned and kicked him face first into the wall. I charged to give him another blow, but he pulled out his knife and slashed me across the chest. The pain stung horribly as my nerves reconfigured and rejoined. The man looked at my wound bewildered, his brown eyes bored into mine.

"What - are you?"

"I have many names, but most call me a monster." I hissed as I slammed the pest against the wall. He hung there helplessly a few inches from the ground. The man opened his mouth to utter a few more words.

"I ask again, and I want a better answer, WHAT are you!" He demanded.

"I told you before, a human rises with the sun, but I rise with the moon. I am a mere immortal soul that feasts on your fears and flesh."

"Why won't you answer my question correctly!"

"Why won't you just shut up?" I mocked.

"Just tell me!"

I looked to see that the sun had set fully. I felt a surge of power run through my body as a smile of triumph ran across my face.

"I warned you." I said holding back cries of agony. I doubled over in pain as the mysterious man made a run for it, I tried to go after him, but I was too occupied by my transformation.

I watched as my veins rippled like sidewinders beneath my skin. My brain burned like it was full of acid as my back split to make way for my rows of seats. I felt my multiple limbs protrude through delicate human skin. Locks of luscious black hair fell out as my nose became a long snout. I grew as my skin became red metal that stretched along my body. I became more and more like the thrill ride that I really was, and then every human characteristic on the outside and some internally, faded. I was a roller coaster once again.

I stood upright and howled, signaling a threat to any mortal that dared to mess with me. I suddenly felt a soft hand along my side; I easily recognized it as Clare's.

"We must leave Railrunner; the police will be here any minute!"

"Screw the police!" I said angrily.

"Railrunner look out!" Clare said suddenly pointing in front of her. I looked to see an eighteen wheeler speeding right for us; we had no time to get out of the way neither. Acting on instinct, I wrapped my tail around and over Clare. I only had enough time to see that the man that I was just fighting with was driving. I held up my wheels and waited for the impact of the truck. When it did, my body felt like it had been hit by a tidal wave. My wheels screamed as the truck pushed me by sheer force into the wall. I shoved the truck back in return, tiring to keep it from crushing Clare who was still screaming underneath my tail.

The air began to smell of burnt rubber, badly. It was overpowering, making everyone cough and gag. I knew this had to end; it couldn't go on any longer and I wasn't letting it. I forced a roar that was overheard by even the truck's massive engine. I then set the motor ablaze. The truck caught on fire; there was little time before the flames reached the gas tank. I turned around and swiftly picked up Clare. I looked back to see that I was too late; I doubled over to shield Clare just as the semi exploded.

When the smoke cleared from the gigantic blast, I got up to see that Clare was unharmed to my relief.

"Thanks for saving me." She uttered still a bit shaken.

"Why do you always get yourself into trouble!" I laughed.

She looked at me bluntly for a minute, I started to fear that I had said something wrong. To my surprise she began to laugh along with me, but our moment was short lived as sirens sounded very near us.

"Thunderbark and the others!" I said putting Clare onto my back and running for the clearing. I stopped completely when I saw Thunderbark arching his back and snarling at dozens of cops.

"Stay down." I whispered to Clare. She immediately obeyed as I joined Thunderbark. Every officer seemed to gasp in surprise as they glanced from Thunderbark to me. The white coaster then turned and began to speak harshly under his breath.

"Screw the police! What the hell were you thinking? Now you got all of us in trouble!"

I only growled in response. I roared loudly again, hoping to scare them off without harming any of them. That did not work because they fired. We immediately ran. Sly and Buddy escaped in my Hummer with all of our belongings, including mine. Us rides ran off into the night, and I was expecting Thunderbark to be very angry with me.

Chapter 57
Fire & Ice

We continued to run until the sirens faded off into the night. We stopped to pause in the middle of an empty street. I controlled my breath as I rested for a split second, but out of the corner of my eye I saw Thunderbark narrowing his at me. The icy blue in them turned as dark as the deep abyss. It was apparent he was very angry at me and could snap at any moment. He was holding in his rage and soon he was about to release all of it upon me.

"Where to now?" Merrylegs asked.

For the first time Thunderbark did not step up and say anything, he stayed in his own cone of silence. I looked around at the street signs. The intersection was very clear in my mind, especially because I was on the road that I took to my old workplace.

"We can stay at the old cake factory." I suggested, waiting for Thunderbark to speak up, but to my dismay he didn't.

"Isn't it still in business, Railrunner?" Static asked.

"No, they shut it down. That is why we got fired." I said. My mind suddenly coming back to the day that I began to look for work, right after I heard the two horrible last words your boss says to you.

"Let's go then. We need to get lost quick if we do not want the cops to find us." Merrylegs said as Thunderbark cringed at her last words.

The factory turned out to be about three miles down the road. We now stood at the edge of its chain-linked fence looking up at. It was not a pretty or spectacular sight. The whole perimeter was overgrown with weeds. No car sat in the parking lot that was now scarred with cracks in the pavement. It was clear that from the view through the cracked windows that the machines were rusted. The whole factory looked to have been abandoned for years instead of months.

I stood and waved a set of wheels before the chain link fence. It pulled away from its ties in a roll. I then ducked under and led everyone inside the factory's grounds. Sly parked the Hummer behind a gathering of thick trees, and then he grabbed our belongings from the trunk. I immediately took my bag from him and went to the back door. Thunderbark followed me silently; his head still hung low holding it all back. I expected him to go off like a bomb any second as I entered the warm building and switched on the lights.

Every machine was covered in cobwebs and dust. Everything seemed to be untouched. I hung my bag on a nearby hook as everyone else entered the factory. Looking among the gears and conveyor belts brought back memories, memories that only came faintly.

"Whelp, make yourselves at home." I mumbled out as I turned to see Thunderbark staring at my face with his wheels clenched in fist. I sighed, I had been right.

"Go ahead and say it, you know you want to." I said sternly and also grabbing everyone's attention. Thunderbark then laid a wheel firmly on my chest and glared into my eyes with solid anger.

"*You have got to be the dumbest roller coaster I've ever met!*" he hissed.

"What the hell is your problem, Thunderbark!"

"*My problem? My problem is I'm tired of you being a smartass! All you ever do is drink and choose to do the stupidest of decisions!*"

"Shut up Thunderbark!" I retorted.

"*No! The stunt you pulled back there delayed us and put every innocent human in danger!*"

"FOR YOUR INFORMATION I WAS SAVING CLARE! IT IS NOT MY FAULT THAT WE GOT CAUGHT UP IN THE SITUATION!" I yelled at him. My wheels were trembling in anger, I tried to walk away to cool off, but Thunderbark started it up again.

"YOU KNOW RAILRUNNER, I SOMETIMES WONDER HOW YOU GOT TO BE SO STUBBORN!"

"HMMM - WHY DON'T YOU ASK THE GUY THAT ACTIVATED ME! AFTER ALL, HE KNEW ME EVER SINCE I WAS BORN!" I screamed back at him.

"I'M TIRED OF YOU ACTING THIS WAY!" he roared.

"I SHOULD HAVE LEFT YOUR ASS ROT IN THAT CELL!" I snarled.

"MAYBE!"

I turned around to face him again, a lump in my throat formed as I prepared to yell again.

"I DON'T KNOW WHAT MY MOTHER WAS THINKING WHEN SHE MADE *YOU* MY GODFATHER! BECAUSE YOU SURE AREN'T ONE!"

Thunderbark went silent; he only looked at me in disbelief. He then turned his attention to the floor while I breathed hard from the argument. The white roller coaster then went into an office and pulled a few desks together and lay on top of them. He then dimmed the lights in the small room. Everyone's eyes were wearing into me. I turned and snorted in disgust, and then I leaped from the first to the second floor. I didn't look back as I entered my boss's old observation tower. I sat in the corner like a kid with a dunce cap on, and it sure felt like it too.

"What have I just done!"

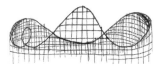

For the past hour I layed on the iron floor under my cloak with my left eye barely peeking out as I rolled an empty fire extinguisher back and forth across the room. During the passed time I found myself bingeing on old cake. It wasn't the greatest by any standard, but I could stomach anything. It was somewhat funny that I never did binge eating during my years as a human; guess it was a roller coaster habit, after all my stress levels had been through the roof lately. However my thoughts on what I had said to Thunderbark earlier consumed nearly all of the time I spent grieving.

As I sat there pondering on my next move, I heard footsteps coming up the metal stairs. Could it possibly be Thunderbark? Couldn't be because the steps were light. Static hated going up stairs so it was not him. It was probably either Merrylegs or Clare. Within seconds they both entered the room cautiously.

"Railrunner?" asked Clare looking around the corner.

"Come in." I said not moving a muscle. Clare and Merrylegs walked inside nervously. They both stopped and stood in the center of the cramped room.

"One of you can go tell Thunderbark that he can kill me if he wants." I said rolling onto my back. I moved the trench coat out of the way to see them both staring at me with their eyes full of worry. Clare came over and sat on my chest, as Merrylegs moved even closer.

"We are certainly not going to tell him to kill you Railrunner."

"I started the whole thing! I caused us to lose precious time! Now that I screwed up, the cops know that there are more of us!" I said in protest.

"Railrunner! Get a hold of yourself and calm down!" Merrylegs said in return.

I took a deep breath and sighed. "What is Thunderbark up to?"

"He has just been reading a book of his." Clare said softly.

"Thunderbark hates me." I said crossing my arms.

"He is just upset." Merrylegs said.

"I need to apologize; I caused the whole mess and the argument. Merrylegs can you tell Thunderbark that I wish to do that? Basically ask him for his permission?"

Merrylegs nodded and trotted out of the room. Clare lay down fully onto me, her head about a foot from my chin. She looked around the room at the empty cake boxes.

"Did you eat all of those?" she said almost laughing.

"Yeah, I'm guilty."

"How come you ate the cake and not my pancakes?"

"You know about that!"

"Yes, Huck got a belly ache."

"I guess I was upset and started to consume whatever was available."

Clare began to laugh again, and then it became silent once more. All we could hear was the scuffling around by our troop downstairs. I sighed and let my head fall backwards against a metal support. Clare rolled over onto her belly, her frail body rising up and down along with my chest as I inhaled and exhaled.

"I bet Thunderbark is too angry to speak with me," I said starting the conversation again.

"I think, in my opinion, Thunderbark seems like a forgiver." Clare said.

I breathed heavily, my chest rumbled as my breath blew Clare's hair back. It hovered for a split second before it fell loosely around her broad shoulders. Her nose flared and she waved her hand around.

"Your breath isn't all that pleasant, it kind of smells bitter, no offence." Clare giggled.

"I know don't rub it in." I laughed. I didn't mind Clare saying my breath stunk; we sort of did stuff like that to each other all the time.

"Oh well, as I was saying I think Thunderbark just got mad because he cares about you."

I raised an eyebrow. "He sort of has a funny way of showing it sometimes." I replied.

"If I remember correctly, you said that the rides from Amusement Park Between come from the real world when they are put into storage because they are no longer used, am I correct?"

"Yes, right on the dot."

"Well, technically speaking, Thunderbark never, you know, had a true dad. Other than the guy who kept him, but I guess that doesn't count."

"Are you saying that Thunderbark is trying to be a good guardian, but he doesn't know if he is doing it correctly?" I questioned.

"Yeah, he seems unsure about it. Kind of like he doesn't know if he is doing it right or wrong."

"I see, it is sort of like trying to tell the difference between fire and ice."

"You are funny, but you're on the right track."

Merrylegs suddenly walked into the cramped room. She showed no expression across her face.

"Well?" I asked curiously.

"I think he is still a little upset, but he did say yes."

I nodded in response as Clare climbed off of me. I stood upright and popped my back. I then exited the tower with Merrylegs and Clare not far behind. I walked in a trance down the iron stairs trying to concur up some words to say to Thunderbark.

Chapter 58
No Trespassing

I motioned toward the office door; the words I was to speak repeated themselves inside my head like an incantation. My blood ran cold within my piping hot veins as I grasped the old door knob. I slowly peeked my head inside to see that Thunderbark held his great head low over a thick book. His small beard and long eyebrows draped downward making him look old even though he was immortal. Thunderbark's overall appearance made him look like a Chinese master.

"Yes, Railrunner?" he said finally realizing that I was there.

"I have something to say," I muttered.

"You may go ahead." Thunderbark replied looking up.

"I'm really sorry for what I said earlier. I am just - extremely stressed out right now about everything that is going to happen."

Thunderbark looked into my eyes with his. Their icy blue coloring began to return. Unexpectedly, a small smile crept across Thunderbark's face.

"I can understand why you act so crude sometimes; I know what you are talking about so I am not angry. You have gone through a lot Railrunner, and I accept your apology. I'm very glad you brought up the courage to do so."

"Thanks for understanding."

"You're welcome. Now, I'm going to share with you a new discovery I have just come across. I believe it will bring your hopes up." Thunderbark said turning the pages of the book. I watched the crinkled paper fall repeatedly as he flipped through them. Then Thunderbark stopped on page five hundred. Two words that were in bold letters pronounced their selves on the page very clearly.

Vadaier Sorum

I knew only one of the words. Sorum meant curse, but I had no clue to what the other word meant.

"What is this Thunderbark?" I asked.

"As everyone knows, no human can enter Amusement Park Between, but I came across a curse that only a coaster can perform. Railrunner, you have the power to turn Clare into -."

"A roller coaster." I said finishing his sentence. The words catching in my mouth.

"Yes."

My mind started to race again. Clare had a chance! She could live! Clare could come to my world! Be with me and have the gift of immortality! My own kind!

"I'm going to carry that out as soon as possible," I said a little to wrapped up in my own thoughts.

"I'm afraid Railrunner; it does not work that way."

"What do you mean?" I said thudding to reality.

"It is a bit more complicated than one would think. There are certain standards to the curse."

"What are they?" I said leaning against an exposed pipe.

"First of all, Clare has to be willing to give up of being human blood. Remember this, she cannot ever go back! What is done can never be undone!"

"Got it."

"Second, the curse can only be performed on her dying breath."

"So -," I said sliding down onto the floor. "I have to let her suffer before she -."

"I'm afraid so, Railrunner."

It became dead quiet in the musty room. I sat and thought about the situation, racking my wheels on the floor as I did so. Thunderbark looked at me, waiting for an answer. I turned my attention to him and nodded as my response.

"How do I actually turn her into a roller coaster?"

"Railrunner you have to - bite her." He said swallowing hard.

"Bite her?" I questioned, not sure if I had heard him right.

"Yes."

I thought hard about the fact. It felt so criminal to bite someone so innocent, more so my girlfriend. I wished that biting her was extraneous. Yet, I had to, I could not let Clare squander away! Our love did not have to be forbidden once my tooth pierced her soft skin.

"I'll do it Thunderbark." I said at last.

"Good, I think you will be very happy with your decision later. Now here are a few things you might want to know. Usually when a roller coaster bites its victim on their last breath, the human will turn into the exact type and color. A red however, is very different. You get to choose the type of coaster and color."

"Because as always, there can only be one red."

"Exactly." Thunderbark said with a big grin across his face.

"I'm very glad you told me about this Thunderbark. I'm happy there is a way." I thanked him.

Suddenly my leather began to prickle. I heard steps on the rooftop, and they were not ordinary, I recognized them before. This time I would be thirsty for revenge. I growled deeply in my chest. Thunderbark looked at me in alarm. He too began to listen intently, and then he started to growl along with me.

"Looks like we have a visitor." He said with a grim expression on his face.

"It's Freakshow." I said storming out of the office. Thunderbark followed close behind me. We entered the factory floor and everyone turned their attention to us. They stood there assuming something was wrong, and indeed there was.

"How do you know it is her?" Thunderbark questioned.

"Let's just say I have a good memory." I replied looking up at the tin ceiling.

"What is going on, Railrunner?" Clare said running to me frightened.

"Clare you need to find somewhere safe to hide. Just do it and don't ask why!" I said as the footsteps stopped. Clare nodded and ran for safety along with Buddy and Sly. I sniffed; I could now smell her awful scent. I prepared for a sudden attack; just in case Ironwheel was with her. It became silent and eerie, nothing moved a muscle, and all I could hear was my shallow breathing and the rapid pounding of my heart.

Without warning, the tin roof caved in and Freakshow landed on top of the oven laughing maniacally.

"Only a roller coaster can kill a roller coaster," she mocked.

"I'm sorry, but I am allergic to your bullshit," I said through clenched teeth. "Where is Ironwheel!"

"Awww, the great red is a bit eager, but anything for my fans. Ironwheel is not hunting you down, he knows your rage will draw you to him." She said as she made her voice elusive.

I quickly read Freakshow's mind, she was actually telling the truth. Her ignorant words made me angrier by the second.

"I'm surprised you lived *freak*, but are you ready for round two?" I snickered.

"*More than ready!*" Freakshow hissed.

I shot forward like a jet and hit her full force. The collision made both of us fly back into a pile of unused boxes. I quickly stood up and moved the boxes out of my way and prepared to face her again. She staggered to her feet, slightly woozy from the heavy blow. She turned to me with a smirk wiped across her face.

"You are quite the heavyweighter," she laughed.

"Glad you think so. I'm good at wrestling." I replied. "Now let me show you how good I am at fencing!" I shouted as I extracted my long claws.

Freakshow quickly exposed her jagged steel claws. We swung at each other at the same time, but our claws interlocked within themselves. I yanked them free and cut a set of Freakshow's off in the process. She stared at the damage that was done for a split second; then she shrieked like a banshee.

"You will pay dearly for that!" Freakshow roared. Then she unexpectedly grinned. To my surprise out of the other wheel sets of her second car grew more claws. Freakshow laughed deep in her throat as she pointed them to me. I found myself staring at Freakshow in disbelief. I had never seen THAT before, perhaps it was her special talent.

"What's the matter, Railrunner? Scared of your demise?"

"You are really starting to piss me off."

Freakshow didn't reply, she swung her claws at me, but at the last second I shifted out of the way. Her middle claw went into a big red button on a control panel, making the factory roar to life.

I realized that I could use this to my advantage. I knew what made these machines tick!

"Good thing I'm an engineer!" I said charging back to the factory floor. I jumped on a conveyor belt. Freakshow soon joined me on the assembly line. She snarled menacingly, her restraints vibrating in anger. I quickly pulled a wire that hung above me, flour rained down onto Freakshow, making her unable to see.

I quickly moved again, suddenly instinct took over as I heard Freakshow follow me. I weaved between giant five ton gas tanks that sat in rows towards the back of the factory. Freakshow slowed her pace and stood in the middle of the walkway.

"Where are you red!" she said as she shook the flour off of her.

I smiled to myself. It was predator against prey again. Dueling the enemy once more. A pure bred against a mixed breed. A classic case of good verses evil.

"Over here mutt." I said darting just before Freakshow moved to my previous hiding place. I was positioned behind her now in back of one of the large tanks. It seemed as if I was reliving the whole incident of the ordeal I had with Captain Vick in the garage. This time however, I wasn't playing with matches; I was fooling with a gun.

I watched Freakshow for several seconds; she looked frantically around for me. She snarled in frustration. Suddenly Merrylegs stood in the middle of the aisle. Why was she being so silly! Merrylegs stood up to roller coasters as if they were statues, more or less me when I was in a foul mood. To Freakshow, in her view, she was nothing but a toy.

Merrylegs looked over to where I was occult, and then she reared back and neighed loudly. Freakshow then spun around to face her, and I realized Merrylegs was setting her up. I placed my wheels under the tanker before me; gathering strength, I shoved it toward the mismatched coaster. The gas tank slid across the floor like a freight train, then it caught her by surprise and pinned her to the wall.

Before she could free herself, I ran out of hiding and grasped her shoulders. I flung Freakshow into the main room again. She sat up quickly and prepared to strike, but Thunderbark suddenly appeared behind her. He grabbed an iron chain and wrapped it around her neck, and then Thunderbark pulled out one of the rifles he purchased at the pawn shop earlier, except that it had been modified. Thunderbark fired the repurposed weapon into her arm. I watched in awe as her blood leaked out all over the floor, how come it wasn't healing? Then I remembered that Thunderbark spoke of a way to kill a coaster with a gun, could this have been it?

Thunderbark held Freakshow firmly, she trashed wildly trying to free herself, but she was only making it worse. I walked casually up to Freakshow and stood towering above her. She stopped struggling and looked at me with her strange eyes. I raised my claws and aimed them toward her heart. She watched my every move, and this time she was actually afraid.

"Do you really have the courage to kill me, Railrunner?" she questioned with a bizarre expression on her face. I did not reply; I only raised my claws higher.

"Do you really want to stab me in the heart like I did your mother?" The comment made revenge flow though my veins, but still I did not reply.

"To bad about her, she was a thrill to kill." Freakshow laughed quietly.

I roared loudly in pure rage and brought my claws down. They penetrated through her metal hide and into her cold heart. She let out no cries of agony or despair. Freakshow simply fell backward into a puddle of her own blood.

"It was a thrill to kill you." I finally answered.

Chapter 59
Risky Business

I stood there over Freakshow's blood soaked body. The last few words she said before her death angered me to no extent. My mother's death now seemed like a constant encumbrance now that I finally learned and understood it completely. One by one I had destroyed the Fallen incessantly, and now there was only one left, the dreaded Ironwheel. I wanted the evil ones blood on my wheels now more than ever.

"Nice work Railrunner." Thunderbark congratulated me. "Now it seems that there is just one more vermin to exterminate."

"Ironwheel." I hissed. Thunderbark looked at me worried.

"What is the -."

"I'm suffering from a severe case of bipolarness. Revenge is all that is on my mind right now. I'll get it soon and I will make damn sure I do!"

"Railrunner, remember your temper and language."

"I don't give a rip about my temper." I growled.

"Railrunner!" Thunderbark replied in one of his disgusted tones. I sighed and took a deep breath and let it come out in a long satisfied whoosh.

"Sorry, I guess I am a bit upset with what Freakshow said. I have a question for you though, how did you make that gun actually harm her?"

"I didn't really do anything to the gun; I just did something to the bullets." He chuckled.

"What? How in the hell did you bypass the principle of what kills a roller coaster?"

"Again Railrunner, I didn't. I made my own bullets. I took an ordinary knife, not my claws, and cut bits and pieces of my metal off."

"That was dumb."

"No it wasn't, I knew it would grow back in a matter of seconds since I used something other than myself to detach it. While you were up in your tower, I secretly shaped these so they would fit in the gun barrel." He said pulling out one of the white bullets. They were very well crafted for a wood coaster who could not bend metal.

"Nifty." I finally spoke.

"Now, I suggest we all get some rest. I will dispose of Freakshow's body so no human or machine can find her." Thunderbark said as he began to pull her body outside.

"Do you need help?" I asked grabbing her tail.

"No, Railrunner, you need your sleep." Thunderbark sighed.

"Fine then." I said laying her tail back down. I bid everyone good night and headed up the iron stairs. Clare followed me at my side. She suddenly grasped my wheels like holding hands. She squeezed very tightly as I looked at her astonished.

"Can I stay with you?" she whispered.

"Of course, why?"

"I'm scared."

An hour later Clare was asleep on my chest, my warm metal comforting her. I however, was awake thinking; pondering up my next idea. My brain filled with many plans, but none of them seemed to be the solution. Clare started to quiver in her sleep. I put my arms around her to serve as blanket and Clare seemed to sigh in relief. I then returned to my ever flowing thoughts. Suddenly I came up with one that just might work, but it was hazardous.

The following morning I awoke with Clare still on my bare chest. She suddenly began to stir, and then Clare got up and yawned.

"This is awkward," she said quickly climbing off of me. She flipped her hair as I got up and put on my hoodie. I zipped it up and then ran my fingers through my black hair.

"Did you sleep well at all?" I asked her.

"I actually sleep good even though I was on metal that was as hot as an oven." She smiled.

"Wait a minute - are you calling me hot?"

"Ahem." Said a voice. Both Clare and I spun around quickly to see Merrylegs standing in the doorway.

"How long were you watching?" I asked.

"A few minutes before you woke up." She smiled.

"You're creepy." I replied.

"What I just heard was creepy." Merrylegs retorted. "Thunderbark and the others are downstairs waiting on you both to join us for breakfast."

"Thank you Merrylegs, we will be there in a second." Clare said cheerfully. Merrylegs then nodded and exited the tower. Clare then turned to me slightly giggling. "As we were saying, yes I did."

"So I am attractive then?"

"I thought we decided that a long time ago."

"Oh, that's right we did! I remember me saying that you were beautiful."

"I remember that." Clare said with a smile. Then I thought of what Thunderbark told me last night, now would be the time to ask her.

"Hey Clare?"

"Yes, Railrunner?"

"If you were a roller coaster what type and color would you be?"

"Well - I would be a steel coaster and I would be light purple. Why did you ask?"

"I was just wondering that's all."

"Hmmm, do you want to head downstairs now?" she asked.

"Yeah, I'm starving." I replied as I followed her out of the tower. Did Clare want to be a roller coaster? I should have made my bribe more straightforward, yet Clare answered my question. Maybe she was willing to give up being human after all. I should get some more out of her first.

"Clare?" I whispered as we stood right outside the tower door.

"Yes, do you have another question for me?" she grinned.

"Kind of. If you had the choice of being human and being a roller coaster; which would you take?"

"Why are you asking me these questions Railrunner?" she demanded.

"I just would like to know."

"Well, most of the time I do wish I was a coaster to tell you the truth." She said as she started her way down the stairs. In the back of my mind only one word pronounced itself, perfect.

Thunderbark and the rest of our alliance sat in the conference room at the far corner of the cake factory. Thunderbark sat the end of the large table as the head honcho. Next to him was Merrylegs and Static. Buddy and Sly were across from each other. Clare and I sat side by side. I looked down to see that a plate of soup was in front of us. I grasped the spoon and dipped it into the broth. I raised it to my mouth and sipped it up. My taste buds actually found a liking to it.

"What is this?" I asked Thunderbark.

"My specialty." He replied grinning.

"It is good, what is in it?" Clare asked.

"Well, it is just a little bit of deer meat form a buck that I saw running around last night." He said as Clare froze at the sound of his words. "In the broth there juices from a cow's gut, I butchered him last night also." He continued as Clare's color began to drain from her face. She held up her hand to signal Thunderbark to stop.

"How can you eat this!" she said.

Thunderbark simply laughed one of his belly laughs. "This is a delicacy to us, and real world meat is perfect for this dish."

"Thank you Thunderbark." Clare started unexpectedly. "It was nice of you to make me something." She said with a small smile.

"You don't have to eat it; there are some frozen meals in the fridge back there. I checked the dates and they are all good."

Clare nodded and left the room. I looked down to see that I had already consumed the whole bowl. I then cleared my throat and prepared to break my plan to Thunderbark.

"Do you wish to speak, Railrunner?" he asked looking up from his plate.

"As a matter of fact I do. I have a plan that could help us find Ironwheel." I said standing and pacing to and fro.

"Go ahead then."

"Okay, Ironwheel is waiting for me; I think I know just how to locate him."

"How?"

"Well - we need some help from Captain Vick."

"WHAT!" Thunderbark said standing up suddenly.

"Think about it! Vick has troops and forces crawling all over the city. If I could strike a deal with him, his grudge on us could -."

"Get to the point." Thunderbark demanded.

"All right, I could trick Vick into helping us by telling him everything he wants to know."

"That is so stupid!"

"I'm not telling him the truth Thunderbark, I'm lying about it. To convince him even more, I'll give him one of the guns you modified and put in the wrong bullets."

Thunderbark was silent; he scratched his scruffy chin as he thought quietly to himself.

"It could work." He said at last. "But I think you are going to have to carry this out."

"Trust me Thunderbark; I know exactly what I'm doing." I said grinning from ear to ear.

Within the next hour, I was ready. The large gun was tucked away inside my bag and I carried a cell phone to contact Thunderbark to keep him posted. I walked into the crisp morning air and across the cracked concrete. The Hummer was still in the exact place that it was the night before. After waltzing through the weeds, I opened the door and started the engine. I then put the SUV into gear and drove it through the hole in the fence we had made the previous evening.

I tried to adjust the seat belt properly, but it was quite difficult with the real coaster gun tucked away inside my hoodie. It was a good thing I had it on safety so it wouldn't shoot on accident and kill me. It felt as if I was an ex con, with loaded guns and an armored car at my disposal, plus my secret weapon that was well hidden.

My decision was to look for a pay phone so Captain Vick wouldn't be able to trace my call. I drove about eight miles or so and still there was none in sight. Perhaps the reason why was because I was in the richest part of town and everyone was expected to have cell phones. If I drove a few miles further, I could have a better chance. But suddenly my plan changed when I saw a lonely old pay phone in the middle of a deserted parking lot. Without hesitation, I pulled in and got out of my car. I looked around before taking the phone off the receiver and putting some spare change into the coin slot. I wanted to laugh as I dialed the number; it was like I was making a prank call. I wasn't actually pranking him on the phone; I was just pulling a fast one. Finally someone answered.

"Hello how may I help you?" asked the voice at the other end of the line.

"I would like to speak to Captain Vick, it is an emergency."

"May I know your name sir?"

I thought for a second and smiled.

"Rodney Philips." I said almost snickering into the receiver.

The voice went silent. Then I heard a great deal of scuffling around and a small whisper of an argument. At last my target came to the phone.

"Yes? "

"This is Railrunner." I said.

"Nice to hear from you coaster," Captain Vick replied.

"It is a thrill to hear your voice Captain, it has been so long." I said with my voice being as smooth as velvet.

"Why are you calling me?" he said harshly.

"I have a proposition actually - for you Captain."

"What kind?" he demanded.

"One that you will find satisfying. I suggest you keep recording so you can remember."

"Fine, tell me your demands, Railrunner." He sighed.

"Wonderful! I will tell you everything you wish to know, including how to kill a roller coaster. I just need for you to meet me in Mystic

Park - *alone*. Under the steel coaster at eight o'clock sharp. Remember, no one else except you, I only trust you, Captain." I finished.

"I will." He said deeply into the receiver. I smiled silently to myself and hung up the phone. I then pulled out my cell and dialed Thunderbark's number. While it rang I climbed into the Hummer and started it again, its rumbling purr echoing into the woods.

"Well, Railrunner?" Thunderbark answered.

"Stage one is complete. Captain Vick was easier to reel in than I thought."

"Good, what was your stage two?"

"I'll get him to meet me in Mystic Park tonight, that way I am at my most powerful point."

"Nice one, very clever on your part. You are heading to Mystic Park now?"

"Yes," I said pulling out of the parking lot and onto the road. "I'm actually very close to it, probably a few miles."

"Good, call me when you find out anything else. I wish you luck, Railrunner."

"Thanks." I replied clicking the phone shut. I stopped at a red light and waited. A police car pulled up beside me. I quickly put on some sunglasses and a baseball cap, that way if the officer looked over he couldn't know it was me. I turned up the radio and started to listen to music, making me seem like a normal human. The officer looked over, only to glance at me enjoying myself for a split second before the light changed green. He quickly sped away without suspecting me of anything.

As I drove I kept my accessories and music on, just in case any more police showed up. I started to think of how I was to word things. Captain Vick paid to close attention to details; I would have to be less specific but to the point. I tapped my fingers on the steering wheel trying to think. After a few minutes I contemplated some pretty convincing lies; just as I pulled into the employee parking lot of Mystic Park.

I creaked the door open and stepped onto the park's turf. The classic ripple of pain went across my back as my fingers and toes tingled. I looked to the steel coaster track, my heart started to beat faster.

"This is going to be interesting."

Chapter 60
Friend or Foe?

I hurried to the trunk of the Hummer and grabbed the bag containing the false gun. I threw the sash around my shoulder and slammed the trunk shut. I then walked back to the driver's side and snagged the keys from the ignition. I walked up to the tall chain link fence that surrounded the park's perimeter. Normally, I would have climbed up the fence in less than two seconds, but in this case that was impossible because Captain Vick had to have a way in. So there was no other choice but to open the back gate and keep it unlocked.

I easily located the entrance and shoved my key into the rusted lock. It finally snapped and the gate reluctantly creaked open. I entered silently, discreet like a ninja. I took one last look over my shoulder to see if any one followed or saw me, with no one in sight, I ventured deep into Mystic Park.

My muscles strengthened beneath my skin as I moved between the silent rides of Mystic Park. At this time of year, the park was usually buzzing with employees that worked on assembling new additions, but due to my presence and screw-ups, the park delayed any constriction on new rides. That might have been a good idea on their part.

My keen ears picked up a rustling noise not to far from where I was standing. I quickly pulled my hood over my head and pulled out my gun. I started to move quicker among the shadows towards the coaster track. I veered into a dark alley between two gift shops. Before I made it to the end, a guard walked out in front of me.

"What are you doing here!" he demanded raising his club and waving it around like a caveman. I charged to him, but before he could swing I put the gun to his forehead. I watched in amusement as beads of sweat rolled down his face.

"Don't make any sudden moves," I demanded. The frightened guard simply nodded. This poor man could not see Captain Vick and I this evening, I would have to dispose of him. Like lightning, I flipped the gun into the air. I then used the handle and clobbered him on the side of the head. The guard fell to the ground knocked out cold. I flipped the gun around and stuck it through my belt and then pulled out my cell phone.

"Yes?" Thunderbark answered.

"Hey, why didn't you tell me there were guards here!" I said whispering angrily into the phone.

"Guards? There isn't supposed to be any walking around this time of year. I guess they stepped up security since you arrived. Do you see any more?"

"Not at the moment, no."

"Well, there is probably only one or two; Mystic Park never goes overboard with guards in the cold months." He said.

"I hope you are right, Thunderbark."

"Just in case I'm wrong - I would hurry to the rails." He said sternly.

"Right, thanks. I will keep in touch."

"Copy that," he replied hanging up.

I was alone again in the park. Thunderbark was right, I needed to get to the track fast. It would be much easier to do things as a roller coaster than it would as a human.

I started to jog; I had a funny feeling in the pit of my stomach that there were more of them than I expected. I rounded a corner to discover that I had a good reason to have a hunch. Four security guards stood in a circle discussing matters. I froze, but they had not seen me yet. I snuck quietly ahead, unfortunately I wasn't looking where I was going and hit a trash can. It banged on the ground loudly and all of the waste spilled out onto the walk. My head shot up to see all of the men's eyes on me.

"Excuse me sir, what are you doing here?" a chubby guard spoke as he walked to me. The others followed him welding clubs.

"Well -," was all I could mutter through my lips.

"I ask you again, what are you doing here?" he said laying his club on my chest. I glared down at the plastic rod lying on my black hoodie. I smiled and raised my pierced eyebrow.

"You don't want to see me furious." I replied under my breath.

"All right no more funny stuff," the guard said as another handcuffed me behind the back. This charade was getting old.

"You boys probably don't want to be doing that." I said giving the head guard a deadly gaze. The guard pushed me from behind, forcing me to walk forward.

"Move your ass!" he said frustrated.

I had enough. I yanked my arms and broke the hand cuffs in two, their links falling to the concrete. I hit the man in front of me in the jaw, knocking him senseless to the ground. He placed his hand over his bloody mouth and his face twisted into a sour expression.

"Get him!" He yelled as I turned and ran for the track; hitting a man with his own club in the process. The remaining guards thundered after me as I moved blindly, my heart pounding like a drum.

I swerved in and out of buildings, leaping over crates and containers with precision. I could feel my limbs tingle and the Augu Ra grew hot against my bare chest. A shot of pain went down my spine rapidly. I stopped and ducked behind an information kiosk. I sat and went on with continuous labored breathing. My heart rate was sky high as my skin burned. My limbs tingled and shook as I saw my skin start to generate a red tint. I looked up to see that the rails were not but a few feet away. I forced myself to my feet, and glanced behind my back to see one of the guards running so fast that there was no way of stopping him. At the last second, I held out my arm. The ignorant fool ran straight into it, busting his nose.

Without hesitating for another second, I ran for the rails. I jumped high into the air and landed on my hands and feet onto the cold metal track. Immediately the change started to occur. My veins moved like snakes beneath my skin. The rattling and cracking of my ribs sounded as tall black seats rose from my back. My tailbone extended as my nose pushed forward into a snout. Fingers fused together forming my heavy wheels as my eyes turned to their scarlet and amber appearance. The change began to slow and soon it stopped. I arose slowly and turned to see the men cowering like toddlers.

I snarled from underneath my cloak's hood. Several of the men ran for their lives without looking back.

"You." That fat security guard said pointing. "You demon!"

"I told you that you would not want to see furious." I laughed. The guard jumped to his feet and sprinted away. Funny that I actually was letting one of my victims escape. It wouldn't matter if they called the real police since they were coming anyway. I pounced down from my perch and searched for a well suited meeting place. A few moments later, I found a nice shaded spot under the lift hill. I positioned myself and got as comfortable as I could possibly get. All I could to do now was wait for the Captain.

Finally night had fallen upon the real world. Fireflies flickered among the trees as bats swooped down from the dark sky to satisfy their hunger. The nights here, in the real world, did not seem as magical as the ones in Amusement Park Between. There, the night life was just as active as the day. Here however, there was nothing interesting to be heard but the occasional siren.

I stood, leaning against one of the supports. Time had ticked by and Captain Vick was nowhere to be seen.

"Why is he running behind!" I growled. I began to think, maybe Vick was planning a sneak attack. Could he have perhaps have troops lying in wait for the perfect time to strike? My negative thoughts were silenced once my ears picked the click of a car door.

I pulled my hood over my face, and then I zeroed in on where I heard the clang of the door. I allowed myself to hear Vick's solid footsteps on the pavement. I heard the crackle of his breath in the wind, and him scuffle around; finally finding the park's entrance. I felt myself smile with anticipation, I then tilted my head back and howled like a wolf; pushing the Captain's greed and curiosity further.

Captain Vick finally came into view, he wandered between buildings, and he kept his hand over a pistol that was in his holder. At last he spotted me and walked my way.

"Do you humans always show up fashionably late?" I said as he stopped about a meter from me.

"Evening Railrunner, to answer your question we actually obey the traffic laws." He replied chuckling a little.

"If you can't tell, I'm not made for the road." I sneered.

"Well, are you going to tell me everything I need to know?" Vick said as he crossed his arms.

"After you agree to - a bargain."

"What? I didn't -."

"Listen Captain, we need your help."

"Help?" he said confused.

"Yes. But first I need to know if I can trust you, remember I can tell if you are lying. Here are some facts that will guide you to the correct decision. One, you despise me tearing up this city. Two, is that you simply want me and my allies gone. But most of all, you want humans to be safe."

"Hmmm - still why I should help."

"There is an even greater threat that will destroy both our worlds if we don't stop him. His name is Ironwheel and he will enslave the human race and destroy the rest of my kind if he gets the chance." I said stern but gentle. Vick looked at me and I sensed a pinch of harmony in his green eyes. Perhaps I was getting somewhere.

"Tell me what I must do."

"Simple, I need you to patrol the city and call me if you see him." I said holding out a set of wheels. Captain Vick looked at them hesitating, then he placed his hand where I desired it to be, shaking on it.

"Nice to see a human choosing wisely." I grinned as I took my hood off.

"There are so many questions that I wish to ask you, Railrunner." He said.

"Yet my answers are limited." I replied. "I still have things to learn as well as you do."

"So be it." He replied. While he stood, I searched inside him. I looked for lie upon lie, but found none. The truth overpowered everything, Captain Vick was being serious. Suddenly instinct came back into play, but this time it was my better one. I would tell the Captain the truth, but not all of it on the behalf of Amusement Park Between. After all, it wasn't like he could read minds.

"What is it that you wish to know first?" I asked him.

"I want to know - where you came from."

"Tall order, but I can squeeze it in. Where to begin? Oh yes, in my world I am the only red roller coaster there is. I am the only one that was born and not built. The red is always destined for a purpose. It was made for stopping a terrible event that is to occur in our world's future. Now my story, Ironwheel came to power after he arrived at our world. He had the deepest of hatred for humans, but he also loved having control. He soon became king after he sent out his followers to kill any ride that stood in his way. A red roller coaster that was called Moonblood, had the destiny to kill him, but he failed. Ironwheel slaughtered him in a brutal battle."

"Hmmm, so where do you come in exactly?"

"Ten harrowing years went by and our world lived in fear. Then, err - after my mother's discovery that I was coming, the rides your men claimed to see last night watched over my mother until my arrival. However, for some odd reason the moment when the red is born, every coaster knows of its existence. Including damn Ironwheel. They took me to the real world to make sure I would be safe from the army that was sent after us. Thirty six years later, I'm here with my allies hunting him down."

"That's it then?"

"All of it that I know. Any questions?" I replied leaning on the support.

"Yes how did you're -."

"Don't ask because I don't even know how!"

"Forget it. You did say on the phone that you had a weapon that could kill a roller coaster, is there a way I could see it?" he asked lighting up a cigarette.

I pulled the large gun out of my bag, right away Vick's eyebrows went up. I had a really good lie conquered up for this one.

"This gun was made to kill only Ironwheel. You see, I am the only thing that can slay him and vice versa. The bullets are made from my metal so they will do damage." I said handing him the gun, holding back a snicker. Captain Vick tucked the gun away in a large briefcase that he had on him.

"One more thing," he said turning to me. "Where do all the rides in your world come from if they are not born like you?"

"I told you already Captain, my answers are limited and I still have a lot to learn." I replied knowing that he would ask that question.

"Very well then," he sighed. "Before I depart, can you give me a brief description of Ironwheel's appearance?"

"Certainly, he is a big black roller coaster with silver tattoos all over him. Ironwheel has numerous piercings, trust me you can't miss him."

"Thanks and your number, Railrunner?"

I smiled and tossed him the phone. He looked at it strangely.

"I'm not exactly listed, but I do like to tinker with things. That phone will only call my buddy's, just press one." I said with a smile. I watched the Captain put it into his bag and then he said farewell. He looked up for an answer, but I was already gone.

Fatal Attraction

He felt the life slipping from his grasp. He lay, staring up at his calling card, the moon. His body was in great pain far worse that any mortal could imagine. He shut his eyes in agony as the one he loved stood above him sobbing, and time ticked by slowly.

Chapter 61
Moondance

I continued to run through the trees, never stopping to look back at Captain Vick. I was very surprised he would give in so easily. Maybe, perhaps, he was tired of the whole charade. I wouldn't blame him, I too, was sick of all the chaos.

I finally reached the old factory after only a few minutes. I moved quickly across the cracked lot. Steam bellowed out from the manholes, filling the air with a dense mist, which I upset as I passed through. Out of the so called "fog" emerged Thunderbark's familiar white figure. His mouth was twisted with worry and his icy eyes flickered.

"Railrunner? What in the world happened? You never called."

"I'll answer everything once we go inside. Trust me, you will be pleased."

Thunderbark flashed a smile then followed me into the warm factory. Everyone sat around doing as they pleased. Buddy and Sly played cards just as they always did. Static balanced a rusty rod on his cable, twirling it around like a baton. Merrylegs and Clare stayed in a continuous conversation. However, all their heads snapped to our direction once we entered the factory floor.

"Well?" Static asked, eager for the answer.

"Mission complete." I said sitting onto the conveyer belt.

"What did the captain say?" Thunderbark said while he sat in front of me.

"Well, first we sort of tossed out some remarks, and then I made him shake on a deal. I told him the legend of our world -."

"You told him about Amusement Park Between!" Thunderbark said angrily.

"No! I didn't tell him what our world was called! I just told him some facts but I left out the main details."

"Okay then, sorry for interrupting." Thunderbark said sitting back down.

"What I did was this; he agreed to call us when he saw Ironwheel. I in turn, gave him the fake gun with the false bullets. I told Captain Vick that they were made too kill Ironwheel only, if you know what I'm getting at."

Thunderbark smiled a broad grin. His grey eyebrows rose as he began to stroke his small beard. He started to chuckle from deep down in his chest.

"That, Railrunner was the greatest bullshit I've ever seen anybody pull off!" he laughed.

Thunderbark then went to chat with Static and Merrylegs. I however had something else on my mind. I motioned for Clare; she looked at me with one of her soft smiles.

"Yes, Railrunner?" she asked.

"How about you and I go on a little date?"

"What!" she whispered shocked. "Now! To where?"

"It is a secret, but I think you'll like it. I find it quite magical."

"All right, but first I need to change -."

"You don't need to do that! Just come on!" I said urging her to climb aboard while Thunderbark and the others weren't looking. Clare looked back to where they stood, she then hopped onto my back and the both of us snuck out the door into the night.

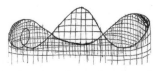

I bounded through the woods with Clare bouncing and laughing upon me. This was like the night that I first got in control and Clare and I ran through the forest to avoid the police. This time however it was for a completely different reason, a good reason.

I stopped in a clearing and Clare climbed off of my back. She glanced around a little confused. She then turned and gave me a baffled look.

"Are we here?" Clare asked.

"No, but I want the place to be extra special and to be a surprise." I said pulling out a blindfold and handing it to her. Clare raised an eyebrow and took the bandanna from my hand.

"We better not be going to a restaurant, I'm on a diet." She laughed as she felt her way back to her seat.

"Don't worry; restaurants have policies such as no animals allowed. I'm sure that includes talking roller coasters that could kill you in a matter of seconds." I said looking at her with one of my crooked smiles. Clare simply giggled and pulled my over the shoulder restraint down. With a single thrust we were off again. She had no clue to where I was taking her, Mystic Park. Tonight, she would receive the ride of a lifetime on a living coaster.

I entered Mystic Park as I did in the morning, only realizing that I had left my Hummer in the employee lot. At the moment that did not matter. I brought Clare through the border, and ever so surely, made my way to the rails.

As I neared the track, my body quivered with power. It shook Clare a little bit, startling her.

"What was that?" she asked.

I didn't really want Clare to know that we were here just yet and she knew I gained power from being in any park.

"I have indigestion," I lied.

"Come on Railrunner, that wasn't it!" she laughed a little as she played with my mind.

"Adrenaline rush." I said quickly coming up with another explanation.

"Whatever you say." She sighed as I entered the station. I began to climb up the lift hill slowly on the steps. Clare shifted in her seat.

"Hey Railrunner, what are you doing?" she said slightly suspicious.

"You will see, now take off your blindfold." I smiled.

I watched Clare out of the corner of my eye. Her frail fingers grasped tightly around the knot. Then she slowly pulled off the blindfold, but her eyes were still closed.

"You can open your eyes, it's not that scary." I chucked, my toying laughter rumbling deep in my chest. Clare then opened her eyes and her jaw dropped.

"Oh my, you can't be serious!" she said excited.

"I am. Now remember, I got you. You don't have to worry about a single thing."

"Why do you say that?" she said, but I didn't reply. I threw myself forward, down the hill. Clare let out a deafening scream, but then it turned into laughter. I landed with a bang on the rails, power running through my body like electricity. I rocketed up the follow up hill, leaving the track again doing a horizontal twist in midair. Then I landed at the hill's base, Clare whooping with laughter. I then went up another hill, but this time I flung Clare in the air. She yelled my name at the top of her lungs, but I judged her position and where she would land. Just before she hit the tracks, I jumped and caught her in the exact same seat she sat in. Clare unexpectedly laughed.

"Is this what it is like to be you!" she said as we raced along the trees.

I nodded and roared as I continued along at illegal speeds. Clare was enjoying it, and the words that she just spoken proved that she wanted to be a coaster. I sped full tilt towards a corkscrew. I glided through the first inversion, leaping out of it and onto the track sections further ahead. Clare enjoyed every moment. Soon, she would be rolling with me, forever, but only if I slayed the beast.

I coasted into the station and slowed to a halt. Clare hopped off and stood trembling with so much excitement that she seemed to have drunk a dozen cups of coffee.

"THAT WAS AMAZING!" she said with her eyes open to their full extent. "That was better than riding in a race car!"

"Glad you liked it." I grinned.

"Thanks for the date, Railrunner. I had a blast!"

"You're welcome, want to do it again?"

"Hell yes!" she said hopping back on, and I began the whole voyage again.

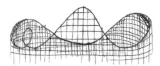

It was midnight and Clare and I lay exhausted from the numerous rounds in the loop. She sat on my chest as we stared up at the moon that glowed like a giant candle. Her thick blonde hair glittered in the light, looking like millions of tiny diamonds.

"It looks like there will be a full moon tomorrow night." She spoke softly.

"Indeed." I replied looking at the vibrant orb. I thought silently to myself. Tomorrow would be the perfect time to turn Clare into a roller coaster. She wouldn't have to go through the same horrible process that I did.

"Railrunner?" Clare suddenly asked.

"Yes?"

"Are you like a king in your world?"

"I don't know." I replied a bit baffled.

"It seems that the rides consider you as one."

"I can't think of myself as a king."

"Don't be silly! To me you are a king. Railrunner, ruler of the rails!" she laughed.

"Then the ruler of the rails dons you as his queen." I replied. Both of us broke out in a chorus of laughter. "Wait, if Ironwheel is King now, I must be a prince." I said as I thought more technically.

"Can I still be your princess?" She giggled.

"Of coarse," I replied. But in the not so far distance my name was called. I easily recognized who it belonged to.

"You hear that?" Clare asked.

"Yeah, it's Merrylegs. Looks like playtime is over." I mumbled.

"That's all right; it was about time we headed back anyway." Clare sighed as we climbed down from the loop.

We began to walk towards the source of Merrylegs's voice. Clare stayed ever so close to me. I put an arm around her shoulder as we moved along the path.

"You think Thunderbark will be angry?"

"Probably, but I'll think of an excuse."

"What do you have in mind?" she asked looking up at me.

I bit my lip in hesitation. Clare could not know the truth! I quickly searched my long list and found one of the oldest among them.

"I'll think of something by then." I finally spoke.

"Might want to think of a good one that's really convincing. Thunderbark is smart."

"I know, he figures out my master plans really quickly."

"Railrunner you are witty, you'll think of something." She said as I exchanged a sly smile in return.

We finally found Merrylegs as our paths crossed. She pranced among the lantern lit path with her red mane flowing freely in the wind. Her yellow "skin" gleamed like gold.

"We've been worried about you two! I knew you both would be here somewhere and turned out I was correct."

"Thunderbark is mad isn't he?" I groaned.

"I couldn't tell actually. His facial expression was difficult to read." Merrylegs replied as she led us out of the park. Her words made me feel so unease; Thunderbark and I could get into another big ugly argument. I did however, have the real reason why I left with Clare on my mind.

We soon returned to the factory grounds and my heart was pounding in my chest. What was Thunderbark going to do with me? I started to think of all the possibilities. At this point in time, Thunderbark could be capable of anything.

Merrylegs and Clare entered the factory unaccounted. I stood there hesitating in the doorway. My mind now could only process the mere thought of Thunderbark yelling in my face. He would probably say: *Why did you do that! You could have been ambushed by Ironwheel! Why did you disobey me! Yadda, yadda, yadda, did I dare go on?*

"Railrunner, you coming?" asked Merrylegs.

"I guess," I sighed as I walked in. I looked around for Thunderbark and soon found him behind the table in the meeting room. He tapped his wheels on the table recessively. His creature eyes burned dark blue as he never took them off while I entered the room. I stood behind the large table and glared down at my stomach.

"Listen I had -."

"Why?" Thunderbark said shaking his head from side to side, his eyes never detaching from me. "Why, Railrunner do you repeatedly disobey me so much?" he said in a bitter tone.

"Do you really want to know the truth?"

"I would love to." He said almost hissing.

"I went with Clare to the rails to figure out if she wanted to be a roller coaster or not! I'm happy to find out that she does!" I shot back.

Thunderbark did not reply, he just remained silent. He stared at the wall biting his lip and crossing his arms. He let out one of his long all too familiar sighs as he looked back at me.

"Sorry, but It would have been nice if you told me where you were going." He finally spoke.

"I do have to admit I was wrong on that one, I should have told you. I wasn't thinking clearly." I admitted.

"There was a big reason why I worried so much and got as angry as I did." He said sounding extremely serious.

"What?"

"I have a feeling that something is going to occur tomorrow, and it is not going to be good."

Chapter 62
Calling Card

Blood seemed to be smeared everywhere. I dripped from gashes across my metal. I looked down to see that I stood over Clare's body. I put a wheel on her bruised head, her breath shortened with each she drew. She held up her hand and muttered out my name. My mind almost collapsed when I realized what was going on. Clare's arm fell to the pavement in slow motion; her head fell backward as she struggled to take a breath. I then bent down in what seemed like suspended animation. I opened my mouth and edged closer. Then, my bloody tooth touched her cold skin.

I snapped awake to see everyone crowding around me. I sat up to discover that I was very dizzy and coated in sweat. I breathed hard, but it didn't seem like I could get a lick of air. I opened my mouth and tried to swallow it in, but my throat felt swollen. I started to cough and gag.

"Railrunner!" I heard Thunderbark yell as I collapsed back to the floor.

My eyesight went blurry and I felt my limbs go limp. Thunderbark pressed his ice-cold wheels onto my forehead. I felt myself slipping back into unconsciousness.

"Railrunner can you hear me!" Thunderbark yelled in my ear. I looked at him but I could not see his face, only a blob of white. I opened my mouth and tried to speak but no words emerged.

"His pupils are extremely dilated, what does that mean?" Sly asked Thunderbark.

"To him, it could mean he could go into a coma at any second!" Thunderbark called back. I heard Clare crying in the background as my senses faded even more. Then I barely heard Merrylegs's hooves as she came into the tower.

"Is that it?" Thunderbark asked her.

"Yes," Merrylegs replied.

"Thank you." Thunderbark said as he opened my mouth. A thick liquid slithered down my throat as he tilted my head back. I forced myself to swallow. Almost immediately I felt my strength come back. I sat up to see that my vision was restored and everyone around me was frightened, especially Clare.

"Railrunner?" Thunderbark questioned.

"I'm fine," I replied. "It was one of those dreams again."

Thunderbark helped me up; I staggered a bit and struggled to get my footing. I wiped the sweat off of my forehead and motioned for Clare. I wrapped my arm around her and she buried her face into my chest.

"Why are you crying?" I asked her. "I'm all right now, there is nothing to worry about."

"You scared me to death! You looked like you were having a seizure! What was that?" she said still trembling.

"Well - it was a nightmare. I sort of can tell the future when I have one. I hate it."

"I can understand why you hate it, but what did you see?"

My blood started to freeze; I walked out of the tower and sat on the stairs. I put my wheels on my head and shut my eyes in frustration. Because of Ironwheel, I thought. The whole thing was his burden upon me. Horrible thoughts and ugly words started to scream through my head. It felt as if all the unwanted facts were rattling my skull. Ironwheel became more and more of an aversion by the second, boiling my blood from its frozen state.

"Railrunner?" spoke Clare, but her words were faint.

I stood and roared in pure rage, shaking the tin roof greatly. My roar got the rides attention and startled the ones that were human. I thundered down the stairs but Thunderbark leaped in front of me, blocking my path. He grabbed my shoulders and made me look straight in his eyes.

"Hey! Settle down! Railrunner, it will all be resolved in no time. She will be fine." He finished whispering so Clare could not hear. My anger started to cool.

"You're right Thunderbark. I'll go and get some sleep now." I said with a nervous smile. I started to descend up the stairs, Clare waiting for me at the top. She followed as I entered the tower once again.

"What's wrong." She said softly as she stood in the doorway.

I didn't answer, I just looked at her skinny body thinking of what it was to become.

"Railrunner is there something wrong with you - I mean are you feeling all right?"

"Sorry, I'm fine, I just need rest."

"I wish you would tell me."

"You don't want to hear it," I blurted out without thinking.

"I want to." She replied sitting near me.

"I can't tell you - it is against the laws." I said making up something spur of the moment.

"Oh, okay I'll quit asking then. Good night Railrunner." Clare said lying at the other end of the room still fearful that I would dream again and roll over her. I began to let my eyelids grow heavy, but I still had the nightmare on my mind.

I woke up to the sun's rays warming my skin. I looked around to see that Clare had already gotten prepared and had gone downstairs. I quickly slipped on my hoodie and shoes then walked through the doorway and rounded to the iron stairs. Everyone stood at the factory floor; oddly they all seemed alert. Something probably happened.

"What's going on?" I asked Thunderbark.

He put on his cream cowboy hat and pulled out the cell phone. He looked at me in a somewhat triumphant stare.

"Looks like Captain Vick sent out a patrol for Ironwheel."

"When?"

"Just a moment ago. We could cruse around the city and wait to see if they call." He replied.

"That's a good idea I suppose."

"That's our plan?" asked Static.

"That is what we are going to have to work with, yes."

In the shadows of an alley, walked a mysterious cloaked figure with a steel cane. He was silent as he paced along, only the tapping of his cane could be heard. He moved with a hunch and all that could be seen was his mouth and neck. Other than his mouth was his heavily scared hand that gripped around the cane, whose handle was in the shape of a roller coaster head with fangs barred.

Behind the man appeared two teenage boys. They exchanged wicked glances before they approached the man.

"Excuse us sir." They laughed. The man turned slowly, breathing harshly as his dewlap like neck vibrated with each breath. The man did not answer as he stared at the two boys with his fingers tapping on the cane's handle.

"What's your name?" the taller boy taunted.

"It is Iro." The man replied in his rugged and scarred voice.

The shorter and chubbier boy suddenly snatched the cane from Iro. He and his partner laughed over and over.

"How do you like that Iro!" the boy laughed. But then his enjoyment faded as he realized that Iro had not fallen. The two boys looked at him befuddled. Iro straitened up, his back making horrible crackling noises, out of his hunched over position. He slowly raised his hand to his hood. Iro slipped it off to reveal his heavily pierced and tattooed face. But the only thing the boys gazed at in horror was his pupiless red eyes.

"Don't you boys just love gimmicks?" he said in his mangled and bone chilling voice. "Allow me to reintroduce myself, I am King Ironwheel!" he finished laughing maniacally. The boys dropped the cane and prepared to run, but before they could even take a single step, Ironwheel lunged to sink his teeth into their necks.

The monster in disguise stood up wiping the blood off his lips. He growled in his throat and flexed his fingers then popped his neck.

"No one is to stand in my way. Especially not Railrunner. That red roller coaster will get what's coming to him." He sneered.

+ + +

I sat quietly in the passenger seat as Thunderbark drove the Hummer. I fiddled with the GPS, setting it on coordinates that we were not intending on reaching. I tapped my left foot on the floor of the Hummer to the beat of a song that was barely heard at low volume. Every once in a while I would glance out the window to look for potential trouble. I toyed with the volume on the navigation device, making the voice of the director go up and down.

"You're getting on my nerves, Railrunner." Thunderbark said not taking his eyes off the road.

"Sorry, just nervous." I replied putting the GPS away.

"We all are." Thunderbark replied finally turning to me. He only looked for a brief second before returning his focus back to the road. He sighed as he clutched the phone in his hand. Thunderbark then turned onto another stretch; people stared at us as we drove by.

"Where do you think Ironwheel is hiding?" I asked him.

"In the shadows or among the innocent." He said looking at the pedestrians.

"Ever seen Ironwheel's human form, Thunderbark?" I asked as we came to a stopped intersection. Thunderbark looked at the stoplight strangely, and then he started to step on the gas petal slightly.

"Hey hold on! You're not supposed to go on that signal." I laughed as he slammed on the brakes. It was quite obvious that Thunderbark drove hardly at all.

"Humph, a roller coaster has no use for traffic lights," he grumbled. "I hate those things."

I snickered in response to his comment, because he was right. "You can go now, the light is green." I said still laughing. Thunderbark sighed and started off again, still grumbling.

"Yeah, coasters have no use for traffic signs either." He said waving his finger at me and starting to giggle. The rides in the backseat started to follow along with Thunderbark's joking remarks.

339

Suddenly it happened, the phone rang.

It all became silent in the SUV as all of us stared blankly at the cell phone. Thunderbark flipped it opened and prepared to speak.

"Yes?" he asked nervously.

"It's me again; I need your entire troop to report to the police station immediately. We may have found some crucial evidence linking to Ironwheel."

"We're on our way captain." Thunderbark replied snapping the phone shut.

"Which way to the station?" he asked as he pointed to the GPS. I brought it up in just a few seconds, the path we had to take highlighted in yellow.

"Just follow the yellow brick road." I replied.

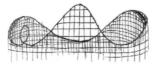

Minutes later we arrived at the police station where Thunderbark took up two parking spots and nearly ran over a trashcan in the process. Thunderbark climbed out and stuffed a gun into his belt. I knew the reason why he was choosing to do so and I did not blame him. In fact I did the same thing and so did everyone that was on board.

"You do the talking, Railrunner." He said coming around to meet me. "Best that we all be alert," he said as he began to head for the front door.

"Do you think the men here will know of our alliance with the Captain?" Merrylegs asked as she walked behind me.

"Of course, Vick has a big mouth." I replied as I traveled through the door with Thunderbark. All of the officers' heads turned to us as we stormed in. They could only stare scared stiff at the rifles in our team's hands.

"Ladies and gentlemen, we are not here to harm you we just have guns for our protection. The real reason why we are here is that we have a scheduled appointment with the Captain." I said slightly leery that they would draw their weapons and fire upon us. Then Vick appeared in the lobby from the doorway. He then smiled slightly and waved his hand as a gesture to me.

"Evening Mr. Railrunner." He said motioning for me to follow him to his office.

"Nice to see you are still in agreement," I replied as we put down our weapons. I then walked up to Vick, he stared at me a little unease as we walked down the hall.

"A little change in perspective," I laughed. "Now you called saying you had news am I correct?"

"Yes," he replied as all of us entered his paneled office. Captain Vick walked over and sat in a leather executive chair. "Temporary office." He said pulling out files from a nearby cabinet. Then he spun around and layed several papers onto the great wooden desk. The files were criminal records of two young boys, not even past the age of seventeen.

"Do you know any of these boys, Railrunner?"

"No."

"They were both convicted felons of theft. These two criminals were killed in cold blood about four hours before. One witness came forth not but thirty minutes ago with a brief description of the suspect."

"What did he look like?" I said as I slapped the files back onto the table's wooden surface.

"The witness said the man was dressed in a black cloak. He had peircings and many tattoos and carried a cane."

"Anything else?" I said impatiently.

"The biggest clues were that the cane's handle was in the shape of a coaster's head and that there was something funny with his eyes." Vick said standing up out of his seat. Right then and there I knew that the cloaked man was indeed Ironwheel in his human form.

"Where was he seen?" I asked him.

"Near the Kingsley Building. On Brook Street to be precise."

Without hesitating a second longer I turned back to Vick and started to give my word. "Send out your squads, all of them, we're going hunting." I finished as Thunderbark, Merrylegs, and Static sped out the door. Captain Vick immediately got on the intercom and gave the order. He then got on his phone and dialed a crucial number.

"Release the troops! Operation "TWISTED" is now in effect! Sound the alarm, follow convoy and stop for nothing!" he said yelling into the receiver. I didn't stand around any longer; I ran outside and hopped into the driver's side of the Hummer. I started the engine and revved the SUV in reverse. I followed the line of squad vehicles out onto the road.

Now it was almost time to get Amusement Park Between's revenge, it was getting closer and closer to the point where I would sink my teeth into Ironwheel's throat.

Chapter 63
The Fun Begins

Helicopters flew overhead as sirens blared through the city. Red and blue lights reflected in our faces as panicking humans fled. Deep down in my mind I knew this was it, time to take things back, to restore order, and to give new life. This was where everything mattered. There had to be no screw-ups what so ever.

"You think Ironwheel will be there?" I said turning to Thunderbark.

"I think so. One thing Ironwheel does not do is back away from a challenge." He said with his voice full of worry.

"Ironwheel will do anything." Merrylegs mumbled as she watched the police cruisers drive by.

"It's time you silenced him Railrunner," Static said, being supportive.

"Thanks for the info," I replied to them. "I'll keep that in mind while I'm kicking his ass."

"That's the spirit." Thunderbark said with a smirk on his face.

The convoy rolled on several more miles. In this city, there were only three tall objects: the Kingsley building, the clock tower, and the coaster tracks of Mystic Park. Ironwheel was probably on top of the ten-story office building looking down, smiling wickedly as we advanced. I lost my short train of thought as the building appeared at the end of the street. I looked through the sunroof expecting to see him standing at the building's edge. Sure enough, I was right.

"He's there." I simply spoke. Thunderbark looked up, following my gaze.

"Told you so." He replied.

The convoy circled the building in a barricade. Officers climbed out of the many trucks and cars and aimed their rifles at the top of the building. All of my allies climbed out of the car to stand by my side. Captain Vick ran over talking rapidly into his walkie-talkie.

"Sky patrol is confirming that he is up there on the roof top. When can you intercept?"

I turned to Thunderbark and the others. I looked at Clare, I thought of everything we had been through over the past several months. This could be the last time I could see her truly human.

"Thunderbark?"

"Yes, Railrunner?"

"Watch Clare and the others." I said as I grabbed Clare and pressed my lips to hers. Our kiss was very real, and very meaningful. Hopefully it wasn't the final one. I then let her go.

"I love you." She said with a small tear streaming down her cheek.

"I love you too, Clare." I replied. Then I turned and grasped the Augu Ra. It glowed hot and let loose a blinding light. Immediately I felt myself begin to change. My skin tore free and exposed my red hot metal. Seats ripped through my back as my eyes changed. I grew quickly into the creature that I truly was, shedding my disguise. Bigger and bigger, losing every aspect of looking human. Then the imminent change stopped and I threw back my head and emitted a behemoth of a roar, so great it trembled even the largest armored truck.

I darted into the building. I took a brief look around for a way up. I spotted an elevator at the end of the lobby. I ran over and pried its doors open. I looked beyond and into the elevator shaft. I extended my claws and started to scale up it, they dug deep into the concrete walls, every so often the tops of my seats would scrape the wall behind me, but that did not matter one bit. All that did was Ironwheel.

At last I reached the doors that led to the roof. I took my other arms and used them as support to hold myself up as I began to pry the sliding doors open. They bent easily under tons of pressure that my body exerted. When they were fully open, I crawled up and out, onto the roof.

Ironwheel still stood as a human at the building's edge, but he wouldn't be human for long. I crept closer, but Ironwheel never turned around to face me. He knows I'm here, I thought, he just wants to play with me first.

"Did Thunderbark ever tell you what happens to reds that are put in storage or destroyed?" Ironwheel suddenly spoke, but he still did not turn around.

I made no attempt to answer, I just growled.

"Well they say their fire-red metal turns black as ashes."

So Ironwheel was once a red? My mind tried to process the mere thought. Why had Thunderbark not told me? Then Ironwheel turned around to look at me with his soulless eyes. He smiled in pure evil.

"That is what I plan to do with you Railrunner, turn you into a pile of useless ashes." He chuckled to himself.

"I'm warning you." I said letting a smirk appear on my face.

"Why?"

I laughed to myself. I then prepared to make my move.

"You don't want to see me furious." I said just a tad bit louder than a whisper. A split second later I lunged, pushing both of us off the edge and hurtling towards the ground. Immediately, Ironwheel changed into his ride form, and the both of us started to go at it in our freefall. I raked my claws across Ironwheel's belly as he hit me with heavy blows. I whizzed my head around to see that the earth was not but just a few feet below us. I quickly grabbed Ironwheel and spun him so he hit the ground first.

Finally we impacted, cracking the concrete. Ironwheel threw me off into a nearby squad truck. I quickly stood back up and faced him. He shot off a lightning bolt, but I was in the perfect position to redirect it. I caught the bolt and sent it back, double time, to Ironwheel who ducked at the last second. Then we both charged at each other like raging bulls. Teeth clashed against our opponent. I clamped down on his neck as he did on my back. Pain went through me, but it only fueled my anger even more.

I ripped and tore at Ironwheel, my teeth chomping down all over him, the enemy's blood leaking into my mouth. Oh so very satisfying. Ironwheel then grabbed hold and slammed me to the ground.

"You worthless swine!" he yelled as he prepared to sink his teeth into my throat. Suddenly a missile flew through the air and hit Ironwheel in the side, knocking him off. I got to my wheels and went for him once more, but before I could even lay a claw on him, Thunderbark leaped onto his back. I watched not knowing what to think as the two rolled over and over. Ironwheel swung toward Thunderbark, his claw sliced across his chest making Thunderbark cry in agonizing pain. I couldn't stand to see this sight any longer.

I sprang and sunk my claws into Ironwheel's back. He immediately released Thunderbark and started for me again. I sliced my claws across his face, spewing blood all over the road. Captain Vick fired bullets at Ironwheel, but I knew that wouldn't help since I gave him the false gun. Ironwheel didn't care; all he was focused on was me as I was to him.

Suddenly Ironwheel swung his tail and hit me in the ribs. The blow knocked the wind out of me and into one of the columns at the Kingsley building's entrance. I forced my eyes open to see Thunderbark lying about fifty feet from me. Blood gushed out of the wound on his chest. His snow white metal stared to stain red as he tried to get to his wheels. Thunderbark raised his arm and generated a flame; miraculously he began to weld the slash back together, tears streamed down his eyes as he did. I ran over to him and tried to help him up.

"What are you doing! Railrunner, I will be all right you -."

Thunderbark was cut off by Ironwheel's deep laughter. I turned to see the king holding Clare in his wheels. Clare screamed horrendously, her eyes looking at me with total horror. The squad teams put down their guns, afraid of hitting helpless Clare. Static raised his cable and sent an electrical shock through Ironwheel. He snarled and flung Static away as Merrylegs rammed her horn into him. Sadly, she too was pushed.

"I don't know what is more pathetic Railrunner, you or your followers." Ironwheel chuckled. Clare looked at Ironwheel with a touch of anger. She then kicked him, but it didn't do any good at all. "That tickles," Ironwheel mocked. "Railrunner, I think your girlfriend will make a lovely rug for my throne room." He laughed as Clare started to scream again. I roared in pure antagonism as my blood began to boil once again.

"*You're pissing me off.*" I hissed.

"Sorry, but I think it is time that I took Clare for a little date," Ironwheel said as he fled. I didn't need to think anything over, I charged after him. I heard the rattle of wheels and hooves as Thunderbark and the others followed me. I ran full throttle, now was the time to see all I predicted unfold and let the horror show begin.

Chapter 64
Proportionate

I thundered across the pavement after Clare and Ironwheel. My nightmares gave me the upper hand this time around. I knew exactly where he and Clare were headed and that was the clock tower on the west side of town. I thought any minute from now I would have to bite Clare, making her be mine forever in other words.

The road to the tower started to back up from fleeing cars. I swerved onto the wrong side of the road and continued from there. I shoved large trucks that had been abandoned out of my wake. They fell onto the road like rocks as I and my allies passed through.

"Are we heading to the place in your dream!" Thunderbark shouted over the honking of cars on the other side of the freeway.

"Yes we are," I replied as I pushed an eighteen wheeler out onto the shoulder of the road.

"Not to anger you, but how accurate are your dreams?" he continued.

"A hundred percent." I said turning to give him a reassuring smile. I spun around to see that more abandoned cars littered the road way, seeing this, Thunderbark snorted behind me in disgust.

"Let's travel through the Lower Fifth, I know that it is a shortcut." Thunderbark said as he changed direction. I made my shift along with him, the Lower Fifth was an underground tunnel that led to downtown. Thunderbark was correct, it was a shortcut.

We now ran along a stretch of road that was under construction. It was pitted with holes and was besieged with construction vehicles. Static and Merrylegs pushed harder in avoiding obstacles as Thunderbark and I glided through. The mangled concrete finally opened up into a large tunnel. The Lower Fifth consisted of many different roads that led through the underground only to be separated by barriers or walls. All in all it was a messy maze only to have road signs to guide you.

"Which way!" Static yelled, his voice echoing throughout the tunnel.

I stopped and sniffed for Ironwheel's reeking scent, sure enough it was easily noticeable.

"Follow me!" I yelled as I took off again. My heart pumped rapidly as my muscles tightened and loosened. My lungs took in massive amounts of air as I ran. My nostrils flared as my wheels thudded lightly across the asphalt. At the speed I was going, which was faster than any normal real world coaster, would make a sports car look like a dune buggy with a flat.

Thunderbark met up beside me, sailing over a disabled car in the process. He seemed to still be leaking blood from the slash along his chest even after he welded it up. He seemed to be fighting the pain along with me; the both of us were too determined. His long eyebrows as small beard blew in the rushing wind making the dragon appearance return. His light blue eyes frosted in fury, changing color to the change in light. It was nice to have such faithful support running beside me, let alone a family member.

I then took my focus off Thunderbark and back to the road before me. My heart fluttered in my chest as I saw a garbage truck blocking the exit, in which it was impossible for neither of us to squeeze through.

"Nice of choice for a shortcut, Thunderbark!" I said crudely. Thunderbark only looked at the obstruction and laughed. With a sudden burst of speed, he sped on ahead. Thunderbark charged at the truck like a rhino. He then rammed it from underneath, pushing the cab up into the ceiling. Shards from the truck flew all over the place as Thunderbark trust the garbage truck up and out. He turned to grin like a kid who had just been given candy at me. If an impact to the truck came from a bus, both vehicles would have suffered severe damage. Thunderbark stood there in mint condition.

"You were saying?" he demanded.

"Nothing," I replied as I bolted past him and back out into the surface world. I heard Thunderbark and the others laugh behind me as they followed along, but then their laughter faded as they saw Ironwheel emerge from the south and begin to scale the clock tower. I stopped and stared at him as he carried the screaming Clare. I gulped, I knew the time was almost here.

"Thunderbark can you make me a promise?" I said turning in his direction.

"Yes I can Railrunner." He replied looking at me with agony and hints of wonder in his ice eyes.

"Promise me that you will not - catch Clare." I said with the words halfway getting caught in my throat.

"I promise," Thunderbark said bowing his head. "Railrunner?" he asked looking deeply at me again.

"Yes?" I replied pondering what else there was for him to say at this very moment in time.

"Forget that little thing I told you about love two and a half months ago." He said with a slight smile.

I returned a grin; Thunderbark had finally given in to Clare. He realized that love never truly is broken apart, no matter what obstacles get in the way. I looked at all of them briefly for a minute and then turned and headed for the tower. Ironwheel clung to its top as he toyed around with Clare, holding her out acting like he was going to drop her as she made shrieks of terror. Ironwheel was making a mistake, the more he made me mad, the worse it was going to be for him.

I ran across the clearing and dug my claws into the brick surface of the clock tower. Hyped on anger and rage, my heart began to pound. I thrust one arm forward and then another, scaling the tower a few feet at a time. Above Ironwheel laughed maniacally, he was going to get it. He had it coming to him for decades, with his nasty habit of wanting to watch Amusement Park Between drown in its own blood. Now the tables were turned, Ironwheel would be drowning in his.

Ironwheel was now ten yards from my grasp. I snarled, daring him to make a move. I had to be careful about the situation as the thought of the dreams and Clare came into mind. I would settle the score with Ironwheel, but at the moment, time was not quite right. He looked down onto me with his hellish eyes and snickered.

"What's this? A sudden act of courage, Railrunner?" Ironwheel said in a deep and ravenous tone. "You're a fool for caring so dearly about this pitiful human. Cockroaches the simpletons are. To humans, their own species is kin, but in their eyes, you're just a freak. A monster in other words. A death machine. We all are Railrunner, the abominations nature never intended." He finished laughing quietly to himself.

"That is because you do not know the goodness in them," I replied struggling to keep a hold of the clock tower's surface.

"Goodness! Ha! Apparently you have gone off the rails a few times. Humans don't give a damn about nothing! All they do is use you till you're nothing but a metal frame! Or in my case, play too rough and be too ignorant to notice what the hell they are doing!"

"You're wrong!" I said through clenched teeth.

Ironwheel simply laughed. Clare cried for help again. Ironwheel raised her up to be eye level with him. He then roared in her face and Clare let loose bloodcurdling screams. In the back of my mind, I knew what was going to happen and where this was leading.

"Hear her scream!" Ironwheel bellowed.

"Let her go!" I yelled, knowing my words would set off a chain reaction. Ironwheel looked at me, he smiled, showing all of his yellowed and blood stained teeth.

"I have some advice for you, Railrunner. Learn to choose your words better!" he laughed. I could only watch as he suspended Clare in midair by the collar on the back of her jacket. One by one, his wheels came off the purple fabric. With one last yank, Clare detached from him, beginning her fall, to her death.

"RRRRRAAAAAIIIILLLRRRUUNNER!" Clare screamed as she fell through the cold air. I watched her only to realize that the time had come. Clare would enter her new life soon enough. I reached out for her, Clare reached out for me, but her frail arms could not extend far enough. I watched her, realizing that she was falling to her certain doom. This was the eclipse of our lives, a point where everything was in a haze. Clare grew closer to the ground, my heart pounded more rapidly. Then it skipped a beat as she hit with a horrible crack.

Ironwheel laughed as I leaped down from the tower and ran to her broken body. Ironwheel jumped off the tower, landing a few meters from me. I stood over Clare and snarled at Ironwheel like a dog. The black coaster smiled and pretended like he did not even care.

"I would love to watch you mourn, but I have things to do and things to gain." He finished chuckling and racing off into the night.

I turned my attention to Clare. I cupped my wheels under her head. She was alive, but only just. Blood seeped out of her cut and wounds onto the concrete. She stared up at me with her eyes, growing dull with every altered breath. I lay my head upon her chest and listened to her fading heartbeat, growing weaker every second. I tilted my head back and let out a long howl of sorrow. Thunderbark, Merrylegs, and Static rushed over to Clare's side. Thunderbark looked at me trying to say something, but he could barely talk.

"She - will. Clare has chosen right. You know what to do Railrunner." Thunderbark muttered still looking at Clare's face that was turning paler.

I looked down at Clare, who shifted slightly. She looked up at me with eyes that dimmed greatly.

"R...R...Railrunner?" she uttered, her voice trailing off.

"Yes Clare?" I said letting an icy tear roll out from the corner of my eye.

"I...love...you." She sighed. I lay my head to her chest and let out sobs. I could not stand to see her in pain. I raised my head and looked at her again. Clare's breath shortened, she looked up with her eyes closing. I knew what I had to do. I winced as I leaned in close to her neck; my hot breath against her skin. I opened my mouth and edged in closer, watching Clare's chest rise for a final time. I pressed my tooth on her skin, its sharp point piercing through. I began to pump venom into her near dead body. I kept it up for ten long seconds, and finally could not stand it any longer.

I rose up and looked at her, she was lifeless. I turned to Thunderbark worried as hell. I looked back at Clare to see that she had not moved. I focused in on Thunderbark again. Sadness hit me like an earthquake.

"It is not working is it?" I asked with tears filling the corners of my eyes and my voice muffled.

He looked at me and then bent down and sniffed her body. "She should be all right. It takes a minute or so for the curse to completely consume her."

My spirit began to soar; Clare was to survive after all. Now all there was to do was linger.

I stood there unmoving, waiting for her to awake and change. Thunderbark and the others stood a few feet back from Clare. Merrylegs every so often, would edge forward to see if she had a hint of life in her. Static jittered with unease too. Thunderbark only waited patiently not saying a word. I was with Static and Merrylegs on this one, to excited and on the edge of my seat.

Suddenly a strange noise came from Clare. I bent down to investigate. Clare's wounds started to shrink until they were no longer visible. Her skin started to turn a lilac tint and her hair began to fall out. The horrible sound of cracking bones made her extend her limbs out as if a jolt of electricity ran through her. Clare's skin began to stretch as her body began to grow. Her eyes suddenly flew open, but they were no longer human; they were the classic cat-like appearance. Yellow orbs with the telltale slit.

I watched her change in awe. I had never actually seen a transformation, let alone my own. Clare's was different; I watched it as if it was on a screen. I started to take a few steps back as she took up too much space. Then her transformation completed the final details, and then she became a full fledged roller coaster. Just the way she wanted.

Clare slowly stood up and howled. I felt myself move in closer. She still had her back turned to me so I took further observation. Clare was a purple steel coaster, lilac as her base color with dark purple lines that swirled, forming little figures and patterns all over her body. Clare was small for a roller coaster, probably because her puny size as a human. Overall, she was even more beautiful as a coaster. Finally, I thought, we were balanced.

"Clare?" I asked.

She spun around quickly, but then I then discovered I had forgotten something. A roller coaster only gained control on their first full moon at its peak in the sky. I gulped and prepared myself. Clare peeled back her lips and snarled, her white pointed teeth shinning in the light. Her muscles tensed up as she prepared to strike. Then her yellow eyes looked to the moon, and she paused. I turned my attention to what she gazed at. I sighed in relief to find that the moon was at its highest.

Clare then began the phase where she would "rid the demon". She began to jerk and double over in agony again, but that step was quickly resolved. Clare sat hunched over staring at the ground breathing harshly. I ran over and helped Clare to her new sets of wheels. She raised her head and looked at me deep in the eyes.

"Railrunner." She said. Her voice was ever so lovely; it was such a mystic tone, more beautiful than the gentle melody of a violin.

"Nice to see you again," I smiled. Clare emitted a small grin. She then put her wheels on her forehead and sighed.

"I feel weird," she said. Funny, she had not realized what she was yet. I held back a giggle. "Do you think I'm fat? I feel like I've gained weight, a lot of weight."

"No, but what do you think?" I said biting my lip.

"What do you mean, Railrunner?" she asked confused. "I just said that I feel really strange that's all."

"I don't know quite how to say this, but -."

Clare interrupted with a laugh. "If you're going to say something just -" she stopped as soon as she looked down to see her chest and belly. Her eyes widened as she held up a set of wheels, looking at them speechless. Clare then felt her head, letting her wheels run across smooth leather seats. She then glanced back at me, standing there smiling like a little girl.

"I'm - a roller coaster." She said. She then grinned the biggest grin I had seen from her and gave me a hug, and this time I could hug her back without crushing her.

"Oh, I'm so happy! Thank you!" she exclaimed.

"You're welcome," I replied.

Thunderbark and the others came over and met the both of us.

"Railrunner is lucky to have you. I'm happy to say that you are now able to spend the rest of your life with him in Amusement Park Between. However, before we return to our home, Railrunner you have some unfinished business to take care of." Thunderbark said to us with a courageous look. I glared ahead to realize that Thunderbark was correct. It was the time that I had longed for so terribly, it had finally come. The time to get revenge.

Chapter 65
Ruler of the Rails

Clare looked at me after Thunderbark had made his short speech and nodded her head in approval. I glanced back at Thunderbark; he too, made a gesture for me to advance.

"You go, Amusement Park Between needs you." Merrylegs said.

"She is right Railrunner, we will follow close behind. I know you will do well." He said bowing his white head. I replied with a quick nod and took a good look at all of them. I finally turned and bolted back into the cruel world of the city.

I ran faster and faster, I wasn't going to give Ironwheel anymore time. I already knew where the evil king was headed due to what his last words were. Ironwheel was going to Mystic Park; he was to get power from the rails. His plan was to reach his full potential and dominate the citizens in the real world. He would then transport them to Amusement Park Between to use them as slaves as well as the rides. He would even create a new army. I had made my decision long ago that wouldn't happen. Ironwheel was on death row, according to me.

I continued my pursuit; I looked behind me to see my allies dragging behind. Apparently Clare was not used to running on more than two feet. I however, had their blessing to move on, and I was taking it with no questions asked.

Finally the gateway to Mystic Park was in sight among the dark horizon. I surged further forward and soon leaped over the iron entrance, sailing into the park's grounds, or as it was now known, the "danger zone". I paused and took a breather, I went on high alert. Ironwheel could be leering deep in the shadows waiting for the perfect moment for an ambush. I sniffed, tasting the air for his sick scent. It wasn't that hard to distinguish from all of the natural odors around. It was coming from the designated eating areas of the park. Ironwheel must be messing around thinking he has all the time in the world, I thought.

Thunderbark and the others soon caught up to me, Clare seemed excited about her new found body, but the others were completely serious.

"He is here," Thunderbark said sniffing the air.

"I know," I replied. "Stay close." I said as I advanced forward. Thunderbark did not protest this time. He knew this job was made for me.

I followed Ironwheel's scent deep into the park. I stood near the rickety old ferris wheel that I used so many moons ago to spy on the police. Perhaps it would come in handy now, I thought as I lightly stepped over to it. I began to scale it as I once did, cautiously and carefully. The ferris wheel wasn't made for this at all, certainly not as a jungle gym for few thousand pound living roller coaster. I reached the top and slowly positioned myself just right. The giant wheel swayed under my weight, I expected it to give way and topple over at any moment. However, I easily spotted Ironwheel walking among the food courts, sneaking around like a raccoon. At the moment he was completely unaware of my presence. He turned with his back facing me and began to ransack one of the shops. I then had an idea that would catch him completely off guard.

I slowly, but surely, climbed down to the inner area of the wheel. I stood at the bottom on the inside. The wheel was positioned just right to roll towards Ironwheel. I grasped the ride's sides, I could break the ferris wheel from it's bearings with one big jerk. I took a deep breath and then trust myself forward. Luckily the wheel broke free with a crack. I ran forward inside the ferris wheel, just like a giant hamster. I may have created a Fallen, but I could be destroying another.

The detached Ferris Wheel rolled forward, toppling over trees and other immovable objects, thankfully not hitting any more rides, at least not yet. The wheel rolled into the food court and Ironwheel turned around in surprise.

"What goes around comes around!" I yelled. Ironwheel had no time to move out of the way, he was hit and almost completely rolled over. Suddenly the wheel began to tip, taking me with it. I quickly jumped out just a few seconds before it crashed to the ground. My little plan was working.

"Railrunner!" Ironwheel hissed. I spun around quickly to see him low to the ground stalking forward.

"Ironwheel," I growled, extracting my claws.

"See," He began. "We are part of the same great game! Brothers by species! Think about that Railrunner! You have no chance! Every red that existed in the same time frame as me failed their mission; I scored first! You Railrunner will fall! Fail just like the others before you!"

"Listen, I told you before, I'm allergic to bullshit, and you don't want to make me furious. Simple as that." I replied giving him a deadly glare.

Ironwheel let out a nasty snarl, dripping saliva as he did. Without warning he sprung and sunk his fangs into one of my legs. The pain was excruciating, horrible and unbearable. I quickly swung my claws into one of his front seats, the steel piercing all the way through. Ironwheel immediately let go and howled in agony, blood seeping everywhere and down the side of his face. I roared in rage! Pure adulterated rage! I swung again, cutting him along his side. Ironwheel hesitated and then bolted, making a beeline for the track.

"NO!" I yelled in anger as I sprinted after him. I raced after Ironwheel and was hot on his wheels. I could not let him reach the track! If he did, who knows what would happen!

My wheels scrapped the concrete as I charged after him angrily. My bitten leg stung each time I put weight on it. Venom was probably pulsing through my blood at the very second, but I had to push that aside. Nothing mattered at the moment except Ironwheel's death.

The black coaster was several yards ahead of me as we continued the chase through the park. He exerted his stampede into the section where Mystic Park housed its thrill rides. Most of their pods and vehicles had long been put into storage, leaving only the "skeleton". Ironwheel rocketed up onto a building as I pursued him, following his action a split second later, I unfortunately fell short with my claws digging deep into the shingled roof. I hurriedly hauled myself up and over. To my disappointment, Ironwheel had traveled further ahead, and was almost to the track.

"Idiot!" I shouted, scolding myself for the faulty move. Like a bat outta hell, I surged forward. Ironwheel was now just a few feet from the track; to my unfortunate despair, Ironwheel was winning the race. I pumped my legs and urged myself forward; my sudden burst of speed was working.

"Prepare to be schooled!" Ironwheel suddenly laughed. He then leaped into the lift hill's scaffolding. Ironwheel scaled upwards, performing ridiculous feats of agility. I skidded to a halt as I watched him succeed, hating myself to the extreme. Ironwheel reached the peak and climbed onto the maintenance stair way. He tauntingly hovered a set of wheels over the rails.

"You know the saying nice guys finish last right?" he laughed. Ironwheel then took the big step onto the rails.

"Oh hell no!" I said as I watched the apparent change in him begin. His muscles bulged beneath his metal hide as he roared in pleasure. Ironwheel glared at me and then raised his arm, I knew that sign well, he was aiming to hit me with one heak of a blast of lightning. Quickly thinking, I leaped onto the low stretch of track just before a bolt rained down upon me. I ran along the rails to give me a push. Then I started to roll among them. Power rattled me in ways that I could not fully describe.

Somewhere above, Ironwheel laughed maniacally as he shot off more lightning bolts as if he was a raging storm. I watched out of the corner of my eye as I saw them barely missing me. Their heat, burning my leather. I tried to ignore the pain from the burns and my leg as I passed through a tunnel. I leaped from the tunnel's mouth onto the apex of the loop. Ironwheel turned and readied another attack, but I made my move first. A bolt of lightning hit him square in the chest, but strangely enough he did not die on impact.

"It's the rails." I said to myself realizing the truth. Ironwheel cried in anger and sent a fireball back at me in return. I ducked and landed back onto the right side of the rails once again. Ironwheel still protected his self-acclaimed turf by sending down lightning shards. Another bolt sailed to my position as I rolled across the brake run. I jumped, but the bolt shot under me, searing my stomach. I fell off into a tall patch of grass in pain. I put my wheels across the burn on my belly. A small quantity of blood smeared off onto them. I stared up at Ironwheel who was still perched on the lift hill. I growled deep in my throat, he had brought me to the breaking point.

My muscles tensed inside my legs as I prepared to pounce. Ironwheel turned his back from me thinking I ran into the tall weeds. Seizing the perfect chance, I released the potential energy that I had stored to leap to the top of the lift hill. I landed next to the black roller coaster and sunk my claws into his side. Ironwheel turned and wailed, and then he swung his big arms, hitting me with a heavy blow with his claws just under my neck. Bright red blood ran down my chest as I lit him up with a blazing fist. He stumbled backwards, but then lunged forward knocking me to the tracks. He hit me like a human punching another. I felt my body grow weaker as the seconds passed.

"You're a joke Railrunner! No better than the ones before you!" he laughed.

I snarled and swung my tail, knocking him to the side. I then bit him on his arm. Ironwheel then released more of his fury by punching me on my burn. I stepped backward and clutched my stomach. I looked up to see Ironwheel crashing down onto me with his tail. I quickly rose out of the way and slashed him across the nose. He turned and spat the blood out that had drained into his mouth. I leaned on the guardrail grasping belly and leg, which were both bleeding horribly. Blood flowed heavily from the cut along my neck as well. I was growing weak from both the venom and wounds. I felt that any moment that something was going to give.

Ironwheel suddenly turned around again, emitting a violent snarl. He went for me, but I reached out and shot a bolt of lightning. Ironwheel fell backward, sliding halfway down the lift hill. I continued to lean against the guard rail for support. I was feeling dizzy and lightheaded. In my mind I knew that Ironwheel was winning. The king suddenly ran back up the hill, Gathering every ounce of strength I had, I charged. I raised my arm ready to electrocute him. Suddenly a ripping pain ran through my third car. It was so intense that I almost blacked out then and there. I looked down to see one of Ironwheel's claws sticking into my belly. I looked up in his face, his eyes burning with a deep hatred of me.

"Like I told you, nice guys finish last." He giggled into my ear. He then punched me in the chest, I fell backward, but I realized that I wasn't hitting with a hard bang on the track. I was spiraling back down to earth.

I landed with a thud in the tall grass against a rock. I tried to get up, but I couldn't move. I looked across my underside to see that blood was soaked all over me. My stab wound gushing the red liquid all over on the ground. I felt my eyelids grow heavy as I let out a moan of defeat.

I pressed my wheels against the wound on my belly, applying pressure, but it did not work. I looked up to see Ironwheel destroying targets from miles away. I leaned backward and let myself go limp as the pain got worse. My vision began to blur as I let out another moan for help.

Suddenly my ears picked up a great deal of rustling around. Then Clare bent over me as Thunderbark came to my aid. Merrylegs and Static joined Clare in worry. The new coaster placed her wheels on either side of my face. I was forced to look up at her, but I could not see her entirely.

"Railrunner stay with us!" I heard her say. Clare then pressed her wheels onto the slash below my jaw. Thunderbark in the meanwhile examined my wound.

"How... bad... is... it?" I asked with my voice fizzling out at some moments as my breath shuttered in my chest. Thunderbark didn't answer; he turned to Merrylegs and looked at her in fear.

"Well?" she asked quietly.

"It looks as if Ironwheel's claw barely missed vital organs. Still, the wound is very serious." He muttered to her.

"Will he make it?" asked Clare.

Thunderbark looked at her with a blank expression, and then dipped his head low. His eyes scanned across my body once again. He then looked back at Clare and let out a long sigh.

"The way I see it - Railrunner has a ten percent chance."

"So!" Clare said angrily. "You're saying he may not live!"

"I don't know... even if I welded his metal back together... the wounds are just so deep that... I don't know." Thunderbark said as he placed his wheels on the stab wound again. I let out a cry of agony as the tender gash throbbed from his slightest touch.

"PLEASE!" I cried. "Don't - it hurts!" I yelled as all of my strength started to drain from me completely. Thunderbark looked at me face to face with sad eyes. He came over and sat beside me. My wheels began to singe and vibrate as I felt my blood run cold. I felt my stomach churn and twist into a knot. My body jerked from relentless pain. I started to break out in a sweat. Then Thunderbark took a set of my wheels and held it tightly, a slight tear formed in the corner of his eye.

"Listen Railrunner, you did well. You are the greatest warrior I have ever come to know."

I couldn't even nod in response the pain was so bad, even worse than transforming pain. I felt everything within me grow dull. Everything was giving way just as I thought. That was when I knew I was at my demise.

"Stay with me!" Clare screamed as I let my eyelids close. I felt myself falling into the "air lock" once again.

"I love you." I whispered to her. "I always will."

Clare began to cry. Suddenly I felt a set of lips touch mine. I realized that they belong to Clare as she pressed harder. She was kissing me for the first time that we were equal enough to do it right. Her kiss felt - magical, putting a tad bit more energy back into my dying body.

I opened my eyes slightly to see everyone bowing their heads, all except for Static, who was fishing through my bag.

"There has to be something in here to help!" he said frustrated.

"Static it's-." Thunderbark said trailing off as he stared with wide eyes at the vile of blue liquid that the bumper car held in his cable. Thunderbark quickly took it from him, his lips drawing into an unexpected smile. I blinked to focus on the vile; I then recognized it as the one that Moonhoof had given to me.

"I was hoping for a miracle, and I got it." Thunderbark said pulling the cork out from the lip.

"What is that?' Merrylegs asked him.

"It is a little something called Liquid Revival. I never knew Railrunner had it. This must be the last of it in existence." Thunderbark announced.

"What does it do?" Static said.

"Well, it heals all wounds no matter how bad, plus it makes him immune to any attack from any coaster," he smiled.

Clare then tilted back my head and opened my mouth as Thunderbark raised the vile to my lips. My sore throat felt the cool concoction flow downward. Within a few seconds the vile was completely empty. There was no immediate change at all. Could Thunderbark have been wrong? Suddenly without warning, a surge of power ran though my body, making my eyes fly open. My metal and innards tingled as they began to heal up. I arose suddenly and made the others scoot out of the way.

My body pumped with anger and rage. My seats rose up higher like an angry cat's hair. I growled and snarled in my chest. I felt stronger than ever, like I could destroy, obliterate, or kill anything.

"Nice to see you back from the brink." Thunderbark spoke.

"It's nice to be here," I growled in response as I returned to Ironwheel. "Hey bastard!" I yelled to the arrogant coaster who was still at the top of the hill. He turned at looked at me in surprise.

"I thought I put you in your grave where you belonged!" he called back.

"No," I hissed through barred teeth as I shook in fury. "IT'S GAME ON!"

My instinct suddenly came into play as I got on all of my wheels and took a deep breath. I then opened my mouth and released a roar unlike any other. It was louder, bigger, but most of all grander. It had a completely different tone than all the others that sounded from me. Thunderbark and the others looked in awe but yet slightly startled. Ironwheel simply looked at me in fear, and I loved every minute of it. My roar seemed to never end; it was so powerful now that it was releasing shockwaves. I finally felt the powerful behemoth fade, and finally it stopped. Then the earth began to quake, I glanced around wondering what I had just done. Every ride, electrical object, every machine vibrated and shook. Then I turned my attention back to my enemy, who was holding onto the guard rail to keep from being knocked off. Suddenly the track broke apart, but to my surprise as well as anybody else's, the track was moving. It wrapped a section around Ironwheel, trapping him.

"What in the world -." I heard Merrylegs say behind me. I turned to see that every ride and every machine was moving, or in other words alive. They rose out of their foundations and began to walk toward us, on wires or supports. Even cars and trucks rolled into the park. My mind began to comprehend on what Thunderbark had said about special talents. Perhaps this was mine.

The track creaked and swayed, I could not stand in the same spot for much longer. I jumped onto a moving piece of track and then onto the lift hill. I stood at the peak, the track had Ironwheel pinned to it, the rails wrapping around his shoulders. Still, Ironwheel trashed wildly trying to get away. I looked down to see the chain lift running smoothly, it gave me an idea.

I leaped from the hill again, the track bended the way I wanted it to, almost like I could control it. I knew already that coasters could take over rides, but that was only for simple things like speed and not making the whole thing do my every will.

I arrived at the base of the first hill to the chain lift system. I extracted my claws and cut the chain loose, this way it could use it as a rope. I then threw my body into the air, swinging around like a monkey on a vine, sailing over the top of the hill and then started back down counter clockwise. The chain caught Ironwheel and completely fixed him to the track, but I wasn't through with that yet. I rotated around a few more times before using up all the chain and smacking back down at the lifthill's top.

Ironwheel was wrapped up like a mummy, the chain was so tight that he could not move even an inch. I walked up to him slowly, staring him in the eye, letting him get the full effect of fear. Ironwheel growled, but he made no threat to me. I bent down to stoop to his level.

"You know, when I very first transformed into the creature that I am, I found out that I could smell fear. Ironwheel, you seem to have a great deal of it lingering from you." I said calmly. "This is kind of like a student being punished by the principal. However it is not principal with the "pal" it should be the one spelled p-r-i-n-c-p-l-e. So, it is where the "student" is being punished by the principle of justice."

Ironwheel could only glare as I rose up again and pointed both of my first sets of wheels at him. It was official; the time had come. I began to think heavily of Clare, a flame aroused in my left set of wheels, in the other I concentrated on rage. A spark of lightning formed in the opposite, where I was bending the two elements at the same time.

Ironwheel's expression faded into pure terror, something that the evil king probably never witnessed. I swung my arms back, making the flames and electricity grow, then like a boomerang brought them back. Two streams of lightning and fire hit him straight in the chest. Ironwheel screamed in pain and suffering. His black metal started to melt away, exposing his ribs and other organs. The two beams crossed creating a deadly combination, rotting Ironwheel from inside out. Soon all of my enemy's metal melted from his body and his flesh was fully cooked. Ironwheel was nothing but a pile of burnt bones that turned to ash as soon as I stopped. I had done it.

I looked at the pile of ashes with a smirk across my face; I tilted my head back and roared in triumph. Then I leaped down from the lift hill, landing in front of my allies. Clare came up and hugged me.

"Railrunner you did it!" She exclaimed.

"Well done, ruler of the rails." Thunderbark said as he placed a set of wheels onto my shoulder. All I could do was emit a crooked smile.

Chapter 66
Home Again

"Is Amusement Park Between now free?" I asked Thunderbark.

He laughed. "Of coarse it is! You killed Ironwheel, fulfilled the prophecy! Railrunner I knew you had it in you all along. You've accomplished so much! Like for one defeating an evil tyrant who enslaved us all, discovering the fourth thing on how to become a coaster in daylight, and finding your special talent." Thunderbark finished looking at all the living machines around us.

"You're right Thunderbark, why did I even ask! Now, I wonder how I'm supposed to return these guys to their homes." I said pointing at the machines. On that note they all turned around and headed back to wherever it was that they came from. The track groaned and resituated into its normal unliving self as well as other rides. I laughed, "I guess that's how!"

"That reminds me Railrunner, before *we* go home; Clare has to have a proper name." Thunderbark suddenly spoke.

"A name?" Clare asked confused. "I already have a name."

"Ah, but it is a human name. For now on you use that name when you are indeed human. Anybody here have any suggestions?" Thunderbark said turning to us.

We all sort of sat there looking from one another and back at Clare. I then thought of something.

"How about "track" being at the end part of her name like my mothers?"

"That sounds good," Clare said.

"What about Venomtrack?" Merrylegs suggested.

"Naw." Clare said shaking her head from side to side.

"Flowertrack?" Thunderbark joked.

"No!" Clare laughed.

"Magictrack?" I asked her.

"Sounds cheesy." Clare replied.

For a while we kept guessing names, Clare denied every one of them. She would either say that they were to dumb or that they did not fit her at all. Another thing was that everyone was making educated guesses except for Static who was hung up in thought. Suddenly Static cleared his throat to get our attention.

"I think I might have one." He said scratching his head with his cable.

"What is it, Static?" Merrylegs asked him.

"How about Shadowtrack?"

Clare was silent. She simply stared at Static with one eyebrow raised. I looked from her to him trying to decide who would speak first.

"I like it," Clare said with a smile. "Thank you Static."

"You're welcome," he replied happily.

"So, Shadowtrack it is then," I grinned at her.

"You bet."

"I guess it is now full speed ahead to Amusement Park Between then?" Merrylegs asked.

"Yup," Thunderbark said as he walked toward the water park that housed the portal. I picked up the bag and slung it over my shoulder as I walked along side of Shadowtrack. I then remembered Captain Vick. I opened the bag and pressed one on the cell phone. It rang for a minute and then finally the Captain answered.

"Hello?"

"It's Railrunner, let me say that you don't have to worry about us anymore. Ironwheel has been taken down."

I heard him cheer with excitement on the other end of the line. He was so loud that he made Shadowtrack giggle.

"Thank you! Sorry for all the trouble, Railrunner. To let you know, I have cleared all your charges and the army's presence will be reported as a training exercise. So the secret is safe."

"Thanks and, you won't be hearing from us no more, by the way, sorry for destroying your car on my way out of here."

"WWWWHHHAAATTT -." I didn't hear the rest after I clicked the phone shut. I tossed the cell phone over my shoulder and into one of the wading pools. Shadowtrack looked at me and laughed.

"You destroyed Vicks car!"

"No, I was just messing with him," I replied with a smirk.

She continued to giggle and then leaned on me as we walked behind the others, our hot metal touching.

"So, what is Amusement Park Between like again?"

"Why are you asking me that when you will be there in a minute or two!"

"I can't wait!" Shadowtrack laughed.

"Looks like you don't have to." I said as we stood with Thunderbark at the edge of the spa, or in other words the portal to home.

"Shall we?" Thunderbark said as he jumped and disappeared into the glowing pool. Merrylegs immediately followed after him as well as Static. Then it was our turn.

"You might want to hold your breath. Just keep close to me and you will be fine." I said taking a set of her wheels. Shadowtrack and I then motioned for the edge of the portal, both of us took our breath and then made the plunge.

Water swarmed around the two of us, surrounding our bodies in a relaxing sensation. I opened my eyes to see Shadowtrack looking back at me with her eyes full of wonder and anticipation. I looked up to see that the water grew lighter above us. I motioned for her to follow me as we made our way to the surface. Shadowtrack struggled at first, but then she found they key to swimming. She soon arrived next to me, matching my speed. In the next second, we surfaced into the bright light.

I got to my wheels and helped Shadowtrack out of the water. She had her eyes closed as we walked to where Thunderbark and the others stood waiting for us. All of them seemed to have a smile on their face.

"You can open them now," I told her, chuckling slightly.

Shadowtrack slowly did as she was told, and her jaw dropped when she saw the vast forest and mountains. The Acterbahnn that cut through the land and the tall buildings of the distant cities.

"You live here!"

"Yep," I replied taking in a breath of the freshest air. Merrylegs and Static scampered down the grassy hill in the direction of the temple. Merrylegs turned and motioned for Shadowtrack to follow her. Reluctantly she did, the purple coaster looked at me when she was halfway between either of us before she ran along with them. Now it was only Thunderbark and I who stood at the hill overlooking Amusement Park Between.

"It is good to be back." Thunderbark sighed.

"It truly is," I said turning to him.

"I guess now we should spread the word that there is a new king," he said with a smirk. I knew right away whom he was referring to.

"I'm no king," I replied.

"I don't think you can deny that. I didn't mention the last part of the prophecy."

"What do you mean?"

"Well, after the red defeats the black, the red takes his place as king." He said with a sly grin.

I looked at him for a good long while; maybe it wouldn't be so bad.

"Fine, I'll take the oath as king if you say so, Thunderbark."

"That's cool with me sire," he said in return.

"I'm just Railrunner and nothing else," I smiled at him.

"If you say so, Railrunner. Meet you at the temple." He said as he disappeared down the hill.

I took one good long look at Amusement Park Between. I started to think quietly to myself, we were finally home in heaven, in my little kingdom. Where the impossible becomes possible and the explainable becomes unexplainable, but most of all, where the twisted rule.

About the Author and the Illustrator

Miranda Leek

Miranda Leek lives in the small town of Rockvale, Tennessee. Her love of art, writing, and roller coasters inspired Miranda, at the tender age of seventeen, to write Twisted; in which started as a simple experience and a few ideas, tuned into wonderful fully illustrated book that could be read over and over.

Please visit www.mirandasmagic.com to view more of Miranda's work including the works of Twisted in their original form.

Also Be On The Lookout For Book 2 In The Twisted Series:

VERTIGO

Breinigsville, PA USA
18 August 2010
243817BV00003B/17/P